Calloway County

(270) 753-2288

www.callowaycountylibrary.org

FEB 2 3 2016

Games
Wizards Play

**Diane Duane's
Young Wizards Series**

DIANE DUANE

Games
Wizards Play

Houghton Mifflin Harcourt

Boston   New York

Copyright © 2016 by Diane Duane

All rights reserved. For information about permission
to reproduce selections from this book, write to

trade.permissions@hmhco.com or to trade.permissions@hmhco.com
or to Permissions, Houghton Mifflin Harcourt Publishing Company,
3 Park Avenue, 19th Floor, New York, New York 10016.

Could It Be from KIM POSSIBLE: THE MOVIE.
Words and music by Andrew Gabriel and Cory Lerois © 2005
by Wonderland Music Company, Inc. and Walt Disney Music
Company. All rights reserved. Used by permission.
Reprinted by permission of Hal Leonard Corporation.

www.hmhco.com

Text set in Stempel Garamond LT Std

Library of Congress Cataloging-in-Publication Data
978-054481-981-8

Manufactured in the United States of America
DOC 10 9 8 7 6 5 4 3 2 1
4500573295

Dedicated to Colin Smythe
Publisher, editor, friend
(who knows where the bodies are buried)

Acknowledgments

Heartfelt thanks to the many online friends who follow me on Twitter (@dduane) and Tumblr (dduane.tumblr.com), and whose engagement and encouragement are a daily joy. As the man says: "You keep me right."

Thanks also to John C. Welch, provider of technical assistance that has proved of inestimable value in the production of this book.

Contents

I . . . am about to embark upon a hazardous and technically unexplainable journey . . . to confer, converse, and otherwise hobnob with my brother wizards.

— Oz the Great, *The Wizard of Oz*

When moon and sun stand each in place
And your opponent takes the field,
Look past him to the one you'll face
When all hid truths stand new-revealed.

When that time comes, your only shield
Will be the outward gaze toward space;
The cold will show what sword to wield
Against the fire's and death's embrace.

Still, though your oldest foe should yield,
Beware the last fall of the dice:
Though now an ancient sorrow's healed,
Beware who pays the final price —

And do not miss, 'twixt fire and ice,
Your chance to make the sun rise twice.

— I Ching trigram 30, Fire over Fire:
"Double Brightness"

I am not young enough to know everything.

— Oscar Wilde

Games
Wizards Play

Time fix: Spring 2011

1

Hipparchus

✳

KIT RODRIGUEZ LAY SPRAWLED in the gray dirt, staring in shock at the fire-blackened book that had just landed open side down in front of him. His stomach flip-flopped as he realized that very close by, another wizard lay dead.

Still smoking gently at its charred edges, the other wizard's manual, a thick, beat-up paperback with a cracked spine, slowly started to vanish. Sheer horrified fascination made it hard for Kit to look away. Only when the manual had finished dissolving did he manage to swallow. His mouth was bone dry, not just because of all the dust flying around, and his heartbeat was hammering in his ears. It was amazing how loud your own heart sounded in these conditions, especially when it might shortly stop without warning.

Kit, you still with us? said a voice that sounded like it was speaking from inside his head.

"Uh, yeah," Kit said under his breath. "Don't think it'd be real smart to move right this minute. I'm pinned down."

Lissa is too, said another voice. *You're below effective numbers now, Kit. We can pull you guys out of there —*

"No chance," Kit said. "Job's not done yet! You think I'm leaving before we finish what Ritchie gave it all up for?"

The moment's silence that followed was broken only by the shudder of the impacts hitting the ground around them. *How many have we got moving now?* said a voice from across the battlefield.

Nine of them, said another voice with a distinct twang to it. *They're right over the rim from you right now, so whatever you do, don't —*

A few hundred meters in front of him, an inward-arrowing glint of ferociously unfiltered sunlight flashed off the narrow shape of yet another of the nasty projectiles that had been making Kit's life so interesting for the last ten minutes or so. Hurriedly Kit shoved his face down into the dirt again, and the incoming missile shot by right over his head, literally within a yard or so of his scalp. Under the circumstances he couldn't feel it by air pressure, but its passage pushed his personal shield down harder onto his skull. This wasn't the kind of sensation any wizard in his right mind took lightly, no matter how confident he was about his shielding — and Kit was a lot less confident about it than he'd been half an hour ago.

He held still, waiting for the explosion from behind him. For several long moments nothing happened. Then everything rocked. The ground beneath Kit rippled, shaking apart in chunks along spiderweb cracks as the blast wave from the missile's explosion burst through it. In the wave's wake, the air inside the larger bubble of Kit's secondary shield instantly filled with kicked-up gray-white dust that obscured everything, as if he'd suddenly been teleported into the center of a frosted lightbulb. He concentrated on not breathing until the shaking stopped and the dust started to settle.

Kit? Kit!!

He didn't answer right away, because he didn't trust himself to breathe the air around him yet. After a few moments the dust had settled low enough for him to carefully put his head above the dust level. "I'm still here, it's okay!" he said. "And no *way* am I moving! Not ready for Timeheart right this minute." He gulped air and levered himself up on his elbows to look over the edge of rocks in front of him. There was little to see except more dust, kicked up low across the plain by dimly seen mechanical shapes. "What about Lissa? She was right behind me —"

I moved, said that lighter voice. *Good thing, or I'd be where Ritchie is now.* As usual, she sounded way too calm for what was going on around her.

Kit sighed in unnerved relief. His only other team member, Walt, had been taken out moments before Ritchie had. But Lissa's survival alone wasn't likely to be enough to make the difference here: mere numbers weren't going to help. "You get the reading you were after on this new stuff they're lobbing at us?"

The shells've got some kind of hyperblooey in them, Lissa said. *Boosted composite chemical and micronuke explosive surrounded by a tamping field. But the explosive's not the problem. The squeeze-field's where the real action is. It's a double-tasked starcore compression spell that's also holding the components of the fusion triggers apart. That's how they're getting so much oomph out of these things.*

"Hybrid tech," Kit muttered. "I really, *really* hate it when people hook wizardry up to explosives. The results cannot be anything but ugly . . ."

Wouldn't argue, Lissa said. *Since we don't have time.*

From his position across the crater came a familiar voice: Ronan. *Five minutes,* he said.

Sweat started popping out all over Kit. The other team was dead quiet, which suggested that they had some sort of solution to what was going on and were about to implement it. *You think they know what you know?* he said privately to Lissa.

I'm not sure, Lissa said. *Couldn't get a clear reading until that last one came real close.*

And you're sure of your results?

Pretty sure. If you want me to make absolutely certain, why not stand up and see if you can attract another?

Pass! Kit said.

Four minutes thirty . . . said Ronan.

The hair stood up on the back of Kit's neck at the thought of what would start breaking loose in four minutes, that being the best-case estimate for when the alien force would push past their defensive perimeter and get at the base on the far side of the crater. The place was full of civilians, none of whom were going to be terribly prepared to be overrun by aliens. And Kit wasn't sure whether whatever the other team was working on was going to make a difference — *So we have to do* something. *Change the equation somehow. If not ours, then theirs —*

The idea hit him completely without warning, and there was no time to waste mulling it over to see if it was too stupid to suggest. *How about this?* Kit said to Lissa. *Those tamping fields on the missiles they haven't launched yet . . . what do you think would happen if they went off prematurely?*

What, you mean if we tried to make them complete their squeeze cycle early and blow? No way, that'd take more power than we've both got —

No. I mean, what if the squeeze-fields shut off. Went away —

Calloway County Public Library
710 Main Street
Murray, Kentucky 42071
(270) 753-2288
www.callowaycountylibrary.org

There was a long pause. Then, *Ooooo*, Lissa said, with the appreciative and anticipatory sound of someone about to open a particularly nice present.

Kit grinned. *Can you build the spell in about a minute?*

A much shorter pause this time. *Got an off-the-rack solution that'll work if I tweak it right.*

Great! Set it up. I'll feed you power.

Lissa went quiet. Kit pushed himself farther up and peered over the rim of the crater again — the bottom of a landscape overarched by the hard black sky of Moon-based day, the stars washed out by sunglare and the shifting, situational glitter of still-suspended moondust that had been kicked up too high and hard to come down yet. The alien war machines that had been shooting at his group were now stalking and rolling far closer to Kit's position across the rubble-strewn basin at the nameless crater's bottom — a stretch of lunar terrain that had been fairly smooth and uncratered until the machines' arrival via rogue worldgate a few hours ago and their meeting with the two wizardly teams that had been sent out to stop them. *Problem is, two teams were never going to be enough*, Kit thought. *Guess I should be grateful Neets couldn't get free for this —*

Three minutes, Ronan said, sounding grim.

You guys got anything? said Matt, from his team's site on the other side of the crater. He sounded freaked, but not so much so that Kit couldn't hear the beginnings of a note of triumph in his voice. *They* do *have something*, Kit thought. *Only question is how fatal it's going to be, and who to —*

For the moment Kit didn't answer. *Liss — ?!*

Just a few seconds more!

Kit swallowed. *Matt*, he said, *this might be a good time to store some last words . . .*

The silence on the other side had an unnerved quality to it; a wizard could do a lot with his or her last words. But then Lissa whispered, *Ready for you.*

The crack-shattered dirt under Kit's nose came alive with a small, remote segment of the spell diagram she'd just constructed — a two-foot-wide circle packed full of closely written lines of light, hovering just above the moondust. Kit hurriedly checked the curves and curls of his name in the Speech to make sure that Lissa had transcribed it correctly, then took a deep breath and slapped his right hand down into the middle of the spell diagram, in the receptor/connector area she'd left open for him, and spoke the agreed confirmation word in the Speech. In the next instant he felt the power leap out of him and flow into Lissa's spell as she said its final word and turned it loose. Then Kit flopped down on his chest again, limp as a wrung-out rag.

Last words? Matt said.

After letting all that power go, Kit was too weak

to do much but grin in anticipation. *Don't count your chickens . . . !* he said.

And a second later the crater came alive with a scatter of explosions that made the previous missile impacts look small and stingy by comparison. Kit peered over the crater rim again, being very careful — because suddenly the neighboring vacuum wasn't just full of dust, but also of rocks and twisted pieces of shiny metal rocketing away from multiple explosion centers in the crater.

Kit took a couple more breaths and started to feel a little recovered from the stress of doing a heavy powerfeed without much prep. *Or maybe it's just seeing the results . . . !* he thought. *Can I stand up without falling down?* He pushed himself up onto hands and knees and then stood, staggering only a bit. Since his personal force shield was hardened against radiation as well as mere physical impacts, he wasn't worried about standing up to see how those nuclear explosions were playing out in vacuum and one-sixth g. Even without air to carry what would have been the deafening multiple roars of their detonation, the effect was still impressive. Nine giant dust-streaked glow-inside balloons were now scattered around the crater in various stages of expansion and glaring brightness, each one growing and roiling like something alive, burning and angry. As Kit watched them, something shiny hit him about chest-high. His shield flared, dissipating the impact's energy, and the thing that had hit him bounced down into the moondust at his feet. He peered down and saw that it was the pointy end of some kind of mechanical claw, twisted out of shape and molten at the edges, the metal still bubbling and exhaling vapor into the vacuum.

Behind him, standing up in her own crater, Lissa was fist-punching the air, or where the air would normally have been, and hooting with delight. From the team on the other side, the silence held for only a few more moments: then the groaning started. "What the heck was *that?*" "What did they *do??*"

And possibly most satisfying, the complaints were followed by a low chuckle from the scenario designer. *Okay,* Ronan said, *intervention's complete at fourteen oh five local, and that's a clear win for Kit and Lissa. Let's get everyone together over at Mid-Hipparchus for the debrief, and let the dust here settle . . .*

Kit said the four or five words in the Speech that reclaimed the air inside his outer shield into compressed storage, then the half-sentence that killed his outer force field. Off across the big crater he'd been peering into, the simulated nuclear explosions were being decommissioned — the dust that had been the only physically real thing about them now snowing gently back down onto the lunar surface. Shortly, even if any other people besides wizards had been up on the Moon right now, there would be no sign that anything unusual had happened here.

Kit carefully bounced up the slope behind him to where Lissa had just killed her own outer force bubble, this making it a lot easier to jump around in triumph without interference. Lissa might look somewhat tall and gangly under normal circumstances, but up here in the low gravity her bouncing acquired an unusual grace that made it seem like second nature — an effect assisted by the orange jumpsuit she always wore to these sessions, which made her resemble an escaped astronaut. Her short fair hair crackled and stood up a little with static as she bounced and waved her arms in the air.

It was hard not to get caught up in such sheer evil glee. As Kit came up with her, Lissa put up one hand for a high-five: both their shields flared with the impact, so that though there couldn't be any sound, there was at least a brief flash. "They were *useless*," Lissa said, and spun around about a meter off the ground in a one-sixth gee dance of triumph. "Useless beyond *words!* They had nothing and we saved their butts. Or if they did have anything, they left it way too late. Oh, are they going to hate us!"

"Not if we don't *gloat* too much," Kit said, hoping earnestly that she'd take the point just this once. But even as he said it, the moondust on the ground around Lissa flared blue-white with the wizardry of the personal transit circle she'd dropped around her as she came down, and she vanished.

He sighed and glanced around, watching the way the dust thrown up by the explosions out in the middle of the crater continued sifting silverly toward the lunar surface. The effect was like watching delicately fluffy snow come down, since the bright-side static tended to make the falling dust clump when there'd been a lot of local activity. Ronan had scheduled this session for relatively late in the two-week lunar "day," both in an attempt to keep the dust from being a problem and to make sure there were plenty of shadows, which made it a lot easier to see surface details when you were running around shooting at things. The dust, as usual, had its own ideas, but the view couldn't be otherwise faulted, now that the action was over and there was time to appreciate it. Above the far crater wall, Earth hung gibbous, a cloud-streaked, wet blue jewel three-quarters full, and its dazzling brilliance was ever so slightly fuzzed around the edges by the faint, faint haze of high static-propelled dust that the first astronauts had been so surprised to see —

Is it possible that you're still *hanging around there sightseeing, crater boy?* said the ironic voice inside his head. *Can we please get on with this? Matt's pitching such a fit, and I'd hate for you to miss it.*

Kit grinned. *Meaning,* he thought, *that he's giving*

Ronan a lot of grief, and Ro doesn't want to have to soak it all up himself... "On my way," Kit said.

His own "beam-me-up-Scotty" spell had long since had the coordinates for the assembly point in the middle of the sprawling Hipparchus crater complex plugged into it. Now Kit said the words that brought the spell to life in a circle on the ground around him, turned once to scan the white-glowing symbols and make sure the Wizard's Knot that completed the circle was tight, and then said the activator clause out loud.

In the airless environment, the normal silence that fell around a working spell — the sound of the universe listening to what you wanted — was much harder to detect. It became more something you felt on your skin, the protecting force field having no power to shield you from the basic forces that powered both it and everything else in existence. Kit could feel the universe pushing in around him as he spoke: paying attention, bearing down on him the way the overshooting missile had pushed down on his force field before. At its greatest pressure, everything went dark —

Then everything flashed bright again as Kit came out in the middle of another patch of pale dusty terrain. Here a gravel-strewn plain stretched away to the foreshortened horizon in every direction, with only the occasional hump or low rille to break the bright-streaked flatness. This was normal for Hipparchus, which was a very old crater and very beat-up because of its age. Its rim was mostly flattened down to low hills by meteor strikes; its main basin had long ago been flooded by black basalt lava, then cracked into gravel over many millennia by countless microme-teorite impacts and the extremes of heat and cold. The only feature of interest anywhere nearby was a low cloud of dust a few hundred yards away and to Kit's right. In it half-seen human shapes were moving around fast, while hard bright lines of colored light zapped up out of the cloud. Theoretically this group had come up here as spectators, but with some of the people involved — particularly Darryl — Kit had always suspected it wouldn't take long before a session of laser tag broke out.

Much closer, off to Kit's left and near a cluster of big grainy gray boulders, a small crowd was gathered. Most of them were talking hard, though there was no way to be sure what they were saying outside the bubble-thin skin of the communal force field dome that was holding in their shared air. Kit had his suspi-cions, though.

He bounced over to them in the shallow jumpwalk that astronauts and wizards passing through learned in a hurry on the Moon. Leaning against the big-gest boulder, in the middle of the group, was Ronan Nolan, tall and dark and angular in his usual black leather jacket and black shirt and faded black jeans. Lissa was there, laughing and shaking her head at Matt

Kingston, who was wearing one of his trademark loud Hawaiian shirts and long baggy khaki shorts. He was holding his open wizard's manual under Lissa's nose and pointing at something on the page with an aggrieved expression, but Lissa wasn't looking at it, just waving Matt away and laughing. Ritchie was there, too, leaning against Lissa's boulder and looking short and dark and a lot less dead than he had ten minutes before. Also gathered around were some of the rest of Matt's team — tall, thin, dark Ahmed, and those two blond girls who always turned up together, one tall and broad, the other short and skinny. *Which one is Heléne and which one's Jeannine? I can never remember* — Kit lifted a hand in greeting and glanced around. "Where's Walt?"

Ronan gestured toward the nearby dustcloud. "He got bored with being dead," he said in that south-Dublin drawl of his, "so he's off getting that way again with the laser tag crowd."

"Glutton for punishment," Ritchie said, pulling off his jacket and shaking it in what looked like the most recent of many attempts to get rid of the moondust that had buried him when the next-to-last missile strike took him out.

Ronan waved away the dust. "So listen, Kit: Matt's having some trouble with your solution —"

"Not with the solution, *that* worked okay, more than okay, who could miss the way everything in sight blew up? But you ran over the time limit!" Matt was a little abrasive at the best of times, but in situations like this the Aussie in his voice sometimes got so sharp and shrill that when he talked fast it was tough to follow him. "Ronan said that once the scenario hit the T-minus-five point, everybody had to either enact their solution or hand over to the next team —"

Kit shook his head and reached out sideways, and his hand vanished up to the wrist in the empty space off to his right as he felt around in his otherspace pocket for his own manual. "Wasn't what he said at all," Kit said as he pulled his manual out and flipped it open, paging through to the section where the scenario details and guidelines were stored. "And if you'd read this stuff more than once before you get here, it could be useful, because your memory's not exactly perfect —"

The usual argument promptly got under way. Matt was what Ronan liked to call a "rules lawyer": not a bad loser as such, but if things didn't go the way he thought they should have during a war game, he had a gift for finding all kinds of things wrong with the setup — failed communications, some part of the rules that you hadn't spelled out, as if you were talking to a kindergartner, a tiny point of logic that was blatantly obvious to everyone else but which suddenly made no sense to Matt. "You should have started your wizardry going before the five-minute limit, and if you weren't ready you had to clear the next team to go, because —"

"That way you'd have had the next three whole minutes to grandstand over the big complex spell structure you'd built and you were powering up on," Lissa said from on top of the boulder where she sat, arching her neck so that she gazed down at Matt as if from a great ironic height. "All the drama, all the tension! Like watching the bomb in a spy movie count down until you pull the big save out of the bag just as the bad guys are gonna break through into the base."

"We'd have been so impressed," Kit said. "And you'd have made a big deal over it for *days!* Except you know what? You were still building the spell."

Matt scowled. "And you were rushing your construction, too, so when you finally finished it, it wasn't fast enough on the execution end," Lissa said. "And so we had time to execute ours first, and beat you, and *that's* the *size* of *that!*" She started fist-pumping again, with both fists this time, doing a little sitting-down victory dance on the rock and briefly losing contact with it in the light gravity.

Both the blond wizards gave Matt a wry, amused told-you-so look that suggested Lissa's analysis was on the money. Matt rolled his eyes and turned to Ronan. "That shouldn't matter! And if you weren't leaving enough wiggle room in the rules so that your buddies'd pick up the hint and figure out how to squeeze through them —"

Kit gave Matt an annoyed look. "Just because Ronan and I hang out," Kit said, "doesn't mean we spend any of that time plotting sleazy ways to win. What'd be the point?"

Matt had the grace to look embarrassed. "Okay, sorry, I meant that if our thing had executed —"

"*If* the Lone Power had wheels, it'd be an SUV," Hélene said. "Matt, let it go!"

Matt said a few words in the Speech which when delivered in his present tone weren't designed to slow down entropy. "But it never had a chance," he said to Kit, "because you started your own little drama. The whole 'last words' thing — you *played* me!"

Lissa spluttered with laughter again, drumming the side of the boulder with her heels. "Yes we did!"

Matt glared at Ronan. "And you let them!"

Ronan looked angelically unconcerned. "Hey, I just designed the setup. How you moved through it was *your* business."

Matt kept on protesting. But Kit doubted this was going to go on much longer, as Jeannine and Heléne were already laughing and poking Matt in good-natured mockery, and the rest of his team were giving him looks plainly suggesting that he give it up. Ronan just stood there in patient-umpire mode and let Matt run down, while Kit stood there scuffing at the regolith underfoot and pretending to pay attention.

Finally Matt simply waved his hands in the air in a "Whatever . . ." gesture and shook his head. "Fine, let it stand."

Ronan glanced around. "Anything else need discussion?"

Heads shook no around the two teams. "Then if we can please get our schedules sorted out for next time?" Ronan said. "As some of us have other things to do besides get our pants full of moondust . . ."

Those who used physical versions of the wizard's manual got them out, and heads were lowered over various books and codices and electronic devices as people started synchronizing their calendars and looking for matching gaps in their busy lives. As this process went forward Kit glanced from one wizard to another of the two teams, privately appreciating them . . . a process he wouldn't have admitted to unless pushed. They were a diverse and motley crew — some of them, like Matt, Kit had met in the heat of the Pullulus crisis that had threatened so much of known space, leaving younger wizards alone to deal with the deadly darkness that was eating away the stars. Others, like Lissa, had become involved months back on the fringes of the project to discover what had happened to the long-lost Martian species, and had met up with Kit after he'd found himself stuck right in the center of it. In every case they were people Kit liked a lot, though they could be irritating in ways that were still taking him a while to get used to. Fortunately most of them were also enough fun to be around that Kit was finding it easy to get past the annoyances. Lissa in particular was the kind of person you'd like a lot even if she weren't also a wizard —

"Ahem," Ronan said rather loudly, right in Kit's ear. Kit jumped. "It helps if you're looking at something besides the weather report for Aldebaran IVa. Not real great this time of year anyway, till the red giant comes out of that pesky expansion phase. JD2455702.10: Can you do that? Everybody else can."

"Uh —" Kit flipped hastily through his manual to the calendar page.

"Say you can," Matt said, "because you're running it." His grin was entirely amused.

For the moment Kit was too thrown off the beat to give Ronan the look he wanted to. It was Ronan who'd started organizing this get-together-and-run-a-nightmare-scenario group. As a result he was in charge not only of coordinating everyone's schedules — since the long-distance teleporting meant that the group had to pool enough energy to power the transit spells — but also of assigning whose turn it was to design and stage the next nightmare. *You,* he said privately to Ronan, *are cruel.*

But effective. Since now Matt, who thought maybe I was giving you an easy time, is changing his mind . . .

Kit made a face. "Morning or afternoon?"

Jeannine giggled that low, throaty giggle of hers. "There's sort of no way point ten can be anything *but* afternoon . . ."

"Yeah, right," Kit said. He looked at his manual half in resignation, as the schedule grid for that day was empty; though a number of days after it were grayed out and the word "Provisional" was branded across them. *What is that?* Kit thought, peering at it. *Must have set something up with Neets when neither of us was sure whether we were going to go ahead with it. Pity this date couldn't have fallen in there.* He made a face. *But if it did, Matt'd probably take it as proof that we've got some evil plot against him . . .* "Okay," Kit said. "Let's do it."

Everyone started putting their stuff away. "Right," Ronan said. "Ten minutes for you to get yourselves sorted and then we'll do the jump down to Tower Hill . . ."

"Thought we were routing through Grand Central this time," Lissa said.

Ronan shook his head. "Had to change it. The GCT gating team's scheduled some kind of emergency maintenance for this afternoon. The North American crowd gets a free transfer back to Penn from London, so if anybody wants to do a little sightseeing. . . ."

People started jumping down from boulders and getting ready to head out. Matt sidled over to Kit. "Look, just so you know — it was just procedural stuff I was complaining about. It was still pretty hot, what you did."

"Thanks," Kit said.

"But don't think I'm gonna let you have any slack next session when it comes around to critiquing time!"

Kit laughed at him. "Why should you? That's not what this is about."

"And as for you," Matt said to Ronan, who was still trying to get the moondust off his usually impeccable black clothing, "we still need to talk about why you're never on *my* side when this stuff happens."

"What," Ronan said, "just because you pulled a magic spear out of my chest and saved my life, I should cut you a special break? Dream on, ya gob."

Matt made a face and threw his hands up in the air. "Later," he said, and bounced off after Lissa.

"It's amazing you keep on doing this," Kit said under his breath.

"I love the aggro," Ronan said, and kept on brushing.

"You must."

They looked over at the remaining dustcloud off to the side, from which beams and chunks of lunar surface were still flying out more or less constantly. "What *are* they doing in there?"

"Beyond some kind of laser tag, not sure I want to find out," Ronan said. "Looks like mindless violence to me."

"Wizardry's biggest hurling fan considers *that* mindless violence?" Kit said, and laughed. "Right."

"Not *my* fault if you've not got the chops to come out and try it sometime."

Kit shook his head, putting his manual away. "Thanks, I like my head where it is. Any sport with legends about nine-year-olds killing each other and getting bumped *up* in the leagues for it? Not for me!"

Ronan merely smiled sardonically, stretching and gazing around him at the slowly deepening lunar afternoon. "And I only get two *weeks* to put a scenario together?" Kit said.

"I did warn you," Ronan said. Kit made a face. Ronan snickered. "You'll be fine. . . .You know, though, you gave me a bad moment there . . ."

"I gave *you* a bad moment??"

"Your 'last words' thing," Ronan said. "The scenario wasn't set up for that."

Kit gave him a thoughtful look. "Oh? Seems like an omission, especially when a wizard could get so much power out of that move."

"Never occurred to me that anyone on *these* teams would use it," Ronan muttered. "You never-say-die types, after all, it wouldn't normally occur —"

Kit burst out laughing. "Oh, come on, what were *you* all about six months back? Make sure you put it in next time, 'cause I want to see what happens when someone *does* use it." Ronan gave him a grim look. "But while we're handing out compliments — that was nice, that bit with the burnt manual. In an ugly way."

"Yeah. Heard of that once."

"But you've never seen it."

"Never want to, either."

"We came close once . . ."

Ronan looked away. "Yeah. Not the kind of memory you dwell on, you know?"

Off to their left, something down close to ground level flashed bright in the afternoon light: another dustcloud, gently expanding from a single focus point. "*Now* what," Ronan said under his breath — then paused as the sphere of moondust kicked out from around a half-seen figure and started to settle in a circle around it. Kit and Ronan both stared, for the figure was that of a human adult.

The guy, a tall, thin shape, waved at them and started bouncing over. "Anybody you know?" Ronan said.

"Nope," Kit said as the adult wizard paused just outside the main air bubble to size up the force field spell and match it with his own. A faint line of fieldglow sprang up around the edges of his silhouette as the two spells synched up and he passed through. "Hey, *dai stihó*," he said, as he got close enough to be heard without shouting. "Didn't interrupt anything, did I?"

They shook their heads as the newcomer bounced to a stop near them, peering around. He was in his late thirties or thereabouts, in jeans and short-sleeved shirt with a neat goatee; he looked at Ronan for a moment as if he was trying to place him, then glanced back at Kit. "No, it's fine, cousin, you're well met," Kit said, mystified. "We were just finishing up here."

"Alien invasion," Ronan said.

The wizard looked around, taking in the settling dust as well as the dustcloud off to one side, which, far from settling, was kicking up worse than ever. "I take it we won?"

Kit snickered. "Might still be some discussion going on about that."

The wizard chuckled, then looked around again, his attention more on the empty landscape this time. "How's the surface around here?"

"Level," Ronan said. "For this neighborhood. And pretty firm. That's why I picked it. You're welcome to my survey logs."

"Thanks."

"Is there some kind of problem?" Kit said, for the

wizard's eyes were darting between the two of them and the surrounding landscape.

"Problem? No, sorry, no way! Just having a look at the area."

"What for?" Ronan said.

"Well, considering how much use the place has been getting lately," he said, "it might be getting some more shortly. Pre-event prep work. They sent me up to do a suitability check."

"They?"

The guy looked at them quizzically. "You seriously haven't heard? . . . No, guess you were busy. Checked your manual lately?"

Kit and Ronan swapped bemused looks. "For updates? Uh, no," Kit said.

The older wizard suddenly acquired a grin that spread straight across his face. "You might want to take a moment," he said. "Don't mind me, I'll just get on with this."

He bounced away across the landscape. Kit and Ronan stared at each other for a second more. Then Ronan shut his eyes to access the Knowledge in his own style, and Kit grabbed for his manual.

It might have been nerves that made Kit fumble the manual and drop it. It bounced, and he managed to grab it again on the way back up, at about knee level, and flipped it open. Sure enough, the edges of the section on general-event notification were flashing softly. His mouth started to go dry; the flashing reminded him too much of the way his manual had looked when the Pullulus overran Earth's solar system not long ago. But the flashing had been red that time. This was a much cooler and more informational-looking blue.

He tipped the pages open to that central section, and the blue flashing dimmed down immediately. The page he was looking at withdrew what it had been displaying — some general weather notification to wizards working in the central Pacific — and a new page's worth of words rose to the surface and settled themselves in place.

To: Rodriguez, Christopher K.

From: Planetary event coordination (Sol/Sol III/IIIa)

JD: 2455686.00

Re: 1241st Interventional Development, Assessment and Adjudication Sessions

Dear Kit,

On behalf of the Powers That Be and Their local representatives: cordial greetings!

This is to inform you that you have been nominated by a regional supervisory steering subcommittee as an assessor- and enabler-candidate for the initial assessment and joint evaluation phase of the upcoming IDAA main session, beginning on JD 2455692.7 and terminating on or about JD 2455713.00.

This nomination is entirely elective, and you are under no compulsion to participate. However, your errantry history is such that your participation would be extremely welcome, both in terms of the value of your past contributions and the experience which you will be invited to share with the session's intake of qualifying participants.

If you do elect to participate, we would ask at this point that you check your schedule to make sure there are no personal event conflicts or other attendance issues during the dates we have blocked for you, and confirm back the open status of your schedule to the appointments and development-assignment committees before JD 2455689.00. Please note that you will not be called to active errantry during your blocked-out dates should you choose to attend and participate. This dispensation will be extended to you through the finals stages should a candidate with whom you are associated be elected into the semis or finals.

Attendance at the IDAA sessions implies subsidized coverage for all associated necessary intersystem transits, and this subsidy will also be extended to you through the finals stages if necessary due to advisory duties or if you simply wish to attend.

We look forward to your response to this invitation at your earliest convenience.

Dai stihó,

Owen Dalwhinnie

for Irina Mladen, Planetary Wizard for Sol III/IIIa

cc: Swale, Thomas B., Romeo, Carl, Callahan, Juanita L. —

Bewildered, Kit scanned on down the note at a very long list of cc's and attached documents. Looking over Kit's shoulder, Ronan started to swear, and not in the Speech either; it was something extremely venomous in Irish. At least most of it was Irish, but there were many heartfelt insertions of the F word in between. "What the fecking *feck!*" Ronan shouted, and stalked away waving his arms, then bounced back, kicking rocks. "How do you even *rate?* Why do I even bother keeping on breathing! What's the point of this whole sodding existence? I ask you!"

Kit looked at Ronan with some concern. "What? What's *your* problem?"

Ronan clutched his head and then waved his arms around some more. "You benighted muppet, has your reading comprehension taken the day off? Is it possible you don't understand what you've got there? It's only an opt-in for the *Invitational,* you total twitmuffin!"

Twitmuffin? Kit got a feeling asking for definitions wouldn't be a smart move right now, as Ronan was genuinely worked up. "Is this good?" he said, and started reading down the page again, trying to make sense of what he was seeing.

Ronan laughed again, but this time it was a helpless sound, like someone being kind to the intellectually challenged. "Let me explain it to you . . ."

2

Coney Island

✷

THE SOUTH SHORE OF LONG ISLAND can properly be described as starting just east of New York's Staten Island, where the southern side of Brooklyn meets the Great South Bay at the outward-jutting spit of land called Coney Island.

The nautical charts don't show it as such, of course. This area is part of the huge, busy expanse of New York Harbor, and the charts are slashed up and down and across the wide white stripes of transit lanes and shipping lanes, and dotted with channel and bottom soundings, with buoy markers, and the little dashed circles that indicate underwater wrecks or danger areas. Only close to shore do things quiet down to a scatter of numbers — the distance to the seafloor in fathoms — with here and there a notation about submerged pilings or obstructions. One of these areas,

Coney Island Channel, runs for a mile or so south-
eastward from the tiny peninsula's farthest western
edge at Norton Point.

Just inshore from the even 20-foot depth of the
channel is Coney Island proper. From out on the water,
the beachfront amusement park itself is only a small
part of the view, the biggest of the thrill rides standing
up like an awkward scarlet mushroom near the longest
of the piers that stick out into the water. Farther to
the west, a double handful of twenty- or thirty-story
apartment buildings catch the light reflected off the
water on bright afternoons, their windows blindingly
afire with gridded squares of Sun.

Nita broke surface and put her head above water,
and the glance of that hot white light caught her right
in the starboard eye and blinded it.

"*Ow*," she said, wincing, and submerged again, or
tried to. For a moment nothing happened except that
her tail beat the water behind her into foam, which
was annoying ... especially out here. She was no
more than three hundred meters from one of the busiest waterways in the whole New York metropolitan
area, and she had no particular desire to be run over
by some chartered pleasure craft or returning fishing
boat because she was having a tail malfunction.

"Dammit," Nita said under her breath, and stopped
thrashing. Then she rolled over on her back to float

and think while scratching idly at the barnacles on her belly with one long pectoral fin. "S'reee," she sang into the water, "this thing's still not working . . ."

"The same problem as before?" inquired a voice floating up from underneath her. "Or something new?"

"New. It's the tail this time."

The voice said something very rude and crass in a long string of squeaks and squeals that sounded like a violin having its neck wrung. "I guess we should be grateful that it keeps failing in *different* ways each time . . ."

"Speak for yourself," Nita said in a low, long humpback wail. She flipped both pectoral fins sideways and used their weight to roll over again, putting herself once more belly-down, and one more time tried to flip her tail up. She managed at least to lean in to the nose-downward orientation for beginning a dive, but the tail hung above the water and waved around in utter uselessness. There was a weird jittering feel to the movement, like the kind of thigh-muscle spasm Nita got sometimes after gym period when she'd just done an extra round of the quarter-mile track and pushed herself too hard.

Just hold still, she told the tail, despite her increasing nervousness at hanging there like someone doing a handstand half in and half out of the water. *Am I just going to fall over sideways again, or backwards —* But the stillness was starting to pay off as Nita slowly and carefully exhaled and let some of her buoyancy go, and she slid farther and farther down until the tail was halfway under, then nearly all the way, then just the flukes sticking out in the air —

Finally she was fully submerged. Nita kept sinking down through the silvery-green water toward where the others were waiting. S'reee was closest to the surface, half rolled over and watching her with concern out of her port-side eye. Hanging more upright just below her, and watching Nita carefully, was one of S'reee's colleagues, a reticent and routinely cranky right-whale wizard called Uu'tsch, who had the heaviest encrustation of barnacles she'd ever seen on a living being. Farther down, swimming back and forth in a casual and theoretically unconcerned manner, was a third humpback, S'reee's friend Hwiii'sh. At least "friend" was the best word Nita could find for him at the moment. While the Speech had all kinds of words for relationships, most of the ones Nita had been researching recently were for relationships with other wizards, and Hwiii'sh wasn't one. He was a food critic — a concept that had confused Nita significantly when she first started getting to grips with it.

She tried working the tail again, and this time it started to respond, though not evenly: she could still feel a jittering in the muscles on the right side, and that bothered her. "Did you have time to run a diagnostic while you were up there?" Uu'tsch said in his creaky voice.

"No," Nita said, "mostly I was trying to make sure I wasn't going to get run over by something I couldn't hear coming! Or see real well." It was a problem in these waters. There was so much low-level sound from the never-ending big ship and small-craft traffic in the main New York Harbor channels that surprisingly large boats could sneak up on you if you were unwary and the conditions were right. And hearing aside, there was still a big spot of sunscorch interfering with her vision: a humpback's eyes weren't designed for looking at so concentrated a reflection of sunlight as she'd caught from those apartment-building windows.

Nita tried to just relax and let herself drift farther down through the murky water toward the diagnostic spell circle that S'reee and Uu'tsch had laid out on the sandy bottom. The humpback whaleshape she was wearing was normally one she had little trouble with; she'd become fairly expert at this particular shapechange over time, it being made easier by the blood she'd shared with S'reee back when Nita had first become involved in the Song of the Twelve. However, the shape she was wearing today, though it might superficially have looked the same, was something else entirely. It wasn't a result of a shape-change spell she'd worked herself. She was wearing a whalesark, and after the last couple of hours' work it was driving her just about nuts.

Whalesarks were rare — since they could only be made from the donated nervous systems of whales near death — and they required a lot of complicated maintenance. And more complicated yet was the business of building them from scratch. The harvesting alone was a harrowing business, as emotional for the donor and his or her pod as it would have been for any human organ donor and family. And then came the business of mating the sophisticated and incredibly delicate net of preserved bioelectricity and other forces to the wizardry that would stabilize it. Once that was done the sark became a tool that could be used by life forms other than cetacean ones to become a whale for relatively extended periods, while being spared the stresses, dangers, and energy drain of doing a full shape-change oneself.

The business of engineering a whalesark was far beyond Nita's present competence. Not that it would be that way forever: she was getting interested. *And you need* something *to do when the visionary talent isn't working,* she'd thought. But she'd accidentally stumbled into the troubleshooting and maintenance end of things one afternoon while catching some rays out at the end of the jetty past the old Coast Guard station near Jones Beach and idly chatting with S'reee, who was taking the afternoon off from more serious work. It occurred to them both at more or less the same time, while they were talking over some of the things that had happened years ago during the Song of the Twelve, that — as far as troubleshooting unruly sarks was concerned — in Nita, the local cetacean wizards had the ideal candidate for the job. She knew perfectly well what a whale's body should feel like, having worked in one repeatedly and under considerable stress. But Nita was also noncetacean by birth, and would be perfectly set up to report on how a sark behaved for a human or other wizard who needed to work inside it.

So over the last year or so, Nita had more or less become the Western Hemisphere's go-to girl for troubleshooting malfunctioning whalesarks. It was never an easy job, though. And running in a new donation was always challenging, as it wasn't uncommon for donors to have had physical problems when they died. The neural "memory" of these problems had to be carefully disentangled from the bioelectric structure of the whalesark before it could be mated to the necessary support and control wizardries and commissioned for active service. And then there was always debugging to do after the wizardries were added. You might know how the spell was meant to affect a basic nervous system, but each one was unique, and every one Nita had worked with so far had found a way to pop some new and intriguing problem when it was in the precommissioning stages.

This one, though, was pushing the envelope of new-and-intriguing problems to the point where it was starting to frustrate Nita, because every time they solved one problem, something else came up. "Guys," she sang to the others as she dropped down toward them, "might be we've got a problem with the spell matrix itself. I think something's going on with the passthrough network that runs your intention through the spell proper and into the virtual neuronal net."

Under his barnacles, Uu'tsch started to bristle. It was more than just an idiom with him: the skin movement beneath the crust that ran all along his back and halfway down his sides could be seen as a kind of ripple, as if the barnacles were scales. "If you're suggesting that the underlying structure is faulty —"

"I didn't hear any suggestions about *fault* as such," S'reee said. "But we know the donor was having neurological problems when he moved on. It could be a phantom neurasthenia problem: we've seen that before when the nervous system's shadow wasn't quite clear yet that it was dead."

"Yes, well, that's hardly *my* fault —"

Here we go, Nita thought. She sighed out a few bubbles and swam away rather cautiously, because her tail was still misbehaving. Today, as in previous sessions, S'reee had been spending more time handling Uu'tsch than she had the whalesark. *She's sounding kind of resigned to it,* Nita thought, and wished she were half as good at the resignation thing, because Uu'tsch was starting to get on her nerves. *But he's such a stick, sometimes. So rigid. And always ready to think you're criticizing him.* "Tell me he's not going to mess up everything you've been doing!" came the whisper from just below and behind her.

Nita rolled her outboard eye — which took some doing, as whales' eyes aren't really built for rolling — and waited for Hwiii'sh to come up on her inboard side. She waved her tail at him in a gesture that among humpbacks was roughly the equivalent of someone patting you reassuringly on the shoulder. "Calm down," she said. "We're way past any possible messing-up stage. It's not like anything's going to explode."

Hwiii'sh let out a few bubbles, sort of a sigh of relief. "He's just so *edgy* all the time . . ."

"Well," Nita said, and then spent a moment more thinking about what else to say. It wasn't that she didn't agree with Hwiii'sh, to some extent; it was more that it didn't seem smart to let him know that. She'd been surprised to discover how fascinated he was by the wizards S'reee worked with — especially the human ones. And though the business of errantry had occasionally brought her to places where wizards were celebrities, this was the first time she'd ever had someone constantly trying to hang around with her because they thought wizardry made her cool. It was kind of odd.

"It's just that he's absolutely dedicated to getting it right," Nita said finally, since that was true enough. "And he's got to be feeling some pressure. He's the one who knows most about how to build the substructure wizardry, and if it doesn't work right the first time, I think it makes him feel, well, less than effective."

"That makes sense," Hwiii'sh said after a pause. "But it's good of you to be so easy on him when he snapped at you."

Nita laughed. "If that was snapping, I've had way worse," she said. "It's okay, we're good."

She angled back around toward where the others were examining the complex spell-sphere that they'd anchored to one spot in the water, and was relieved to feel Hwiii'sh hang back as she got closer. "'Ree, I was having a thought," Nita said, singing quietly so as not to intrude too much on Uu'tsch's thoughts as he leaned in to examine the inner structures of the spell, nearer the core of the sphere. "The sark started misbehaving worse when I was closer to the surface. In fact, it was having the most trouble when I was out of the water."

"Not very useful for a life form that breathes air," S'reee said, as she and Nita swam a little aside. There was a faint glow around S'reee's fins, indicative of some diagnostic spell of her own that she'd been running; but it was on hold at the moment. "This is so annoying. I thought we had the main-system interleaving handled by now . . ."

Nita tried to shake her head "I don't know" and found herself wiggling side to side a bit aimlessly, which made her laugh out a big stream of bubbles. It always took her a couple of hours' steady work to stop trying to do human body-language things with the whale body, whether she was fully shape-changed or just wearing a sark. "Well, this one's been one big long game of annoy-an-anemone, hasn't it. Fix one thing, something else pops up."

S'reee groaned a small laugh herself. Along with some earlier discussions of what went on at Coney Island had come some attempts to explain Whac-A-Mole, and some unlikely undersea versions of the game had been invented. "It's too true. Poor Uu'tsch's nerves are in shreds."

"Noticed that." Nita turned upside down, thinking. "There's trouble with the optical circuitry too. Didn't we build in a filter for bright light already? I don't remember it giving me so much trouble the last time. But nothing cut in when I was topside."

"I'd have to check the history-and-error logs, but I'm sure we did."

"Something to do with the pressure-handling

routines, then? We made lots of changes in that last time, just before we had to break up, and I wasn't sure I understood all the more technical stuff. A little out of my depth there . . ."

S'reee imitated Nita's bubble of amusement, for all the cetacean versions of the Speech had the idiom. "It's worth checking. There was definitely a lot of tweaking going on."

The two of them swam back toward the spell globe. "Uu'tsch," S'reee said, "hNii't's noticed something. All these newer problems get more troublesome near the surface. Could this be —"

"Something bathygenic?" Uu'tsch held quite still, considering, as everyone leaned down to peer more closely at the spell diagram. "We did an awful lot of work on the depth-and-pressure routines last time . . ."

Moments later he had his big nose stuck deep into one of the wizardry's secondary cores, and the surface of the boundary sphere started sporadically shivering with pale golden light, bright against the wavering blue of the shallows. "All right," S'reee said, sounding resigned now in an entirely different way, "this is the part where we float around and watch him do things he's way too excited to explain in real time . . ."

"The logs'll catch the details," Nita said. She was getting a sense that this mantra went a long way toward keeping S'reee calm, especially when so much of her own composure was being sacrificed to keep the participants in this exercise tranquil. "So tell me." She leaned sideways to go skin-to-skin to S'reee, so she could discuss things with her so softly as not to be heard by anyone else in the nearby water. "Hwiii'sh hasn't missed a single one of these sessions, has he? Most rational beings who're not wizards would be bored out of their skulls by now."

S'reee produced a tiny moan of amusement. "Well. Rationality is relative . . ."

This was a thought that had already occurred to Nita. *S'reee is way smarter than Hwiii'sh,* she'd thought more than once, *no matter how complex it is to analyze regional backflavors in krill. There is something about this I'm not getting . . .* "And you'd have sent him on his way a long while back if him being here bothered you. So what's the attraction?"

S'reee blew some ruminative bubbles. "Well, it's not *just* that he's very handsome. Or that he has a nice personality. There's more to it than that . . ."

"Or that he has the hots for you because you're a wizard."

S'reee gave Nita an ironic look. "Okay, it might have started that way. But there's more going on."

"You're just not sure what."

"No, and I'm giving it some time. This kind of thing — if you try taking it apart to see what makes it go —"

"Or *not* go —" Nita said, casting an eye toward Uu'tsch.

"— then you might not be able to get it back together again. Or once you did, it might not work the same way. Or at all."

"Mmm," Nita said. *Funny that those are thoughts I've been having lately, too* . . . S'reee had been seeing Hwiii'sh for some months now. But to Nita's way of thinking the "seeing" was sounding suspiciously like dating, and she suspected that S'reee and Hwiii'sh were thinking seriously about starting a pod. *And where do they go with that once they get the two of them sorted out? A pod's usually three. Do they go around auditioning third parties, or do they* . . .

Nita stopped herself, suddenly feeling strongly that whale sex wasn't something she wanted to get into just now. The issue of human sex was entirely too much on her mind as it was: not exactly in her mental backyard yet, but nonetheless looming on the horizon. "'Ree," Nita said after a moment, because she wasn't sure how well this subject was going to cross the species boundary, "is there any chance you've noticed —"

"*Aha!*" Uu'tsch howled, and S'reee and Nita spasmed a couple meters away from each other with the sheer volume and shock of the noise.

"We'll hope that's a solution," S'reee said, exchanging a glance of mutual annoyance with Nita. The two of them turned and swam back to the spell globe, where one part of one of the secondary cores was flaring brighter as Uu'tsch teased a long string of words in the Speech out of it.

"Just as I thought," Uu'tsch said as they swam up. He'd already turned his attention to the long drift of Speech glowing faintly golden in the water. Sparks of light swelled here and there on the strand, like the air-bladder nodes on a strand of kelp, and pulsed gently at slightly different rhythms. "The pressure differential routines had a conflict with the virtual blood chemistry regimen, the part that serves the virtual ADP in the musculature and the —"

"Complicated parts of the sark, yes," S'reee said in some haste. "That's a nice piece of analysis, Uu'tsch."

"— and so of course that means there was nothing wrong with the spell matrix at all, that's just fine, nothing worse than a connectivity issue between it and the depth management routines." He threw Nita a look — literally a side eye, from way down deep in the crust of barnacles on that side. "Won't take more than a few days to troubleshoot."

It's just magic the way without saying a word he makes his wonderfulness somehow still be my *fault,* Nita thought. *Powers That Be but I am done with this guy. Isn't it wonderful that I'm going to be working with him for the immediate forever?* Still, somehow she managed to keep herself from bubbling in exasperation. "That's great. When do you think you might be ready for me to take this out for a run again?"

Everyone got the inturned expression that meant they were communing with the Sea in order to have a look at their schedules. Nita closed her eyes and did the same, as the sark had a manual-emulation routine built into it so that wizards wearing it could use the Sea as a manual the way a cetacean wizard did.

Then Nita exhaled in quiet annoyance, as all she was getting was a huge vague roar of data with a sort of edge of excitement around the boundaries of it. *One more thing that still needs work, and no point in mentioning it to Uu'tsch right now, he'll just get cranky . . .* "You guys mind if I get out of this?" she said. "I know my own system better . . ."

"No, no, go right ahead," Uu'tsch said, vague, paying no particular attention to Nita. S'reee simply shrugged her fins at Nita, an amused gesture.

Nita said the brief spell that brought her preprogrammed force field bubble into being around the whale-body, and got the get-rid-of-the-water routine ready. Then she tugged the loose spell-thread that hung out of the whalesark's wizardry, saying the single very long and involved word that undid it — as complicated a construct as might have been expected when you wanted to make absolutely sure it wasn't something you could say accidentally. The whale-shape around her collapsed in a brief storm of light as it released some of the unused wizardly power that had been keeping it online, and as it did the water-expulsion wizardry instantly came up and teleported the water inside Nita's force bubble outside of it, replacing it with the air that was normally stored in the force field's own onboard claudication. A second later she was standing in her bathing suit at the bottom of her force field sphere, dripping a little, with the decommissioned whalesark draped over one arm like a shawl of sea-blue glows and glitters.

She threw the weightless thing over one shoulder so as to have her hands free, reached sideways in the air to unzip the between-spaces claudication that followed her around when she was on active errantry, and reached into it to dig out her wizard's manual. The usual brief fumbling and feeling around ensued — a claudication has something of a gift for filling up with stuff — in this case pens and thumb drives and a couple of paperbacks and a half-eaten roll of LifeSavers that had gotten in there somehow. *Now, where has it — it should be within reach, oh wait, is* this *where my hairbrush went? Well, that's a relief —*

Aha. Finally Nita felt the familiar shape and pulled her manual out. The scheduling pages in the back were highlighted at the edges: she riffled through to them. "Okay," she said. "What are we talking about here? Next Tuesday?"

And she stopped, because some page edges farther along were blinking. "Wait, what the —" She hastily flipped pages to that section. "Oh, *now* what?" she muttered in the general direction of whoever among the Powers That Be might have been listening. "Can't you see I'm busy here? I swear, every time I start getting settled into some kind of schedule, it's 'Oh no, we'd better get *Nita* in here to fix everything up.' Aren't there like half a billion *other* wizards on the planet who you could . . ."

She trailed off. "What?" S'reee said, peering through Nita's force bubble.

Nita turned around and waved her manual at S'reee. "Do you know anything about this?"

"This *what?*"

"Whatever an 'Invitational' is," Nita said, irritated. "I honestly don't need another work thing right now!"

S'reee stared, then burst out laughing at her. "h'Niiit, you're kidding me, surely?" She waved her flukes around in a bemused way. At least that was how Nita was reading it. She was no specialist yet in whale body language, and being in a sperm-whalesark when you were trying to read humpback kinesics didn't confer any particular advantages.

"Not on purpose," Nita said. "What is it, some kind of meeting?"

"Honestly, I have to wonder whether you and K!t

have been kept way too busy, that you don't know about this! Never mind, one thing at a time. Next Tuesday?"

Nita paged back again. "No, I've got class," she said. Her school had recently gone split-scheduled, and she was still having trouble getting used to being in class only in the mornings on some days and only in the afternoons on others. "Mmmm . . . Thursday? Some time in the morning be okay?"

The others agreed; even Uu'tsch didn't sound too put out. They settled on ten a.m., which was early enough for Nita on a day when there wasn't some urgent reason to be up earlier, and the group broke up, Nita passing the shut-down whalesark back to Uu'tsch through her force bubble. "You go on ahead, Hwii'ish," S'reee said to her companion as the others left. "I'll find you by sound in a bit. Look for me about halfway down Third Isle."

"Sure," he said. "Swim well, hNii't!"

"You too, big guy."

"You've got a fan there," S'reee said, very low, as Hwii'ish made his way off eastward through the water and finally disappeared from view.

"Yeah, I've been noticing that. Look, let's go up top," Nita said. "I'll dump the bubble and go whale."

S'reee snorted out her blowhole. "You're such a poet," she said, and headed for the surface.

Nita reached out to the surface of her force bubble

and told it through touch to float itself up to the surface. As the two of them bobbed up together, Nita dismissed the force shield — which left her in nothing but a one-piece bathing suit, well out into the Great South Bay, in weather that could only be described as "springlike" with great generosity. "Oooh, bad-idea-bad-idea-*bad-idea!*" she gasped.

S'reee was throwing Nita an amused look even as Nita felt around in her head for the shape-change spell that had become so second nature for her since she and S'reee had shared blood all that while back. "You feel water temperatures like a cetid even when you're primate-skinned," S'reee said. "My fault, I guess . . ."

Nita's teeth were chattering so hard she had to stop twice to clamp down on her jaw muscles so she could get the words of the spell out right. But as the last word slid out, suddenly everything smoothed itself over, the water was warm, and Nita's nose was ten feet in front of her eyes again, where it belonged. *In this shape, anyway . . .*

She let out a long moan of a sigh. "Better," Nita said. "'Third Isle?' What's that, Fire Island?"

"That's right. Over by —" S'reee briefly went quiet, correlating her own internal mapping against human conventions via the Sea. "Sunken Forest, you call it."

"That's a pretty good ways from here," Nita said as she got her fins working again. After you'd spent an afternoon in a whalesark, it took a while sometimes to remind yourself about how your own whale-shape normally worked. It was like the way your gait changed after you switched out of highish heels back into sneakers.

S'reee waved a fin in a shrug as they started eastward. "Hwii'ish likes to swim fast," she said.

"You mean he likes to think you can't catch up with him if he swims fast." Nita snickered a string of bubbles as they submerged together.

"Well," S'reee said, under her breath, but not correcting Nita.

"And you *like* letting him think you can't."

S'reee rolled her starboard-side eye at Nita. "Every now and then," she said, "I disabuse him of the notion."

Nita laughed. "I just bet you do."

She concentrated on sinking deeper, bathing herself in the restful dark green of the near-shore Bay and listening to the sounds of the near-offshore waters; the buzz of distant pleasure-boat motors, the soft groans and clicks and whistles of various marine life drifting up from the ocean floor some forty feet below them, the distant calls of other whales, like murmurs half heard across a busy room. "Look," Nita said, "now that we're out of singing distance . . ."

"You're going to ask me what's going on with Uu'tsch and his personal hygiene problem."

"Oh God." Nita went hot all over with embarrassment. "Did he know I was thinking that? I'll die *right here.*"

"I can think of better reasons for dying," S'reee said, sounding a bit dry again, and Nita had to laugh; genuine death *had* been a lot closer to both of them, when they were first working together years back, for reasons much more worthwhile than embarrassment. "But no, I doubt it. He's no expert on human thought or body language. The truth is, he doesn't see much of anything but himself and wizardry. The rest of us are just a nuisance to him, and as for the barnacles, I'm not even sure he notices them. I don't ask. He's a genius at what he does. Everybody who works with him just lets him get on with it." She chuckled. "Which is why no one makes a big deal of us going well into the Busy Water and halfway to Barnegat to consult him. He's the talent: need goes where the talent is . . ."

"Okay. I was just trying not to stare."

"Just what we all do. But I'm not sure he even notices *us* doing it, frankly. He's so wrapped up in himself and his work."

Nita felt a lot better. "Fine. Now what *is* this Invitational thing? Last time I saw something like this, Dairine had signed me up for an interplanetary student exchange . . ."

"Your excursus, that's right. No, that was just a working holiday! This is completely different. Not about work as such. In fact it's an honor."

"*Oh, no,*" Nita said immediately.

S'reee bubbled a laugh into the water. "All right, and kind of a challenge too! But you can turn it down if you want to."

Nita had her own thoughts about that, even though she'd hardly heard anything yet. The Powers had a sneaky way of getting you to do things for them even when you'd sworn you absolutely weren't going to. "Okay," she said as they slipped into the barrier-island waters just east of Coney Island, "what's it about?"

"Well. You know that not everything one hears from the Sea, or that you get from your manuals, comes straight from the Powers That Be."

"Sure," Nita said. "Wizards contribute lots of spells and raw data. General knowledge, reports on local conditions . . ."

"Of course. Well, it's important that such contributions don't just happen by accident, or under stress. Wizards have a responsibility to further the Art, and part of that is making sure the new up-and-coming talent is getting the support it needs."

"At wizardry in general? That's what the Advisory- and Senior-level wizards were for, I thought."

"That's only part of it. Because when you're

a younger wizard, who wants to be listening to Advisories all the time? They're so *old*."

Nita burst out laughing at that. "Oh, yeah, look at *you!* Who was a Senior just now, oh ancient one?"

"As if I didn't get rid of *that* title as fast as I could!" S'reee said. "And good riddance. But even among cetaceans, when it comes to long-term learning, we tend to retain better what we learn either by ourselves or from others our own age. Or close to it, anyway."

"So they want us to — what? Start teaching other wizards stuff?"

"Not so much teaching. Well, yes, to a certain extent . . . but it's a mentoring program at heart. Just because someone's incredibly talented doesn't necessarily mean they know what to *do* with it."

"Please," Nita moaned. *"Dairine."*

S'reee bubbled with amusement. "I wasn't going to mention . . ."

The image of a whole crowd of Dairines gathered together in one place was already making Nita twitch. "Anyway," S'reee said, "an Invitational is probably the biggest gathering of wizards you're ever likely to see on a regular basis. Certainly the biggest noncrisis gathering. Once every eleven years the new intake of wizardly talent comes together to show what they can do."

"What, to do spells?"

"Oh, among other things, yes. But not wizardries that've been around for a while. This is as much about new spell design as anything else. The participating wizards display new ways they've found to exploit the forces and elements of the universe. And the Speech, of course."

"Huh," Nita said. "Sounds like some kind of science fair."

S'reee briefly looked puzzled. "I'm not getting a meaningful translation into the Speech on that phrase."

Nita frowned, because she wasn't sure how much of what was involved in a science fair would make sense to a whale even if she found a way to just put it into S'reee's dialect of humpback, let alone the Speech. "It's an educational thing. You do projects that demonstrate some scientific principle. Or else you show how you'd solve a problem using science. The best projects get a prize, usually."

"Oh," S'reee said. "All right, this could be like that. Except while you're doing your demonstration, it's okay to rewrite the laws of science a little bit . . ."

"Well, fine. But why am *I* getting invited to this thing? Is it because of Kit? I see he got an invite too."

"Isn't it obvious? They want you to come in and mentor."

"What?" Nita stared down at that little eye. "Why *me?*"

"I keep talking to you, hNii't, about not going so unconscious about your own credentials," said S'reee. "You dealt with the Lone Power one-on-one, on Its own turf, on your Ordeal. You survived the Song of the Twelve, which isn't exactly a given for *any* of the participants. Not to mention various other minor skirmishes. Mars, just now. Alaalu. The Hesper business."

"We were lucky!"

"You were smart," S'reee said. "The research kind of smart, the *preparedness* kind of smart. Smart is six-tenths of luck. And you played to your strengths, and you took your chances where you could find them. You weren't afraid to improvise, or go for broke."

"I also have a partner," Nita said, "who knows how to be smart for two when *my* smarts break down."

"So there you are," S'reee said. "You understand it. Individually and as a team, the two of you have data and experience worth passing on, wouldn't you say? You could make the difference between some other wizards living or dying because you knew how to help someone hammer the rough edges off the spell that someday was going to help them, or somebody else, survive."

Nita sighed as they turned left and passed slowly by Point Lookout, heading inshore toward the northern side of the waters running inside the Fire Island barrier. "This is a 'pay it forward' thing, isn't it."

"Of course it is. What isn't?"

She could see the low roofs of Freeport and Bay Shore jutting up against the afternoon sky ahead of them. *A lot of things have started out like this,* Nita thought, *really innocently . . . and then turned into something way different before they were done.* Yet she had to admit there was no guarantee that this was going to be one of them. "Well, what do I do now?"

"I'd guess you want to make sure your transport allowance is properly implemented, and check out the apps they've set up for you. Take a few minutes to talk to your Advisories, of course: Sea knows they'll have been down this road before. In fact they probably recommended you for this, so you may want to talk to them about that."

"Take a baseball bat to them, you mean!"

S'reee whistled with amusement as the two of them headed as close toward shore as it was wise for S'reee to go. "And then shove everything else you've got going on into a claudication and forget about it for a while, because you're about to be the busiest you've ever been when you weren't actually saving the universe."

3
Wellakh / Hempstead

✳

THE HUGE HIGH-CEILINGED SPACE was dark, walled in by rough stone. Only its floor was smooth, and mostly dark except where hot orange light fell on it in the center of the room. There, floating perhaps a meter above the floor, hung what appeared to be a giant burning globe of gas twenty meters across, turning slowly and gently in the air. Swarms of sunspots crept slowly across its surface in big clusters and patches: prominences arched out from it into the dark empty air, strained at what seemed to be gravity, fell back again.

In all the ways that mattered, it looked like a sun: specifically, a dark golden-orange subgiant star somewhere between types G and K, perhaps a G6. The only odd thing about it was the way it was throbbing — its surface blooming outward, shivering, then falling back again, shifting the big dark patches of sunspots around so that they drifted farther from one another briefly when the burning surface expanded, then flocked closer together when it collapsed back again.

The only other immediately peculiar aspect of the situation would have been the thin young redheaded girl in capri pants and sneakers and a long floppy purple print top who came stomping around from the far side of the huge burning globe, waving her arms and yelling at the top of her lungs, "Okay, that was *completely* out of bounds, there was *no* need to do that, and *you* may think it was cute, but pulling a cheap stunt like that *absolutely and completely sucks!*"

After a few moments' silence, from behind the stellar simulator two other figures emerged: a big blocky silver-haired man in jeans and a polo shirt, and a much taller and slenderer man with tied-back red hair nearly down to his knees, wearing soft dark-amber trousers and boots and a long open vestlike robe a shade darker. The taller man folded his arms across his chest in a resigned manner and looked at the shorter one, who had shoved his hands into his pockets and was gazing at the far-off ceiling and shaking his head.

"Harold," the taller man said, "pray advise me. Would this be an appropriate response to what we've just seen?"

Dairine's father shrugged. "Was what happened just there something that was *supposed* to happen?"

"No, no, no, no, *NO!*" Dairine shouted, and

stalked away from them, waving her arms in the air. "Don't you two start trying to tag-team me, now, this is the *last* thing I need —"

"I mean, I don't see what the fuss is about," Dairine's dad said. "It didn't blow up anything like as hard as it did the time before last. This looks more like heavy breathing, and it seems to be settling down. So relatively speaking, what you're doing looks like an overreaction."

"If I had been prepared for it, it'd never have happened!"

"Precisely the point," Nelaid said. "This is about how you react when you are *not* prepared."

Dairine whirled and threw a look at Nelaid that (if being a wizard was good for anything) should have vaporized him. Then she whirled away and went stomping off again.

The two men exchanged glances. "Harold," said Nelaid, "is it, do you think, appropriate to discuss anger management strategies at some future date?"

"Nel," said Dairine's dad, sounding completely resigned, "you're on." They watched Dairine with their arms folded, in nearly matching poses, with nearly matching faces.

She stopped herself from coming around for another bout of stomping and paused long enough for a familiar shape to come pacing out of the shadows on numerous mechanical legs. Spot's laptop-body was moving close to the ground and nothing like the normal number of stalked eyes were in evidence: he looked like he was purposely trying to keep a low profile.

No need for you to be doing that, she said silently as she scooped him up.

Yes there is, Spot said, and pulled his eyes in tightly enough to his upper carapace that they vanished into it.

"It is not fair that you won't let me use Spot!" she said to Nelaid, hugging Spot to her as Nelaid and her father headed over to her.

"Fairness does not enter into it," Nelaid said, "because, as I thought I surely must have made plain to you by now, while your mech-based colleague may indeed be specialized hardware, he is *not* specialized enough for this task. And we have been over this a good number of times. The Sunstone is more specialized and far more suitable to purpose when it comes to everyday maintenance of a star than even Spot's most carefully tailored wizardly routines, regardless of how assiduously you have been attempting to alter them to suit your needs. Which are mostly impelled by laziness," he said to Dairine's dad.

"Tell me about it," her dad said, rolling his eyes. "I blame these smartphones, myself. Nobody knows how to just *remember* anything anymore."

Nelaid flashed what Dairine suspected was a very

precisely calculated half-smile. "Wellakhit wizards have been looking for alternate modalities to the Stone for longer than people on your planet have known how to do algebra, and have yet to find *anything* as suitable as this particular orthorhombic silicate crystal for the work of mapping wizardry onto the fine structures of a solar interior. That you expect that *you* will be able to do so simply so that you can allow Spot to handle the imaging and patterning routines for you, rather than learning to build the spell interface inside your own mind while using the Sunstone for templating, is, well, ambitious at the very least. But also rather self-deluding."

"You think 'stubborn' might fit into the description somewhere?" said her dad.

"Oh God, what have I done to *deserve* this?" Dairine muttered.

"That is possibly an issue you will want to take up with Roshaun at some later date," Nelaid said.

Dairine froze.

There was a time, she thought, *when if he'd said something like that to me, I'd either have broken down and cried or punched him out. Now, though — But how can he say his name as if he's just stepped out of the room, as if what* happened *to him hadn't — ?* Dairine's throat went achy in the space of a breath. She *hated* it when that happened and there was no way to control it —

I can't wait *until I'm so much better at this that I can safely tell him just what I think of him!* And she let out a breath of exasperation, more at herself than at him. — *Sometime in the next century, at this rate.* But in the meantime, Spot was squirming to get down. Dairine puffed out an angry breath and crouched down to put him on the floor and let him skitter away. "My son took some time to master the fine detail of structuring the plasma management routines," Nelaid said, sounding completely unaware of Dairine's anger, or (worse) uncaring of it. "It is neither fun nor easy, and it is never going to be. If as you have been saying you intend to fulfill some of his functions for our world as well as his, the technique must be learned as taught before you can go on to try to improve it."

"If it's worth doing," Dairine's dad said, "it's worth doing right. Even when it's a pain in the ass . . ."

One of his favorite sayings, and one she'd been sick of hearing since she was nine. Dairine had been furious at Nelaid, and now she was getting furious at her dad as well. *Exponentially furious,* she thought. *But when they're like this they're more than the sum of their parts, so I get at least the square of how angry I normally am. If we could just have a huge blowup it'd be great, but they just keep calming each other down.*

"Leaving aside the issue of how you operate on the simulator, or the star it represents," said Nelaid, "I see I also still need to impress on you that just because one starts to feel more comfortable with a given star's attributes and characteristics, that is no reason to allow the comfort or familiarity to bleed into one's treatment of other stars that are overtly similar."

"Well, it wouldn't be an issue if you didn't sneakily just *change the simulator's settings* so that —"

"And why would a star on which you are operating normally take the trouble of notifying you before it is about to do something unexpected? The unexpectedness is the whole *point*. There is no more dangerous scenario than the one in which you are absolutely certain that you *know* what will happen. You were plainly quite certain of how the oblique shockfront was going to propagate in that last run, so much so that when the pressure densities of the plasma in the chromosphere underneath it started to change, you discounted the change entirely . . ."

"She did catch it before it blew, though," Dairine's dad said.

"True enough, Harold, but if she had been so careless with *your* star, the resultant derangement of its upper atmosphere, transient though it was, would shortly have done significant damage to the delicate upper levels of your planet's atmosphere. Your climate would have suffered significantly as a result, and the survivors of the weather difficulties that would inevitably have followed would not have thanked Dairine for the increase in skin cancers and the cascade effects such as selective extinctions of species too fragile to cope with the change in lower-atmosphere UV levels."

"Mmm, I take your point."

"I dropped a *decimal point,* okay?" Dairine yelled, clutching at her hair as she swung away from them.

"Pretty heavy one, looks like," her dad said, with a complete lack of sympathy.

It was bad enough when Nelaid got underhanded on her. But when her dad ganged up on her with him . . . *"Aaaaaaaagh!!"*

Her dad and Nelaid sighed and gazed at each other with that *here-she-goes-again* expression. *How is this my life?* Dairine thought, as she struggled to calm herself down. *How can everything be so screwed up when I'm a wizard? And when I have a computer who's also a wizard? And even my sister's a wizard? And my dad's* okay *with all this? And when I also now somehow have a* space *dad?!* Which — not that she would have admitted it to anybody — was incredibly cool, especially since he was also a wizard, might as well be considered the king of his planet, and was deemed so powerful and scary by some of his own people that they routinely tried to assassinate him —

"Dairine."

She blinked. Nelaid had glanced away from her father and was holding a tiny spark of white fire between thumb and forefinger. It was his manifestation of the wizard's manual, and he was studying it the way someone would look at an interesting new bug. "I wonder if this might perhaps be a wise time to finish up." He looked back to her father. "You dislike letting these sessions run too late into afternoon of your local day, which I believe is now well advanced . . ."

Her dad checked his watch. "Closing time's coming on at the shop, yeah," he said, "and there are a couple of things I want to check up on before we lock up for the evening."

Suddenly Dairine felt very tired. It had been a long work session today, partly because her spring break period was ending and this would be the last day for a while that her schedule and Nelaid's would coincide for more than a few hours at once. "Yeah," Dairine said. "Okay."

"I will set up the homeward transport for you outside, then."

"Fine," her dad said. "Come on back with us?" he asked Nelaid. "You did want to have a look at that rhododendron I was telling you about."

"I will see you home, certainly, and after that I am at your disposal. Just give me a few seconds to collapse this."

She and her dad headed for the barred gates that led out onto the terrace as Nelaid turned to decommission the stellar simulator. "And why not?" her dad murmured as they made their way out. "Got some shopping to do as well. No point in boring you with it when *he* likes to come along."

Dairine snickered and went to lean against the chest-high balustrade at the far side of the terrace that surrounded this level of the Sunlords' towering stone-spire palace. It wasn't so long ago that the relationship had seemed not just ridiculous but unlikely. "Perhaps I would understand your personal situation more clearly if I were to see you more often in your own environment?" Nelaid had said. And that had unfortunately seemed too sensible for Dairine to object much, especially if she wanted to keep doing this work with him — the work Roshaun had done and that she wanted to learn, too, as a possible way to find out what had happened to him, and to get him back. So Dairine had said "Okay" and not thought too much more about it, except to hope that her father wouldn't have too much trouble with their home life being occasionally invaded by someone who was more or less equivalent to an alien king.

Then, when her dad and Nelaid met, they not only liked each other a whole lot but knew it *instantly*, and Dairine realized her problems were even more complex than she'd feared. She'd wondered whether wizardry had been involved somehow, except that she knew Nelaid would never stoop to any such thing. He was way too serious and straightforward a wizard to even consider doing anything as potentially invasive as tampering with someone's mind without consent.

He came visiting often enough that they'd begun passing him off as an uncle. *Or, not 'we' did,* Dairine thought. *He did.* "My brother," Dairine had heard her dad say casually to a customer in the shop one afternoon, when she'd walked in after school. Nelaid was standing there with an armful of chrysanthemums, looking around in apparent confusion, while her dad stood behind the counter wrapping some kind of dish arrangement in white-and-gold gift paper. And what was extremely peculiar was that as they stood there — the tall broad-shouldered man with the prematurely silver hair and the very tall slim man with the longish hair that was almost exactly the red-gold of Dairine's own — they really did look like they were related. *And it's not just the disguise-wizardry Nelaid's wearing,* Dairine had thought at the time. *Something else is going on.* Whatever it was, it made the relationship show in their eyes. It was so extremely odd, the whole idea that you could have family on other planets: or that it could have been lying there waiting for you for years and years without you ever expecting it . . .

Except that this isn't the relationship I'm interested in having on another planet! This is just complicating things.

Things got even more complicated after that when her dad and Nelaid started going out shopping together. "If there's a better way to teach you about our culture in a hurry," her dad had said, "I don't know what it'd be." And off they'd gone to the Pathmark supermarket in Baldwin, and if there had been any sight that could spin your brain right around in your head, it was your father the florist standing in front of a heap of cantaloupes with the most senior wizard of a planet hundreds of light-years away, discussing seasons and the way axial tilt affects an area's mean solar radiation, and how to use the little depression at the bottom of the melon that you pressed into to make sure it was ripe. It was weird enough to Dairine that Nelaid considered her father to be some kind of potential spiritual leader because he worked with plants. *Though Wellakh people have always been a bit plant crazy. I guess you have to be when that's where the oxygen comes from and the vegetation's all that's kept your planet habitable after a flare . . .*

"So," said Nelaid as he came through the gate into the body of the peak and waved it shut after him, heading out across the terrace to them. He had changed into charcoal trousers, a white shirt, and a navy blazer, with his hair still tied back but looking much shorter, thanks to a fairly simple concealment spell. Dairine had to turn away to hide her amusement — he looked like some kind of rock promoter heading for a casual business lunch.

As Nelaid walked, the polished redstone floor

came alive with buried lines and circles and ellipses in blue light: a complex worldgating spell, densely inter-written with the Speech's long flowing characters and spreading out from where they stood for about twenty meters on either side. "When next we meet collegially, Dairine, we need to spend some more time on the way you have been handling the relationship between the spectral radiance and solar wind mass loss. The sooner this is handled, the sooner we can avoid having to revisit this scenario and go on to something more, well, challenging."

Dairine made her way over to the small, empty transport circle set aside for her inside the larger spell matrix and simply grunted vague agreement... because she was simply reluctant to complain. All her life she'd been infuriated by having teachers who always assumed her to be *dumber* than she was, some trick genius who had a weak spot they'd eventually discover if they just kept poking at her long enough. Nothing had prepared her for a teacher who routinely expected her to be far *smarter* than she was, and seemed intent on breaking her of the bad habit of taking it easy. *And wow, I love that. Not that I'll ever let him know. He'd just get as smug and insufferable as Roshaun...*

And her heart clenched. Dairine held her breath for a moment from reflex, then let it go. *It's getting to the point where I can think his name without it being painful...*

Her dad went over to stand in his own locator circle and gazed around at the spell diagram. "This costs a lot of energy normally, doesn't it?"

Nelaid, making his way to his own circle, glanced over at Dairine's dad. "What?"

"This form of transport. Otherwise the kids'd be doing it every day."

"Oh." Nelaid chuckled. "Yes, especially when such distances are involved. But a Planetary has wide latitude in requesting such transport allotments from the Aethyrs, especially when one or more planets' infrastructural benefits are concerned. And this training is good for both your stellar system and mine, in terms of augmenting local expertise. So the authorization was not hard to come by."

"We need this, do we?"

"Oh, your world has its specialists," Nelaid said, "some of them very gifted. Naturally we've conferred from time to time. Your star, however, has been under unusual pressure in recent years. In particular, the direct attentions of the Lost Aethyr: the one your people call the Lone Power."

"That time the Sun went out . . ." Dairine's dad said.

"Yes. Any star that had been through *that* kind of punishment might be expected to behave badly afterward: so having extra oversight in the neighborhood is seen as a good thing. And wizards native to Wellakh have over the millennia developed an unusual level of expertise in dealing with aberration in nongiant stars on the main sequence: Thahit has a history of being somewhat badly behaved indeed at intervals."

"'Somewhat'? You mean like slagging half the planet down with a single flare?" Dairine muttered.

"I have seen worse," Nelaid said. "If you're fortunate, *you* never will. Ready?" He checked to make sure they were both well inside their circles. The transport pattern flared into life around them —

— and when it died down again, they were standing in the dim brown light of a garden shed.

The backyard of Dairine's dad's flower shop was a paved area backing onto the alley where most of the deliveries arrived. In the high solid wooden wall there was a sliding gate that would open wide enough to let a van or small truck drive in, and off to one side was the shed in which they now stood. It was surrounded by the heaps of wooden crates that some flowers and supplies came in, stacked up to wait for the next flower delivery guy to take them away, and with the long thick-walled cardboard boxes in which more fragile cut flowers like roses and lilies got delivered. The crates were picked up for recycling once a week, after Dairine's dad spent an afternoon of what he referred to as "line dancing," stomping them flat before tying them up in bundles. The area wasn't particularly tidy: it tended to get scattered with floral stakes, busted-off chunks of arrangement foam, the scraps of ribbons and paper that missed being thrown into the recycling bin, and all the other detritus that piled up around a florist's business if the owner was too busy to sweep the floor more than once every few days. It was definitely not the type of place that made you think the shed in the corner, the one with the dust-obscured little windows and the door with rusty hinges, had a worldgate acceptor site in it.

"Clear?" said her dad, peering out the side window.

"Yeah," Dairine said, squinting out through the one in the door. It was hard to see through it, but that was kind of the point.

"No sign of Mike?"

"I think he's inside." She saw something move past the shop's rear window, the one in the workroom beside the walk-in fridge: a pair of arms completely laden down with a stack of long white boxes. "Yeah."

"Okay." He reached past her to pop open the catch of the door. "Go on and distract him. Nel, give me a couple moments, then come on in."

"As you say."

Her dad headed softly out, then opened the back gate so that Mike would think they'd come in that way. Dairine headed for the back door of the shop's workroom. "Hey, Mike!"

Her dad's assistant, a tall, skinny, auburn-haired

stringbean of a guy in jeans and an Islanders sweat-shirt, put his head through the tacky bead curtain that divided the front of the store from the back. "Hey, Dair!" he said. "Great timing, I was just going to start locking up."

"It's okay, I think Dad'll do it," she said as her father came in behind her.

"Mikey, did we get those boxes of mums that I — Oh, I see we did." It would have been impossible not to see the thirty or so boxes of mums, which took up almost the entire floor space in the back of the shop and blocked access to both of the sinks and the stainless steel worktops.

"Yeah, I was getting set to go stack them in the walk-in."

Her dad glanced at his watch. "It's after five," he said. "You go on. You know how your mom gets if I make you miss dinner."

Mike laughed. "But what about the mums?"

"Leave them there. I'll take care of them and the rest of the unloading."

"Right, Mr. C. See you in the morning!"

"Eightish, okay?"

"Okay!" The front door slammed.

Dairine came out of the back room in time to see her dad walk up to the front door, turn the key in it, flip the CLOSED sign around to face out, and pull the blinds on the door and the shop window.

"Daddy, what about these boxes?" Dairine said, almost thankful to have something to do besides ride herd on a star that had been purposely programmed to blow up on her.

"Most of these need to go into the walk-in," her dad said. "These white ones, oh, and that red one, there's boutonniere material in those, leave them out for the moment. Don't try to pick up more than one, you'll throw your back out . . ."

She edged between some of the boxes to put Spot down in a spare space on one of the countertops as Nelaid slipped in through the back door, paused, and took a deep breath. "It smells of life in here," he said, smiling. Glancing around, he added, "Quite crowded with it, in fact."

"So true. And to keep it that way we need to get the boxes into the cooler . . ."

There was a knock on the frame of the rear door. Everyone looked up, alert and surprised, and then relaxed, because it was Tom Swale standing there — wearing a business suit, unusual for him, and slipping out of the suit jacket while they watched. "Hey," he said. "Thought I might catch you. Harry, can I give you a hand with those?"

"Not worried about your shirt? Well, okay, here, grab the top few. What brings you here?"

"Saw your worldgate go off, and something else has come up. Good evening, *sa ke Nelaid*."

"And to you, Advisory *ke Swaal*. Busy day?"

"Getting busier all the time," Tom said. "Where do you want these, Harry?"

For a few moments nothing much went on except getting the long cardboard carnation boxes up off the floor and onto every available surface. "Yeah, that's right — No, not on top of the fridge, it blocks the vent — Oh," Dairine's dad said then, starting to laugh as a pile of boxes went past him without anyone physically carrying them: but behind them Nelaid was nudging them gently along through the air with one finger. "Now there's a trick I wish somebody would teach me."

"A fair amount of other data would be needed as well," said Nelaid, "and possibly a change of career . . ."

"A little late for that," Dairine's dad said. "Maybe I could just get you in every other weekend . . ."

The laughter got lost in more shuffling around of boxes. "This has to be the whole East Coast's mum supply, Harry," Tom said as he stacked his last few. "Long weekend, I take it."

"Two weddings, two funerals," Dairine's dad said. "I'll be in here very early tomorrow."

"Good thing I caught you now, then," said Tom.

Dairine's dad threw her a thoughtful glance as he reached for the water hose that ran from the work sink and started filling the first of a stack of tall plastic flower buckets. "Should I be scared to ask?"

"I did not *do* anything," Dairine said in exasperation.

"Didn't say you did," said Tom.

She breathed out. "So if it's not something I did, what *is* it?"

"Something you haven't done yet."

Her father and Nelaid stared at each other, and then Nelaid burst out laughing. "Have the Aethyrs installed a new, more efficient youth-disciplinary system then?" he said. "Will we now be sanctioning misbehaving wizards *ahead* of the fact?"

Tom laughed too. "I could see where it might save on paperwork. But no." He looked at Dairine. "You haven't checked your manual today?"

"I've been kind of busy. *Not blowing things up*," Dairine said with a glare at her dad and Nelaid, intent on getting just a little more mileage out of this truism if she could.

"Well," Tom said, "we were thinking of giving you the opportunity — offering you the opportunity, anyway," he said, with a sideways glance at Dairine's dad, "to blow up something else."

Dairine couldn't help it if the look she turned on him was suspicious. "What's that supposed to mean?"

"Take a look at the scheduling in the manual," Tom said, "while I give your dad a bit more of a lowdown."

She pulled her manual out, stared at the blinking page edges, and cracked it open in a hurry. "I take it you're speaking figuratively," Dairine's dad said, pushing the last few stacked boxes into line and then turning to lean his back against the stack.

"I'm *hoping* I will be," Tom said with a dry grin, "but with these things you can never tell."

"These things being?"

"I'm having my manual functions copy a précis of this data to your phone," Tom said. "But pending your approval, I've nominated both Nita and Dairine as potential mentors for a wizardly event that's going to start happening in the next couple weeks. It won't be dangerous; they'll probably both be more closely supervised than they have been when doing almost anything since they became wizards. There'll be a lot of senior personnel around for this — a lot of attention to what they're doing. By adults."

"Meaning you?" her dad said as he pulled the lever to crack open the door of the walk-in fridge.

"Strangely enough, no. Or not directly. I've got other duties during this period, and so does Carl. Though we'll check in from time to time, since there are attendees we've nominated. The event's educational; in a way it's about training the next generation of consultant wizards. By publicly recognizing the talent of some of the up-and-coming generation, we're looking to get some of the newer wizards to think about making the research and development end of wizardry the main thrust of their careers."

Dairine's dad tilted his head to one side, looking interested. "So this is like a jobs fair?"

"Yes, but more than just that. A lot of networking goes on, and a lot of, well, showing off." Tom chuckled. "Any time you put a group of gifted teenagers in the same place, in a situation where it's a *virtue* to show off what they can do — well, you can imagine."

"Probably no, I can't," Dairine's dad said. But she felt reassured to see him smiling when she glanced up from her manual.

"As I said, we've got a lot of safeguards in place to minimize the risk for everybody. Especially because some of the candidates will be working with spells at a very theoretical level, and it's always smart to make sure that if the spell starts to execute in a way that its designer didn't intend, the effects can be contained. Believe me, there's a lot of attention on that, since most of the best spells, the ones that are the most useful tools for wizards in the field, have dangerous aspects."

"How large is the intake, Advisory?" Nelaid said.

"Three hundred candidate entrants, plus or minus twenty," Dairine said, already halfway through the pages that had been blinking at her. She was starting to break out in a sweat, she was getting so excited, but she was determined not to give any sign of how she felt just yet.

Tom nodded. "Assuming we get about eighty

percent uptake on the invitations. Each entrant's assigned at least one mentor a few years older than they are, or same age but smarter. We keep the ages close: candidates learn better from younger mentors than older ones." He looked at Dairine's dad again. "While we recommend assignments, the Powers do the final matching for the closest fit and the best results."

"So if a candidate wants to dump their mentor," Dairine asked, "they can do that?"

"Or the mentor can step away from the relationship with the candidate," Tom said. "Though it doesn't happen often. Even if there's some initial tension, the pairings are sufficiently appropriate for each other that they normally make it through to the final stages of competition."

The word "competition" got down the back of Dairine's neck and just buzzed there in her spine, very pleasantly. "What's the prize?"

Her dad and Nelaid and Tom exchanged an amused look. "A year's coaching relationship with Earth's Planetary Wizard," Tom said. "You remember her, Harry. She came to the barbecue at your place after the Mars business. Irina Mladen."

"The nice blond lady with the baby and the parakeet? Of course." He smiled. "She made sure she had my burger recipe before she left."

"There you go," Tom said. "That's her."

Dairine dropped her gaze back to her manual,

thinking, *Yes, the woman who could destroy the earth with a couple of sentences' worth of the Speech and a word or two with the planet's core . . . !* She closed her manual, resisting the urge to slap it shut in a fury. "How is it," she said, trying not to sound too tightly angry, "that *I* never got to be in a competition like this as a candidate?"

"Bad timing, I'm afraid," Tom said. "Experience has shown that it's not all that productive to hold the Invitational more than once every eleven years. So that's how it's done. Anyway, even if you were eligible to compete in this cycle, that's no guarantee that you'd be chosen as a candidate." He gave her a look that was maybe just a little too knowing. "Even for the most successful candidates, this isn't just about winning. It's more about getting to know more wizards than just your local circle. Wizardry as it's practiced on Earth is a very networky business; the sooner you learn how to get quickly into contact and work effectively with people you've only known for a very short time, the better it is for everyone. There are years when the stuff that goes on around the edges of the Invitational turns out to be more important than the events themselves. There's no way to find out unless you play . . ."

"So what you're telling me," Dairine's dad said, "is that she's going to be riding herd on someone else to make sure *they* don't blow something up."

"Could very well be," Tom said. "Candidates tend

to be matched with mentors who'll know, or recognize, how they're most likely to screw up, and can keep it from happening."

"Well . . ." Dairine's dad folded his arms over his chest.

Dairine's insides immediately went cold. *No, no, he's going to say no and I need this, I have to go to this — !* "Dad . . ." she said, and then stopped herself.

His gaze, which had drifted in a vague, noncommittal way along the floor, now flicked up to meet hers. In his eyes Dairine could see the potential grin that he hadn't let out onto his face as yet. "Well." He shifted his gaze sideways to delay it. "Nel, what do you think? Can she be spared from her lessons for a while?"

Dairine held her breath. Nelaid's face was always much harder to read than her father's, for various reasons — chief among them his alien facial kinesics, or the carefully guarded mindset of a man who while in office rarely saw a tenday or half a month go by without someone trying to assassinate him. That gaze now rested very consideringly on Dairine. "What do you think, *petech*? Do you think recent behavior warrants it?"

Apprentice, he'd just called her. Meaning that this was one of those trick questions. Dairine groaned inside. If she went humble and agreed with Nelaid, or said what she thought he wanted her to say, he was likely to kill this whole prospect. *Which would be horrible,* thought Dairine, *since this sounds like the most interesting thing that's happened since, well, since the world needed saving the last time! A whole bunch of new people — wizards I don't know, people who'll take me* seriously. *And maybe put me onto some spell or something that I've missed, something that'll help me find out what I want to know about more than anything else, the one thing that matters —*

"Spinning your wheels there?" her dad said. The grin was still not showing on his face, and Dairine knew it would be fatal to try to force it there. And her mind was still racing. She honestly did grudge any time away from the work she was doing with Wellakh's star-simulator and with Thahit itself. Gradually she'd been reaching some possible conclusions about what might have caused Roshaun's bizarre and untimely disappearance from the surface of the Moon at the end of the Pullulus War. *But sometimes it makes sense to switch tracks. Especially when the one you're on seems to go on forever and ever with no real results, just wishes and hopes and staring at the ceiling in the middle of the night, missing his goofy face with the lollipop sticking out of it . . .*

Nelaid said, "Harold, we are surely unkind to leave her in these agonies for so long." He glanced at Tom. "If your Advisory has gone so far as to recommend you for this role, and the Powers have gone so far as to second the recommendation, or confirm it, then there is no point in second-guessing them. If you find this appropriate, Harold, then I daresay I can manage my star's well-being for a few weeks until my apprentice is at leisure again."

Dairine let out the breath she hadn't realized she was holding, and grinned.

"How long's this last, Tom?" Dairine's dad said.

"Three weeks, give or take. There's an informal plenary session to start, then a couple of orientation days for everyone to get to know each other. After that, informal spell assessments lead up to the eighth-finals, where spells are judged against each other theoretically for relative effectiveness. Quarter-finals are for 'proof of concept,' the demonstration of single elements of wizardries. That culls out another half of the competitors. All this time the mentors and candi-dates are working together — they sort out their own schedules and meet whenever they think they need to. After that, semifinals in front of a panel of twenty or so wizards at Advisory or Senior level. Two thirds of the competitors are set aside there. After that, three rounds of pre-finals go forward in groups of fifteen or twenty. And finally, five wizards do their full spell implementations at the big final session on the Moon."

"Safer there, is it?" said Dairine's dad.

Tom raised his eyebrows. "If something gets out

of hand," he said, "just as well that it happens over on the 'dark side,' especially these days. We have to work around the various lunar orbiters, and we usually put a stealth shield over the proceedings to be safe. Not that most of the spells even show, from space. But better to be sure."

"And this can be worked around school, I take it?"

"Oh, yes. In your case, I see that your kids' school has just gone to split sessions: that'll make things easier for the three of them." Dairine's head came up again at that. "Oh, yes, Kit's in it, too: he and Nita are a team on this as usual," said Tom. "I have to go see his dad and mom after we're done here. But otherwise, except for the big events, it's up to the mentors and candidates how and where they meet. And of course worldwide worldgating travel's subsidized for this, for the duration. It's a bit of a perk."

Dairine's dad nodded. "So I get to go to this?" he said to Dairine. "When you make the final, or your candidate does." And he grinned. Dairine grinned back.

"Sure you do," Tom said. "You count as vital support personnel. No one would think of keeping you away."

Tom dusted his hands off and picked up his jacket again. "So I'll be on my way," he said. "Unless there are any more boxes you need moved?"

"Nope," Dairine's dad said. "We're sorted here."

"Later, then." And absolutely without noise, Tom vanished.

Dairine let out a long breath, staring at where he'd been. When she looked back at them, her dad and Nelaid were both smiling at her. "You two are *so mean to me*," she said. "You were *always* going to say yes! You just let me stand here and *squirm*."

Nelaid looked at Harold, arched an eyebrow. "Has anyone considered introducing the concept of gratitude to this planet?" he started to say, and then was cut off suddenly on finding himself wearing Dairine around his middle, hugging him hard. The *whoof* of the breath going out of him was satisfying.

Her dad was the next victim, but he had a few moments to prepare. "You're going to *love* this," she said into his chest.

"Just make sure *you* do," he replied, hugging her back. "That's the whole point."

Not the whole one, Dairine thought. *But it'll do . . .*

4

Antarctica / Knox Coast

✳

"WHAT DO YOU WEAR for Antarctica?"

Carmela stood in the doorway of Nita's bedroom, looking in with considerable confusion at the clothes hanging about in the air. In some cases they were *literally* hanging — like the ones that were floating about on their hangers because Nita hadn't bothered to remove them before the clothes emerged from her closet. Tops and pants and skirts were so thick in the space between her and Carmela that Nita could hardly see anything of Carmela but her feet.

"Would it be out of bounds for me to pass a comment here?" said Kit's partially unseen sister.

"You can pass a comment, you can pass go," Nita said, pushing through a tangle of tops of various colors. "You can pass anything you like — and maybe you can pass me those pants. Yeah, those right there . . ."

Carmela moved among the floating garments like

someone making her way through the down-hanging branches of a thickly grown forest. "These ones?" She plucked a pair of white Capri pants out of the air and held them up between her hands, turning them back and forth. "These are from *last year,* Neets."

"I know."

"And are you *sure* about wearing white to Antarctica this time of year? It's getting on toward fall. We must be close to their version of Labor Day. Assuming they *have* that down there. But then again, no one owns the place, do they?"

Nita had to stop and laugh, pushing her hair back out of her face. "Antarctica? They *say* they don't. Or at least, international law says they don't. But all the big countries spend their time working around that one. Everybody's got a scientific base somewhere down there, and while there *are* people doing science, sometimes they're accidentally acting as cover for some secret weapons thing or some such . . . And everyone pretends it's not happening and quietly spies on each other every way they can."

"And probably nobody pays any attention to Labor Day. Well, you still don't get to wear these pants. Your legs aren't the same length they were last year. And besides, Dairine is having a Capri-pants phase right now, and the last thing you want to look like at a party is your little sister."

"Oh, God," Nita muttered, "this is turning into

a nightmare. I can't make up my mind about *anything.*"

Carmela chucked the white pedal pushers onto
Nita's bed, then flopped down on it herself and
watched Nita push her clothes around in the air. "Why
the stress levels?" she said. "You're going to be there
for — it's not even a day, is it?"

"Afternoon until evening," Nita said.

Carmela rolled over on her back and looked at her
upside down. "So throw a few things in a bag and go!
This fussing is atypical for you."

Nita rubbed her face, then dropped her hands helplessly and sat down on the windowsill. "Everything's
so *different* all of a sudden," she said. "And it makes
no sense, because nothing is that different."

"Well," Carmela said, with the air of someone
walking on eggshells, "*one* thing. The B word."

Nita moaned. "There are moments," she said,
"when I wake up and it's the truest thing in the world.
And there are others when I wake up and think, *What
the hell have I done?* I don't know how to be, I can't
think what to say, I freeze up." She made a disgusted
face. "I *blush.*"

"Saves on makeup," Carmela said.

Nita snorted. "Only if you can get it to stay in the
same place all the time."

"And you're going to tell me," Carmela said, "that

my baby brother is just cruising right along as if nothing's happened."

By and large, this was entirely too true. Nita sighed. "Look. I need a baseline. How many boyfriends have you *actually* had?"

Carmela waved a hand airily about. "Many have auditioned for the position," she said. "Very few have *achieved* that lofty status."

Nita couldn't restrain the snicker. "Possibly because their having achieved it still doesn't stop you from flirting with everything else that moves."

"What, I should limit my options? Flirtation does not necessarily imply a lesser level of commitment."

"And this is why you're in demand for interstellar negotiations," Nita said. "Because you can come out with a sentence like that, and people *believe* it."

Carmela simply smiled and didn't deny anything. "So how many?" Nita said.

"Three, maybe four. No, three, I've stopped counting Bill, he turns out to have just been a self-obsessed dork." Carmela let out a long sigh that suggested she was more disappointed with herself than with him. "I was way too much for him to handle."

Nita refrained from sharing the opinion that for most beings in their local universe, Carmela fell into that category. "Did any of them ever make you spin your wheels like this?"

"That was usually the signal to get rid of them," Carmela said. "I don't mind butterflies in the stomach, but when they start getting big enough to be mistaken for helicopters, I believe in cutting my losses and getting out while I can."

"Well. With Kit —"

Carmela waved her arms. "There's a sentence that'll go on and on. Leave it for now. You need to get yourself together or you're going to be late for this thing. Worse, *I'm* going to be late for this thing, and I refuse to miss a chance to see people treating Kit like a superhero. Why're you having so much trouble deciding?"

"Well . . . there are going to be so many *other people* there. And I don't know who they're going to be! Or I know in a *general* way, but I don't know how they're going to be dressed. I don't want to make a bad first impression, but I'm not sure what a good first impression's going to look like! There'll be kids there from all over the planet, all ages, wearing all kinds of things, and I just — I don't *know!*" Nita waved her arms. "Should I look serious? Should I look playful? Should I try to stand out? Should I try *not* to stand out? I don't want anyone thinking I'm a showoff —"

Carmela shook her head and bounced off the bed, pushing the floating clothes off to one side and another. "Forget this stuff," she said. "We can both spare half an hour. Let's go to the Crossings and buy you something completely new. Stuff from the Crossings is always classy, and new is always good for taking your mind off yourself when you're nervous."

"Oh, God, 'Mela, are you kidding? No *way* there's time —"

Carmela flung her arms wide. "Will you listen to her, Universe? She has *no time* to go a few thousand light-years to buy some clothes. There are *so* many things wrong with that sentence, I scarcely know where to begin." Then Carmela sighed. "But you know what? This isn't about the other kids, or the weird new people, or how you're going to look in front of them. This is about *him*, isn't it?"

That was a thought that brought Nita up short. She opened her mouth, then realized she wasn't sure what to say.

"Yeah," Carmela said. "Because otherwise, if things were what we laughably think of as normal around here, you'd be completely busy obsessing over whoever this new kid is you're mentoring and how the two of you are going to keep him in line." She paused. "Is it a 'him'?"

"Yeah. I think he's from San Francisco."

"You *think*." Carmela looked bemused. "Since when do you not *know* everything about something like this? You are the queen of research and you've known about this Invitational thing for days, and this guy for nearly as long! But instead you're standing here overthinking yourself into a hole in the ground about how the way you dress might make people think about *Kit!* Aren't you?"

Nita couldn't find a single way to refute this line of reasoning. *Which frankly doesn't look good . . .* she thought. *Am I such a total wuss? This is awful.*

"Well, forget that," Carmela said. "Because why would you dress for him? You dress for *you*, and let the boys or whatever fall where they may. Here, this flowery dress with the V-neck —" She pushed her way to it and seized it out of the air. "You know you like this one! It does the swirl thing when you spin around. Add those leggings under it, that lace camisole thing, put on some flats in case you're planning on falling down a crevasse or something, and then finish this *up.*"

Nita hesitated. "I'm wondering if it makes me look too . . . girly."

Carmela's eyes went wide. "How are we even having this conversation? I remember you standing there in the Crossings with that magic gun thing and picking off nasty aliens one after another like Clint Eastwood —"

Nita could remember it too, and the memory was not pleasant. "I hated that."

"I know, you kept apologizing. Okay, maybe not something that Eastwood would have done. But still! Very *you*, and your reactions didn't ruin your aim, either. And now you're standing here worrying that a flowery dress is somehow going to damage your intergalactic image?! Wow, have *you* got the wrong number."

Nita slumped against the cool of the window. "It's just that there've been a couple of, I don't know, strange moments with Kit lately —"

"When you've been around my little brother as long as I have, you'll see that *most* of his moments are strange. The wizardry's just been a blip."

Nita put her eyebrows up at that, but still had to smile. "I thought he might come out with me to check out this whalesark — I told you I was working on that? — and he comes out with this line about 'No, don't have time, but you know, I've been thinking I should get out there again, get back in touch with my nature side . . .'"

"*His nature side!*" Carmela snorted with laughter. "What is he *talking* about?"

"Well, look where he was just the other day when the news came down. Off shooting up the Moon . . . His gaming group's into this very tech-wizardly stuff at the moment. Though the last session might not have gone as smoothly as he was expecting. I hear one of his team's been giving him trouble." Nita laughed under her breath and then assumed someone else's face and voice. "'Where's Nita, are you *excluding* her from this, don't tell me you see this as some kind of *boy* thing . . .'" She grinned. "Lissa's like a buzz saw. All edges and *spinning.* You don't mess with Lissa . . ."

"Yet Little Brother keeps doing that," Carmela said. "Could be a sign that he's as confused as you are right now? But seriously: 'his nature side'? Like the Moon's not nature."

"Yeah, well, you know how some of the guys at school are. They talk like worrying about how the planet's doing is stupid, like it's . . ."

"I can hear the world 'girly' hovering in the air." Carmela rolled her eyes. "Idiots."

"But it wasn't just that one thing." Nita sighed. "Every now and then it seems like stuff that never bothered him before is becoming an issue. Roles . . . what people think . . ."

Carmela narrowed her eyes. "The only people whose opinions matter here are your fellow wizards', yeah?" Nita opened her mouth. "And *not about your clothes!* We're past that now. There're going to be a lot of people at this thing who think of you as *famous.* Your dress is not going to be the issue. *Nita Callahan* is going to be the issue! The only thing you have to worry about is how to smile graciously while not tripping over the bodies of everybody who wants to worship at your feet."

"That's . . . an interesting image."

"Yeah. As I said, wear flats. No point in injuring them with heels while they're abasing themselves."

Nita pushed away from the window with a smile and started pulling her clothes back down out of the air, the ones on hangers first. "Seriously, though . . ." She shook her head. "You think things'll get easier when you finally break down and say it. 'Boyfriend.' And then you find your troubles have just begun . . ."

"Oh, Neets! 'Troubles'!"

Nita laughed too. "Too grim?"

"You should hear yourself." Carmela started pulling down some of the floating clothes and folding them neatly over one arm. "You're having a crisis of confidence. That's all."

"Don't tell me *you've* ever had one of those."

"Yeah. I thought I was wrong about something, once. I got over it."

Nita burst out laughing. "It's just . . . This is when I'm supposed to be giving someone else advice about how to do stuff. Not the best time for a crisis, you know?"

"Knowing the way your life runs," Carmela said, folding another top over her arm, "something much more gripping and involved will come up almost immediately and you'll forget all about this."

"Good." Nita let out a breath. "Because the idea that I'm getting cold feet embarrasses me."

Carmela waved a hand again, dismissive. "That's not where you are. I think maybe your feet are just now warming up. You know what I mean? The two of you have been through a lot. And now suddenly it happens that you're in this part of your life where everybody starts paying so much attention to Life Plans and what you're going to do with yourself from now on until the end of time, and everything starts feeling so permanent."

"Or not permanent," Nita said very softly.

Carmela went quiet and just looked at Nita for a moment. "You're afraid that just saying it has jinxed it somehow. That what you had was perfect, and you've screwed it up."

Nita paused, then nodded. "Even though he said 'about time.'"

"And he hasn't said it since, I bet."

Nita shook her head. Then she laughed at herself. "I must sound so needy."

"No. You know what the problem is? You two are too used to reading each other's minds in a crisis. You hit the talking part and you choke. And here I thought wizardry was all about, you know, *Speech.*"

They looked at each other and then both burst out laughing at the same time. "Come on," Nita said. "We ought to get out of here in the next hour or so. Your worldgate or mine? I've got a subsidy."

"Let's take mine. As it happens, I know the entity who's in *charge* of your subsidy, and you want to make sure he's got you hooked up to the VIP handling routines."

Nita grinned and picked up the camisole and leggings Carmela had pointed out to her. "Is Sker'ret going to be there himself, you think?"

"In the later stages, yeah. It's a big deal, and the Earth worldgates are kind of special in the master gating system: he'll be wanting to make sure that Chur doesn't get overloaded again."

"Let's go, then. Can't keep the talented new intake of wizards waiting."

"Are you kidding?" Carmela said. "They can't start till we get there."

They popped out together into an area that looked suspiciously like a gating cluster at the Crossings — a shining white floor, patterned with glowing blue hexagonal shapes, each one big enough to hold five or six people comfortably. Nita glanced around, trying to get a grasp of the space around them. The central part was roughly circular, about the size of the main concourse in Grand Central Terminal; the ceiling was much higher, and translucent. It let in the light of the bright Antarctic day, and it was intricately carved with shapes whose fine details were mostly lost at this distance. But somebody had plainly spent a whole lot of time doing those carvings. Figures of animals and aliens and heaven knew what else were spread out over it in groups and clusters, while between them the ceiling surface was delicately patterned with geometric shapes and what might have been long sentences in the Speech, carved into the ice. "Holy cow," Nita said under her breath. "Somebody's got a lot of time on their hands . . ."

"Not that anybody's paying much attention to it," Carmela observed. She waved an arm. Nita turned toward the center of the big space — the gating hexes having been emplaced well off to one side, where they wouldn't interfere with people socializing — and saw that a whole lot of that was going on under the highest part of the ice dome. There were easily a thousand people milling around, the cacophony of their voices rattling off the ice in the enclosed space. "Wow," Nita said again. "This is a big deal, isn't it?"

"You'd know better than I would," Carmela said. "But look who's here!"

Nita smiled as she caught sight of the low-slung shape breaking away from the crowd, because for a change it was almost easy to see him coming. Normally when you met the Master of the Crossings these days, it was in the midst of thousands of other aliens of every kind. But here there was nobody but the humans, and him. Sker'ret came pouring himself along the white-ice floor toward them, stalked eyes gazing all around him as he came, segmented legs working, and a glimpse of his gleaming segmented magenta carapace reflecting itself in the icy surface. *You'd think he'd be slipping around on this more,* Nita thought, and scuffed one shoe against the floor. *But no, looks like they've put a high-friction field on this. Good. Somebody's thought it through . . .*

And then he was in among the hexes with them, rearing up half his body to throw a bunch of those segmented legs around Nita. She laughed, and hugged him back. It was like getting into a clinch with a very friendly coat rack. "Sker'ret, baby," she said, "are you getting *bigger* again? Have you had another molt?"

"Two," Sker'ret said, "but who's counting?" He chuckled, producing a sound like pebbles rattling in a tin can. "We've loosened up dietary regulations at the Crossings for my people since I've been running things. And after all, the Stationmaster has to set a good example . . ."

"Well, I'd say you haven't been slow about that," Carmela said, taking her turn to hug him. "You have to be twice the size you were this time last year. You're going to be taller than Filif soon!"

"That'll take some doing," Sker'ret said, "because — have you seen him recently?"

"Don't tell me I need to take him ornament shopping *again*," Carmela said, with entirely too much relish.

"But I'm surprised to see *you* at one of these dos," Nita said, reaching out to rub the top of Sker'ret's head between the eyestalks. "Has to seem like the Little League from your point of view."

"Oh, no," Sker'ret said. "This is the type of professional engagement that needs serious legs-on handling. When subsidized worldgating transport on a given world picks up for short periods, the way it's going to pick up here — especially a world with Crossings-legacy worldgates, old naturally occurring ones like Chur that're finicky to deal with — then I have to be here to keep some eyes on things. At least until I'm sure the ancillary systems I've installed, the automation and so forth, are running smoothly." And then he laughed again. "Besides, I have friends involved in this competition. People whose basement I've lived in. Couldn't miss *that* for the worlds! Though I can't let other worlds in our work group know about that, because they'd get jealous and start screaming that I was showing favoritism —"

"Well, let them scream," Carmela said, looking smug. "Their problem if they can't cope with the realities of interstellar politics."

From off to one side, some hard rock started echoing off the roof — something very metal-sounding, with a dark multivoiced rap overlay that sounded like it might have been in French. Beyond the area from which the music was coming, some large tables were spread out — *probably the buffet,* Nita thought. But her stomach was churning, and the thought of food just wasn't working for her. *Why am I so intimi-*

dated by this? she thought. *I've been in much more dangerous places, seen a lot worse . . .*

"Wondered when you were getting here," came a voice from off to their left. "Did you come via the Galactic Rim or something? Oh, hi, Sker'—"

Nita turned, then stared at the apparition strolling up to them. Over dark leggings and dark flats and a long, silky, unconstructed above-the-knee tunic in a green that was so dark it was almost black, Dairine was wearing an ankle-length shawl-collared open vest — Wellakhit casual wear, in a heavier silky stuff of a more forest-green shade. It did nothing whatsoever to hide the heavy gold torc at her throat with its centered yellow gem, the gleam of it cooler than usual in this icelight. *Dammit,* Nita thought, *and now all of a sudden I look underdressed.* She also noted (and tried not to show that she noted) something Dairine was wearing wrapped twice around her narrow wrist as a bracelet. It was a double chain of emeralds strung on what at first glance appeared to be a faintly green-glowing chain. But the second glance showed this to be not a physical thing, but a construct of pure energy: simply a single sentence in the Speech, impossible to read for the smallness and fineness of the characters, and elegantly intertwined through itself like braided wire.

"Nice," Nita said, glancing at the Sunstone again

as Spot came ambling across the floor behind Dairine on his many legs, his lid-carapace burnished shining black and gleaming in the cool radiance from the sky-light. "Pulling rank, are we?"

Dairine shrugged. "If you've got some pull some-where, you may as well wear the trappings. It's a qual-ification. And a pretty one, so why not?" She looked Nita up and down. "You don't look too bad, anyway. But then you've got the Crossings' best hominid styl-ist working you over."

Nita had to laugh at that, and Carmela preened with the expression of someone who found the assess-ment accurate. "You didn't sound last night like you were going to be in that much of a hurry getting here, with all the talk about 'boring forced socialization.' Surprised to find you here early."

Dairine grinned mischievously. "Well, once I found out this was being held in the UFO Caves, no way was I going to be fashionably late . . ."

"The what?" Nita stared around her.

Dairine burst out laughing. "There were these conspiracy guys online . . . you know, the people who see a UFO under every rock . . ."

"And not the real ones."

"Yeah. They were looking at some Google Earth imagery and decided they thought they saw ice caves down here with UFOs buried in them. Now naturally as soon as you hear something like that, you start wondering, so some wizards from Australia came down to check into it. Who knew, maybe somebody from off planet *did* get lost or confused and crash here, and need help. You have to check." Dairine shrugged.

"It probably wouldn't have been, though," Nita said. "Who uses *ships* for interstellar travel if they can avoid it? When worldgating tech's so widespread, it's just silly."

"Yeah, well, no accounting for taste, is there? Anyway, it turned out that the buried spaceship was just an optical illusion. Something to do with the angle of sunlight the day the satellite took the picture. But then the Aussie group thought this would be a great place to come down and party, where no one could see, and it was close to them."

"A thousand miles is close?" Carmela said.

Dairine shrugged again. "It is if you're Australian. So they did a tectonics study and an environmental assessment and they checked out the stability of the ice shelf, and it turned out to be okay for use as a temporary facility. So they built this." She looked around in admiration. "Or hollowed it out, anyway. And then the artists got loose . . ."

"Kind of amazing," Nita said.

"If you've only been in this part, you haven't seen *anything*." Dairine looked as smugly delighted as if it had all been her own work. "There's a whole laser tag complex a level down. They've duplicated some of the sets from *Alien,* there's a Hall of Statues . . ."

"I'll make a note," Nita said. "Listen, have you seen —"

"Neets?"

The familiar voice brought her head up, and she looked around, not seeing him —

And then she saw him, and her mouth went dry. Kit had broken away from the crowd and was heading toward them. *It's just a blazer,* she thought. *And he had those jeans on yesterday —* But now there was a white shirt open at the neck, and *when did he get this tall, how have I been missing this,* and he'd done something with his hair, and —

Nita swallowed, dry. "Hey," she said.

Dairine, however, burst out laughing. "Kit, come on," she said, "don't you think the antenna sort of spoils the line?"

Kit, who had looked very cool and tall and unruffled until then, broke the spell by turning to look over his own shoulder at his own butt, or at least he tried to. His Edsel-antenna wand was sticking out of his pocket. "Yeah, well. Think of it as an icebreaker." He looked over at Nita. "Didn't mean to be late. I had the dryer set wrong, had to pull the jeans out and give them some help . . ."

Dairine snickered. "So domestic," she said, and

headed away. "I'm gonna hit the buffet until they start things going."

"Wait for me!" Carmela said. "I missed my lunch!"

The two of them made their way back toward the crowd, vanished into it. "So how does this go now?" Nita said, eager to talk about something that would get her away from the subject of how tongue-tied she'd nearly gone just now at the sight of someone she'd seen nearly every day for years. *I have got to manage this somehow, it's all gotten so weird . . .*

Kit shoved his hands in his pockets, rocked on his heels a little. "Well, I saw from my manual that you'd signed off on reading the orientation pack, so I thought you'd be ready to lecture me on what to do first . . ."

"Lecture!" Nita laughed at him. "Don't push your luck."

He grinned at her. "Okay. We know his name, we've seen his picture, we've read the title of his spell project —"

Nita smiled, unimpressed. "Don't think I've seen a longer string of jargon in the Speech since I first cracked the manual," she said. It had taken her nearly ten minutes of brain-bending effort and a bemused consultation with Bobo The Very Offended-Sounding Voice Of Wizardry to come up with a rough translation of their mentee's project into English: *An innovative approach to subversion of magnetohydrodynamic peri-odicity spikes in solar peak periods, with attention to robust crisis intervention in coronal oscillatory periods and spectrum tweaking, damage inhibition in Earth's upper ionospheric layers, and LEO-inclusive derange-ment prevention.* Bobo's comment regarding some of the compound-word neologisms in the title when they'd finished working it out together had been suc-cinct: *You get a feeling he doesn't think the Speech has long* enough *words.*

Kit made an amused "Hmf" noise. "Like it's not a tactic everybody tries once when they're in a science fair. Or maybe twice."

Nita threw him a look. "You're never going to let me off the hook about that wind turbine thing, are you?"

"Not after what it did to Mr. Vasquez's toupee," Kit said, "nope."

Nita snickered. "So what next then? Do we go hunt him down and accuse him of overstating his case, or wait till he finds us?"

"I don't know about accusing him of anything just yet," Kit said. "But the overview made it sound like they wanted us to wait on the introductions until the Powers That Be had had their say."

Nita's eyes widened. "You're not saying that *they're —*"

"What?" Kit grinned. "Going to be here? Hardly. Just the Planetary. After all, she's the door prize . . ."

"Then come on and let's go talk to some of these people." Nita was starting to get her composure back. "Maybe we'll see someone we know."

They wandered around and did indeed find here and there a few people they knew: mostly other younger wizards the two of them had run into last year during the Pullulus crisis, when older wizards had lost their power and the business of running and saving the planet had devolved abruptly onto the "next generation." During this process Nita had briefly misplaced Kit while in the act of picking up a bottle of some mysterious fruit-flavored mineral water from a buffet table (*Pitanga flavor?* What *in the Powers' name is a* pitanga?) when behind her she heard a pair of voices that she recognized immediately both from their extreme similarity to each other and because half the time they were talking over each other and the rest of it they were speaking in near unison.

She grinned and turned. "Is that Tu and Ngu?!" Nita said, turning to find the twychild arguing cheerfully and enthusiastically over a plate of some kind of alien hors d'oeuvres that was hovering in the air between them. (At least it seemed likely these were alien: Earth was short on blue food. *And the minute*

Kit finds these here, it's going to be even shorter on it . . . !)

Tran Liem Tuyet and Tran Hung Nguyet had each shot up by about a foot, and where the last time she'd seen them they had been in a sort of tunic-like Vietnamese casual wear, now Nguyet had gone for a hoodie-and-skirt-over-jeans look, and Tuyet was wearing a suit (though apparently just a T-shirt under it, and a tie just vaguely knotted and thrown over his shoulder). Their heads came up in unison and the two of them swung toward Nita with broad smiles on their faces.

"Is that *Nita?!*"

"Powers That Be in a bucket, are you *mentoring?*"

"You ancient *thing!*"

"Look at all her gray hairs."

"Well, look at *yours* then," Nita said, laughing, and there was some truth to it, since Nguyet had installed a prominent and showy silver streak in her long dark hair above her forehead and off to one side of her part. The hors d'oeuvres plate was waved away to drift lonely in the air while the twins grabbed her and hugged her, and Nita hugged them back. "Come on, you two are such babies, I thought you'd be competing!"

"Hah!"

"Nope, none of that for us."

"We're mentoring a group —"

"A set of quadruplets from Chile, would you believe?"

"— not *twychild*-twins, of course, they don't do the augmentative-wizardry thing —"

"But they've got some new take on group work, it's fabulous, it's like time-sharing —"

"Holographic spell management —"

"But that's just cool organizational stuff. Knowing you, you and Kit've scored yourself some kind of super-dangerous talent who needs controlling —"

Nita had to laugh. "No," she said, "as far as we can tell it's a rabid spacecraft fan who's mostly interested in keeping communications satellites from being fried. In fact his précis was technical enough that I won't mind an explanation."

"Too technical for *you?*"

"Is the world ready?"

They were laughing together and deep in the midst of further gossip by the time Kit drifted back, and then there was more laughing and hugging and some teasing about height. "I thought I was gonna at least get taller than you!" Tuyet said to Kit in a tone of cheerfully aggrieved complaint, "and now what do I find but you've pulled *this* sneaky trick! There is no justice. None."

"No one's gonna care how tall I am next to you," Kit said, "when you're doing stuff like *that* with your tie. Wannabe fashion plate . . ."

"Bean pole!"

"Brain box! Having trouble finding oxygen all the way up here? Come on, breathe deep, assert yourself . . ."

Nita and Nguyet raised their eyebrows at each other as the boys got increasingly creative with their mockery, in the way that only people who've lived through life-or-death situations together can. "Do you have any idea . . ." Nita said.

"Who're being pushed as the hot picks for winning?"

"Actually," Nita said, "I was going to ask you if you knew what in the world a pitanga is. But seriously, how do you start picking a winner out of three hundred people whose projects the judges haven't even *looked* at yet?"

Nguyet wiggled her high, slender eyebrows at Nita. "There are a lot of maths freaks and statistics wranglers in this group," she said. "Some of them, I don't even know names for what kinds of wizards they are . . . but they're strong on the predictive end, and they've gotten real excitable since the individual prospectuses went up." She gave Nita a sideways look. "Thought you might have stumbled across some inside stuff while reviewing the material."

"For this? No, I wouldn't even —"

A sudden flash of image went across Nita's gaze, as if someone had swept the lens of a screen projector past her. An image of Carmela, very upset about something, looking at Nita with the oddest expression, almost disbelieving somehow —

"— begin to know how to make a noneducated guess . . ." her mouth kept saying, and then Nita ran out of steam, feeling shocked.

"You okay?" Nguyet said, and looked over her shoulder, then over Nita's shoulder. "See somebody you know?"

"Uh, no." Nita shook her head. "Just a weird moment —"

Around them the music started to fade, and the crowd started glancing around expectantly. "Uh oh, here we go!" Nguyet said, and a second or so later Kit and Tuyet were looking over their shoulders at the heart of the crowd.

It was pushing aside, people murmuring and melting back so as to leave a roughly circular space open inside it. A small blond woman stepped into the center of the group.

A silence fell around her. No one called for it — nothing so crass. All that was happening was everyone responding to the sense of sudden power in their midst. The Planetary Wizard for Earth just stood there quietly, looking at the crowd surrounding her at a more-than-respectful distance.

Nita was amused to see Irina Mladen for once not in the kind of floral housedress she'd seemed to favor the couple of times that their paths had last crossed, but in a very businesslike pantsuit, the type of thing you might wear to a job interview; navy blue, low heels, a white shirt. But Irina also had something at her neck, hard to see, that glinted sharply blue — exactly the shade of blue that Earth's seas would look like from space. In a flower-patterned sling, her baby — *must find out what his name is!* Nita thought — hung at her side and gazed curiously around at the gathering. On her opposite shoulder perched the little yellow parakeet who seemed to go everywhere with her, peering around as alertly as the baby. It briefly stood on one leg to ruffle up the feathers behind its ear with one claw, made a quiet scratchy sound, and settled down against her neck again.

"Colleagues and cousins," Irina said, "associates who've come from great distances and from just up the road — you're all very welcome. In the names of the Powers with whom and for whom we work in overseeing this planet, I want to thank you for making the time in your busy schedules to be a part of this proceeding, which is probably the biggest since that famous one in Babylon — the one back ten millennia or so, when Julian dates hadn't yet been invented and we were still reckoning everything in fractions of a Simurgh year."

A soft laugh traveled around the room among some of the older attendees. "Your presence here," Irina said, "is an indication of your commitment to help the rest of us do our work better — the most important work there is: serving Life in this world, and incidentally in others. But, like charity, the best work for others starts at home. Here, on your own ground, those of you who're competing in the Invitational will have a chance to demonstrate to your peers, and to those working at more central levels, the best of what you've learned and engineered to make wizardry better."

She began to stroll casually around the space that had opened up around her. "Today and tonight we'll have a chance to get to know one another better. You'll have an opportunity to meet up for the first time with the wizards you're going to be working with for the next few weeks, and to get a sense of what others in the community are doing — a sense that we're hoping will be helpful to you whether you make it through into the later competition stages, or are obliged to step aside due to criterion-based outsorting."

And then Irina cracked a grin as she looked out into the crowd. "I spent nearly half a day looking for a slicker or at least kinder way to phrase 'getting chucked out on your butt.'" She smiled. "Because that's what it felt like to me when *I* was deselected from the Invitational in 1992. I went down in the eighth-finals, and at the time I didn't think it was possible for *anything* worse to happen to me for the rest of my life. Of course, then I got made Planetary." Another laugh went around the group, but there was a slightly uneasy edge to it. "So if you do get outsorted, please don't assume that your life is over. A surprising number of our former competitors come back later as mentors . . . or are so busy with other things that happened to them secondary to the Invitational that they don't have time to waste further angst on it."

She walked around some more, looking into the sea of faces as she did. "As usual," Irina said, "you know that the honor the Powers That Be have bestowed on us as wizards is not entirely without its challenges. That old saying that the Powers will not send you any challenge for which you are not prepared —" She shook her head. "Unfortunately that saying was invented by someone who wasn't a wizard. We know perfectly well that the universe has *never* worried about sending us challenges for which we are not prepared. But the Powers that manage this universe bloody well expect us to *get* prepared, if we're capable. All of wizardry, if looked at one way, is a never-ending game of catch-up. The Invitational, and similar events in other worlds near and far, are all attempts to get ahead of the game."

Irina paused in her walking. "More to the point, it's about encouraging you and other wizards like you not only to use the manual, to use the knowledge that we share in many modalities, but to *contribute* to it as well. We're all of us together in a business that can wear you down, wear you out, or kill you dead, without a little help from your friends. And though thousands of wizards worldwide do independent networking every day, giving each other help and advice on their own initiative, we've found it useful to hothouse the process every now and then. Wizards who work actively with other wizards in a primary role of spell design and implementation need to be accustomed to working fast in crisis conditions — and so, in that sense, the next three weeks, for some of you, are going to read like one long crisis."

Irina laughed softly. "Not that you can't have fun at the same time, of course. What's that famous line from the sports show on one continent? 'The thrill of victory and the agony of defeat' — well, we hope the agony can be kept to a minimum. To assist you in that regard, we have acting as mentors some of the best and most effective younger wizards of recent years. They come here unified in the intention to help you produce results that will mean other wizards won't have to go through the crap *they* did."

At that a much louder ripple of laughter spread through the group, and Irina joined it. "So if the next three weeks seem cutthroat to some of you, and if you feel your mentors and your fellow competitors are driving you hard, that's exactly the way it should be. Our oldest competitor, the One who'll be here and whom you will *not* see — *that* One, too, is cutthroat in Its habits. That's the One whose actions and intentions we can never afford to turn our backs on. The next three weeks are designed to get right in Its face."

Irina looked around at the crowd, the smile on her face a touch feral now. "No matter what the final result at the end of this proceeding, for the competitors and their support teams, you need to know that our always-present invisible friend — and greeting and defiance to *you*," she said, her gaze sweeping around the group —"will be constantly infuriated by what you do. If you choose to frame some of what will happen here as *Its* fault, well, you wouldn't be wrong. Some of you will go home bruised. No one will blame you for taking your annoyance out on It later. Indeed, we encourage it.

"But those of you who make it into any one of the finals stages may assume that Its attention will be on you in somewhat increased amounts from here on in. That's one of the reasons the winner will be working with me for the following year. Anyone who displays such a level of accomplishment so publicly in a wizardly gathering of this kind is entitled to protection after the fact. And we, the Seniors and others involved in the assessment and oversight structures of the Invitational, want you to know that we're not going to hang you out to dry after you win."

There was a soft murmur at that. "So," Irina said. "The thing for you to do now is get to know each other. *Some* of each other anyway: there are so many of you here! Some of you will know members of the mentor group, having heard of their work. Some of you won't have a clue and are here to make friends — and that's fine too; friendship is a thing of incalculable power. There are times it'll keep you going when you can't find anything else in the manual that seems to do any good. I hope to greet as many of you as I can before other duties call me away. In the meantime, on behalf of the supervisory structure of the wizards of Sol III, known as Earth and by many other names among our own kind and others, I declare this event, the twelve hundred and forty-first Invitational, to be in progress. Enjoy yourselves, stir around, and I'll see you all at the finals!"

Irina received a patter of applause as she stepped out of the circle. It sounded somewhat subdued, but Nita strangely could understand that; applauding Earth's Planetary seemed almost too obvious a gesture. And then, as she turned to Kit, Nita noticed with some surprise that nearly all the wizards in the center of the ice-cavern had little glowing lights hovering over their heads.

Kit started to laugh, as did various other people in the room, possibly for the same reason. "Look," he said under his breath, "we're all in *The Sims . . .*"

"And these lead us to whoever we're supposed to be meeting?" Nita said, cocking an eye up at her own glowing light, which like Kit's was faintly blue.

It was wobbling rhythmically in the air with a little *thataway, thataway, thataway* kind of movement that seemed to be indicating a spot past the buffet tables.

"Yeah, looks that way. Shall we?"

Together they started in that direction. The whole crowd scene had turned from a jumble of bodies standing mostly still to a seething confusion through which kids were pushing every which way, everyone wearing that searching-for-a-face expression familiar at airports and train stations. Occasionally one of these people would come up against a red light that matched it in shape and size and the two parties would pause; hands would be shaken, or there would be bows or other styles of greeting, and both parties would look at each other with interest, though (it seemed to Nita) also, in a lot of cases, a certain wariness. *Because who knows what they're getting in one of these situations, at least right at the beginning?*

"Getting warmer," Kit said, glancing up at Nita's floating indicator: it was flashing faster now, "pointing" more emphatically.

"Yeah," Nita said, looking at Kit's. "Is that — Wait, he must have moved. Left, I think."

"Yeah, over by the buffet again . . ."

They made their way farther through the crowd. "Funny," Nita murmured, "I think he stopped again."

"Yeah. Still, we're close. See how bright these are getting now, he must be —"

"Right there," Nita said, pointing toward the end of one of the buffet tables, where a tall young man was standing.

He really *was* tall, Nita thought: right up there with Ronan, despite being a couple of years younger. *Pushing six feet, easy . . . and so lean.* It was odd how the impact of both the height and the leanness was so much greater in person. She'd seen an image of him in the manual when going over his précis, and the usual height/weight hard data, but it hadn't made anything like the same kind of impression on her as he was making at the moment. His dark hair was longish and shaggy, covering his ears; his carriage a little slumped, but at first glance it looked like an attitude thing rather than something chronically postural. *Stress,* Nita thought. *Well, why not? All of us are twitching.*

He watched her and Kit approach with a much more overstated version of that wary look Nita had seen on some of the people here. She searched briefly in memory for what his stance and affect reminded her of, and then thought of the guys she'd seen on one of the websites she sometimes caught Dairine secretly drooling over, a site devoted to Asian boy bands. Photogenic, sullen, definitely trying to look hard to get. *And then there are the clothes,* Nita thought. *Not that you expected him to be in some kind of traditional gear, why would he be, but* — He was wearing designer jeans, a white V-neck T-shirt, a bright floral shirt over that, and a black leather jacket over *that*, cut high to let as much of the Hawaiian shirt show as possible. Big boots, something like patent-leather Doc Martens, and — *Is that* lace *on the tops of his socks?*

It *was* lace. Neon orange lace, even more blindingly orange than some of the flowers on his Hawaiian shirt. *Better keep Tuyet away from this one,* she found herself thinking. *Too much competition on the clothes side. Come to think of it, better keep* Carmela *away from this one, too.* Because their mentee was definitely quite handsome, though not in the usual ways: his face was slightly longer than it looked like it should have been for its width, but the tilt of his eyes made it all work, and also the depth of their color, a dark, deep brown.

But the looks aren't all that's going on. There was power here: considerable power. *Bobo?* Nita said silently.

Five point six, said Wizardry itself in her ear, assessing. *Plus or minus point six. And on a slow climb. Hormonal, long term. Final status when the hormones settle, somewhere around six point nine, maybe seven.*

Nita breathed out. *And he's what? Fifteen going on sixteen? Wow . . . So why's he looking at us like he thinks Kit might bite him in the leg?*

The guy leaned there against the table and watched them come. As they got within chatting distance, their guide-lights went out — confirmation, if any was needed, that their little group's members had found one another.

He stuck out his hand to Kit. "Penn Shao-Feng," he said. *"Dai stihó —"*

"Dai," Kit said. "Kit Rodriguez. My partner, Nita Callahan —"

"Hello," Penn said, glancing at her, then back at Kit. "Nice to meet you."

Not nice enough for me to be offered a handshake, was the first thing that went through Nita's mind. *Don't I rate a* dai?

Or am I just being hypersensitive?

"Want to grab a drink and sit down somewhere?" Kit said, gesturing toward the ice-cavern's walls, where all kinds of force-shielded seating had been carved into the bodies of numerous niches and cavelets.

"Uh, not right now, thanks though," Penn said. "Listen, did you see where Irina went?"

"Uh," Nita said, startled by complete confusion into politeness. "I'm sure she's still around somewhere. They said she was going to hang out for a while after the introduction."

"They said? You don't know?"

Nita stood there trying to make sense of the odd, slightly mocking expression Penn was leveling at her.

"If I could read a Planetary's mind," she said, recovering, "I don't know that I'd advertise the fact, because there might be some pushback about spreading that around. So no, I *don't* know. But then we're only two of about a thousand other people who'd love to drag her off somewhere and monopolize her attention. Think you've got a shot?"

Kit threw a *Did you just say that?* look at her. Nita ignored it, waiting to see what Penn would say.

Instead he ran a bored-looking hand through his hair and turned away from Nita toward Kit, as if what she'd said wasn't even worth engaging with. "Look, why don't I get in touch with you tomorrow and we can set up a meeting," he said. "You can come out and see me in San Fran; I'll put the coordinates in your manuals. I've got a nice place, you'll like it, it's quiet, and we can take an hour and you can have a look at what I'm doing. Yeah? Kind of busy tonight."

Doing what else *besides meeting with the people who're supposed to be helping you* win *this?* Nita thought. She opened her mouth —

"Sure," Kit said, and Nita had the brief satisfaction of noticing that his voice sounded tight around the edges. "Fine. Tomorrow, then. *Dai . . .*" And though Nita thought he'd been about to turn and walk away, Kit stood still with a casual sort of look bent on Penn, and waited.

"Yeah, *dai*," Penn said after a moment, then turned himself around and stalked off.

Nita and Kit stood there for a moment more, then looked at each other.

"Is it just me," Kit said, "or were we just not only blown off but totally disrespected by someone wearing *that shirt?*"

Nita shook her head. "Fashion statement," she said.

Kit made a sarcastic sound at the back of his throat. "A statement that he thinks fashion beats style."

"Ooh. A little judgmental, there? Maybe he's not the blazer type." She gazed after Penn. "I could be wrong, but I think he's been through one of those fashion streets in Japan, you know? Where they're big into mixing and matching everything on the planet."

"I wouldn't know," Kit said. "That's more 'Mela's department. But wear a *Hawaiian shirt* to something like this? When you're not Hawaiian? I don't know that I feel that sure of my dress sense. And I'm not sure I ever will . . ."

"You need more coaching from Carmela, maybe."

"Please, as if she needs to know that. Life with her is bizarre enough already."

Nita stood there watching Penn push farther into the crowd; his height wouldn't allow him to vanish completely at close range. *Well, maybe it's nerves . . .*

"Come on," Nita said, "let's go look for Dairine and see if she drew a better hand than we did."

Kit gave her a brief look. "Kind of a snap judgment from you . . ."

"Sounds like I'm not the only one, either. But who knows, we might even find someone more mature. Or less self-absorbed."

Very quietly, Kit started snickering. "He has no idea what he's in for, does he."

"What?"

"I know that tone of voice. Like you're absolutely intending to be kind to somebody, but it'll be the sort of kindness that's gonna kill them."

It was embarrassing to have to admit that killing was somewhat on Nita's mind. "Seriously," she said under her breath, "who comes to an event like this and *acts* like that?"

"Someone who's sure he's the hottest thing on the street," Kit said. "Or thinks he is. And doesn't mind who gets annoyed by the shade he's throwing." He gave Penn a sidelong look, and watched him head off through the crowd.

Nita snorted. "Or else he's trying to make a strong first impression. Well, he has."

"Maybe he's stressed," Kit said. "Or freaked at meeting us."

"*Us!*"

"Yeah, well." Kit shrugged. "Looked at your précis in the manual lately? The version of it that someone sees when they don't have the right association levels set? Who knows . . . it could be intimidating."

Nita shook her head. "Intimidated by *us?*"

"If you were young and not real sure of yourself . . ."

"The way *he's* not sure of himself? Give me a break."

"I've seen stranger coping methods . . ."

Nita sighed. It wasn't fair to let their first impressions of Penn get in the way of what they'd all come here to do. And the Powers were behind their assignment: there had to be *something* about them that this kid needed. "You're probably right," she said. "This is stressy for everybody, there's all this —" She waved a hand. "Frustrated wizardry in the room. Or maybe 'frustrated' is the wrong word. Eager."

"Competitive," Kit said.

Nita nodded slowly, because he was right. And it was something she wasn't used to seeing where wizardry was concerned. Almost since she'd been called to the Art, all the wizards Nita had ever found herself working with were intent on getting the job done, whatever it took — very often at the expense of their own egos and their own stress. *This is already looking like a different kind of scenario,* she thought, *and I'm not sure I'm going to like it much.*

"Still . . ." she said.

"Thinking out loud, Neets?" Kit said. "Or talking to Bobo, maybe?"

"No," she said, "just myself." She threw a sidelong look at him, then glanced back to look for Penn in the crowd, but he had finally vanished. "But I have a feeling you're going to be hearing a lot of that in the next few weeks . . ." she said, with a sigh. "Come on," she said. "Let's go have some pitanga juice."

"Some what?"

"It's over by the blue food."

"*What?* You're on!"

Dairine stood off to one side, listening to Irina's speech and trying not to get too impatient as she waited for the payoff: the moment when she'd get a sense of how much of a winner or loser her mentee was going to be.

The manual had given her little besides the bare facts: *Merhnaz Farrahi, Mumbai, India, specialty: geomancy, seismics.* Dairine's initial reaction had been approval. *Good specialty for that part of the world . . . there are never enough earthquake wranglers who've got the skill and smarts to stop the worst ones.* But beyond that . . . who knew? The manual was not going to give you personality data. Dairine had tried to get it to do that, once or twice, when looking over the précis of a few of the other competitors. Some of their spells were so unusual that they made her want to know them better. *And who knows,* Dairine thought, *if I meet my mentee and she's boring, then afterward I'll go hunt some of those guys up. At least the networking might be productive.*

It was odd, though. The flush of excitement she'd felt in her dad's shop on learning she would be included in this — after the inevitable annoyance at being thrown into it on such short notice — was fading. It was always good to meet other wizards when there wasn't a calamity under way. There were some nice people out there on errantry, and hearing from them personally about the places they'd been and the cool things they'd done was endlessly more fascinating than just reading about it in the manual.

She thought again of the hectic, edgy excitement and camaraderie of the great gathering on the Moon at the beginning of the Pullulus War. Everyone had been terrified but up for it. *Having to save the universe,* Dairine thought, *tends to put you on your best game . . . assuming it doesn't also make you want to dig a hole and hide.* In any case, there had been no leisure for hiding at that point. Everyone had thrown intervention groups together the best they could, headed out into space, and started tracking down the weapon that would bring the Lone Power's plans to an end.

This was a much different business; more structured, more leisurely, and less deadly. It was going to be engaging enough, but probably not all that exciting, except with the manufactured sort of stimulation that comes with staged competitions everywhere. Which was just as well, because she had other things to be thinking about right now. *So funny,* Dairine thought. *There are probably kids on the planet who would give* anything *to be here right now. And where do* I *want to be?*

She smiled to herself. No matter how much of a pain in the butt her dad and Nelaid could be when they were tag-teaming her, if there was anywhere she wanted to be right now, it was in Sunplace, on Wellakh, on the terrace of that high spire of stone, leaning over the rail there . . .

And not alone.

In memory she leaned there again, and Roshaun was next to her. The interlude they'd shared before the terrible events on the Moon at the conclusion of the Pullulus War had been so brief that at times Dairine had to go back and check her manual to see whether one thing or another had actually happened. *Did I really lean here with you, with our elbows banging together, so that you kept nudging me and I kept nudging you, and we were both doing it to annoy each other, and it didn't do anything but make us both laugh? That bus ride we took to the mall, did you really have one of those lollipops sticking out of your face then? When we were sitting on the steps that one evening, and the lilacs were out . . . were you really looking at me the way I thought you were?*

And then came their time on the Moon. Not the Moon on the day when everything went wrong: but the Moon when she took him there, after first pointing it out to him in the sky. *That whole thing got splashed out of the Earth, a long time ago. And it was just the right size to form up . . . Really? By how small a chance you had a Moon at all, then . . . Yeah, we use it as a paradigm for how sometimes you get incredibly lucky. The way things do go right sometimes.*

Except that things had then gone most spectacularly wrong.

My best friend. Truly *the* best friend: the one who couldn't be mistaken for anything else — the one who had to be your best friend because there was simply no other way you could be putting up with him on a regular basis. The infuriating, hilarious, smart, ignorant, stuck-up creature with his ridiculous snotty bearing and his formal ways and flashy clothes; the young King who (once he got the position) didn't *want* to be a king at all, but who resigned himself to doing it as well as it could be done because that was the way he handled things. The terrifyingly competent wizard, the guy who refused to take anyone's crap but would laugh at *her* with that supercilious look when she delivered it to him by the truckload. The one who never took her seriously. The one who *always* took her seriously.

Roshaun. Where the hell are you?

It was the silent cry that started every day and ended every one. Sometimes Dairine heard it in her sleep; sometimes the rawness of it woke her up. She would lie there in the frontier between dream and awakening, knowing she was at home in bed, but also knowing that she was kneeling in the cold dust of the Moon with the Sunstone in her hands, someone else's Sunstone, the heavy collar and the bright gem that had simply parted company with him somehow and now lay there in the talcum-powdery, gunpowder-smelling moondust. And the stones hurt her knees, but not as much as her chest hurt because he had been there and now he was gone.

Not dead. That much she knew (though her own cowardice had kept her from being sure about that for a long time). But not alive, either. Something had happened to his physical body: it had seemingly been burned away in the terrible wash of coronal energies that Roshaun had tried to turn against the Pullulus as it closed in around Earth. *And the worst thing about it,* Dairine thought, *was that it made no difference, at the end.* The power that would end the Pullulus came from another direction entirely.

Well, maybe it's not true that it made no *difference,* she thought. *He bought Kit and Ponch time to make it happen.* But at the end of it, Roshaun was still gone.

But not forever. That resolution, too, came at the beginning of every day and the end of every one. *I'll find you,* she thought. *I don't care how long it takes...*

There was a patter of applause going around the room as Irina finished her speech. *Okay,* Dairine thought, *let's find out how terrible this is going to be.* She put Spot down. "See anybody?" she said.

Not yet.

About a quarter of the way around the room, Dairine could see Kit and Nita making their way toward the side of one of buffet tables. *So they're taken care of now,* she thought as she saw them come to a halt in front of a skinny dark-haired guy even taller than Kit. *That's going to be interesting,* she thought. Kit was very proud of his height: sometimes she wondered if Nita had noticed how incredibly happy he'd been when his middle-school growth spurt began, or realized how he'd hated being short —

"Uh, excuse me?"

A very soft voice, very shy sounding, pulled Dairine out of her thoughts. She blinked. Standing in front of her, twisting her hands together, was a dark-haired girl of maybe fourteen. She was wearing long dark trousers with a kind of blue watered-silk overcoat on top, and had a big, geometrically patterned scarf in blue and white wrapped around her head and shoulders.

"Hi there," Dairine said.

The girl was looking at her with the oddest expression of near astonishment. "Are you Dairine Callahan?"

"Uh, yeah. And you're — Mehrnaz? Did I pronounce it right?"

"Yes, yes you did —" She said it as if this was an amazing thing. And then she *blushed*.

"Well, *dai stihó*."

The girl opened her mouth, then shut it again, and it took her a moment more to manage words. "Is there some mistake?" she said at last.

Now what in the world does she mean by that —? "Mistake!"

"I mean, are you absolutely sure you were assigned to me?"

What, she doesn't like *the idea for some reason or other?* Dairine, already on edge, was just about ready to let her have it. But the girl's face was so scared, and looked so little like that of someone who was trying to be offensive, that she held her fire for the moment.

"Well," Dairine said, and pointed above her head. "Little blue light . . ." Then she pointed to the girl's. "Little red light . . ." She shrugged as both of them went out. "And I think we have to assume the wizardry's working right, because otherwise a lot more people would be complaining."

That shy face was suddenly transfigured with laughter. "Oh, Powers," Mehrnaz murmured. "It's true, it's really true, isn't it? It's you! The one who *wouldn't move the planet.*"

Dairine was confused. Then, suddenly, the memory of a long-ago phone conversation, from after her Ordeal, came back to her. "No," she said. "It was fine right where it was." Yet there was no avoiding the stab of frustration that came to her now as she thought of the time when she could have done something like that, even *would* have done it if the reason had been right. "But seriously," she said, "since when do they let privileged communications like that out into the manual?" And she had to laugh. "If it's there, though, I guess it can't have been that privileged. Maybe I had the comms permissions set up wrong. It was kind of an exciting time . . ."

"And you were so *awesome,*" Mehrnaz said. "*Are* so awesome! I can't believe it! It's such an *honor* to be paired up with you."

"Uh, okay," Dairine said, astonished. This was not the way she'd imagined this was going to go. She'd expected to be bored by whoever she met. *But who thinks I'm amazing? Even Roshaun never . . .*

She shook her head. *Wrong thing to be thinking about right now.* Meanwhile, Mehrnaz seemed content just to stand in front of Dairine in wonder: and the idea struck her as faintly ridiculous. "So you're the one who wants to take earthquakes apart from underneath," she said.

"You looked at my spell!" Mehrnaz said.

"I read the précis," Dairine said. "*Spot* read the spell, and we discussed it in general terms. Some pretty complex stuff there —"

Mehrnaz's eyes went wide: she followed Dairine's glance down. Spot had spidered over to crouch down in front of Mehrnaz, and was looking at her with all his eyes. "This is him!"

"Yes, it is," Dairine said, and she had to smile, because this was all going so differently from what she'd expected. "Look . . . why don't we go find someplace to sit down, and you can start telling me more about it, okay?"

"Yes, absolutely yes!" And without another word Mehrnaz was heading off toward the far side of the ice cave in search of an empty conversation niche, while looking back over her shoulder every few feet with a big grin at Dairine.

I have a fan, she thought. *This is truly weird.*

We *have a fan,* Spot said, scurrying past her.

All Dairine could do was laugh and go after the two of them, because the excitement to which she'd said goodbye was rising again. *Okay,* she said to the Powers. *I'm game. Even though You knew I was busy, You got me into this. So let's see what happens . . .*

5

San Francisco

✳

KIT HAD NEVER BEEN to the City by the Bay, as much because of a lack of time and opportunity as of power. It was surprising how busy a wizard could get, between errantry and school and family business; you might think you had infinite power to go anywhere you liked — just build the transport spell and go — but then you found that it didn't work out that way. Everything took energy, and sometimes what with one thing and another there wasn't enough to spare.

Now, though, standing here on the high point Nita had chosen for their long jump from Grand Central, he was sorry he'd put it off this long. They had come out "high on a hill," the kind of place where the song suggested you were supposed to leave your heart. The view of the ocean alone would have been enough to make the trip worthwhile for Kit. Way ahead of them, way past the Bay and the famous orangey bridge, the

Pacific Ocean stretched out vast and quiet and glittering, dappled with shadows and patches of light left by the low clouds sliding over it. It was an ocean Kit could look at without feeling the slight chill up his spine that the sight of the Atlantic at home always gave him. *Not that we didn't do good things there,* Kit thought. *But there were a lot of bad things that could have happened . . . and some of them got way, way too close.*

He sighed. This, though, was different. "I can see why people would want to live here," he said, "even with the earthquakes."

Next to him, Nita rubbed her arms a little. It was cold up here in the wind, colder than either of them had expected. "I don't know about the earthquakes," Nita said, looking northward at the San Francisco skyline. "I'd rather the Earth held still."

"Yeah," Kit said, "it's probably preferable. So where is he exactly?"

She gestured with her chin. "Right down there," she said. Houses climbed a good way up the hill where they stood, following the curves of the narrow streets from side to side as they angled steeply up the slope. It looked like an old, well-established neighborhood. And, from what Kit knew about the area, probably an expensive one. "High-rent district," he said under his breath.

"It looks that way," Nita said. "We'll find out." She glanced down at the transit circle glowing on the ground at their feet. "You ready? I'll jump us down. There's a park nearby with some ornamental plantings where we won't be seen."

"This is what happens when your dad's a gardener, isn't it?" Kit muttered. "We always wind up in the shrubs somewhere."

Then he cursed himself silently. *What is it?* Kit thought. *What's going on with me that makes everything I say in the last couple few weeks come out sounding like it means something dirty?*

Nita threw him an amused look. "Stop it," she said.

"I know. I know. I just can't seem to —"

"I don't mean *that!*" she said. "Stop freaking out about it." And she snickered. "Because it's happening to me too."

"Oh," Kit said. "Okay . . ."

"So let's jump now," she said, "because the shrubs have nothing to fear from us. Right?"

"Right."

She reached down toward the transit circle; a line of light ran up from it to the charm bracelet on her wrist. Nita wound her fingers around the bracelet, tugged.

A second later, they were indeed in the shrubbery. It was so thick and overarching a patch of rhododendrons that there was no possibility anyone could have seen them. But there was a trampled-down patch in the middle. "I have a feeling wizards use this a lot," Kit said.

"Or somebody does," Nita said, and grinned at him.

It was beginning to occur to Kit that the changed circumstances that the two of them were dealing with were going to have the side effect of giving them a whole lot more things to joke about. *And that can't be bad . . .*

They made their way cautiously out of the undergrowth, Nita pausing at the edge to look around before she waved Kit out behind her. "Don't want anybody thinking we were doing what you're *afraid* they might think we were doing," she said, giving him a sidewise glance.

"No, of course not . . ."

Together they headed across a carefully groomed park with swings and slides and a graveled running path through it, and finally down into a street lined on both sides with two- or three-story houses painted in bright colors. "I swear I've seen this street on TV," Kit said. "In some commercial. Or on a postcard somewhere."

"It could be," Nita said. "Or on some old TV show . . ."

"Yeah," Kit said. "What's the house number again?"

"Thirty-five."

"There it is, then," Kit said. It was across from where they stood; a white house with a slight overhang over its garage, a red-tiled roof, and a broad picture window looking out on the street.

They crossed over and went up the steps to the front door, and rang the doorbell. A few moments later it opened for them, and there was Penn, dressed in a floppy T-shirt and surfer jams and sandals, his hair rumpled, as if he'd been asleep. "Hey," he said. "*Dai.* Come on in."

They stepped into a long, quarry-tiled hall with various big heavy oak doors leading off it, white stuccoed walls, and pale oak beams crossing the ceiling at intervals: down at the end of the hall they could see into a bright north-facing room with a large table and some chairs in it, possibly a kitchen. "Is there anybody here we should know about?" Kit asked.

"What?" Penn said, yawning and scrubbing one hand through his hair. "Oh, no, don't worry about that, it's just me here and they're all out at work."

He looks like he just got out of bed, Kit thought. *If I was expecting company, I'd at least be up for a while before they showed up!* But it was early to start getting so judgmental. They'd barely met. There was no telling what kinds of pressure he was under at home.

"So where are we going to be working?" Nita said.

Once again, Penn looked at her as if he had no idea what she was doing there. "Uh, downstairs in the media room. Come on," he said, and led them down a spiral staircase to the lower level of the house.

They followed him down the polished oak steps into a room with some large plush sofas and easy chairs over in one corner and a huge entertainment center up against the wall across from them, with a gigantic screen and a wet bar off to one side. The fourth wall was nothing but a huge picture window looking out across that glorious northern vantage of the Golden Gate and the sea.

"Wow," Nita said. "That is *some view*."

"Thanks," Penn said, smiling at her for the first time. "We like it. You guys want something to drink? Beer? Wine? Soda?"

It occurred to Kit that it was early to be offering them wine or beer, both in terms of their drinking ages and the time of day — not to mention that the very concept of drinking while doing any kind of wizardry gave him the shivers. You might as well juggle loaded guns. "Uh, if you've got something like mineral water, that would be nice. Neets?"

"Yeah," she said, "same for me, please."

Penn went to the wet bar, got a couple of plastic spring water bottles out of the small refrigerator below it, and handed one to each of them. "There you go. Listen, sorry about yesterday —" He looked briefly sheepish. "I have a problem with crowds sometimes."

"It's all right," Kit said. "It got a bit intense there."

And for Kit, so it had: he wasn't used to wizards in such large numbers. *Or rather, I kept thinking about the Moon . . .* went through his mind.

He pushed the thought aside for the moment. *Someday it'll get easier. It may take a while. But someday . . .*

Meanwhile Nita was carefully cracking the cap off her bottle of mineral water. "Would it be overstepping to ask what your folks do?" she said to Penn.

"They own a small supermarket chain," he said. "Asian groceries, sundries, that kind of thing. Import-export."

"Not wizards, then," Kit said.

Penn laughed out loud. "Oh God, no, that would be one of the *last* things they'd want. One of the reasons they left China, as a matter of fact. Too much magic in our neighborhood." He had picked up a mineral water of his own; now he swigged from it. "Anyway, don't worry, you won't be seeing them. Even if they do get home early, they won't come down here while I'm working."

"You're out to them?" Nita said.

"Yeah. My dad always knew it might happen to me, and my stepmom got over the shock pretty quick." He smiled. "They were hoping *I* wouldn't be a wizard, to tell you the truth . . ." He shook his head. "But the tendency's strong on my grandfather's side of the family. My dad thought of it as such an old-country kind of thing: he was glad it skipped him, and he thought it might skip me, too. When we immigrated over here and my Ordeal happened anyway, they were pretty disappointed." Penn shrugged. "But they got past it."

An old-country kind of thing. Kit tucked that concept away for future examination. He knew that because of China's great age as a nexus of cultures, the concept of wizardry had had a very long time to become embedded into it, and as a result, in places China was much more accepting of the concept of magic than many other parts of the world. It hardly meant that you could run down the street throwing wizardry around without consequences. But the thought that magic could exist, *did* exist, was apparently working in the background for a lot of people. It hadn't occurred to him that this might create more problems than it solved.

"Well," Kit said, "why don't we get to work? The thing for us all to do, now, is figure out how we can best be of help to you. Help you structure your research ... assist you with implementing the wizardry you're working on. Or if you've got some logistical or ethical issues that you want to flesh out around your project." While going through his own orientation pack, Kit had been surprised to discover that the part of the presentation that dealt with spell justification and intervention rationale was something that a lot of candidates didn't spend enough time on. There were plenty of people who simply thought a hot new energy spell was a great idea and didn't deal with the emotional and ethical impact statements surrounding it until it was almost too late. When they were standing up in front of a panel of Senior Wizards, having to defend their rationale from attack on all sides, those who had neglected this part of the project soon wished they hadn't.

"Well, theoretically you're supposed to be helping me sort out any problems with the spell," Penn said. He ambled over to a nearby coffee table that had a few books on it, including one with a leather binding and Chinese characters embossed and gilded on the front of it. This he flipped casually open and glanced down at a two-page spread that Kit could see was covered from side to side with the graceful curlicued script of the Speech. "Except that there aren't any problems."

Kit kept himself from throwing Nita the look he wanted to. *Give him the benefit of the doubt . . .* "That's a great state to be in," he said. "Especially so early on in the process. Why not spread out the basic diagram for us and we'll have a look."

Penn's expression went profoundly suspicious. "Yeah, sure. How do I know you're not interested in swiping some of the sensitive elements?"

Kit glanced at Nita in astonishment. Nita gave him an "I saw this coming" look, with a smile, and said nothing.

Kit turned back to Penn. "To use for *what,* exactly?" he said.

"Yeah," Nita said, and chuckled. "It's not like I run out the door in the morning thinking *Ooh, wow, I really feel the need to divert the solar wind today!*"

Penn smiled at her skeptically. "Good one," he said. "But, realistically, this is going to be kind of technical for you, wouldn't you think? I thought you were more into the birds-and-bees kind of wizardry. The nature end of things."

Nita's mouth quirked up on one side. "There's quite a lot of nature," she said softly. "And quite a lot of it is . . . *technical.*"

Kit kept still, as he didn't think he'd ever before heard Nita put a twist on the word "technical" that practically turned it into a drawn knife. "But go ahead," she said, and there was more humor in her voice now. "Let's see how much technicality you've got packed away in this thing." She stuffed her hands in her jeans pockets and looked unconcerned.

Kit swallowed as inconspicuously as he could. He had a very strong feeling that something quite untoward had just barely missed happening. *What worries me, though,* he thought, *is that Penn didn't even see it . . .*

For the moment, though, it didn't matter. "Right," Penn said, "here it is!"

He waved his arms in a grandiose gesture. The

burning blue lines and circles and angles of a spell diagram flooded out from his manual on the side table. The diagram covered the floor and then reared upward into the upper half of a sphere that closed over all their heads like a diminutive dome.

The first thing Kit noticed was that large parts of the spell diagram were missing. The wizardly construct arching over and around them was sketchy, more of a schematic than a full diagram. There was a large, empty core-sphere at the heart of the thing, the spot where the routines meant to handle interaction with the Sun's distant surface would go. The core had big spell-powering receptor sites faired into it all over its surface, and some time had been spent on the multiple energy-scoop wizardries associated with them.

"Okay," Nita said, before Kit could even get his mouth open, "I see where this is going." She walked into the heart of the spell, reached out for the core-sphere — about the size of a big beach ball — and picked it up in her hands. "Now this has some possibilities. You take this construct, shove it from wherever you are into a small temporospatial tube, and drop it out the other side of that into the Sun's chromosphere. So you can implement it from anywhere, which is good." She turned the "beach ball" over in her hands. "All these receptors pull raw energy straight out of the solar atmosphere, so the spell, except for the verbal Speech parts and the intentional components, is powered by what you're using it to control. That's elegant. And all *you* have to do is bootstrap it with the basic spoken wizardry and your own intention, then turn it loose."

She paused, then, and turned slowly once in a complete circle, looking over the rest of the visible spell diagram that was drawn on the dome over and around them. "So far, so good. But after that the spell's got a whole lot of work to do, and you haven't yet indicated how you intend to power *that*. What you're planning to do is to warp the prestorm coronal structure into a kind of funnel shape over the area where you're working, and then shoot the high-speed energy particles of the wind off in another direction, like water out the neck of the funnel. Which is fine. Now, I see the control sectors over here —"

She walked over to one side of the dome, pointing at and tracing with one finger a number of fairly complex angular structures, densely interwritten with the Speech. "And these are a nice idea, too. But you're not going to be able to power them directly off the Sun, as you've already got one set of directives doing that in the spell; you can't run them both at once in such tight quarters. At the very least, you've got to spin off another entire core for the control structures. It's going to cost you more energy: maybe fifty percent more than what you thought you were originally going to spend. A solo-working wizard who has to do this spell on short notice and without prep is going to be useless for anything for a day or so afterward. So you've got to either repurpose this spell for group work or scale it back. If you scale it, it won't be able to handle as much of the corona as you're indicating you'd like to do here, but it'll still be useful as sort of a fire extinguisher that a wizard can deploy while waiting for the heavy assistance, the fire trucks, to arrive."

She turned around where she stood, looking at the other diagrams and annotations in the Speech that were written over the surface of the dome. "It's a start," Nita said. She wandered back toward Kit and Penn, and casually tossed Penn the beach ball of his spell-core. He caught it and staggered, not expecting the extra ten pounds' worth of gravitational force that Nita had quietly imparted to it on the fly while he wasn't paying attention. "Now all you have to do is fill in the rest of this stuff," she said, waving her hands at the dome, which was about two-thirds empty space. "It's interesting, though, even though generally this is more in my sister's line of work."

"Your sister's a wizard?" Penn looked surprised. "Older than you? Younger?"

Oh, God, Kit thought, *he doesn't even know.*

"Younger, yeah." Nita produced a cockeyed smile full of meaning that Kit suspected Penn was completely unequipped to parse. "You two should meet." The smile got a touch more feral. "It'd be fun."

"So that's the structural side," Kit said. "Looking

at it simply as a concept, I can't see any problems. It's a great idea, and I see no reason why it shouldn't work. In fact, you have to wonder why no one's done it before! Which I guess is a good sign."

Penn preened himself a little. "I thought so," he said, "you know? It had that feeling of . . . *inevitability* about it." He grinned.

Oh, Powers That Be, Kit thought, *lend me your bucket that I might stick my head in it and not have to listen to this guy's ego parading itself around the room!* He was surprised by how much this was getting to him. *Have I simply not noticed how lucky I am not to have a life full of people who all think they're the best thing since sliced bread? Even Carmela seems low-key next to this guy.*

Aloud, though, Kit merely said, "Well, what's not inevitable yet is that this is going to be ready for you to perform it in front of thousands of people in a couple of weeks. You're short on structure right now. I know you're, well, concerned about the sensitive aspects. Fine. You don't know us, we don't know you — or at least we didn't before a day ago. But at the same time, the Powers That Be sent us to you. I'd *hope* that would suggest to you that your content's safe with us. We are not just some random wizards you met in the street."

Kit watched Penn's face work as he thought that over. *I can't believe,* Kit thought, *that he's genuinely wondering whether the Powers That Be are screwing him over.*

"All the same," Penn said, "before the Cull stage, why do more diagramming than to the proof-of-concept level? If I go through, I've got five days or a week before the eighth-finals. Plenty of time to fill in the holes. Why knock myself out? No one else is going to."

"I wouldn't put any money on that," Nita said. "Better do the work early and have time to fix it if something goes wrong."

"Don't see how much could," Penn said. "But maybe you'd like to backstop me." He looked at Nita admiringly.

The look she gave him back was one of amused pity. "Oh, Penn," she said, "if you want me to do your homework for you, you're going to have to ask me *way* more nicely than that. The soulful look hasn't worked on me since — second grade? Maybe third. But meantime? Not a chance. You're going to want to get started the minute we walk out the door, because you've got a *lot* to do before Cull Day."

Penn smirked and turned away. "You had your chance," he said. "Guess you'll have to watch and learn."

"Guess I will," Nita said. "Is there a bathroom down here somewhere?"

"First door on your right."

"Thanks." She left the room.

After a few moments Penn said, "Just one question real fast. You passed her all that stuff, didn't you? You're just giving her a boost."

Kit stared at him. "What?"

"None of that stuff was in her specialty. I looked that up! She does —" He waved his hands around. "Visiony stuff. And whales, lately. I don't think we need her around for that."

How can anyone be this clueless? And what use is a wizard who doesn't read? "I don't need to pass her anything, Penn. For one thing —" There were about *thirty* things, but Kit was controlling himself hard, aware that his annoyance if let loose could make him get rude with someone in whose house he was a guest. "Besides a ton of brains, she happens to have the spirit of wizardry stuck in her head."

Penn put his eyebrows up. "Ahhh. No wonder she's so fast at working out what makes a spell tick."

Kit frowned. "She's fast at working out spells because she's *smart*." His thoughts went back suddenly to a round patch of ground inside a freeway exchange, a long time ago, and the image of the girl looking silently down at him. Out of the memory he said, "And she's also really good at making friends."

"I bet she is," Penn said softly.

Kit didn't quite know how to take that. Half of

Penn's utterances were accompanied by a smirk, as if he considered everything that came out of his mouth to be at least potentially funny. *Well,* Kit thought, *you're not half as funny as you think you are.*

"She made friends with a hundred-foot-long great white shark once," Kit said. "That looks like the gold standard of friend making to *me.* But if you're going to stand there making what-do-we-need-her-for noises, well, better check with the Powers That Be, because *they're* the ones who insisted she be here. Theoretically, to give you a fighting chance of winning. Want to cut us loose and go it alone? Say the word."

He pointedly turned his attention back to the spell diagram on the floor, half wishing that Penn would say, *Yeah, I don't need you.* But instead Penn hurriedly came around in front of him, saying, "Hey, Kit, listen. No offense, right? It's just important to shake out who's doing what early on. Easy to get confused about something like that."

Because you're assuming I'm *doing the heavy lifting in this team,* Kit thought. *It's going to be so much fun to watch you keep making that kind of mistake . . .*

"*So* easy to get confused," Kit said. Down the hall, a toilet flushed; a door opened.

A few seconds later, Nita brushed through the dome of the spell diagram. "So," she said. "What's the plan?"

"I'd say we need to meet at least a couple times this week," Kit said, "to see how Penn gets along with filling in these blanks. Tuesday?"

Penn pulled out an iPhone, did a few thumb-touches to its screen. "Tuesday's good," he said. "Your time zone or mine?"

"Ours sounds good," Nita said. "About point three suit you?"

"Sounds excellent." Penn put his phone away, reached out to Kit for a handshake. Then he held his hand out to Nita.

Kit watched Nita look thoughtfully at the hand for a second. Then she took it.

Penn lifted her hand, bowed over it, kissed it. "I'm so sorry," he said. "I misjudged you."

"Yes, I'd say you did," Nita said. She recovered her hand without any undue show of haste, and unexpectedly offered the other one to Kit.

He hesitated only a second before taking it, hoping the uncertainty didn't show. Nita looked at him. "Shrubbery?" she said.

"Shrubbery," said Kit.

They vanished from Penn's house with less air displacement than might have been caused by a passing butterfly.

A few moments later they were in among the rhododendrons, and Nita was scrubbing the hand Penn had kissed against her jeans. She was also laughing in sheer disbelief. "What — the hell — was *that?*" she gasped.

"The cheesiest line ever uttered by a living being?" Kit said, laughing too. "Listen, the next time we see the Powers, we absolutely need to knock them on their butts. What have they *stuck* us with here?"

"An ego on legs," Nita said, still laughing helplessly. "That spell had better be useful for *something*, because if I come down with the chronic cooties because of that —" She flapped the offended hand around in front of her. "Oh, God, Kit, I need antiseptic. What a waste of *time!*"

The two of them laughed a while more until they ran out of breath. "But not a waste of power, I guess," Kit said. "Because here we are, on Their business. And we wouldn't be here if this wasn't for something useful."

"Yeah . . . yeah." Nita sighed and leaned against the exposed trunk of one of the rhododendrons. "While I was in the bathroom, I heard what you were saying."

Kit flushed hot. "Okay," he said, "but I had to, right? What kind of person would I be if I'd stood there and let him trash-talk you?"

"You shouldn't feel like you have to protect me," Nita said. "This is like being out in the playground again, except this playground's full of wizards. Believe me, if I needed to tear Penn a new one, I would."

"You almost did," Kit said.

"Yeah," Nita said, "and I would've had reason. Oh, God, Kit. *'The birds and the bees' . . . !*"

They laughed again together for a moment. Kit felt some of that uneasy tightness go out of his chest. "But honestly, this guy exhausts me," Kit said. "Everything he says is a brag, an insult, or an innuendo. What is his *problem?*"

"Trouble at home, maybe? There's some evidence for that. Hormonal junk? Nerves?" And she rolled her eyes. "Or maybe he's just an asshole."

Kit laughed again. "Have we been living a sheltered existence, or something? Because this isn't the kind of wizard we normally run into . . ."

"It's true," Nita said, in a musing sort of way. "We don't know that many asshole wizards."

"Ronan."

"Oh, come on! Ronan is not an asshole."

"All right, he's just annoying. But he still gets the job done."

"Problem is, I think Penn has a chance of doing that, too."

"Being annoying?"

"Of course, but I meant getting the job done."

Kit tilted his head back and blew out a thoughtful breath. "Assuming he can *do* what he spends most of his time claiming he can do . . . But now you're standing up for him?"

"And why not?" Nita said. "We're mentors; isn't

that what we're supposed to be doing? This guy has talent. I don't think there's any doubt of that. If there was, he wouldn't be in this at all — the Powers would never have invited him! And he's got something to contribute here: a good idea. So far, though, that's pretty much *all* he's got. Good spell execution is more than just the outlines."

"Yeah. If he's going to make it past the Cull, even, he's gonna have to fill in a lot more of those holes."

Nita nodded. "If today's any indication, then what we've got to do is help him learn to navigate around his jerk tendencies. Keep him appropriate, keep him focused. Which is going to be a full-time job." She shook her head. "But I wasn't kidding. I'm trying to work out why the Powers even wanted *me* in on this. Seems like a waste of time."

"What? Why do you *think?* Because we're a team."

"Well, for one thing, it's more Dairine's specialty. Why didn't they hook him up with her?"

"Because he wouldn't have survived kissing her hand?"

Nita laughed, but she also rolled her eyes. "If I find out that the Powers That Be have sent me along on this thing to cure somebody of their *sexism,* they and I may have words afterward. Because this is going to get on my nerves."

"Well," Kit said, more quietly, "you know the principle. 'All is done for each . . . '"

"Yeah, well," Nita said. "It sounds good in theory. But when you find out that *you're* the tool being used to do the 'all,' your perspective changes." She frowned. "Penn needs serious education. At the very least, he needs to be socialized with other wizards so he doesn't come off like an idiot! And I don't know about you, but I was looking at the base schematic for his spell and it was all over the place. I don't know who taught him to compose . . ."

"Well, we've both got the advantage of working with someone who specializes in spell composition. Tom's been doing that . . . *how* long now? Decades. Since he wasn't too much older than us, I think. If Penn is self-taught — working only with the manual and the general style guides in there — maybe it's no surprise he's sloppy around the edges."

Nita sighed. "We've got our work cut out for us. Let's go. I want to wash my hand."

Kit hesitated, hoping it wouldn't show. Then he held his hand out to her. "Grand Central?" he said.

Nita looked thoughtfully at Kit's hand: then took it, with the smallest smile. "Grand Central," she said.

They vanished.

It was night, and Nita was standing all by herself in the middle of a big, dark field. She could smell grass; fresh-cut, so fresh that a lawnmower might have been by in the last few minutes.

So that's interesting, Nita thought. *But where the hell am I?*

The silence around her, though, *that* got her attention. *If I'm outside*, she thought, *if there's a lawn-mower, then why can't I hear anything else? If it was nighttime, and there was a lawn to be mowed, then there would be insects.* But she couldn't hear anything of the kind.

Nita held still, and closed her eyes. *All right*, she thought, *one thing at a time. This is a vision. Let's see where it goes.*

You think that's going to help? said a voice nearby in the darkness. *The real problem is that you're trying to treat this* rationally.

And since when is being rational a problem? Nita asked.

It's not the rationality by itself, the voice said. *It's where it leads you.*

Fine. Where should I be going, then?

The way you fear to go, the voice said.

The chill that ran down the back of Nita's neck had nothing to do with the night, or the dew falling on the cut grass. "Bobo," Nita said, looking around her, "is that you? Thought we had an agreement that you weren't going to get *into* one of these. It gets too confusing."

As she spoke, she suddenly became aware of a faint light out at the edge of things. She turned to try to get an idea of where it was coming from, and realized that she was completely surrounded by it. She couldn't see any source, either — it was as if the light was downhill from her in all directions.

Bobo's not here, said another voice. It wasn't one that she was familiar with — which somehow the first voice had been. This one was low and sad, and sounded deeply troubled.

She could understand why it was troubled, because Bobo was *always* here. In fact the idea that Bobo wasn't answering her began filling Nita with alarm. In the waking world there were times when she could go days without speaking to him, sometimes even without thinking about him; but when she called on him, he never failed to answer. And now that it felt as if he was *needed* here —

Well, Nita thought. *This is weird.* But she wasn't going to start crying for him like a baby missing her toy. She'd coped without him before, and she would do it again.

"All right," Nita said. "Is there something you want to tell me? I'm listening."

A second later the light got brighter, distracting her. Nita looked around and realized that the faint radiance encircling her was just that; a circle, sharp and cleanly drawn. It lay faintly glowing on the grass, right out at the edge of her vision, but the circularity of it was plain to see — as if someone had walked around her with one of those chalking machines they use at football games. There were, however, no irregularities or bumps or wiggles in this circle. It was unnervingly perfect. And as she was continuing a slow turn in which she examined it, the blue-white glow of it, for any slightest wiggle or bend, another voice spoke up.

And this one was strange, *strange.* It was a hiss, almost, like someone speaking with breath but no voice, the breath a soft roar oddly like the roar of flames up a fireplace chimney. But very low, afraid to be heard, almost unwilling to be heard. *It's late,* the new voice said. *Very late. Too late, maybe.*

"What's the matter?" Nita said. "Let me help!"

You can't help, the fiery voice said. *He's the only one who can help, and he's not here. Why isn't he here? He was supposed to be here. How else can we be freed?*

The hair rose on the back of Nita's neck. *This is bad,* she thought, feeling the sense of fear and pain that the other voice was trying to hide, and failing. It was too young, that was the problem. It wasn't supposed to be by itself. *He* was supposed to be here. Nita swallowed, unnerved. "Bobo?" she said, and then more loudly, not quite shouting it. "Bobo!"

"Where is he?" said another voice in the darkness, and this one she knew: it was Kit. "We need him now, Neets, can't you get in here?"

A moment later, another voice chimed in. It was Carmela's. "Not this time, Neets," she said. "He can't help. Kit can't help. You're the only one. And you have to help find where both of them are. If you don't find them both, it won't be any good, they'll *destroy* each other if it's not done right — *!*"

Nita tried to swallow, but her mouth was dry. As she struggled for words, she suddenly realized that the circle was closer around her, now; closer *to* her. It had been nearly out to the horizon before, or at least the light associated with it had been. Now it was maybe — what? Fifty yards away? And it was pulsing — buzzing, or humming, making an odd sizzling noise. It was brighter, too.

The cold down the back of her neck felt more like heat now, prickly heat. The darkness about the field where she was standing had somehow got darker. There were no stars in it, none. It was not like it had been when the Pullulus came through, when there were stars on one side of the sky and the darkness on the other side that was trying to eat them. Here there was simply darkness. Even the ugly un-sky of the Lone One's alternate Manhattan had not been this desolate. This was an emptiness that was chillingly complete. It was not a place from which stars had been disbarred or eradicated; it was a place in which they had never existed at all.

"Bobo's not here," said one voice. And, "Bobo can't help," said another. Nita's eyes widened. *Was that Penn? What's* Penn *doing here?*

And then still another voice, much darker, much deeper, spoke. It said, "And you know what the joke is this time?"

At that, Nita went cold all over. She knew *that* voice entirely too well. "Oh, go on," she shouted into the dark, in no mood to sound conciliatory. She'd had it up to here with the Lone Power's jokes. "You know you want to tell me —"

"But I'm on your side this time," it said, with a sort of sad, wounded sarcasm.

"Oh, tell me another one," Nita muttered. But that was apparently the wrong thing to say. The circle that had been fifty yards or so away was now maybe five yards away, closer, brighter, buzzing more malevolently. Heard at closer range, the noise it was making had become more uncanny. It sounded peculiarly mechanical, as if tiny racecars were running a deadly serious race around and around it. *What do they call those?* Nita thought, trying to remember the name of the long, thin cars that go so fast around special tracks, or on big races through many cities. *Formula — something.* Racing wasn't something Nita normally paid much attention to, but now she could hear the wasplike whine of miniature cars circling. Except the sound was higher now, fainter, more piercing.

"Not that it's going to matter to you, or to her, or to him," said the darkest voice. "Especially not to *him*.

His attention will be elsewhere. So you should make the most of this brief pastorale, because he's going to come to his senses, and it won't last long."

"Who?" Nita said. "Bobo? Kit? Penn? You know, sometimes you get too obscure for your own good."

"But not this time," said that very dark voice. And it was laughing at her — laughter that she'd heard before when things had not gone well. As it laughed again, the circle had drawn in even closer, was lying right around her feet, hemming her in. She couldn't move out, couldn't step away, couldn't escape. The whining noise it made scaled up and up. Desperately she reached out for what hadn't been there before, a hand to hold, and found nothing: just empty air.

"For a change," the dark voice said, "obscurity is not on my list. My only limitation in communicating with you is your unwillingness to engage. Isn't it delicious? The only thing that will keep you from saving them is *you*."

"I'll break through," Nita said. "I will!"

"But will you do it in time?" the Lone Power said. "Not if you don't become at least somewhat more flexible. But that's always been your problem, hasn't it? Stubborn Nita, always so sure of what she thinks, refusing to compromise. Compromise is going to be right at the heart of this one, and you will probably walk right past it because you're so determined to have your own way."

A long, thoughtful pause followed. "Because it's not your style to let somebody else walk into the fire, is it? You've still got some guilt about that. But that'll be a problem for another day. Right now, there's something closer at hand. And it's going to be so much fun watching you figure it out. If you can."

"Well, if you're going to be on my side, then maybe you should just tell me the answer!" *After all,* the thought came to Nita out of nowhere, *if it works on the Transcendent Pig . . .*

The circle was gone from below. It was around her throat now, like a choker necklace, strangling her, stopping the words in her mouth and the breath in her body. Her hands went up to tear at it. But she couldn't get so much as a fingertip underneath it, and she gasped and her vision started to go, while right under her ears the maddening whine and buzz of the tiny cars became the only sound in the world. "I'm telling you the answer all the time," the Lone Power said. "But will you hear it?" She could almost hear It shrug. "Doesn't matter, not really," It continued. "Or rather, it'll matter to another. Not to me. You're stuck with me. If you won't walk into the fire, *he'll* be stuck with me, too." Then a long, soft laugh. "And if you *do* get him to walk into it," It said, "then you've just managed to get somebody else to die for you, haven't you?"

She couldn't breathe. She couldn't move. The voice kept speaking to her, but she couldn't hear it over the excruciating buzz of something going very very fast in circles. Wheezing for breath, Nita tore at her throat, choking, as everything went black —

And she woke up.

She was sitting bolt upright in bed, still panting for air. "Sweet Powers above, below, and sideways, what the hell was *that?*" she whispered as soon as she had breath enough to do so. *"Bobo??"*

You told me not to wake you during these, Bobo said calmly. *I would've liked to, especially since you were calling for me, but you* did *specifically countermand that. Want to give some thought to rewriting the night-vision routine?*

"God," Nita said, "don't tempt me." She tried calming her breathing. It wasn't easy.

I recorded it, Bobo said, *but as usual there's nothing but sound and imagery. You're going to have to add subjective context.*

"I honestly do *not* want to do that right now!"

White Queen memorandum . . . Bobo replied.

Instantly, inside Nita's head, a picture of an engraving from the old version of *Through the Looking Glass* appeared, with the White King and the White Queen; the White King saying, "The horror of that moment I shall never, never forget!" and the White Queen, completely unconcerned by his distress, saying, "You will, though, if you don't make a memorandum of it!"

Nita sighed. "Nobody likes a smartass, Bobo . . ."

Your note, not mine . . .

"Fine. Can I go pee first?"

Five minutes, Bobo said, *and think about it while you're there. I'll take dictation on the context and under-dialogue while you're brushing your teeth.*

She rolled out of bed, groaning. "Wizardry is *mean* to me," she muttered. "I'm gonna *tell*."

At the back of her head, Wizardry snickered unsympathetically, and Nita muttered to herself and made for the bathroom.

6

Mumbai

✳

IT WAS PECULIAR, Dairine thought, that as a wizard you could go thousands of light-years away from
home, even millions, and not get all that nervous
about it. But go halfway across your own planet and
you started to twitch.

Her own nervousness annoyed her. *I've traveled
distances that some human beings can't even conceive
of,* she thought. *I've been out practically to the information event horizon, the place beyond which things
can barely be said to* exist. *I have* buddies *out there.
And now I've got someone I know in Bombay — no,
Mumbai,* she corrected herself — *and I'm losing my
grip. What's the matter with me?*

Dairine stood in front of the mirror in her bedroom, finishing up the business of getting dressed.
The unusual thing for her was that she was doing it at

midnight, and was already resisting the temptation to yawn.

"You ought to give us timeslides," she'd said to Tom when she'd gone over to his place to discuss this visit with him.

He'd given her a look of incredulous amusement. "Let me get this straight. You want us to selectively derange the structure of local space-time and risk a cascade of possible temporal paradoxes so that you don't have to have your personal sleep schedule messed up?"

"You gave Nita and Kit one for their Ordeal when they asked!"

"Actually, that was *because* they were on their Ordeal," Tom replied. He was leaning against his dining room table with his arms folded and his legs crossed at the ankle, and his whole demeanor radiated a disinclination to take Dairine seriously. "And the suggestion came from us. Carl has latitude to offer such instrumentalities to probationary wizards if he thinks it's appropriate, which he did — as the Powers gave him to understand that Nita and Kit's ability to return from their trip at the same time they left would prove useful. And as it happens, it did. In *your* case, however, a timeslide would serve no such purpose. And seeing that *you* were the one who suggested that the two of you meet up at your mentee's place —"

"The orientation pack said that was a good thing,

because people are more comfortable on their own ground!"

"That is completely true," Tom said. "It was very smart of you to pick up on that suggestion. And no, the Powers are *not* going to give you a timeslide as a reward for being considerate. In fact if I were acting for them and I were going to give you anything right about now, it would be be a recommendation that you start stocking up on coffee."

Frustrated, Dairine had scowled at him. "I thought coffee was supposed to stunt your growth."

"Urban myth," Tom said, heading over to sit down at his desk in the living room again. He flipped his laptop open, his expression intimating he'd had about enough of Dairine for one day. "Invented by a guy at the beginning of the twentieth century who was trying to sell people on his new grain-based coffee substitute. There are various other reasons why someone your age might want to avoid overdoing the caffeine-based beverages, but stunting your growth would not be one of them."

"Tom," Dairine whined, "they're *nine and a half hours ahead* of us!"

"And you did that without even looking at the manual!" Tom said, tapping at his laptop's keyboard and not looking up. "My faith in young people's ability to do mind math is completely restored."

Dairine paused, frowning. "What happened to the other half-hour?"

Tom shook his head. "Lost in translation? Take it up with the world temporal steering commitee. Maybe one of them has some time-share scam going."

She sighed. When Tom got snarky like this, it was impossible to get anything useful out of him.

"I can hear you thinking how nonforthcoming I'm being at the moment," Tom said. "But spare a thought for the other thirty or forty people who've been in here this morning already, looking for advice and assistance with Invitational issues." He sighed. "And the thirty or forty who'll come after you've left, before I get anywhere near my lunch. I'm a very popular man today . . ."

Dairine had to laugh at that. "Okay," she said. "I'll get off your case now."

"Please and thank you!"

She was heading for the door when Tom paused in his typing, staring at the laptop screen. "One thought," he said, "just in passing. You might find it useful to have a personal invisibility spell loaded up for when you arrive."

She studied him curiously. "Okay," she said. "Anything else?"

"There's a Dutch instant coffee that's nice," Tom said, still not looking up. "Sort of a big coffee crystal, very smooth. Can't think of the name right now, Carl always buys it. Glass jar. If you look in the cupboard . . ."

"Thanks so *very* much," Dairine said, rolling her eyes, and got out of there.

She spent some time before she left consulting both her manual and the Internet to see how people dressed in Mumbai. After all, she and Mehrnaz might wind up going out somewhere; there wasn't any point in sticking out or looking like a tourist. After checking some images online, Dairine spent a while rummaging around in her closet and her drawers and finally settled on a light, high-collared, long-sleeved summery white tunic from a few years back. It still fit, even if it was shorter on her than it used to be. Over jeans it would be okay.

She hadn't really started to get ready until her dad came back from the shop around nine that night, quite late for him: apparently he had to start getting himself together for a Tuesday night wedding. *At the rate he's going,* Dairine thought, *he's gonna have to hire somebody else to help in the store. Mike won't be enough.* She was grateful, though, that business had picked up so much lately. After their mom had died, when he'd got past the initial shock, there had been a time when her dad had insisted on being in the shop all day, handling every order, burying himself in the work.

He'd lost weight and worn himself out. Both Nita and Dairine had worried a lot about him, because simply *telling* him that he needed to slow down had had no effect.

It had been a bad time for all of them, but slowly their lives had worked themselves into a new kind of normalcy — insofar as anything about life could be normal when two of the three people in a family were wizards — and their dad's work habits had evened out, too. *As much because he just couldn't keep doing that any more, I guess. His body wouldn't put up with it.* And, Dairine had suspected at the time, it had also occurred to their dad that if he put himself in the hospital by abusing himself, he wouldn't be taking very good care of his daughters. Shortly he'd hired Mike, and started training him in what needed to be done in the store. Mike was smart and he liked the work, and (as important, to Dairine's way of thinking) liked their dad. *So that part of life had started to get normal, at least.*

She grabbed her hairbrush off her dresser, brushed her hair back, and fumbled around in her dresser drawer to find a scrunchie for it: *better not have it flapping around in the breeze when you're in a strange new place where you might want to move fast.* In the midst of putting her hair up, Spot came spidering in. "Ready?" she said.

Of course. You?

"Nearly." And then she looked at herself in the mirror, and dropped her hands. "No . . ."

No?

Dairine sighed. "I kind of feel like I'm leaving Nelaid flat. You know what I mean?"

I'm not very sure. As I remember, he told you that you ought to do this thing.

"Yeah, well. When he and Dad get in one of those tag-teaming moods, sometimes it's not so easy to figure out what they're thinking separately."

She gave the scrunchie one final twist and sat down on her bed while Spot clambered up onto it and looked at her thoughtfully with several stalked-up eyes. *Stopping your work with him right now troubles you,* he said.

She nodded. "It's just . . . I don't know. So much of what he's teaching me, I started out having to parrot it back to him. Do what he was doing. But it's getting to the point where I'm beginning to understand the theory." She reached up and fiddled with her hair again. "I keep seeing something he does, or sometimes I'll be hearing something Nelaid's talking about, truly *hearing* it instead of just listening to it, and it'll remind me of something or other Roshaun said to me once."

Something specific?

"No . . . Except yes. Once or twice," Dairine murmured, her gaze going unfocused as in her mind she saw herself walking around the stellar simulator, staring at it, at its many readouts of the subtle and complex forces in play inside Thahit or Earth's Sun, and listening to what Nelaid was telling her about them. And something he said would unexpectedly trigger the sound of Roshaun's voice saying something very similar. Then her insides would flare up with the thought, *That,* that *was something important. But* why *was it important?* And then half the time she'd lose the thread of whatever it was about in a flood of sheer relief that she could *remember* what his voice sounded like, that she hadn't forgotten how he sounded. The thought of forgetting Roshaun's voice woke Dairine up sweating cold, some nights.

But you can't remember what it was about, Spot said.

"No," she said, and sighed. "I wonder sometimes, am I imagining it? But I don't think so." Dairine frowned. "There's something . . . something *useful* that I've been missing. Something we've been getting close to, when I'm working with the simulator. We've been doing a lot of work on stellar kernel stuff, the star's software . . ." She sighed again. "There's so much data, though, it keeps piling up, and every time I think I might have time to start reviewing it, something else happens and I get distracted . . ."

You don't have to do this, you know. They said you didn't.

"But yeah, I do, because I said I was going to,"

Dairine said. "If I was going to pull out, I should have done it before the meet-and-greet the other night . . . I'm in it now. It's only for a few weeks. And who knows, maybe something'll happen to jog my memory."

Dairine got up, looked herself over in the mirror one last time, and on a hunch reached into the top dresser drawer to rummage around. She pulled out a big dark blue scarf in light, cheap silk, something of her mom's. She kept remembering that Mehrnaz had had her head covered. What religion she might be wasn't any of Dairine's business at this point, but if Mehrnaz felt she needed to wear something like that when she was out in public, then Dairine might wind up in the same situation. And it wouldn't do to differ from her mentee in any way that would attract people's attention. She wound the scarf around her neck a couple of times, knotted it, shoved the ends down her collar, and then turned to pick Spot up off the bed. "Ready to go undercover?"

Ready.

Down at the bed's end was one last thing she thought she might need: a plain brown leather messenger bag with a long strap. Her mom had bought it for her some years back thinking it would be good for schoolbooks, but her mother's concept of what you needed to carry your books to school in was plainly from the distant past, when schools didn't believe in giving you quite so much homework. Dairine slid Spot

into the bag and buckled it shut. "Got those coordinates I selected?"

Located. Ready to initialize.

"Then let's go!"

They popped out in a place Dairine had carefully pre-
selected with the manual, an alleyway within a few
minutes' walk of Mehrnaz's family's apartment. It was
a strange sort of halfway-to-Oz moment: the pave-
ment of the alley where she stood all scattered with
rubbish, barred doors and screen doors opening off
it, walls full of windows reaching up high on either
side and blocking out the light, so that it was almost
dim here, with the hum of overtaxed air-conditioners
drifting down from above. But at the alley's end,
everything was people and vehicles and bikes rushing by in both directions in full sunlight, a gaudy hot
morning light completely unlike what morning light
far north of here would be.

On target? Spot said in her mind. He could most
likely see it through her eyes, but out of courtesy he
often acted as if he couldn't.

"Yeah," Dairine said.

She walked down the alley and out into the street.
But this took her longer than she expected, because
that street — which she'd selected because it seemed
quiet — was extremely busy and crowded. Dairine
had walked New York streets at lunch hour more than

once, but this was far worse than anything she remembered. There seemed to be different rules for how you walked here: people seemed willing to be pushed a lot closer together than they'd been even in the worst crush Dairine could remember at rush hour in the subway. The smells here were different, too: car exhaust, of course — the traffic was crazy — but also bizarre scents and unexpected stinks, people's perfumes and bodies and the smell of food seemingly everywhere. *For me it's the middle of the night,* she thought, her stomach growling emphatically as she went by a storefront where they were frying something spicy-smelling, *so why am I hungry?*

And the whole picture was complicated by the way people stared at her . . . specifically, the way men were staring at her. It wasn't as if that had never happened before, but the gawking she was experiencing now was different from the usual kind. From some of the guys, there was an unpleasant *owning* quality to the gaze they fastened on her: as if they felt they had a right to stare.

At first Dairine handled this exactly the way she would've handled it at home. As she walked, she stared back to let them know she wasn't afraid. But shortly she began to notice that this didn't help. At home, glances would've shifted, eyes would've looked away. Here a lot of them just kept on looking, and some of the men smiled. Dairine did not find the smiles at all nice.

Her first impulse was to use some wizardry to give them something else to think about — like falling on their faces in the crowded street — and see if they could smile at *that*. But she could imagine what Tom's response would be to that kind of behavior. *I'm not here to cause trouble*, she thought. *I'm here to get a job done, and help somebody out, and keep a low profile. If there's some kind of culture-shocky thing going on, for the moment my job is to cope.*

Annoyed, Dairine stepped to one side of the street into the narrow space between a news kiosk and a sweetshop, and said the last few words of the spell she'd been holding ready on Tom's advice. A second later, she was invisible and moving away from there, while one of the nearest men who'd been staring and grinning at her now blinked and tried to figure out what had happened.

Dairine snickered quietly and kept moving, while at the same time being fairly resentful at having to disappear. It was a challenge, moving in circumstances like these when nobody else could see her, but, she reminded herself, it was a challenge she was up for.

She glanced at her watch as they went. "Nearly nine thirty . . ."

Nine twenty-eight. We're close.

Maybe sixty yards ahead of her, Dairine could see the street where she needed to turn. She passed ten or fifteen more storefronts, some shining and modern and some unbelievably ramshackle, bizarrely standing side by side. It was as if the place had history that it was both trying to hang on to and eager to get rid of. Up near the corner where the crazy-busy street met a crazier-busier boulevard, Dairine pressed herself briefly into a doorway out of the relentless flow of people and stood there for a moment to get her breath, shaking her head at the shouting, blazing multilingual cacophony of it all.

Straight ahead on your right, Spot said.

Got it. Let's be uninvisible for a few moments. Not being seen here has its uses, but crossing the street that way strikes me as kind of death wish-y. In particular, a very few moments watching the intersection from here had suggested to Dairine that traffic lights in Mumbai were considered more of a hint or guideline than an actual requirement that anyone *stop.*

Fading in now. Find a spot to be less conspicuous on the other side and I'll fade us out again.

Dairine waited a few seconds for the fade to be complete before shouldering herself out into the crowd of people waiting at the corner for the lights to change. In a matter of seconds she was surrounded by more people coming up on her from behind, and was about to tell herself *Now, don't get all paranoid* when Spot observed, *At five o'clock behind you, someone who wants the bag —*

She felt a hand on the strap even as everyone started

to move out in unison into the intersection. For that she had a wizardry ready, one which had come highly recommended in the manual for wizards on the go in public places when thieves were about. Smiling, Dairine whispered the last few words of the spell and kept walking. *She* couldn't feel any difference, but to the person tugging fruitlessly on the strap of her bag, it now had a virtual weight of several hundred pounds.

Dairine then spun around to walk backwards for a pace or three, smiling what she hoped was a most evil and eldritch smile right into the shocked and uncomprehending face of the thin little woman who'd been attempting to relieve her of Spot's bag. Then Dairine turned back again in the direction in which she'd been headed, pushing farther into the crowd as it crossed the street. As soon as she got up on the sidewalk on the far side she spotted another alleyway not too far ahead, and when she reached it turned into it, giving it just enough of a glimpse to make sure it was empty. *Okay, fade . . .*

A few moments later she peered out of the alley, waiting for a tiny gap in the crowd to slip into. The trick of it seemed to be to make sure you were always moving faster than the people who might bump into you from behind. *Only a couple hundred more yards, right?*

A hundred and fifty-three.

She kept going. This street, though it looked more

upmarket and modern than the one she'd turned off of, still had something of that between-periods struggle going on. But it was hard to say which looked grander — the glossy new shops and apartments, all glass and chrome, or the older buildings, most of which were of carved stone and had a solider, more impressive look to them. *That's probably because they were built to let you know where the money and power were,* Dairine thought. Though her world history unit last year had touched only briefly on India, she had a fairly clear sense of the complexity of the relationship between this country and the power that had once run everything here but now insisted that these days they were both absolutely the best of friends. Dairine made an amused face at the idea. If she knew anything about friendship at all, it was that even when it was true and deep, it was never uncomplicated.

A hundred yards, Spot said. *On your left. There's a sort of little driveway circle in front.*

Dairine nodded: up ahead she saw something that might have been a taxi pull into it. She forged ahead, and as she did so an errant breeze — welcome enough in this heat — blew across in front of her and brought her a smell of something else frying. *I don't know what that is,* she thought, *but I really* want *some.* It smelled like sauteed onions, and it was already talking her stomach out of the idea that it was bad for her to eat so late at night.

Scent analysis, Spot said. *Onion bhaji.*

Oh, God, Dairine said silently. *Make a note of that! Whatever else we do, I'm going out for some of that later.*

Noted. Fifty yards.

Dairine sighed at her growling stomach and kept on walking. And after a few more shiny shopfronts, *Right there,* Spot said. *Across the street.*

Dairine stared at the building. "But that's a hotel!"

Only part of it, Spot said. *There's a private dwelling on the top floor. You'll want to go around the side: there's a private entrance under the archway that leads back toward the parking lot.*

Dairine stared at the building, amazed. The whole front of it was faced in rose-colored marble, with a colonnade of paler marble pillars stretching across the facade. The place was huge, and rose up in about five stories more of carved pink marble, like something out of a film set.

Better move now or you'll get run over, Spot said.

Dairine got bumped from behind, causing consternation among those who stumbled against and into someone who wasn't there, and then against and into each other. A fistfight very nearly broke out behind her, and there was yelling and screaming in several languages, all of which she was able to understand in the Speech. "Wow, people, seriously, *language,*" she said under her breath, and snickered as she slipped out into the space between a couple of parked cars; then, when there was a break in the traffic, across the road.

Dairine's career in wizardry had been eventful enough that a fair number of aliens and hostile others had tried at one time or another to kill her, but when she was safely up on the sidewalk again she found herself thinking that all of them could have taken lessons from the traffic in Mumbai. "Oh God, not even the Crossings at *rush hour . . . !*" She stood there and got her gasping under control.

That may be so, said Spot, *but if you keep standing here you're going to start another fistfight . . .*

Dairine laughed softly and made her way down the side of the half-circle drive that served the front of the hotel, along to where an ornately carved arch in more pink marble sheltered a side entrance and the further drive down into the parking lot behind the building. She slipped behind one of several SUVs parked to one side of the driveway, ducked down, and said the words that would decommission the invisibility spell; then stood up again and headed for the door.

It was large and impressive, carved wood under its own small marble arch. There was a box with a button and an intercom grille set in the side of the arch, and Dairine pressed it.

But instead of a voice speaking, the door opened. Dairine found herself looking up and up at a gentleman in a business suit and a turban. "Yes?"

"I'm here to see Mehrnaz," she said. "I'm Dairine Callahan."

"You're expected, miss," the man said. "Please come in."

He opened the door and Dairine went in past him into a vestibule done in both pink marble and white, with tables up against the walls on which sculptures and huge vases of flowers stood. The effect was still much like being in a hotel, and Dairine wondered if there was some mistake, but the man who now closed the door behind her nodded toward a stairway at the end of the vestibule. "Please go up, miss," he said.

"Thank you," she said, and headed up the stairs.

At the top she paused and looked around in astonishment. The room she'd entered was easily the size of the bottom floor of her whole house. Up here all the marble was white, and between the wide windows that let in the morning light there were framed prints and paintings — modern art, mostly, though there were some portraits as well — and at least one gigantic flat-screen TV down at the far end, with a huge U-shaped white couch in front of it. And from the couch Mehrnaz, in another of her silky overcoat-like tops but without her headscarf, had just jumped up and was coming over to Dairine. "There you are! I was worried about you, why didn't you teleport straight in?"

"Thought I'd walk some of the way," Dairine said. "Local color . . ."

"In this traffic? It's such an awful time for that, and it's hot already. And it's got to be the middle of the night for you, you must be exhausted! How about some tea?"

"Okay. Thanks."

She followed Mehrnaz back to the couch, looking around the big room. Another stairway led up to a higher level: more closed doors of dark carved wood were set into the room's rear wall. Inside the U of the couch was a glass coffee table, scattered with magazines and TV remotes. Mehrnaz picked up one of the remotes, fiddled with it a moment, put it down. "Did you bring your friend?"

"Never go anywhere without him," Dairine said, sitting down and unbuckling the bag.

One of the doors beside the huge TV opened up, and a petite woman in a light- and dark-gold sari came out. "Yes, miss?"

"Lakshmi, will you bring us some tea, please? Thank you."

The woman disappeared. *My God, servants?* Dairine thought. *And did she just use the* remote *to call her? That's a new one.* But for the moment she simply pulled Spot out of the bag — he having pulled in all legs and eyes and anything that made him look like something besides a laptop — and put him down on the table. Then she looked over the back of the sofa at the huge space. "Seriously, Mehrnaz, you ever consider playing football in here?"

Mehrnaz gave her a thoughtful look. "American football or *football* football?"

Dairine burst out laughing. "You could go either way. This is . . . Well, this is incredible! You didn't tell me you lived in the Taj Mahal."

"What?" Mehrnaz laughed at her. "*This?* You should see some of our neighbors' houses. This is just a flat! And not such a big one."

Dairine shook her head. "You think this is *small?*"

"My mother won't let me say 'small,'" Mehrnaz said. "She insists on 'modest' . . . "

The door beside the TV opened again and the lady in the sari reappeared, this time with a tray holding a teapot and cups and saucers and milk and sugar. She put the tray on the table, smiled at Dairine, and flitted away again, closing the door behind her.

Mehrnaz poured a cup for Dairine. "How do you like it?"

"A lot of sugar."

"Brown or white?"

"I'll try the brown. Yeah, two's enough, thanks."

Dairine accepted the cup gratefully, noticed the china in passing — extraordinarily thin and fine with a delicate rose pattern — and took a few sips while thinking, *It's no use, I've got to ask, this is going to drive me crazy.* "Mehrnaz, before we start getting down to work . . . please get me straight on one thing. Are you *rich?*"

Mehrnaz's face went thoughtful while she considered that. That she had to stop to consider it said more to Dairine than almost anything else. "I guess we are," she said. "Not that some of our *neighbors* would think so! They'd say we're just moderately well-to-do. And some of the older ones wouldn't think much of us because they'd say we 'came up from trade.' Worked for money, instead of inheriting it. The nonwizardly side of the family is into IT and cellular telephony."

Dairine shook her head. "I don't get it. How is getting rich from your own work not good?"

Mehrnaz shrugged. "It's sort of a class thing, I suppose."

"Is it like the caste system?"

"Mmm, in a way." Mehrnaz made a helpless expression. "Or just snobbery, maybe. But I don't think most of the family cares about that one way or the other, because the nonwizardly side of the family is very, *very* small. Most of us are wizards. Aunts and uncles and grandparents for a few generations back, and all these cousins —" She laughed. "Not cousins the *hrasht* way. Just *cousins.* There was a wedding, a couple years back, my second-oldest sister, and we sat around and tried to count them all. It was hopeless. We had to stop at two hundred."

"Sometimes I wonder if big families are all the fun they're supposed to be . . ." Dairine said.

Mehrnaz put her teacup down, leaned back against the cushion of the sofa, and rolled her eyes. "Funny you should mention football, because that's what it's like, being stuck in a football match all the time. Everybody running around in all directions, pursuing all these different goals, chasing after all these projects. And everybody who's not doing that themselves is standing on the sidelines and cheering for some of them and booing at the others. It's so *exhausting.*" She covered her face, rubbed it. "What's it like, having just one sister? How many aunts and uncles have you got? Tell me it's only three or four."

"Three, now," Dairine said. "We lost a couple of them young." She sighed. Their uncle Joel had been a particular favorite of hers and Nita's, the source of the Space Pen that Nita loved so much and that had in some ways been at the heart of her getting into wizardry.

"That's such a shame! I'm so sorry," Mehrnaz said.

"It's okay," Dairine said. "It's a long time ago now. Or it seems that way. And as for having just one sis-ter —" She had to smile. "It can still be pretty intense. Especially when she's a wizard and you're not."

"Oh, dear Powers, were you jealous of her?"

Dairine grinned. "You have no idea. But it got bet-ter after she was almost eaten by a shark."

Mehrnaz stared.

"No, I don't mean that being eaten by a shark was going to *make* it better! I mean, after that, They came for me. And I found out that I was being jealous of the wrong things, and that being almost eaten by a shark could be the least of your worries."

Mehrnaz sat there on the sofa shaking her head. "Some of this was in the manual," she said in a hushed voice. "But it sounds so much more *interesting* when you tell it. . . . And yet not so scary."

"It could be scary enough," Dairine said. "Believe me. I'll tell you everything you want to know." She finished her tea and put the cup down, already feeling better from the hit of caffeine. *Though I can see I'm going to have to take Tom's advice . . .* "So you've got to tell me how things work here first. You say most of your family's wizardly . . . so what about the rest of them? Do they know about you?"

"Oh yes," Mehrnaz said. "Everybody knows from when they're little that a lot of the family does magic. It's kind of taken for granted."

"What about the, uh . . ."

"The household staff? Oh, they know. But they really, really like their jobs, so they don't discuss it. In return we take very good care of them — very favorable salaries and benefits packages."

Dairine's eyebrows went up. This was a whole

style of management of the interface between wizardly life and the nonwizardly that she'd never imagined. "Okay. So we don't have to worry about hiding what we're doing."

"In here, not at all. Of course I wouldn't do it in the street —"

Dairine flushed hot. "Uh. Maybe this isn't a great thing, but I just *did* do it in the street."

Mehrnaz looked alarmed. "Do what?"

"Vanished once or twice. I was careful about it . . ."

"Oh, that." She sighed. "We all do that sometimes. Half the time no one even notices. The rest of the time . . ." Mehrnaz shrugged. "What're people going to say? 'I saw some girl disappear in the street today'? Anyone they told would just think they were drunk or on drugs."

"Yeah," Dairine said, "true." She wasn't going to get into the issue of why she'd felt freaked enough to need to do such a thing: they had other things to be thinking about. "Okay," she said, "so we're all set then."

She tapped Spot's lid; he lifted it, and from the sides of his carapace two pairs of eyes came out to look at Dairine and Mehrnaz. Mehrnaz leaned in to peer at him, fascinated and smiling. "Hello!"

Hello, Spot said.

That surprised Dairine somewhat: Spot could

sometimes be quite silent with people he didn't know well. "Spot, would you bring up the abstract of Mehrnaz's spell again?"

His screen went dark, then brought it up: the text page in the Speech that described in general terms what the wizardry was supposed to do. "A strategy for the redirection and diffusion of hypocentric slip-strike fault discharge preexecution by way of selective paradoxical standing wave amplification," Dairine read.

Mehrnaz nodded. "That's it."

"So tell me if I'm getting this right. You're suggesting stopping an earthquake from going off by creating a virtual earthquake that exactly cancels out the way the original's vibrating? And the spell's going to alter itself on the fly to match whatever the quake's doing?"

"Yes! Exactly."

Dairine whistled softly. *Wow,* so *many variables. And so* complicated. *She may look sweet and unassuming but she is* ambitious. "Okay. Spread it out for me and let's take a look," Dairine said, standing up, "and you can talk me through it the way you'll talk the judges through when they come by your stand."

Mehrnaz jumped up from the couch, went out into the middle of the floor, and reached sideways into the air. Half her arm vanished as she felt around inside a pocket temporospatial claudication much like the ones both Dairine and Nita used sometimes. After that she came out with what, to Dairine's surprise, looked like a young girl's locked diary, bound in plastic and splashed with bright colors, most of them shades of pink.

She caught Dairine's expression, and giggled and blushed. "I know what it must look like . . ."

"Don't give it a thought!" Dairine said, laughing too. "Did you see the guy the other night carrying around the controls for an old PlayStation as his manual access? Not to mention that one Canadian guy with the Magic 8 Ball. How you access wizardry is between you and the Powers, and so's what the interface looks like. When you want something different, you'll find it."

Mehrnaz just nodded, looking relieved. "Okay . . ."

She unclasped the book's little strap-lock, riffled through the manual to one particular page, and then reached down into the manual as she'd reached into her otherspace pocket. Out of it she pulled up a glittering webwork of words and lines and diagrams, all swirling softly together like glowing gauze. With a practiced flick of the wrist she cast it shining and spreading out into the air, where it unrolled itself and slowly floated down to settle on the floor.

Dairine grinned. "Slick!" she said. "You get an eight for presentation."

Mehrnaz smiled back at her, though there was something uncertain beneath it. "Really?"

"Absolutely! It's not easy to keep all the linkages together when you're working with a spell graphically like that. If you're not holding the main structures in your head, too, hearing and seeing the words in the Speech, the whole thing comes undone half the time."

"It took a long time to work out how," Mehrnaz said, sounding rather unhappy about that, "and it did keep unraveling . . ."

Dairine shook her head. "Not your problem now. So tell me about it. It's okay to walk on this?"

"Yes, of course. So the idea is this. An earthquake happens when stresses between seismically sensitive structures build up to the point where they have to discharge themselves. Detection via wizardry of faults likely to do significant damage when they discharge has come a long way, as it has in the mainstream scientific scholia. But prediction, even in the very short term, remains troublesome because there are so many variables involved at both the overtly and covertly scientific ends of the spectrum."

Mehrnaz walked around the spell, pointing at various parts of the diagram as she moved. "So this strategy involves installing monitoring routines on one specific type of fault, the oblique — typically the most damaging type of earthquake fault — as its activation heralds tend to be more easily read. It then activates a first-strike sine-mirroring intervention that cancels the worst of the kinetic energy in its earliest possible stages, then siphons off as much as possible of what escapes cancellation into a neutral 'sink space' while alerting supervising wizards to intervene personally and in more detail . . ."

She's good, Dairine thought. *She knows her stuff and she doesn't have trouble with talking about it.* While Mehrnaz spoke, Dairine walked around the edges of her spell and then started working inward, while Spot did the same from the other side, looking the wizardry over for both sense and structure. Though the diagram was extremely intricate, everything looked very tightly knit and grounded. *Well, geomancy, it makes sense . . .*

And her personal style's good. In working with the manual for some time and seeing spells built by other wizards in it, Dairine had realized that there were some people whose spell diagrams were so structurally odd that it was hard to tell what they were doing — sometimes to the point where she needed to ask the manual to redisplay their spell in a default format. Mehrnaz, thankfully, wasn't one of those. Her spell diagram was cleanly laid out, the power structures were offset and isolated from the "executing" structures of the wizardry in what was considered best practice, and the flow of power through the working parts and outward into the executive sections was straightforward and easy to trace. While every spell was supposed to resemble an equation in that all the elements of its exchange of energy with the universe should balance, some spells did this with more grace than others, and Mehrnaz's definitely came down on the graceful side.

Still, there were some unfinished-looking areas and a few peculiarities of design, and Dairine's attention was drawn to one of these fairly quickly. "Okay, hold up a moment. What's that hole over there?"

Mehrnaz peered where she was pointing. "Oh. The lacuna."

"What?"

"You always leave an empty space in one of these spells. The world might want to assert itself."

Dairine restrained a laugh. "Thought the world asserting itself was precisely what you wanted to stop."

"What? No! It doesn't work that way. You always have to leave some wiggle room when you're dealing with the elemental presences . . ."

" . . . I have *no idea* what that means." Only by making them sound like a joke would Dairine ever allow those words out of her mouth.

Mehrnaz raised her eyebrows, perhaps starting to become aware of how rarely such phrases were going to come out of her mentor. "Well. You know how there's a physical expression of a planet's laws and tendencies . . ."

"The kernel, yeah. Sort of a combined firmware-software bundle. My sister works with those."

"Right. Well, there's also an emotional aspect or expression of a planet's tendencies bound into that: the affective bundle, it's called. What people think about the physical world, how they feel about it, and how the planet itself expresses and channels those thoughts and feelings."

"Like the whole idea of the Earth being alive —"

"Well of course it's *alive*," Mehrnaz said, sounding annoyed. "Even popular culture has that concept, which shouldn't be a surprise really." She threw Dairine a look that suggested a private opinion that her mentor seriously needed educating.

Dairine smiled at that. *I think I like the snotty Mehrnaz a lot better than the suck-up one or the shy uncertain one*, she thought. *Then again, that might say more about me than about her . . .* Because behind the idea lay the constant thought of someone else who was snotty but whose style Dairine liked a lot.

She let the thought drop for a moment. "Gaia . . ."

"Yes, Gaia, but this isn't some lovely sweet-natured mommy-Earth wandering around in flowery meadows wearing a big hat and a pretty frock." Mehrnaz's face twisted a bit with disdain. "This is Earth. This is *power*. She *moves*. She demands the *right* to move. And sometimes you have to talk her out of it. But to do that you have to leave space not just for how she is right now, but how she might be in ten minutes, an hour, a week. That's part of why earthquake prediction is so hard.

She moves, all over, everything is moving all the time: it's all *uncertainty.* And setting aside a single bit of the Earth to analyze and intervene in is dangerous. It leaves out all that other movement. And when you construct an equation where some of the variables are going to have to go unspecified at construction time, you'd bloody well better leave some space open. Otherwise the wizardry comes undone like soggy toilet paper."

"Not sure I needed that image."

"It's accurate, though."

Dairine nodded. "Okay. So if the kernel is the ego, sort of, and the affective bundle, the spirit, is the superego . . . then there's sort of an id in here somewhere, too?"

Mehrnaz shuddered. "Yeah, but maybe we don't want to go there right this second. We allow for it in the equation." She pointed at a very dark and tangled set of Speech-symbols over to one side of the spell diagram, bunched up tightly in their own subset circle. "Anyway, you have to leave the lacuna in there to allow for changes in the affective bundle."

"And that's the space over there." Dairine paced over to look at it — a round area in the diagram, not even defined by a circle, but only by the presence of the other structures around it: an empty spot. "That's it? It doesn't look complicated."

"It doesn't need to be. Sometimes a space is just a space. The Earth's full of emptiness, in places. It's not all packed tight, like at the core: not solid. There are *real* lacunae, huge caves that no one will ever see. Some of them contain kinds of life we're not meant to interact with, except very sparsely, very carefully. But most of them are just *empty*." She smiled, and there was something mysterious about the look. "So much of solidity is empty space, right down to the atomic level. The universe is full of holes, and some of the solidest-seeming stuff is the emptiest . . ."

"Sounds kind of Zen."

Mehrnaz sniffed at her. "Zen! Newbie stuff. It's in the *Bhagavad Gita*," she said. "And the holy Qur'an. Emptiness comes *first*. Solidity is a later invention. Emptiness has primacy. It's the most senior thing there is."

Dairine laughed and watched Spot spidering along the lines of the spell diagram, checking it for flaws, examining the tangents and junctures. "You've really got the theory down on this, don't you?"

"It's been on my mind for a long while . . ."

"Well, it's time this got into other people's minds, too."

"It's nice of you to say that." Mehrnaz sat down on a nearby hassock and looked out across the spell diagram the way someone looks across a landscape they're only visiting but would like to live in. "There's only one problem." She sighed deeply. "It's not going to happen."

There was something so hopeless about the words that Dairine couldn't simply refuse to take them seriously. She looked at Merhnaz. "Why not?"

"Because I know I'm probably going to get dropped out at the eighth-finals stage."

Dairine stared at her. "What?" She wasn't going to say that the odds were on Mehrnaz being right: there were, after all, three hundred competitors, and the eighth-finals, "the Cull" as that stage was called casually, was where at least half the weakest projects would be winnowed out.

"I just know I am. Things . . . don't usually work out for me."

The sudden air of dejection that Mehrnaz was now wearing seemed to have come out of nowhere; now she sat looking at the spell diagram with an odd expression of annoyance. Dairine finished looking at the last few elements of the spell under her feet, then made her way over to her.

"You've done a whole lot of work here for someone who's sure they're going to fail out," Dairine said. "This thing . . ." She shook her head. "I can see a few places you might want to polish, but seriously, they're minor. If they threw the eighth-finals in here right now —" Dairine looked around. "And there might be room for it —" Mehrnaz gave her a wan smile. "Then I'd say you had at least an even chance of going through. Which is good, as I'd like to see someone test this live."

Mehrnaz shook her head. "It's very nice of you to say that. I just wish I could believe it."

Dairine pulled over another hassock and sat down by her. "Look, Mehrnaz. If you're so sure you're going to fail, then why bother entering? You could have turned them down if you didn't feel like putting yourself through this. Why are you *in* this thing?"

She shrugged. "I have to be," she said.

Dairine took a breath, tried to figure out what was going on. *Which brings me back to: why am I* not *in this thing?*

The ironic answer *Peaked too soon . . .* breathed through the back of her mind in soft mockery. Dairine could remember a time when *Nothing ever happens fast enough . . .* was the theme song of her life. Now she found herself looking back at that earlier incarnation of herself and saying, *Believe it or not, a time's going to come when you'll beg for things* not *to happen so fast. For your mom to stick around a while longer. For your power to stay at the levels they were when you started. For that particular friend to stay right where he is, exactly the* way *he is. Crazy-making, a pain in the butt . . .*

"Tell me something," Dairine said. "Why'd you get into geomancy in the first place? Because you're seriously good at this."

"You think so? You really think so?"

Dairine held still for a moment. *Who's left you*

in a state that you're asking questions like that? she thought. *Because I think I'd like to kick them.* "Yeah, I really think so! Look, Mehrnaz, if there's something you need to get through your head right now, it's that I'm not going to jerk you around, because neither of us has time to waste on that. If something's working, I'll say so, believe me. If it's not, you'll know about it in a heartbeat. But where wizardry's involved, and where somebody's working at this level, tiptoeing around what needs to be said isn't going to help *anyone.* And the meter's running: it's only — what, four days now until New York, until the eighth-finals?"

"Yes," Mehrnaz murmured.

"So forgive me if I don't waste any more time buttering you up, okay?"

"Okay."

"So why *are* you in this, then? Because it might help if I understood."

"Well." Mehrnaz looked embarrassed, but not terminally so. "It was the endgame, really. Irina."

"Yeah," Dairine said, "I could see the point."

"No, not just that," Mehrnaz said. "It was — You don't understand. It was Irina a long time before this."

Oh no, Dairine thought. *Is this some kind of crush issue? Not that there'd be anything wrong with that, but —*

"How much do you know about her?" Mehrnaz said.

"Well, she's the Planetary —"

"No, no. Not that." Mehrnaz's eyes went wide. "You don't know, do you? Not what she does: what she's *done*. You don't know about San Francisco. You don't know about La Paz. Or Sydney Marianas."

"Wait, how do you mean — ?"

"You don't know about the *earthquakes*. The ones she stopped. By *herself*." And Mehrnaz's voice dropped. "You don't know about *Mazandaran!* That's the one that hit where I used to live, when I was little. It's why we moved here from Iran. So much was destroyed, our whole town was flattened. It broke windows all the way to Tehran. But it could have been so much worse, it could have spread and set off half the faults in the East. But it didn't, because of Irina! She is *so amazing*. You have no *idea* what kind of wizardry that was, what kind of *wizard* she is."

Oh God, Dairine thought, *it's worse than a crush, it's a hero-worship sandwich with gratitude filling. And I thought when we met the other night that I was getting it bad from her!*

. . . So possibly this is not *the time to tell her that Irina was in my backyard not long ago, wheedling my dad for his burger recipe.* "Well —" Dairine said.

"You don't understand." The tremor in Mehrnaz's voice was impossible to mistake for anything but real passion. "I'd do anything, *anything* at a chance to study with her, to work with her. I want to do what she did,

I want to keep people's lives from being *destroyed* like that! Because I've been there." Mehrnaz stared at the floor. "You have no idea what it's like when you wake up in the dark and have to run, run *out,* and things start falling, and when the shaking stops all you want to do is sit down on the couch and cry. But there's no couch, and no house . . . nothing but a pile of bricks and tiles with your whole life buried under them. And past that, nothing but roads twisted up and thrown around like toy car-racing tracks. And then the screaming starts."

Mehrnaz fell silent. "It took me a long time to get the dreams to go away," she said. "The sounds, the aftershocks. The way things *smelled* afterward." She swallowed. "Not until after my Ordeal. I did some work on my head." She looked grim, but very satisfied, and the expression made her face look completely different: younger, fiercer. "But once that was over, I knew what I wanted to do. *This.* And when I found out about the Invitational . . ." She shrugged. "Here I am."

There's something else going on, though. Dairine thought, *something that scares you more than earthquakes. And that's what the problem is. You're going to fail yourself out of this somehow, fail yourself out of a chance at getting something you seriously want, because you're so scared of whatever that other thing is that you're going to make sure you're pushed to one side.*

Well, not if I *can help it.*

"Okay," Dairine said. "Look. If you've come this

far, then you need to stay in, okay? Because it's not just you at stake here: it's other wizards. If you last through the Cull, this spell —" she pointed at the floor —"will go into everybody's manuals as a positively rated prospective intervention. Even if you never take it any further, other people will be able to. You'll have a good chance at saving lives even if you get Culled, because your presentation will get heard. If you give yourself half a chance and work like you think you're going to make it through, the spell will get even more attention, and that's that many more lives you have a chance to save. So you have to stay in, Mehrnaz. It's what you swore to do. It's serving Life." She sighed. "Not always easy . . ." *God, I'm starting to sound like Nita. Let's see if she swallows it, though . . .*

Mehrnaz spent a few moments simply looking at Dairine. "Okay," she said at last.

"Good." Dairine sighed, and Spot, off to one side, shifted and made a soft muttering noise. "Then let's talk about these few rough spots I noticed. I want to make sure I understand everything that's going on before I make you start a polish . . ."

7

Hempstead / Elsewhere

✴

IT WAS JUST BEFORE eight in the morning, and Nita was standing in the kitchen doing the dishes. Partly this was because there weren't enough of them to bother putting in the dishwasher. *Or there are,* Nita thought, *but they'll sit there all day waiting for a full wash to build up, and what if somebody wants to use them?*

The real reason, though, was that she wanted time to think. Since she and Kit had agreed to get involved in the Invitational, things seemed to have gotten very hectic — more so than could be accounted for by what they'd done. She and Kit had had two more sessions with Penn — Or rather, Kit had spent a total of nearly eight hours over two days getting him to fill in the multiple sketchy, incomplete, or half-baked parts of his coronal management spell, while Nita prowled around the edges ignoring Penn's smart remarks and inept attempts to get on her good side.

The trouble is, she thought, *that he has no idea where my good side is. Or why he's on my bad side.* For someone who saw himself as a very cool dude, it was surprising how Penn's attempts to present himself that way kept backfiring. *I still can't believe that he actually kissed my hand.* She rubbed it against her jeans in slightly grossed-out memory, something she'd caught herself doing before. *If he tries that again, I'm going to have to explain things to him.*

. . . Ideally, before Kit does.

She considered that notion, then laughed at herself. *Not really his style,* Nita thought. *What is this, the Middle Ages?* But all the same, she kept running up against behaviors of Penn's that came across as immature. *And he's almost the same age as us. Doesn't he have enough friends at school to help him get a sense of what works with people? Or does he not have enough* friends, *period?*

. . . Or the wrong kinds of friends, it occurred to Nita after a moment. It was easy enough for things to go either way at school. Often enough she'd caught herself sitting through a long afternoon's classes and thinking, *I can't wait for my senior year. Because once I'm there, I will be able to look at most of these people and think, 'In just nine months I'll be done with you and I'll* never *have to see you again!'*

It wasn't that she *disliked* a lot of her fellow students. It was simply that for the most part she had so little in common with them that she might as well have been going to school with members of an alien species. *In fact, generally speaking, I get along* better *with alien species than I do with a lot of these guys.*

Nita laughed at herself as she picked up another small sandwich plate and started scrubbing at it with the abrasive side of the dish sponge. Then she sighed yet again and wondered what she and Kit were going to do about Penn. *It's not that he's not a fairly competent wizard,* she thought. *He made it through his Ordeal, he goes on errantry when he's sent, and he gets the job done.* But beyond that, he didn't seem to be much of a self-starter. Nita had checked her manual with an eye to having a look at Penn's independent projects. What surprised her was that there *weren't* any.

That had left her shaking her head. *What does he do for fun?* The answer seemed to be, *not wizardry.* He liked baseball, and ice hockey, which was slightly remarkable for someone from California; he sang with the choir at his church; he listened to a lot of rock and jazz. And all of these things he would talk about endlessly if you didn't stop him. There were times when you'd be working with him and Penn would want to talk about anything *except* the wizardry you were debugging.

Or, Nita thought, *times when* Kit *will be working with him.* She was still having trouble trying to understand what possible reason Penn might have for not wanting to engage with her except as a girl. *Or his image of a girl,* Nita thought, and put the plate she was washing on the dish rack. *Someone kind of sweet and friendly but not particularly dangerous.* And as she picked up another dish and started scrubbing it, she had to snicker, because if that was Penn's image of her, he was delusional. *It's not like I go around menacing people, exactly. But I've been dangerous enough on occasion. Does that bother him for some reason? And if it does,* why?

She shook her head, rinsed the plate, and added it to the rack. Then she paused, having heard a floorboard creak in the upstairs hall. *Dairine's up . . . Or wait, maybe she's just back.* Her sister's normal working hours had been badly thrown off by her own Invitational work: she'd been in India until nearly breakfast time today.

Nita heard the bathroom door upstairs shut, and reached out to grab the kettle, then filled it up and put it on the stove. From nowhere in particular Dairine had manifested a yen for coffee, and had even gone to the supermarket herself to buy it. *Something her mentee's got her onto, maybe? I should ask.*

Nita went back to the sink and picked up the last dish. *Meanwhile . . . Penn.* They had another meeting set up with him for this afternoon, his time. *On* this *side of things, thank heaven. I'm getting bored with being three hours out of whack half the time. Going off-world is so much easier, you don't have to worry about zonelag . . .* Nita stood there scrubbing, and sighed. *There must be some spells that are good against that . . . I'll look it up.*

Don't bother, Bobo said. *There are several. But they're energy-intensive, and I don't recommend you start using them unless it's an emergency. Fiddling around with your melatonin levels is dicey business.*

Dairine came thumping down the stairs and leaned against the kitchen door, looking blearily at Nita. She was dressed in jeans and a long T-shirt — *again, or still?* Nita wondered. "Water's about to boil," she said.

"Thank you," Dairine said, sounding like she'd prefer to go to sleep right where she stood.

"Go sit down before you fall down," Nita said.

Dairine did that without discussion, which shocked Nita more than almost anything else her sister could've done. Then Dairine put her head down on her arms and blinked at Nita like someone who was finding it too much strain to think, let alone talk.

"You want some of your coffee?"

"Yes."

Nita put the last dish on the rack, pulled two mugs down from the cupboard, and turned off the burner under the kettle. "How much sugar?"

"A lot. Two. Three if you're using a small spoon." She didn't even look up. "Is Daddy here?"

"Nope, left for the shop around seven," Nita said as she got herself a teabag and dropped it in one mug.

Dairine rolled her head on her arms and groaned. "Why do I feel like this?" she said to the table. "I've fought the *Lone Power* and I haven't felt this tired."

"Working hard, maybe?"

Dairine sighed. "Some. Not so much, really, my mentee's smart. But I keep getting the feeling she's keeping something under wraps that's going to pop up at a bad moment." She pushed herself upright, leaned against the back of the dining room chair with her head lolling back.

Nita rummaged in another cupboard for the coffee. "Family stuff?"

"I don't know," Dairine said, her eyes closed. "Haven't seen any of them, it's hard to tell. But I get a feeling it's complicated." She sighed. "I'm not used to family being complicated . . ."

"Maybe we're too nuclear," Nita said, prying the lid off the coffee jar.

Dairine made a slight puff of air that Nita recognized as a substitute for a laugh. "Yeah, but fusion, not fission," she murmured.

Nita snickered. "How much of this do I use?" she said, squinting at the coffee jar.

"Sort of a big teaspoon . . ."

Nita measured it out, poured steaming water. "Lots of milk," said the muffled voice from the table.

Nita took care of that, then put the mug down by Dairine's head and sat down herself with her tea. "What's on the agenda today?" Dairine said, reviving enough to sit up and slurp at her coffee.

"Penn's coming over this afternoon," Nita said. "He's been doing more work on his spell, and we're going to look it over at this end of things."

"In the house?" Dairine said, sounding dubious. "There's not a lot of room."

"No," Nita said, with a slight smile, "not in the house."

Dairine looked at her out of the corner of her eye. "I know that look," she said. "What're you plotting?"

"Well . . ." Nita turned her tea mug around a couple times on the table. "You know, from back when we were working with Mom, I still have access to the aschetic spaces."

Dairine's eyes widened. "The practice universes? No, I didn't know."

Nita nodded. "Had a look at the manual to learn more about Penn, and you know . . . he doesn't seem to have gotten out much. I mean, the High Road isn't to everybody's taste. There's no law that says it *has* to be. But for someone who acts like he's such a big deal —"

"Or thinks he has to act that way?"

"Whichever." Nita shrugged. "Either way, it's a pain in the butt. Anyhow, he doesn't seem to have any circle or group of wizards he works with, not even as casual partners; he doesn't get involved in joint wizardries. And the stuff he *has* done has all been on Earth. Not that that's a hanging offense either." She sighed. "It's just that — Well, with most of the wizards you and I know, the minute they found out there were other planets with life on them, and that you could get at them — *they* were out there like a shot. At least once or twice, if only to see what it was like! But Penn?" She shook her head. "Not once, as far as I can tell."

"Maybe he went on his Ordeal," Dairine said, "and ran into something he didn't like."

"Maybe. But as usual, that's sealed data. No way to find out about it unless he decides to say something, and *I* won't be asking." Nita took a sip of her tea. "Anyway, I'm going to open up a doorway into the Playroom. At least that'll be a little interesting for him, if not exactly off-planet. And we can work without being interrupted. Also, it'll give him a chance to put his spell through a dry run in a place where he can't hurt anything."

"Smart."

"I hope so. I got a segment of the Playroom's space booked for exclusive use late this afternoon — that's the soonest he can get over, which is fine, we're not done with school till around then. I'm going to stealth-shield that whole area way in the back where the sassafras trees are, and anchor the portal there."

"Yeah, I know the spot."

Nita looked at Dairine with slight concern. "I just didn't want you to come back from something and find the energy signature back there had gone peculiar, and then get panicky." *At the thought that somehow, someone had come back without warning, someone you've been missing . . .*

"Like I've got the energy to get panicky about anything right now . . ." Dairine said, gulping down some more coffee.

"It's when you're bleary like this that I start worrying what you might do if you *did* get panicky," Nita said. "Make a note, though, and let Spot know about it, okay? And if you're not busy, stop in, if you want to. I wouldn't mind you looking him over . . . seeing what you think."

"Okay." Dairine guzzled some more of her coffee.

Nita shook her head. "You're really getting into that stuff, aren't you?"

"Yup. Tom's full of good advice," Dairine said.

"Oh, is *that* who got you started. No wonder the jar looked familiar."

Dairine nodded, got up, and headed out with the mug. "You have school this afternoon?" Nita called after her.

"Yeah."

"Okay. I've got a couple of classes starting at three. I'll see you there, then . . ."

No answer; Dairine merely went stomping back up the stairs.

Nita sighed, reached for a dish towel and picked up the first of the dishes from the rack while starting to review the Playroom portal spell in her mind. "Bobo," she said, "text function to Kit's manual?"

Open now. Go . . .

In the upstairs bathroom, Kit was just out of the shower, drying himself off and listening to absolutely nothing.

The house was blessedly quiet. His pop had left for work half an hour ago; his mama was working nights in ICU and wouldn't be home for another half-hour or so. Carmela was asleep, as she too had gone over to afternoon classes at school and on weekdays steadfastly refused to greet the day before ten. *Only time that worldgate in her closet gets any downtime . . .* Kit thought.

He sat down on the toilet lid and sighed, then scrubbed his hands through his hair and tried to stroke it into some kind of shape that wouldn't make him look like an idiot later in the day. *That last haircut . . .* Kit thought. *Not sure it's what I wanted. It keeps sticking up in all the wrong ways.*

Yet at the same time, he remembered turning up in Antarctica the other day after sort of fluffing it up the way the barber had told him to, with some hair gunk, and when he finally tracked her down in that crowd and headed for her, Nita had looked at it and . . . Kit swallowed. He could still see that look. It made his stomach flip.

Is it insane to be still remembering something like that — how she looked at me two days ago?

Nothing's normal *anymore.*

And then he started laughing at himself, there in the quiet. *Like my life's been* any *kind of normal since I picked up that weird book in the secondhand store a few years ago . . .* But he had to admit, as the laughter ran out, that it was still bizarre how just one word could change everything.

Tell the truth, though, Kit thought, *I dared her into saying it.* He'd known that the word had been hanging in the air between them unspoken for a long time. *And also to tell the truth, I was incredibly chicken about it.*

I thought if it just got said . . . then the tension would go away. Because the tension between them had been getting tougher and tougher to bear, for Kit at least. It wasn't as if people at school hadn't been noticing for a long time that there was *something* going on with them. There were kids who were sure it was sex, and (when they hadn't been able to dig up any evidence to confirm this) who then split further into two camps:

those who were sure Kit and Nita were doing something secret and kinky (because why would they hide even being girlfriend and boyfriend otherwise?) and those who were certain that one or the other of them was a virgin who was using the other one as cover.

Gossip, oh God the gossip, you get so sick of it, Kit thought. *How is this any of their business?* But all around them was the pressure to be something that fit into a category everyone could *understand* — crushing, dating, messing around, platonic, religiously celibate, whatever. And the endless stares and the whispers and the knowing laughter, they got so *old.* The urge to stand in the middle of the hall and shout *Yes, yes we* are *doing something together: we save the world! We've done it a bunch of times now, and I think we're getting the hang of it!* — it got strong sometimes, when Kit was feeling particularly tired or goofy. At such times he considered that it was probably a good thing that at least one of the school shrinks knew about wizards.

And he knew Nita felt the pressure as well. Unfairly, it seemed worse for her. The kids who thought she *wasn't* hooking up with Kit thought she was frigid. The ones who *did* think she was hooking up with him thought she was an easy lay — though so far no one had worked up enough courage to say so in Kit's hearing, which was just as well for them.

Problem is, he thought, *sometimes I want to step in*

between her and these jerks but I can't tell for sure when she wants that. Or even if. Certainly they'd saved each other from trouble often enough in the past. And he laughed again at the bland cover-all term "trouble." *Chased around Ireland by stone drow-trolls? Check. Stuck in the middle of a wizards' civil war on Mars? Check. Nearly nuked by Ultimate Evil at the far edge of the visible universe? Been there, done that, got his 'n' hers T-shirts . . .* In fact it was getting to be sort of a joke that he and Nita should work out a schedule to make sure that each of them got an equal opportunity to be the hero, or alternately to be the person who got to feel idiotic about needing to be saved. *But everything's changing,* Kit thought. *Things we might have done six months ago and never thought twice about aren't always the right things to do now.*

And reactions to what we do aren't the same either. Kit remembered how after he and Nita had been at Penn's the other day, on the way back to his house he'd found himself reflectively rubbing the hand she'd held. His first thought on realizing what he was doing had been *Oh stop it, you're pathetic!* But it had been kind of shocking at the time how automatically she'd reached for him after her annoyance at Penn grabbing her hand and getting all smoochy-smoochy with it. Kit had gone quite warm, blushing, and then, feeling humiliated, had thought, *Oh please don't let her see me doing that. Don't let* him *see me doing that!* And as it happened, no one had seen . . . which had been a relief.

Sometimes, though, seeing wasn't the issue. You still *knew.* And more, you suspected that others knew. In particular, Kit kept catching Dairine looking at him . . . just *looking* in an unsettling way. When he'd mentioned Dairine's expression in passing, Nita had laughed it off. "She gets protective of me, you know how she is sometimes . . ." and Kit had very nearly said, *Yeah, and can I have some of that action please?* But he'd kept quiet because he didn't know if that was too much or how Nita would take it, and this was all too *new* and strange now that they were actually talking about it . . .

Except we aren't *actually talking about it much. Mostly we're still dodging it.*

And things are going to keep getting worse for a while. Because in a couple of weeks I've got to go back to where I didn't think it could *get any worse . . .*

It was an odd thing to contemplate, and uncomfortable. Kit had always loved going up to the Moon and sitting there and enjoying the view — either homeward toward Earth, or (on earlier visits to the "dark side") out into the farther universe. Turning his back on the world, occasionally turning his attention outward, as far outward as possible, had been a pleasant thing — challenging without being scary.

Now, though . . . "Scary" did creep in. It was

difficult for Kit at the moment, when he was on the side where Earth didn't show, not to start reliving the events that (locally at least) had ended the Pullulus War. The death of that terrible darkness, the safety of the world, of all the worlds, had been worth it. But there had been awful losses among the wizards and others who'd held the final line. And one loss in particular had left Kit in serious pain.

He looked over at the empty braided-rag rug by the bed, where no one lay upside down with all his feet in the air, snoring. *Your dog,* he kept telling himself, *is not dead. He is in fact the next thing to a god.* But it was one thing knowing Ponch to be immortal, invulnerable, and now present in every dog who lived. It was another thing entirely to have to stand by helplessly watching a terrible battle of powers and spirits that Ponch might not have survived . . . and then, Ponch having beyond belief won that battle, it was a worse thing still to have to watch him go. The friend who had been with Kit since he was little, almost before he could remember . . . Now that space was empty. And all the other dogs in existence, nice as they were, couldn't fill it the way Ponch had done.

Kit remembered how, sometimes when you were small, it was possible to get scared over what later turned out to be nothing. You'd hear your parents fighting, or you'd have done something stupid and gotten yelled at particularly hard, and you'd go to bed so terrified that your stomach tied itself in knots, while you twisted and turned and were sure that the world was over and everything was ruined, never to be right again. But even when Kit was scared and upset and feeling horribly alone because of something like that, Ponch had always been there with his nose in Kit's ear, or licking his face, or looking at him with big worried eyes that said, *Don't be sad; if you have to be, then I have to be sad too!* And all the time Kit was growing up, when Kit was happy, then Ponch was ready to play; and when Kit was unhappy Ponch always *knew* somehow, and would be with him, just *there*.

And then Ponch was gone, and for the first time Kit had a referent for the way Nita felt when her Mom died. Except he couldn't *say* that to anybody, because he could imagine how it'd be taken when it came out. *You're comparing losing your dog to somebody's* mom *dying? How can you even* think *of doing that? How* stupid *are you?* Yet the feelings had to be alike, in some ways — the horrible twist of the gut and the heart as again and again you came up against the absence of that unwavering companionship and acceptance that had always been within call: the love that you knew could be depended on for better or worse, that you knew would *never* abandon you. Suddenly it was missing, but the *habit* of it wasn't. You kept reaching for it and finding nothing, and over and over feeling the sickening impact of the wrongness of that, like a missed step on the stairway of the heart.

Kit leaned his head back against the medicine cabinet above the toilet and stared at the shower tiles, unfocused. *Yeah, I know it's all right. I know he's all right.* Impossibly *all right! . . . But it's not the same as having him here. And the Moon's gonna bring all this up again, hard.*

He sat there a while longer. Then Kit sighed, got up, knotted the towel around him after about the third try, and and reached for his toothbrush. *One thing at a time,* he thought. *If I take my time with this, maybe I can get myself to a place where I won't freak out when I'm up on the far side of the Moon. That'll be good enough.*

Meanwhile . . . Penn. What do we do about Penn? Because if he tries that stunt with Neets again, she's gonna increase entropy all over his butt. Don't think the organizers'll like it if we kill our mentee . . .

Kit started considering ways to prevent that from happening as he headed out of the bathroom and down the hall to his room. No sooner had he gotten in there, though, than he caught sight of something glowing softly and rhythmically on his desk: the page-edges of his manual, pulsing with bluish light. *Oh. Something from Neets —*

He went to the desk, flipped the manual open, and riffled through the pages to the messaging section. One part of it he'd set aside for the Invitational — which had been a smart move, as all the texts and support material tended to pile up pretty quickly — and at the top of the first page, he found a text from Nita: *Got the Playroom booking sorted out*, it said. *5:30 p.m., my backyard.*

"Got that," Kit said, and watched as the words appeared on the page beneath Nita's text. "5:30 it is."

Send? the manual asked a few lines down.

"Send it," Kit said. The page grayed itself out while the Sending herald displayed, then darkened down again, listing Kit's text as sent.

He walked over to his dresser, pulled a drawer open, and started rummaging through it for underwear. "So go to audio," he said to the manual, "and let me take another run at the judging structure for the eighth-finals. How many judges? . . ."

When Penn popped out of nowhere later that afternoon into the shielded space at the end of the backyard, he looked surprised to find himself apparently in the center of a small forest, through which not even the low Sun was managing to shine. "Um," he said, turning around in a circle and taking in the nonview, "we having some kind of field trip?"

Nita smiled, amused, as even without wizardly shielding it was almost impossible to see the neighbors' houses through the undergrowth or past the taller trees. If you hauled a lawn chair out here in nice weather you could feel astonishingly distant from suburbia and the general troubles of the world. But with the shielding up, what little view was visible past the trees was blurred and uncertain — the shield-spell's way of verifying that it was up and working. "You could say that," Nita said. "How's your day been so far?"

"Uh, okay. Thanks. Where's Kit?"

It's going to be so much fun breaking you of this, Nita thought. *Possibly too much fun.* "He'll be along in a few."

"And am I supposed to be laying the spell out here?" Penn stared at the leaf-littered ground. "Kind of, uh, untidy. And cramped."

"The trees don't do active art installations back here anymore," Nita said, "but even so, you're right, there's not a lot of space to stretch. I've got something roomier set up."

"Oh," Penn said, "okay." He folded his arms and leaned against a tree. "Before he gets here — can I ask you a question?"

Nita reached into the otherspace pocket that always hung near her while she was working, and pulled out her manual. "Sure," she said. *Especially since it's prob-*

ably going to be more words than you've said to me since we met.

"Why does Kit let you do so much stuff?"

Let *me?* Nita thought. *This just gets more bizzare all the time . . .*

"I mean," Penn said, "isn't he afraid you're going to get in trouble?"

"All the time," Nita said. And she grinned. "But he knows not to interfere with that, since the job keeps getting done. That's how we work."

"It seems — dangerous."

"It's dangerous for him, too," Nita said. "And believe me, I've got nothing on him when *he* gets in trouble. That's when I get my worrying done. But somehow we come out all right. At least so far . . ." She flipped through her manual, found the spot she needed, and scanned down the page. All the necessary permissions were there. "One thing I need you to do," Nita said, and handed him the manual. "Check your name here and make sure I've got all the other details right."

Penn took the book and looked curiously at the subdiagram that contained his name. He stood quietly for a moment, tracing the long curve of Speech-characters with one finger. "Yeah," he said, "it looks fine."

"You sure?"

"It's fine," Penn said, and passed Nita back her

manual with an expression that looked faintly uneasy. It was the first time she could recall the cocky expression falling off his face. She liked him a lot better without it; he had nice eyes, and they were nicer still when that set expression of certainty wasn't squeezing them small. "Okay," Nita said, and was even more amused by Penn's look of concern as she slapped the manual shut.

"Wait, aren't you going to —"

"Not with that," Nita said, tucking the manual under her arm and taking hold of one of the charms on the bracelet she was wearing. In it, the activator phrase of the spell she needed was stored; at her touch it awakened, waiting for her to speak the trigger phrase. "Ready? Here we go."

She began to speak the long trigger phrase, and glanced around her with satisfaction to see things darkening down around them, to hear that silence settling over the space where she and Penn stood — the sound of the world listening to a wizardry, getting ready to make it come true. When all sound had fallen away, when the light and the trees around them seemed to be dissolving into darkness, Nita spoke the last word of the spell — the one she'd said often enough, when her mother was ill, that she didn't need to read it from her manual anymore.

And with that one word, light flooded back

everywhere except in one wide, vertically poised circle of darkness right before them. Through that circle, a shining white surface stretching away into the distance could be seen: nothing else.

Penn was staring. "Here's where we'll be working," Nita said. "Come on."

She stepped through and stood there once again on that surface that could have been mistaken for a floor, except that it reached seemingly to infinity, as far as the eye could see, and was a condition of that space rather than any made or built thing. Even that place's horizon, out at the edge of vision, was peculiar — the air was perfectly clear, so there was no haze to obscure the distance.

Penn stepped through the doorway behind her, staring around him. "Where *is* this?"

"Not sure the question means anything in terms of location," Nita said. "It's another dimension. A space where wizards come to practice dangerous spells without endangering other people's lives. Thought you might find it useful. Once we're started I'll show you what I made you."

"How big *is* this place?" Penn said from behind her as Nita headed farther into the space.

She spun around once as she walked, considering. "Not sure. Probably the question has an answer — I mean, the space isn't *infinite*, I don't think. But you'd be a long, long time trying to find the other side. If there *is* another side; if there's anything but horizon out past the horizon." Nita smiled. "I'd pack a lunch."

"It's really . . . *flat.*"

"Perfect Euclidean surface," Nita said. "I keep wanting to bring a bike in here sometime and just ride. You'd never have to worry about hills. It's funny, though, the way when you look at it you keep trying to see some kind of bump or rough spot. But there aren't any. It's not like our space. No curvature at all."

When they were about a hundred yards in through the portal, Nita paused and took the opportunity, as she turned again, to glance at Penn. He wasn't exactly green around the gills, but his look of overconfidence was gone.

Almost against her will she felt sorry for him. "This can be a little weird visually," Nita said. "How about if I do a kind of tile floor thing in here? It'll make it easier to focus."

"Okay," Penn said.

There was a strained tone to his voice that made Nita think hurrying up would be a good idea. The physical eccentricity of this space had made her feel ill once or twice when she'd been working here for long periods. It didn't surprise her that Penn might be having a similar response. *And is there the slightest possibility,* she thought as she reached out to the air for the otherspace pocket in which the Playroom's kernel was stored, *that I was sort of hoping that would happen? Shame on me.*

"Here we go," Nita said, finding the spot she wanted and plunging both arms in it up to the elbow. Sometimes habitués of the Playroom hid the kernel from each other as a combination exercise and game — kernel management being one of the main reasons they came here in the first place. But the last user had left the kernel in its default position, convenient to whatever ingress the next user employed to get into the space, and immediately available on demand. Nita pulled the cantaloupe-sized kernel out of the otherspace pocket where it was stored and turned it over in her hands, feeling with slight satisfaction the faint burn and tingle of the energy involved in confining this place's physical laws to one tightly interlaced and exceedingly complex bundle of phrases and statements in the Speech. It looked like a big tangle of yarn made of burning light, and in a hundred colors. Everything a space required in terms of physical constants was here — gravity, mass, distance, time, the control structures for all of them arranged in one handy management bundle.

She turned the kernel over until she caught sight of the one command-strand she wanted, then reached two fingers in and teased it out. The strand had a number of minuscule nodes dotted along it, like beads on a string: presets, some of them featuring bumps or scratches as tactile indicators of what they held. Nita ran her fingers down the strand until she found a node she wanted, on which she could feel the tiny crosshatch markings that indicated the "tiled floor" routine. She squeezed the node, gave it a half twist.

Immediately, the floor right out to the horizons was covered in perfectly symmetrical black and white tiles, glowing in the Playroom's sourceless light. Penn, who had been standing hunched over, now straightened up tentatively and took a deep breath. "Yeah," he said, "that's better."

"No problem," Nita said. She tucked the kernel under one arm and felt around in her jeans pocket for her smartphone. "Funny, though, Kit should be here by now. What time is it?"

Penn pulled his iPhone out, and Nita turned away to hide her smile. *He's got a watch, but why would he look at that . . .* But then Penn's expression turned surprised. "I've got service. Five bars . . . !"

"Why not?" Nita said. "This space is very malleable: it'll do exactly what the managing wizard tells it. And why would I want to disable that nice suite of networking-spell apps that the Invitational gave us? Especially when we're so close to the Cull. What if somebody needed to get hold of us?"

"Yeah, I guess . . ."

"There you are," Kit said as he stepped in through

the portal from Nita's backyard. "Hey, Penn. How do you like it?"

"It's very nice." Penn turned slowly, assessing everything in an amused way. "Kind of minimalist, I guess." His tone of voice suggested that as a decorating strategy, "minimalist" had been declared to be over.

About a minute and a half's worth of off balance, Nita thought. *Not too bad for Penn, I guess.* "I got rid of the furniture for the time being," she said, pulling open the empty air beside her and pushing the kernel into it, out of sight. "Most of it's not for humans, and we can use the extra space."

Kit nodded as he came ambling along and stood next to her. "Thought maybe you'd started without me."

"I thought maybe you'd stopped for dinner."

"Not tonight," Kit said. "Tonight's pizza night. Mama's cooking tomorrow, though." He sighed. "Arroz con pollo. She *would* do it when we're busy."

Nita sighed. Kit's mama didn't cook that much because her work hours were irregular and left her too tired. But a few things, when she had the energy, she cooked brilliantly, and the arroz was one of them. "You couldn't get her to change the day?"

"I tried. No."

They shook their heads more or less in unison and turned back to Penn. "So," Kit said. "This is our last chance for a close look before tomorrow. There were a lot of blanks to fill in when we last sat down, day before yesterday. How do you like where you are now?"

"I like it fine," Penn said, folding his arms. Nita was beginning to loathe that pose; it was a sign that Penn was about to get indignant about something.

Kit waved one arm out at the space. "So let's have a look, then. The floor's yours."

Penn reached into the pocket of his leather jacket, pulled out his manual, flipped it open, peeled a layer of diagram and Speech-charactery off the revealed double-page spread, and dropped it to the floor. The complex diagram that flowed out across the floor from what he dropped did so in flat format, this time, and in a tangle of multiple colors indicating successive revisions and additions.

Nita glanced at Kit out of the corner of her eye, noting without comment that he had finally gotten Penn to stop using 3D versions of the spell diagram for debugging. While they were handsome and impressive, it was too easy to turn your back on some part of one and miss something important — particularly something missing that, when the spell executed, would blow up in your face. "So this is the version you're going to use for the walk-by judging?" Nita said, beginning to stroll around it.

"Yep," Penn said, sounding very pleased with himself.

This diagram was far simpler and clearer than the one Penn had shown them first, which was a good thing. Going by her reading of the judging criteria, the Senior and assessing wizards who'd be examining the spell diagrams of some three hundred contestants were not going to be impressed by presentations that suggested a wizard was more concerned with style than substance. *Not that style's not good,* Nita thought. But a small, clear, compact spell was going to impress them much more than a big, sprawling, splashy one that made you waste time understanding it.

Kit started walking around the diagram from the other direction. "It looks a lot better than it did," he said. "You're still going to want to clean up all these stacked-up revisions, though."

"Sure. That gets done last. Tomorrow morning."

Kit nodded. "And you've got a short, recorded version of your explanation for when you have to be away from this?"

"Yeah. Let me play it for you —"

"Don't bother right now," Kit said. "Let us have it live, because what's going to count most tomorrow night is your presentation. All kinds of people are going to come up and start asking questions about this when you've got it laid out — people our age, people older — and any of them might be judges. The more practice you get, the better. So let's hear the spiel."

Penn brushed his sleeves off and stood up straight. He then beamed the kind of smile that Nita had seen on the hosts of late-night infomercials, and started in. "Esteemed Seniors and assessors, thanks for your time. The spell I've brought for evaluation today is unique in that it proposes an unusually simple and elegant solution to the problem of plasma storms secondary to the Sun's active periods. Now that Earth is surrounded with a halo of vulnerable satellites and a permanently manned space station, it becomes more important than ever to attempt to protect them undetectably from radiation storms that could otherwise cause huge disruptions to modern life on Earth and tragic loss of life in space. If I can direct your attention to the core redistribution assembly partition . . ."

And he was off. Nita listened to him rattle out his introduction very comfortably, as if he'd had a lot of time to think about it and was completely at ease with the details. *And the first part of that might even be true*, she thought. For the moment, though, she turned to a blank page in the messaging portion of her manual as she walked around the spell, and with one finger wrote a note for Kit: *If he's going to work in English instead of the Speech, better make sure he doesn't use the name of that core part as an acronym . . .*

Kit, casually paging through his manual, gazed down, threw Nita a sidelong look, and smiled.

Completely without warning, that smile made her insides squeeze. *Oh cut that out,* she told herself, annoyed. *Do I need to start* distracting *myself from him now? God, I'm hopeless. Never mind, let's mix this up a little.* "What's that part over there do?" Nita said, pointing.

Penn stopped and looked at Kit with an aggrieved expression. "Nobody's going to *interrupt* me like that, are they?"

"Think you'd better count on it," Kit said. "Not *everybody* there's going to be a judge. Some of the attendees won't have a clue what this is about, and if they see you standing there, they're going to *ask* you. And if a judge is around and hears you fudging an answer, or blowing somebody off, you'll lose points. Or maybe get deselected on the spot. So better practice being nice to the hecklers."

Penn grimaced. "So what *is* that?" Nita said.

"I'm glad you asked me that, Juanita," Penn said, and turned the infomercial smile on her full force. "It's a legacy function that has featured in solar intervention wizardries for nearly a thousand years —"

Nita looked at Kit and widened her eyes, mouthing at him, *Juanita?!*

"— and dates back to the time when there was a fairly major shift in the Sun's internal dynamics, around the year 1010. That coincides with something called the Oort Minimum. Now you have to understand that the Sun has active periods and quiet periods . . ."

"Sunspot maxima and minima, thank you, I'm perfectly familiar with those," Nita said. "It's not the Little Ice Age period we're talking about, but seven hundred years or so before. I get it."

"Oh good, that makes this easier. Well, there were some changes in the Sun's subsurface atmospheric speeds and flow patterns then, and the diagram reflects those and 'remembers' them in case those patterns reassert themselves without warning. It's boilerplate, of course, nothing like that's happened for a while, but we leave it in as a nod to a legacy state, on the off chance that it might reassert itself."

Nita nodded. "Okay, good. Let's move on . . ."

Penn picked up smoothly where he'd left off, and kept talking. *I wish we could do something about his delivery,* Nita thought. *I keep thinking he's going to sell me car wax, or a revolutionary new food processor. Like he's afraid to let go and be excited, or enthusiastic in a natural way.* But despite the overly slick delivery, Penn spoke very knowledgeably about what his spell was supposed to do, and how it was supposed to do it. Random questions he handled less gracefully; he really did hate being interrupted. For one fifteen-minute period, Kit and Nita took turns being hecklers, and Nita noticed with interest that Penn hated it even more from Kit than he did from her. But she also noticed that he rose to the challenge, and though she and Kit both got more disruptive and abusive than they could imagine anyone being in this situation, Penn not only kept going, but he started treating it as a joke and actually being funny about it. *That might wind up helping him . . .*

Finally she and Kit ran out of things to pick at, and let Penn finish his presentation. He spoke with such relish about how great it would be to have this thing installed in the Sun and working that when he was done, Nita found herself clapping, and Kit joined in. "Bravo!" Kit said.

Penn bowed theatrically. "Thank you, thankyou-verymuch, I'll be here all week." He bobbed up again, looking smug.

Nita strolled around the diagram toward him, giving it one last look. "Penn, you actually have me convinced about this thing now."

He headed toward her in turn, laughing at her with the aren't-you-a-funny-heckler chuckle that he'd been using, and for the moment Nita didn't mind. "You weren't convinced before? I'm wounded."

"Let's just say it's a family thing," Nita said. "When it comes to tinkering with the local star, I take some convincing. But I think you've done a good job here."

"So do I get some kind of reward for that?" Penn said, grinning.

"Well. Maybe we ought to let you run this spell."

He laughed as if he thought Nita was joking. "Too soon for that, maybe. How would we do it, anyway?"

"There might be a way," Nita said. "Though it would probably be kind of *technical.*"

Kit raised his eyebrows at Nita, the expression saying, *You haven't explained this to him yet?* Oh *boy.*

"Come to think of it," Penn said, "didn't you say when I came in here that you'd made something for me? Haven't seen anything yet."

"You're right," Nita said. "Here." She reached sideways into the otherspace pocket in the air, felt around for the kernel, found that one tagged strand that she'd left hanging out of it, made sure she had the right one, and gently pulled.

Instantly the checkerboard under their feet vanished, leaving the three of them standing above a roiling, roaring sea of fire that stretched from one impossibly distant horizon to the other.

"I made you a Sun," Nita said.

It was as if they stood no more than a few hundred miles above the solar surface. At this height, vast glowing bubbles of boiling red-golden plasma rose up beneath them, slow, huge, impersonally deadly, shouldering up out of the convection layer to jostle and squeeze against one another, give up their heat, and then be pushed down into the depths again. Between the plasma granules, fountains of terrible fire, straight upward-splashing spicules and broadly curved prominences, reared up again and again out of the solar surface, strained away, and were swallowed back into the near-blinding conflagration. From where the three of them seemed to be poised, the corona was far too high above them to see — but the whip-crack hiss and lash of it through near-solar space echoed deafeningly in the emptiness around them, along with the low, furious roar, unending, of the body of the Sun breathing its heat and light and other radiation out into space. For a second it stirred a brief memory for Nita from a recent dream, a voice like the soft roar of fire, but the sound around her quickly drowned the memory out.

Nita stared down into the maelstrom, shaking her head, fascinated and awestruck as always by the huge, uncaring beauty of it. *And this isn't even a very* exciting *specimen, as stars go,* she thought. *But still so cool . . . if that's the word we're looking for.* She grinned, glanced over at Penn to see his reaction.

He was standing there staring down, frozen, his face blank. It took Nita a moment to realize that the expression was one of terror.

For a moment she couldn't move either. *How's he frightened by the environment he designed his spell for? Why would you build something that was going to take you someplace that scared you? You build something you like. The way Dairine did with her volcano at school, that time . . .*

"How *big* is that?" Penn said in a hoarse whisper.

"Full size," Nita said, staying matter-of-fact to see if it would calm him down. "Eight hundred and fifty thousand miles across, give or take . . . Probably about as wide as three and a half trips to the Moon laid end to end. Though I might need to check my math on that."

"But it's not real —"

"It *is* real," Nita said. "It's real *here.* That's the whole point of the aschetic spaces. I told the space to make me a star, and fed it the necessary qualities and coordinates, and it *made* it."

Penn was holding himself still. Anyone who couldn't see his face might have believed he wasn't longing to turn and flee out the portal. Nita saw him throw a glance at it. But then he turned his head away, scowling. *Hanging on hard,* she thought. *But why's he freaking out like this?*

She looked over at Kit to see if he saw what she was seeing: but he was still gazing down at the view beneath their feet. "The sound on this is really good," Kit said, impressed.

"If you could stand there in the coronal medium

without a shield," Nita said, trying to sound casual, "it's exactly what you'd hear . . . for the fifty or sixty milliseconds before you were burnt to ash."

Possibly Kit caught something odd in Nita's voice at that point. He looked over at her, saw her watching Penn staring down into the fire. *Well, this is weird,* his expression said. *Now what?*

She shook her head at him, looked over at Penn again. *I could kill this,* Nita thought. *But Penn hasn't said anything, and I don't get what's going on. Is this something he never expected to see, didn't think through? Sure, his presentation says this wizardry's meant to be dropped into the Sun from a distance. But a wizard who did a spell like this would have to go there at least once and watch it from up close. Watch it go in, and make sure it was doing what you expected . . .*

Never mind. Let's see what he wants to do. "So Penn," Nita said. "If you want to do your spell right now and see how it runs, we could do that. Whatever happens here, it can't hurt us and it can't do anything to Earth."

That finally brought his head up, and Penn looked at Nita with an expression that was nowhere near calm, but at least wasn't frozen in horror. "I, uh," he said after a moment, "I think I might want to work on it some more first."

Uncertainty? From him? Wow. But Nita made sure none of her surprise showed. "Okay," she said. "No problem with that. But when you're ready, this'll be a good place to test, and it's no trouble to bring up —"

"Well," said a voice from near the portal, "isn't *this* an unusual development . . . !"

Oh God, talk about the wrongest moment possible, Nita thought, as Kit's and Penn's heads swung around toward the newcomer. Silhouetted against both the daylight shining in through the portal and the much closer and fiercer daylight coming from right under their feet, Dairine and Spot were ambling across the floor of the practice space side by side, Dairine peering down at the duplicate Sun as she came.

"This is nice," Dairine said. "And not a simulation, either. *Real.*"

"Cloned," Nita said, trying to sound casual.

"Such a good idea," Dairine said. "Gotta talk to Nelaid about this! There could be things you could do with this setup that you could never do with a scaled simulator . . ."

She wandered over to where the three of them were standing around Penn's spell diagram, the glowing multicolor lines of which were nearly invisible against the blast of light from below. Spot came along behind her, having put up a number of stalked eyes to look over the diagram. Nita held her breath: the last thing she needed was for Dairine to start dissecting Penn's work at the moment. *And what a laugh. Ten minutes ago I might not have minded . . .*

"Hmm" was all Dairine said. She turned away toward Nita, digging around in her pockets. "Listen," she said, "I was over at Tom's and he asked me to drop these off for you."

She handed Nita a small, circular token glowing faintly blue on a key ring, then made her way around to Kit. "It's your marker for the Mentors' Picks event tomorrow morning," Dairine said, handing him a twin to what Nita held. "You walk through and drop it into the spells you like the look of. It stamps them with your mentor ID and gives them points toward their selection."

"Thanks," Nita said, pocketing hers.

Dairine, meanwhile, had paused by Kit to take in the diagram again, and then glanced up at Penn. "And you are?"

"Penn Shao-Feng," he said. And then he gave Dairine one of those smarmy smiles, though to Nita's eye there was a more strained quality to it now. "Don't know how much time Juanita's going to have for upchecking other people's spells, though. She'll be too busy getting everyone else to drop their markers on *mine.*"

Why was I even worrying about how he was? Nita

thought. *He's fine. For Penn . . .* But Dairine was now looking over at Nita with barely concealed amusement. *Juanita?* she mouthed.

Nita shrugged. "Penn," she said, "my sister, Dairine. She's mentoring too."

"No kidding!" Penn said brightly. "You don't look old enough to have even had your Ordeal yet —"

Not quite the worst thing you could say to my sister right off the bat, but a real strong contender, Nita thought, her heart sinking for Penn's sake.

"You must be quite the powerful one!"

Aaaand he's two for two. Between the patronizing tone and the significant reduction in Dairine's power levels since her Ordeal — *Oh God, she'll simply destroy him now.*

Dairine looked very deliberately from Penn, to the diagram, to Penn again. "Well, Penn," she said, with the slow, measured delivery one might use when broaching an advanced subject with a five-year-old, "as far as your spell goes, I sort of think that one of the two wizards who brought back the *Book of Night with Moon* from where the Lone Power had it stashed has better things to do than run around the Invitational shilling for *you,* y'know? Especially since she knows perfectly well — though she probably hasn't told you so yet, she's so kindhearted — that if people are looking at your wizardry and it's not generating its own buzz, you're doing it wrong."

Dairine turned away again. "A wizardry has to stand on its own merits. And at first glance, this one doesn't so much stand on its merits as sort of lie there." She looked up. "Neets, do me a favor and kill the background noise?"

Penn stood there with his mouth open, probably at least partly due to the effrontery of someone who could casually refer to the overwhelming visual and aural splendor dominating the practice space as "noise."

"Sure, no problem," Nita said. She reached into the otherspace pocket and turned off the Sun. *And look at that. All of a sudden he's so much more relaxed . . .*

"Interesting," Dairine said, once more starting to stroll around the perimeter of the spell, now laid out as it had been before on the black and white tiles: and as she walked around it, Spot stepped delicately out into the diagram, carefully avoiding any of the lines or Speech-phrases, and looked it over with all his eyes. "Coronal redirection, huh," Dairine said. "Not easy to do with something this minimalistic. Going to have to pump a lot of power into this for it to function."

"The star powers it," Penn said. "If you noticed the accumulators, they're very —"

"Fancy," Dairine said. "If structurally fragile. Well, the overall design has some merit. This could possibly make it through to the quarter-finals, who knows? I kind of hope it does . . ." She was coming around to

Nita's side of the diagram now, and she grinned at her sister. "As it'll give *my* mentee a chance to whip your mentee's butt."

Nita smiled and said nothing.

Penn continued to stand there in shock. "Aren't you going to *defend* me?" he said, turning from Nita to Kit.

Kit was hanging his head and pinching the bridge of his nose as if he was trying to stop himself from sneezing, but Nita knew what he was suppressing and was intent on not triggering him by cracking up herself. She shook her head at Penn. "I've heard that from everybody from the Lone Power on down," Nita said. "But where Dairine's involved, we all get to take our chances."

Dairine grinned and put her head next to Nita's. "I don't want to second-guess you in front of your guy," she said very softly, "but this thing reinvents the wheel a couple of times, and he's probably gonna get called on it."

"That could be my fault," Nita said as softly. "I did an analysis on this some days back, and a lot of the work he's done since then has been about doing what I told him . . ."

Dairine shook her head. "I recognize your style in there. But he's got problems elsewhere. Doubt there'll be time to fix it before tomorrow, but Spot's grabbing the design at the moment. I'll give you some notes later."

"Okay. Thanks."

"Hey, can't have you looking bad out there." Dairine sighed. "But what I don't get is how *you* got this guy and *I* got Mehrnaz. Seems like a mismatch."

Nita shrugged. "Take it up with the Powers," she muttered. "*I* don't pretend to get it! And frankly I'd sooner you had him than *we* did. But there's no swapping out once you've accepted the assignment. I think we're all stuck . . ."

Dairine nodded. "Right. Anyway, check your manual later," she said, rubbing her eyes. "I've gotta go crash for a while. I need to be up at midnight again . . ."

Nita patted Dairine's back absently as her sister turned around, yawning, and Spot came spidering along to her. "See you tomorrow, Kit," she said. "Penn . . ." She waved amiably at him without looking at him. "Good luck. 'Cause you're gonna need it!" And she wandered off toward the portal and vanished through it, Spot clambering after her.

Penn gazed after Dairine, looking both astonished and a bit surly. "Thinks she's pretty hot stuff, doesn't she," he said. He was trying to make it sound like a joke.

"So did the Lone One," Nita said, shaking her head. "It might have had a point, for once . . ."

Kit was looking at Penn as if he felt sorry for him. "Come on," Kit said, "if you don't want to run your spell now then we've done all we can for today. Let's go 'round the corner to my place, have a soda or something, and make plans for tomorrow."

Penn's long, smooth face was pinched-looking, and what was left of his smile was anxious. "No, thanks but no, I have to get back home ... there are some things to do before tomorrow." The expression that had replaced his sulkiness looked to Nita like it was shading toward panic. "So, listen," Penn went on, "I'll message you guys in the morning, okay? And we can figure out where to meet then."

"Uh, sure," Nita said, and didn't know whether Penn had heard her, because he was already out the portal. Barely a second later she heard the *Bang!* of someone in so great a hurry that he didn't use his transit spell to control the noise of the air that slammed into where he'd just been.

Nita turned to look at Kit. "What the hell was *that?*" she said.

Kit shook his head. "The sound of our schedule for the next couple of weeks freeing up?" he said. "Because if he goes into this tomorrow like *that,* he's finished. And so are we."

8

Hempstead / Mumbai

✴

IT WAS AN HOUR or so later before Dairine saw Nita
again. To her credit, Nita had peered into Dairine's
room as quietly as she possibly could, opening the
door just a crack. But all the same it was enough
to snap Dairine out of the doze she'd fallen into,
propped up against the pillows at the head of her
bed. She'd skipped dinner and hadn't bothered to get
undressed — there was no point in it. *I'll do it after I
get back from seeing Mehrnaz,* she'd thought. Right
then, nothing had been so attractive as the prospect of
stretching out and being horizontal for a while. Even
the weight of Spot, hugged to her chest as they com-
muned before she dozed off, hadn't bothered her.

"You asleep?" Nita said, barely above a whisper.

"I wish," Dairine said, while Spot sprouted a couple of bleary-looking stalked eyes out of his lid to gaze
at Nita.

"Did you even eat?"

Dairine rolled her head back and forth against the pillows as Nita slipped in and sat on the edge of her bed. "Too tired right now," Dairine said. "And if I eat and fall asleep, it'll lie there inside me like lead." She sighed and pushed herself up straighter against the pillows.

"You shouldn't get up," Nita said. "You should sleep." She started to stand up. "We can do this in the morning, when you get back."

"No no, wait," Dairine said, rubbing her face. "Let's get it done now. There's some chance your guy might have time to fix it tonight. Assuming he's willing to take direction."

Nita sighed. "Not sure my chromosomes are arranged in the right order for him to do that willingly," she said. "He seems to have this 'why should I listen to *you*, girly' thing going on to the point where it interferes with his reasoning processes."

Dairine groaned. "God, what year does he live in?"

"I don't know," Nita said, "but I think he has a rude awakening coming if he makes it past the Cull."

"Well, that's the whole point, isn't it," Dairine said. She yawned and stroked Spot's lid. "Virtualize the space for us, would you?"

Instantly the walls, the ceiling, even the floor of Dairine's room all went away, replaced by the appearance of a broad, smooth, pale plain, all airbrush-hazed with soft colors, and overarched by the gentle fire of a gigantic barred spiral galaxy.

She caught the sound of Nita taking a sudden breath, and smiled. "That's a new trick," Nita said, craning her neck to look around.

"Think of it as a 3D desktop," Dairine said. "The Mobiles hooked it up for me. They're experimenting with thoughtspeed communications; they need it for the backup they're building."

"You mentioned that a while back," Nita said. "They're trying to back up . . . the whole *universe?*"

"Only this one to start with," Dairine said. "Right now the two main problems are speed and storage space. But at the communications end, they've built me an experimental signal tunnel. My end goes through a wormhole somewhere in local space, and the signal comes out at their end, umpty billion trillion light-years away. Then they encode it for storage on individual electrons in a spare universe full of hyperdense matter, I think they said." She waved her hand. "Don't ask me how the engineering works — I'm just the beta tester."

Nita shook her head in amazement. "As long as they're not asking you for help with their math homework, I guess you're doing okay . . ."

Dairine snickered. "Yeah. Anyway, here's what Spot got from your guy."

Penn's spell appeared spread out over the glassy

superstrate a few yards away, the spell circle enlarged to about twenty feet across to bring up the detail. She pointed at one particularly troublesome spot in the spell construct that Penn planned to drop into the surface of the Sun. "Here's his real problem," she said, and as she pointed at the diagram, a representation of the actual matter/energy structure that the spell would build rose up in front of them: a long, thin, tubular structure with a sort of finny dumbbell head at one end and a trumpet-shaped opening at the other.

"The subsurface structure," Dairine said, and the dumbbell end enlarged, "that's where the trouble is. All those little pinwheely things sticking out of it . . . He wants to install those only a few thousand miles under the surface? Near the boundary layer, where the subsurface convection movement is nearly supersonic? Complete waste of time, because those are *way* too fragile to take plasma currents at that speed. They'd flame out within the first fifteen minutes or so . . . rip themselves up like windmills in a hurricane, and the whole thing would come to pieces."

Dairine yawned again. "The basic idea he's proposing doesn't need to be so depth-specific. Or anything like so sensitive, either. I don't know who he's trying to impress —"

"The judges?"

"If they work with the Sun on a regular basis, they'll just laugh. What you need to get him to do at the very least is redesign these pinwheels to be more robust. Cut their wings back by about half, you'd still get plenty of input off them. But better still, he should pull the fancy fiddly things off and retailor the wizardry to dump the power structures in way deeper."

Nita nodded, reaching up to pull her manual out of the air.

"Don't bother with that," Dairine said. "I'll have Spot copy it to you."

"Thanks," Nita said. She didn't put her manual away, though; she sat with it in her lap, looking at Dairine. "You're being very helpful."

"And you're wondering why."

Dairine looked at Nita for a moment and opened her mouth.

"You don't want me and Kit to look bad, do you," Nita said.

Uh oh, Spot said silently.

Fortunately Nita had already seen sufficient yawning from Dairine in the past few minutes for Dairine to think it wouldn't look suspicious to shut her eyes and lean back against the pillows, rather than meet her sister's eyes and possibly let Nita see what was going through her mind. Ideas such as *Things are weird enough for you and Kit right now. No point in making them even weirder or more stressed.* "Since it seems your guy is a jerk," Dairine said, "no point in letting you have trouble dealing with him at the technical end, too. Not when I can make a suggestion or two, anyway."

Nita nodded. It occurred to Dairine that she looked tired, too. "Is this strictly legal?" she asked after a moment.

Spot made ratchety noise: mechanical laughter. Dairine opened her eyes again, meeting his stalky ones. "I win," he said aloud.

The look Nita gave him was bemused. "Win what?"

Dairine snickered. "Spot bet me that you'd want a rules check before you decided to do anything with the advice."

Nita swatted at Dairine's head, missing on purpose. Dairine didn't even bother moving. "As long as I'm not mentoring him solo, as long as one of you two is directly present in the loop, you're fine," Dairine said. "I checked."

"Okay," Nita said, looking over at the spell again. "Tell me. Without this being fixed . . . what do you think of his chances of making it through the Cull?"

"Without the fix? Not so great. With the fix? Could be better than even."

They both spent a few moments more regarding the spell's general structure. To Dairine's way of thinking, it was nowhere near as tidy as something she or Nita or Kit might have built. And especially, while she was thinking of it, the lovely rigorous structure of

Mehrnaz's spell made this one seem shabby by comparison. *This looks* lumpy, *somehow.* Even after being worked over in line with Nita's suggestions, there were still places in which too much wizardry was crammed into too small a space, and there were barren spots that made no sense. One or two of them reminded her vaguely of the "lacuna" nonstructures that Mehrnaz had built into her anti-earthquake spell. Here, though, the resemblance was accidental: just empty places left that way because the designer hadn't thought ahead.

Dairine yawned again, rubbing her eyes: they felt grainy. "God, I'm sorry . . ." she said.

"Don't be!" Nita said, getting up. "The second opinion's useful."

"But look, you did good with this, for someone who hasn't been working on stellar stuff as much as I have." Dairine pushed herself up against the pillows, as while looking the spell over again she'd slid down. "You're seriously going to make him stay up late and fix this?"

"Thinking about it real hard . . ." Nita shook her head. "Don't know that I can *make* him do anything, but I can strongly suggest it."

"It'll be his fault if he ignores you and gets his butt deselected. Though I get a feeling with the attitude he's got, you might not mind that."

Nita looked somewhat shocked at the suggestion. "Because I think he's a pain in the ass? No." Though then her gaze dropped, and Dairine found herself wondering whether this thought had indeed crossed Nita's mind, to her embarrassment.

But a second later Nita looked up again. "Fifty-fifty," she said, looking over at the spell, "honestly?"

Dairine shrugged. "Well, yeah. In terms of the spell itself. But from the reading they gave us, it looks like whether you pass or fail isn't always about the project, is it? Sometimes it'll be about the wizard. When Seniors and above are doing the judging, you have to assume that the Powers are whispering in at least some of their ears. And when Irina's the prize — can you imagine she's going to let herself be tied down to someone she can't make a big difference for?"

"No," Nita said. "I see your point." She shoved her manual back into her otherspace pocket, then stretched. "Well, I'm not going to be his favorite person in a few minutes."

"Don't think you've been his favorite person since you met," Dairine said.

Nita laughed once, a momentary, sour sound. "You should have seen him trying to fake it, though. The *hand* kissing."

"Surprised he didn't pull back a bloody stump."

"So am I," Nita said, and headed for the door. "You need a wake-up call?"

"No, Spot's got it handled."

"Want coffee before you go?"

"If you want to make some, sure. Thanks."

Nita paused in the doorway as Dairine waved a hand at the floor and banished the Mobile-world landscape. With the hall light on behind her, it was hard to see her sister's face clearly: but the shadow of a smile was there. "Is it *that* obvious," Nita said in a low voice, "what's going on with Kit and me right now?"

"It can probably be seen from space," Dairine said. "But don't let that bother you."

Nita shook her head — the smile definitely betraying itself as the light caught it. Then she pulled the door mostly closed behind her and headed off down the hall.

Dairine lay there for a moment more in the near dark. *Spot*, she said then, *let me see that diagram again.*

It reappeared in the darkness, in reduced form to fit her bedroom floor, and she cocked an annoyed eye at it.

This Penn guy's structure is sloppy, but he's got a flair for this, she thought. *Without even working at it. Which is kind of unfair.* She considered how long it would have taken her to build something like this without Nelaid coaching her through every step, a couple of months ago. *And I am not a stupid person. But this guy burps this up in the space of a couple of days?*

Dairine scowled. Two thoughts were warring in her. One of them was, *If he did this in a hurry, I'd like to see what he could do if he took some time.* The other: *If he did this in a hurry, I'd like to punch him in the nose.*

But why *was he in such a big rush? I don't get it. If this is a specialty for him, and he'd been thinking about it for a while, why not start sooner? Why stress himself out?*

She sighed and let her head flop back against the pillow, waving the diagram away into darkness again. *Not my problem,* she thought. *Got enough of my own.* Mehrnaz's certainty that she was going to fail out of the eighth-finals was still on Dairine's mind.

She lay there smiling about it, convinced that Mehrnaz was completely nuts as far as this went. *I can't wait to see the look on her face when she goes through to the quarter-finals,* Dairine thought. *Because I really think she's going to.*

Dairine sighed, closed her eyes.

Midnight?

"Yeah."

She fell asleep.

This time when Dairine was ready to transport in, she decided not to bother with the scenic route. She had Spot check the downstairs lobby in Mehrnaz's house to make sure that no one was there, then texted her through the manual's communication system: *Be with you in about two minutes, okay?*

That's great! the answer came back. *My mama's here and she wants to meet you before she goes out.*

"Oh great, *parents*," Dairine muttered, and dashed back down to her room to have one last look at herself in the mirror. She'd dug up another longish tunic like the one she'd worn the other day, this one dark blue, and had wound her mom's scarf around her neck again in case she needed it. *Better keep it conservative,* she thought. *But this looks okay.* She made one concession to her own preferences and rolled the tunic's sleeves up to below the elbow, then wondered if she should roll them down again.

No one is going to care about your sleeves, Spot said.

"You can never tell," Dairine said. "Especially when you're not sure you've done enough research yet." She made a face and rolled the sleeves down. Then she picked Spot up. "Do the circle and let's go."

Their transport diagram flared blue around them and they vanished.

It was an entirely different kind of day in Mumbai this time. The sky was a misty, unrelieved gray, and a faint damp drizzle spattered the big windows. But the heat was almost certainly the same outside. Even in here, with the air-conditioning going, Dairine could feel the stickiness in the air as she climbed up the stairs into that great acreage of marble and greeted Mehrnaz. "Sort of a change from last time . . ."

"Yes it is," Mehrnaz said, leading her over to the table in front of the entertainment center; tea was waiting on a tray. "And a surprise. We don't normally get much rain this time of year. But when June comes . . ."

"There's a monsoon, isn't there? You get most of the year's rain at once."

"Hundreds of millimeters every month," Mehrnaz said, "until the season's over. We're not there yet, though! Which is good. I hate that time of year, nothing ever dries out . . ."

"Then you should go somewhere else," Dairine said. "You want dry? There's always the Namib Desert. Or that one in Chile. Even, I don't know, Arizona or New Mexico . . ."

"Um, well," Mehrnaz said, "I don't go off by myself that much. The family doesn't like it."

Dairine put up her eyebrows, but didn't say anything for the moment. "Well," she said, "we've got more to keep us busy right now than the weather. Though the weather report says it's going to be nice and dry in New York the next few days."

"This is going to be *so wonderful,*" Mehrnaz said, dropping her voice to a confidential murmur. "I simply can't wait to go. I've never been to New York before!"

"You'll like it," Dairine said. "If we can find time to get out. There'll be so many super people there, and so much going on — and that's just around the Invitational itself. Wizards from all over are coming in to see the pre-Cull judging, and all the presentations. It's a big deal! So we should get started . . . But I want to make sure you're good on the verbal presentation, because everything else is in great shape."

"You truly think so?"

"Do I *have* to say it in the Speech? What did I tell you about me not wasting my time saying stuff to you that wasn't true?"

"I know," Mehrnaz said, looking shamefaced. "It's just that . . . I'm used to hearing a lot about it when I get things wrong. Not so much when I get them right."

Dairine shook her head, put Spot down on the floor, and let him get out of the way of where the spell circle was going to wind up. "Well, we're changing that, aren't we. So come on — let's get it out there."

Mehrnaz's pink diary-manual was on the back of the sofa in front of the entertainment center. She caught it up, twirled around, flipped her manual open, and pulled the spell diagram off the page. Once again Dairine shook her head to see that smooth and elegant cast of the beautiful, tightly structured array of glowing Speech-words and symbols across the floor, like a fisherman gracefully throwing a net. "I'll never get tired of watching you do that," Dairine said, seeing no point in disguising her admiration as the diagram spread itself out faultlessly one more time. "That is *so cool.* I'm trying to think of a way we can make sure there are judges around when you do it." She snickered. "We need a name for that move."

"If you like," Mehrnaz said, "I could pick it up and put it away at the end of every presentation, and then wait for people to come around before I put it out again."

"Spell casting," Dairine said. "That's the name for it. Once people see it, they're gonna start *asking* you to do it."

Mehrnaz suddenly looked concerned. "Isn't that kind of, I don't know, like showing off?"

Dairine laughed. "You're kidding me, right? The Invitational *is* showing off. You've been *invited* to show off." She grinned. "And I mean, sure, flinging a spell out there like that's kind of stagy, but getting people to notice the wizardry is part of the business here. There's all this competition to be noticed; you have to stand out! And it doesn't mean the spell's any worse for being shown off. It's not like anybody can make a shoddy spell better by doing a big song and dance over it." Dairine looked over the beautifully structured diagram. "Anyway, you've done such a great job on this, it deserves to have people pay attention to it! That way word'll get around about it; people will look for it in their manuals to use it. Wizards with more experience will have a chance to improve on it. It'll have a chance to save more people's lives."

"That would matter so much," Mehrnaz said softly. "To have a chance to do that . . ."

Her intensity made Dairine shiver: *that* intention she understood. "You're going to have more than a chance," Dairine said, but before she could finish the thought, the door next to the entertainment system opened. Through it a small, pretty woman came hastening in: dark-haired, dark-eyed, round-faced and round-bodied, with a sweet smile and a button nose. She had a big, brightly patterned paisley scarf over her head and around her shoulders, and she was wearing long, soft shimmery cream-colored trousers and a tailored, amber-colored coat-tunic like Mehrnaz's that went down to the knee. The effect was made more interesting by the Nikes she was wearing under the pants.

"Is this your friend?" she said to Mehrnaz as she hurried toward them. To Dairine she said, "I'm so glad to meet you! Isn't your hair *wonderful!*"

That hadn't particularly occurred to Dairine, but she smiled. Mehrnaz looked embarrassed, but not mortified. "We don't get a lot of redheads around here," she said. "Mama, this is Dairine Callahan — she's my mentor."

Mehrnaz's mother bowed slightly to Dairine, with her hands folded in front of her. *"Salaam alaikum!"*

Dairine bowed back a little more deeply, having been used to this kind of thing for a while now with

Nelaid. *"Alaikum salaam,"* she said, knowing enough to do that at least. Mehrnaz's mother positively beamed at her.

"This is my mama, Dairine," Mehrnaz said. "Dori Farrahi."

Nelaid's constant insistence on getting the greeting right on meeting another, possibly more senior wizard suddenly came up for consideration. He did keep saying, *It may seem worth nothing initially, but politically it can make a difference later . . .* "Elder sister," Dairine said, "our paths crossing here on errantry's business, I greet you!"

"And such lovely manners! Come sit down now and have some tea." She paused as Spot clambered up onto the sofa cushions beside Dairine. "And who's this?"

"My colleague Spot," Dairine said.

Spot trained some eyes on Dori and then did a kind of squat on all his legs, his approximation of a bow or curtsy. "Charmed," he said out loud.

Mehrnaz's mama beamed at him too. "And aren't you handsome," she said, admiring the stark matte black of his carapace and the Biteless Apple glowing on his lid. "Wouldn't you like something like that, Mehrnaz? Or someone, I should say!" And Dori giggled. It was a funny sound coming out of a woman her age, but cute in its way.

Mehrnaz threw a slightly apologetic look at

Dairine and said, "He's a one-off, Mama; Spot is unique. A being *and* a manual."

"That's so wonderful," Dori said. "And how marvelous that he should come here! Come now, let's have some of this lovely tea."

That was the way things went for a while. Everything was lovely, or gorgeous, or wonderful, or *so tremendous,* or *very exciting* — that was the Invitational — and so on, endlessly. Dairine was beginning to wonder if it was possible for Dori to run out of superlatives, especially at the speed with which she spoke. Assessments and opinions fired out of her as if out of a machine gun. *A very* sweet *machine gun,* Dairine thought. *But it's like she thinks that if she talks fast enough, and doesn't stop, she can keep everyone else from saying anything she doesn't want to hear . . .*

". . . and this is all so *exciting* — would you like another biscuit? Try one of these pink ones, they're lovely — but of course you know we would have had some concerns about Mehrnaz taking part, very general ones of course. It's not exactly that we have any worries about her —"

Yes it is exactly, Dairine found herself thinking.

"— she's been very strictly brought up, she always knows the right thing to do, but she's led, well, something of a sheltered life here and of course even though there are so many wizards in our own family, she hasn't got out that much into the wider community . . ."

And why's that, I wonder? For the moment Dairine kept on smiling and nodding through the stream of chatter, occasionally making useful or encouraging neutral noises. But something about the way Dori's monologue had started was bringing a submerged part of Dairine's mind to an alert state.

All kinds of things routinely came up for discussion while she was doing her stellar management training with Nelaid. Some of these issues Dairine hadn't mentioned to her dad, as she didn't know how far down that road Nelaid had gone with him yet — notably the ones revolving around how, in a place like Wellakh, where a planet's people were in an uneasy and ambivalent relationship with the wizards they'd chosen to lead them, life wasn't necessarily always safe.

So much of what people say is coded, Nelaid had told her one evening while they leaned on that high baluster before Dairine went home at the end of the day's work. *They know what they mean, but unless in great danger or stress will not say it to you straightforwardly. People will couch their meaning in such a manner that you will never be able to say to them, when their truth is finally revealed,* 'You never told me that.' *They will be able to say,* 'But I *did* tell you, just not in so many words! I can't believe you didn't understand what I was talking about!' *And in their own eyes they will be blameless, while you are not. So always look for the code to see what it is truly saying. It will always be there.*

Now, as she kept on nodding and held her cup out to have more tea poured for her, Dairine was realizing that nearly every word that came out of Mehrnaz's mother's mouth meant something else. *And what it's all about is that she's not sure that I'm a safe person to take her baby away. She wants me to prove that I am!*

Dairine's initial urge was to take offense . . . but she caught Mehrnaz looking at her with a pleading expression that said *Don't, please don't, I'm so sorry . . . !* So Dairine took another drink of her tea, and when Dori did too — as even for a wizard it was a challenge to talk while drinking — Dairine said, "You must be so proud! To be invited to one of these is a compliment from the Powers. To Mehrnaz *and* to you."

"It is, isn't it? Though naturally we only agreed to let her go along to this event with the understanding that she'd be very careful not to get in trouble somehow . . ."

The very slight emphasis on the word *trouble* was the giveaway. It was amazing how once you'd kicked yourself into this mode of thinking, you started seeing what someone truly meant underneath the verbal output, as if there were subtitles. *Trouble? No. Danger. From being alone in an unfamiliar place. Probably because of being a girl. Cultural stuff too. Ethnic? Religious? Hard to tell —*

"— and though we have the greatest confidence in her —"

No you don't. In fact, for some reason, you've got none whatsoever. What's that about?

"— and of course she's been properly brought up and knows exactly how to take care of herself —"

When she's locked up safe in the house where nothing bad can happen.

"— we wouldn't want her to get in any difficulty —"

Because you're absolutely sure that she will, somehow.

"— or make any problems of any kind for anybody —"

Because you have absolutely no idea what she might get up to, and you're terrified to let her out of your sight.

"— and make sure she has all the help she needs when she's away in a strange place!"

God, poor Mehrnaz, I bet you have to put up with this all day when you're by yourself with her. You must be about ready to chew through the walls!

At this point Dori stopped for breath long enough for Mehrnaz, who was fidgeting where she sat, to manage to say, "Mama, seriously, everything's going to be fine! There's nothing whatsoever to worry about."

"Well, let's be reasonable, dear —"

Dairine held her face very still, as in her experience any time a conversation with a parent included the phrase "let's be reasonable," it usually indicated they were about to stop being that way.

"— it *is* after all an unfamiliar city, and there are all kinds of people running about with their own agendas, and if you're someplace where you can't find help quickly if you need it, or a way to leave when you're with people you don't know . . ."

"But Dori, you do know from the orientation pack that the whole Invitational venue has manual visioning access," Dairine said, copying her own mom's inimitable calm-yourself-down tone of voice and phrasing. It was very reassuring, and very grown-up, and implied that anyone who was wasting time being concerned about this was silly — but it did it in the kindest sort of way. "The system will help you have a look at Mehrnaz anytime you like." *At least, any time when she's told the system that she doesn't mind being surveilled.* "And it's not like it's exactly a private space. They're holding the spell presentation and evaluation event in the big convention center over by the river. The Javits Center, it's called."

Dori looked astonished. *Which tells me that you didn't read the orientation pack very closely. Or at all. Either you couldn't be bothered, or for some reason you didn't think she was going to go.* "But my goodness,"

Dori said, "how can they possibly do that? Surely there'd be a dreadful commotion if nonwizards could walk right in there and see wizardry happening!"

Dairine laughed. "Well, half the people wouldn't notice. You know how people are when they see something happening that they can't believe! Half the time they forget all about it. But no nonwizards are going to get into the secure areas. They're being spell-shielded so that people who have no business there don't want to go in, and don't notice anything happening. The organizing committee could have staged this part of the Invitational someplace out of the way, but New York's convenient for everybody because of the worldgating complex, and of course it's historically fascinating." Dairine had another sip of tea. "They like to do this stage in a shared space, since it's not dangerous. Last time they did the Cull — the initial deselection — in the Sydney Opera House, and nobody batted an eye. They're in Australia again this time for the semifinals. Canberra." She shrugged as if it was all no big deal.

Dori sat there blinking for a moment and put two more sugars in her tea than she'd been planning to. "Well, that's good to hear," Dori said. "Though still, even in a protected place like that — there will, after all, still be a lot of unfamiliar wizards —"

"Seniors," Dairine said with a put-upon expression, "and Advisories all over the place, peering over our shoulders *all the time* . . ."

"— and some of those wizards will be boys —"

Mehrnaz suddenly became fascinated by the plate of biscuits to her right on the table, so that her face was turned away from her mama's while she considered which one to pick next. Dairine, though, was positioned to see her mentee's panicked expression through Spot's eyes, as he was sitting on Mehrnaz's far side.

Uh huh, Dairine thought. *There we go.* "Boys?" she said, incredulous, and laughed. "Dori, both of us are going to be *way* too busy with this to be thinking about *boys.* We've got work to do."

"Well, yes, but it's always when we're thinking about other matters that things happen, isn't it?"

Dori looked away while saying this, and Dairine became absolutely sure she was thinking, *Because it did with me.*

"That is not going to be allowed to occur," Dairine said. "Boys have their place in life, but not for the next two weeks."

"Ah. And you don't have a boyfriend either, then?"

Dairine looked Dori straight in the eye, and said in the Speech, "I have absolutely no interest in any guy on this planet."

Mehrnaz's mother's eyes widened at the sudden change of language. Then she looked very relieved. "Oh well, that's all right then," she said.

"And I am *not* going to let her get in any trouble,"

Dairine said, once more in the Speech. "I promise you that."

"Well of course you're not, my dear, would the Powers have set you two up otherwise? I'm so glad we understand each other." And the subtext then quieted down enough for that to seem to be the only thing Dori was saying. Except possibly, *I really am relieved.* "Do you girls want some more tea?"

"Not right now, Mama," said Mehrnaz. "We'll ring for Lakshmi if we need anything."

"All right then," her mother said, and smiled fondly at both of them. "I'm keeping you from being busy, aren't I? I'll get out of your way, then; I had some shopping planned for this morning anyway. You two have fun now. It was so *interesting* to meet you, Dairine!"

"You too," Dairine said. *You have no idea.*

Dairine shot Mehrnaz a sideways look and didn't say a thing more until the door closed behind her mentee's mother. Then she spluttered with laughter. "'Have fun!' What's she think we're going to be doing, going halfway around the planet to play with our Barbie dolls?"

Mehrnaz giggled too. "Truly, I don't mean to mock her. She's a wonderful mother." Dairine held her face still: she was having some of her own thoughts about that. Perhaps Mehrnaz suspected as much; her tone went embarrassed again. "Though I *am* sorry she started to give you the Inquisition there. Half the time she treats me like I'm about six. The rest of it, she gives me grief about not acting grown-up enough. And when I do, she scolds me."

Dairine sighed and shook her head. "We all get that, wizards or not."

"But, mostly she's good. Our family is, well, kind of complicated. In some ways, she's sort of the eye of the hurricane." But then Mehrnaz smiled. "And as far as wizardry goes, no one, *no one* can do what she does with food. People talk about magic in the kitchen — well, she *is* the magic. Give her half a chance and she'll cook for you and stuff you until you have no choice but to teleport afterward, because the only other way you can move is to *roll*."

Dairine's stomach chose that moment to growl. "Oh God," she said, "it keeps doing this to me. My body clock is so messed up."

Mehrnaz grabbed the remote. "I'll send for something," she said. "These little biscuity things are never enough, they just make you hungrier . . ."

Her stomach growled again, and Dairine couldn't do anything but laugh. "You know, when I was coming up the street the other day, I smelled — someone was frying *onions* . . ."

"You went by the bhaji shop," Mehrnaz said with a grin. "Oh, you wait. I'll send for a bag. *Two* bags."

Dairine grinned and bounced up off the couch to go look at the spell diagram again. Mehrnaz joined her. "Look how this came down," Dairine said. "Not a line out of place. We are going to make spell casting *the* hot thing of this Invitational. Mehrnaz, I'm telling you, half the people in the quarter-finals are going to be doing it."

"It'll be nice to watch them," Mehrnaz said, her voice very soft.

Dairine gave her a stern look. "I can hear you thinking, and it's not going to go that way. You are *not* going to be a spectator. You are going to be in the middle of it, *competing*."

Mehrnaz turned, confused. "Don't tell me you do psychotropic spelling too! *Mind reading?* That's so smooth! I never even felt you doing that!"

"It wasn't mind reading," Dairine said. "It was prediction." She thought of Nelaid again, and smiled.

"I thought that was your sister," Mehrnaz said, sounding dubious.

"She's a visionary," Dairine said. "The prediction stuff comes and goes: she's still working on it. Kind of a sore point with her, so when you finally meet her, I wouldn't dwell on it. It's been driving her nuts lately."

"Is she no good at it?" said Mehrnaz.

"I get a feeling sometimes she's *too* good," Dairine said, "and it's starting to freak her out. But never mind that right now. Go on, pick a place to stand and let's hear you present again . . ."

• • •

In her dream Nita was standing in the Cavern of Writings on Mars, and the place was afire with wizardry . . . and this was *bad.*

It had often bothered Nita that when she'd first come there in company with Carmela and S'reee, there hadn't been time to appreciate the place as the work of art that it was. The vanished people they were seeking had taken this amazing space, the remains of a single giant bubble of gas buried deep in molten lava, and smoothed the jet-black walls of it to a near-perfect truncated sphere. Then they had written those walls full of history and prophecy and knowledge, deep-graven in ancient angular characters whose meaning had fallen out of the body of wizardly knowledge under the sheer weight of time — of past ages during which no living species had seen or read those characters or even heard of the species that had written them there.

When they'd first found it, the wizardry in the place had been worn down to nearly nothing, almost extinguished by the passage of millennia during which it was never repowered. The words engraved into the walls had been silent, drowned in shadow. But now every character, every diagram carved into those great curved walls burned hot and bright like a light bulb's wire filament, and the place was flushed with their light, a fierce emerald green.

Nita stood in the middle of the huge green-metal

design let into the floor of the Chamber — a calligraphic image of an ancient Martian scorpion-guardian, all wrought about with the curves and tangles of a massive data storage spell. But it was dead now, the last of its embedded power long gone out of it.

She was standing there wondering why this made her feel concerned when someone fled past her toward the walls: ran so closely by her that Nita's hair lifted in the breeze of the person's passing. "What —" Nita started to say, but then she recognized the tall slim shape, the long dark braid whipping to one side as the runner slammed up against the far wall, ramming into it with arms outspread as if trying to catch something. "'Mela? *'Mela!* What's the matter?"

"Gotta find the answer and then get out of here before they find me!" Carmela gasped, feeling her way along the wall. "All the answers are here, all the secrets, I have to find the right one. But I have to do it *now* or they'll find me, Neets. Gotta get out of here first!"

"Who'll find you? What's the matter?"

"One of them's like Kit. Oh God, he *looked* at me, you can't let them look at you, Neets, they'll kill you inside. They'll pull the heart right out of you; you can't look them in the eyes! *Don't look in their eyes,* whatever you do!"

Nita's hair stood up on the back of her neck.

Carmela was the one who was always gaily unafraid, who set her jaw and went in with a grin when things looked bad. But now she was rushing down the length of that wall, skidding to a stop, clutching at the characters and boxy phrases written there, then pushing herself hurriedly away when she didn't find what she wanted. "'Mela, who? Whose eyes? What's it about! Slow down, hold still, just *tell* me!"

Carmela was nothing but a cartoon cutout now, black against the sharp, fierce brilliance of the character she obscured. She twisted away from Nita and kept working her way down that wall in panicky haste, shaking her head, gasping with fear. "Can't slow down, can't hold still, they'll get you and your eyes'll fill up with lies like theirs. Don't let them get Kit, Neets, *please* don't let them get him, he won't be the same afterward! Either they'll kill him and you'll lose him that way or he'll live but he won't be Kit anymore and that'll be even worse —"

Nita's desperation was growing in tandem with Carmela's. "'Mela, stop for a minute, you have to tell me what this is *about!* Who'll get you, what's going on?"

But Carmela wouldn't stop. "The answer's here somewhere. If we can just find it —" And then she stopped, staring at the wall. "Wait! Wait, this is *it* —"

"What is?"

"There!" Carmela swung around, for the first time sounding less terrified. She pointed past Nita, pointed at the floor.

Nita swung around. Behind her the green-metal design embedded in the floor was coming to life, glowing softly at first, then burning brighter and brighter. It went beyond a glow to a blaze, the details of the design lost now in the overall fierce burning of it. The light paled out of green toward white and started to spread, running across the floor at them like lava. It splashed harmlessly past them ankle-high, and ran up against the walls of the Cavern behind them, extinguishing the fire of the carvings above it as if it had sucked all the light and power out of them.

And then the light sank into the floor, through it, left them standing on a surface clear as glass while the burning dropped away below them, the color of it starting to shift. Not white any more but faintly yellow-white, and then more golden. And then Nita and Carmela were standing together over the surface of the Sun as Nita had been yesterday in the practice universe.

"This isn't practice," Carmela said. "This happens first, and it's the real thing. You'll find her, and she'll find him, and it's going to look as if everything's all right, because everyone's going to be so happy! But right after that they're coming for me, Neets, and when they do they'll come for Kit too. You *cannot* let them have him, you hear me? You *can't*." And Carmela came to Nita and grabbed her by her upper arms and actually shook her. Her fingers bit into Nita's biceps so hard they hurt. "Do whatever you have to do to keep him safe. I don't care if they get me instead."

"Nobody's going to get Kit, and nobody's going to get *you!*" Nita said, grabbing Carmela in turn. She was no longer scared but angry, simply *furious* at anything that could turn Carmela into this alternately scared and desperate thing. "I'm not going to let them, whoever they are! Stay with me, we'll fight them!"

And then Carmela dropped her hands and looked sadly at Nita.

"Too late," she said. "They're here."

Under their feet the Sun had begun swarming with dark sunspots, like a mass of black bees, buzzing, clotting over the light, shutting it out. With horrible speed the Sun went almost totally black, the only light able to escape from it shooting upward between the sunspot-clumps like rays of Sun through closed curtains. *It can't do this,* Nita thought in growing panic, *if the Sun goes out again we won't be able to get it to relight, not like the last time —*

All around them the Cavern of Writings filled with a frightening low rushing noise like something vast drawing its last breath, a breath of fire. In the growing rush of sound an awful, tremulous darkness fell. And the thought came to Nita in horror: *No, it can't do that, the Sun's too small to end that way, it can't go n—*

Everything went violently and terminally white, an unbearable onslaught of light like a scream. Except the scream was Carmela's . . .

And then Nita was sitting up in bed and gasping as if there was no air left in the world.

Everything was normal. Outside the venetian blinds of her bedroom window, the light of dawn was growing. Everything was perfectly quiet, perfectly peaceful.

Except for her. Nita wrapped her arms around herself and hung on for dear life, and concentrated on breathing.

This, she thought, *completely* sucks.

An hour or so later, Nita was in the kitchen at the stove, making pancakes to try to take her mind off things. It wasn't working.

Carmela, she thought as she poured a few more circles of batter into the frying pan. *The way she was in that dream . . . it was all wrong.* But something else was off about it, too. Something about the emotional context struck Nita as overstated. *It's like she was acting. Why would she do that?*

. . . Though of course this was a dream-Carmela, so why would anything she did necessarily be strange?

Nita scowled as the pancakes started to cook on one side, and she shook the pan to jar them loose. They kept sticking, which was an irritation, because when they stuck they burned within seconds, and at this rate there wouldn't be enough for both her and Kit when he got here.

And then there was the bit with the Sun, and the voice that had whispered to her before but that now had roared in frustration and long-suppressed rage. . . . *Boy,* that *was freaky. But of course the Sun's on my mind right now. How could it* not *be? And not just because of Penn.* She sighed. *Dairine . . .*

She flipped the pancakes, then under her breath said "Dammit!" They'd burned already. Nita turned down the control for that burner again, but the last time she'd done this the setting had been too low and the pancakes had sat there in the pan refusing to cook except with the residual heat. *What is going* on *with this thing?* she thought. *Please don't let the stove be dying. That's an expense Daddy wouldn't like right now.*

She stood there impatiently tapping the spatula against the edge of the frying pan. *As for Penn,* she thought, *what was going on with him yesterday? Why was he so scared of the Sun?*

Unless he didn't mind the thought of doing things to it at a distance. But when he got close enough to it for it *to do something to* him *. . .* She shook her head, because the question brought her back to her earlier one. *Why would you purposely build a project that was going to scare you? It still doesn't make any sense.*

Nita was pulled out of the moment's distraction by the smell of something burning. "Oh, come on now, *stop that!*" she said. Hurriedly she scooped the four pancakes out of the pan and then put her hand down on the edge of the stove, away from the heat but close enough to the burner for there to be a direct connection between her and the metal. "You could just find a good temperature and *hold* it," she muttered to the stove burner in the Speech. "I don't want to burn any more of these. I'm running out of batter and because *somebody* forgot to get eggs last shopping, I can't make any more!"

The burner silently gave Nita to understand that the heat fluctuations weren't *its* problem: there was something wrong with the house wiring, or maybe the circuitry in the stove. *It* wasn't to blame. *It* got power fed to it, *it* glowed, it did *its* job, the power settings weren't *its* problem —

Nita heard the screen door open. *Oh great,* she thought, *now Kit's going to think I couldn't handle this mechanical thing. Or that I was saving it for him to do something about. Like he's the repairman . . .*

He shut the door behind him, sniffing the air, and came into the kitchen. "Got something burning there, *Juanita,*" Kit said, and started laughing.

"I will *kill* you to make up for not having killed *him*," Nita said, standing there with the batter jug in one hand. "Thought I was going to lose my lunch right then."

"He *is* kind of clueless sometimes," Kit said. "It's not as if it doesn't say in the manual what you prefer to be called."

"Yeah, well, I wonder how much of the reading he's been doing! Some parts he seems to get all right, and the rest of it — it's like he doesn't even bother. Doesn't think it's important enough or something."

Kit shrugged and reached past Nita for one of the pancakes lying on a nearby plate on top of a paper towel. "Maple syrup?" he said, rolling it up expertly.

"Second cupboard over. Assuming that *someone* remembered to buy some."

Kit went rummaging for it. "Her turn to do the shopping this week?"

Nita blew out an exasperated breath and poured the last of the batter into the frying pan. "No problem getting her to go to the Crossings," Nita said. "But the *Pathmark?* Might as well be halfway across the galaxy."

Kit shook his head in a resigned way. "I know where she gets the Crossings thing from . . ." He regarded his pancake as he poured maple syrup on it over the plate that was holding the others. "You decide you need more charcoal in your diet or something?"

"No. The heat in this guy keeps jumping around." She nodded at the burner. "He says it's not his fault, though."

Kit's eyes went unfocused as he ate the first half of his pancake. "Yeah," he said after a moment. "Something to do with his connection to the stove . . . I'm not sure what that's about. Might be a short."

Nita sighed. "Okay."

"But today's *really* big question is, how late did you have to stay up last night getting Penn to make all those changes?"

She blinked. "I didn't stay up at all. Did he do a lot? I saw a note in the manual that he'd been working on the spell diagram, but I didn't check the details right then. I wanted a shower first."

Kit nodded until his mouth wasn't so full. "Yeah, he did a lot. He pulled the main core routine apart, the whole energy-scooping part, and put it back together again in a completely different configuration. Must've taken him all night."

Nita shook her head and flipped the last few pancakes as Kit reached past her and rolled up another one. "How about that."

Kit gave her a slightly sly look. "The manual also said you had a chat session with him."

Nita hadn't bothered copying Kit in on that because she'd foreseen the chat getting either inappropriate or angry, and she wasn't sure she wanted him seeing either result. "It was real short," she said. "I told him the odds were more in his favor if he fixed it, and I told him what Dairine told me. And sure enough, he tried to wheedle me into doing it for him —" Kit rolled his eyes. "Thought I'd die laughing. I said to him, 'You think that's gonna happen, you need your grasp on reality retooled.' Told him we'd see him sometime after the presentations started later today, and I closed the chat down and that was that. End of story."

"Well," Kit said, "he did the job. Or at least he did something. We'll see how it looks when he lays it out." He reached for a third pancake.

"You'd better leave some for me!"

"I'm eating the burnt ones."

"That's all of them!"

"Better hurry up, then." Kit grinned at her.

Nita pulled the last pancakes out of the pan and took the maple syrup away from Kit before he started drinking it (which he'd been known to do). She rolled up the least burnt one, poured syrup in the plate and dunked it. "You satisfied with how Penn did on the verbal presentation stuff?"

Kit nodded. "Yeah. I wish we had another session to do heckling with him, though. He's getting better at handling the interruptions, but he still hates them, and it shows. Wish we could desensitize him."

"He was worse about that with you than he was with me."

Kit reached for a fourth pancake and rolled it up. "I don't know if that's him being competitive with guys, or competitive with me . . . Though why would he be competitive with *me?*" Kit shrugged. "Don't get it."

"Could be both," Nita said. "The way he is with girls . . ."

Kit shook his head. "You really have problems with him, don't you."

"It's his attitude. I honestly don't know what's going on with him. But it's as if he thinks girls are some other species. I wish I had some idea where he gets that from."

"You mean you're *not* another species?"

Nita kicked Kit ever so gently in the shin. "Thanks a lot. Maybe he sees guys as being . . . I don't know, more worthy of competing with? More of a challenge?"

Kit was at that moment finishing his pancake, and shrugged again. Nita grabbed a couple more pancakes, rolled them up together, wiped up what was left of the maple syrup with them and wolfed them down.

"So, you ready?"

"Just want to wash my hands and grab a jacket. Where should we pop out? Right at the Javits? They've got a dedicated 'beam in' spot; Sker'ret installed it yesterday."

"I don't know. It's a nice day. Thought we might go into Grand Central and walk over."

"Not Penn Station?"

"They're doing something to the gates, the manual says. Penn's offline."

"Oh, great. That has to be driving Rhiow nuts." Nita laughed. "You know, we're going to have to have something else to call him if we're going to talk about him and the station at the same time."

"Easy. Penn Station is Big Penn. Our mentee is Little Penn."

"Yeah, in terms of needing to be cut down to size."

"Looks like it's gonna take a few minutes for your blood sugar to sort itself out . . ."

"Shut *up*." But Nita laughed. "Let's go."

9

Manhattan: Javits Center

✱

GRAND CENTRAL TERMINAL at midmorning, for Nita at least, had a surprisingly restful feel. The worst of the morning rush hour was over, the Sun shone in beautifully through the big windows, and lots of people strolled casually or purposefully across the bright, echoing space without there being too much of a feeling of stress or hurry. Nita was quite aware that her own history with this place tended to affect her perceptions; any space tends to look serene when it's not full of angry dinosaurs or about to be trashed by the Lone Power in a bad mood. But that didn't stop her from enjoying the slower pace.

She and Kit transported as usual into the commuter-free "safe space" at the far end of Track 23 just off the Main Concourse — where the onsite worldgating team had the terminal's security cameras permanently spoofed, and a simple on-demand light-bending stealth-spell operated 24/7 to keep any unexpected nonwizards in the area from noticing when the emplaced worldgate operated. As it happened, Nita and Kit arrived during a brief quiet period between train arrivals, and it took only a moment or two for them to make sure no one on adjacent platforms could see them. They were heading toward the edge of the stealth field some meters away when something down low near the floor passed through it and faded into visibility, trotting down the platform toward them: a small black cat with its tail held cheerfully in the air.

"Rhiow!"

"Well, look what the Queen dragged in!" said the most senior of Grand Central's worldgating team as she came up with them in mid-platform, rubbing against one of Kit's shins and then rearing up against Nita's.

"Yeah, and *dai stihó* to you too!" Nita said, reaching down to scratch her between the ears.

Rhiow dropped to all fours again and gazed up at them with big golden eyes. "Cousins, I can't stay, the Lexington gate got stuck in the middle of its maintenance cycle again and I have to go debug it. But it's fine to see you! You're on your way over for the Invitational?"

"Yeah," Kit said. "I saw that Penn Station's gate's down, though. That must be a nuisance for you with all the people coming through . . ."

"Oh no, it's *because* of the Invitational that it's down! Just a temporary service reconfiguration. We can't leave a set of short-term gates operating so close to the permanent gate structures at Penn: they're too territorial, they'd start making trouble for each other. So all the Penn Station worldgate traffic's being rerouted through here for the day. Not such a big deal."

"Oh, that's okay then, I guess," Nita said. "We were worried something was broken."

Rhiow's ears went flat for a moment. "Powers That Be, don't even think it! Things are busy enough as it is."

"Too busy for you to stop by Javits later?" Kit said.

"This evening? Most likely there'll be time. Tell them to save me some of that upstate milk." And she flirted her tail at them and headed briskly on down to the end of the platform again, leaping off of it and vanishing into the dark.

"No problem," Nita called after her. "See you later!"

"Upstate milk?" Kit said as they headed on down the platform in the other direction and the stealth field released them into visibility.

"There's this dairy farm in the Catskills that's been selling milk in one of the city farmers' markets on weekends," Nita said. "She and Hwaith have it bad for this stuff. They keep going on about the cream on top, apparently it's not homogenized . . ."

They made their way up the ramp from the Grand Concourse and out through the bright brass doors into the sunshine, turning right on Forty-second and heading west. Cabs blared horns, trucks rumbled by, a fire engine honked its way past in a blur of red and white, lights flashing and siren yipping as it braked at the intersection of Forty-second and Lex, then slid through against the lights, still yipping. People going both ways on the sidewalk pressed in around them, brushed past them, trailing fragments of conversation over them. "But then I thought, why in the world would I —" "— not going to do *that* —" "I never made that bet with you!" "— starts making fun of my hat and I said, 'You know *nothing,* and anyway this isn't a fedora, it's a *trilby* —'"

"You thought he was going to give you trouble?" Kit said as they paused at the intersection of Forty-second and Madison, waiting for the light.

"Who?"

"Penn. About the chat."

Nita let out an annoyed breath. "Or I was going to give him some, yeah."

The light changed: they headed across. "Not that he wouldn't have had it coming," Kit said.

"Yeah. It's just that — I don't know, I keep getting the feeling that every time I try to have a conversation with him, he's saying one thing and meaning something else." Nita made a face. "Possibly something creepy. Or else he's writing me off as too girly to listen to. No middle ground with him."

Kit looked amused. "You know," he said, "we could turn Lissa loose on him."

She looked at him in surprise. "Wait, is she going to be here?"

"Yeah, I saw her on the incoming visitor list in the manual this morning." Kit grinned. "After ten minutes or so of Lissa in *I'm-talking-tech-to-*you,-*stupid* mode, he'll be *so* grateful for you."

The notion made Nita smile, though there was a slightly sour edge to it. *I should be able to do that to him myself,* she thought. As they came up to the next light at Fifth Avenue, Nita gazed across and leftward at the New York Public Library and the great couchant lions guarding the doors. She was briefly distracted by the idea of them leaping off their pedestals and roaring down Fifth Avenue in the darkness years ago. Then she realized that Kit was watching her with a worried expression. "What?"

"You look pissed off."

"I am," Nita muttered.

"Look —" Kit's expression was slightly nervous. Nita stared at him, confused. "Lissa's not . . . I mean, there's nothing you should —"

Nita thought of what Carmela had said to her a while back: *You two get so used to reading each other's minds that you forget how to talk.* She had to smile: there was truth in it. But she didn't see why she couldn't still tease Kit about it. "For someone who's usually all about finding the right words, you sure get tongue-tied sometimes."

"What I mean is . . ." Then Kit caught Nita's tone and knew that everything was okay, and laughed. "I don't *know* what I mean."

She realized that Kit was looking down at her hand, hanging beside his. His was twitching a little. Nita looked up at him and said, "I know what you mean about not knowing what you mean."

Then they both cracked up. "Do you even *listen* to yourself?" Kit said.

"Been trying not to, lately."

The light changed. Kit reached out and took her hand, and they crossed Fifth together a little awkwardly. *You'd think crossing the street while holding someone's hand would be easier,* Nita thought. *Not the other way around . . .*

"With Penn, though . . ." Nita said after a moment, jumping back a subject as they headed on down Forty-second and past the side of the library. "Who needs any more of that? With all the crap at school —"

"Yeah." Occasionally it seemed as if sometime during the last year or so in school, somebody had thrown a switch, and suddenly talk about sex was *everywhere* (though as far as Nita could tell, there was a lot more talk going on about it than action). And *not* talking about it was as fraught with trouble as talking about it was. If you got into such discussions even as protective coloration, there could be an ugly backlash. Nita had learned the hard way that some people took her refusal to talk about it either as proof she and Kit weren't doing it, or proof that they were. Being hit with both insinuations at once had recently caused Nita to completely forget for several minutes about years of being committed to not increasing entropy. She'd been within a breath of increasing it (generally) all over the athletics field in back of the school, and (specifically) all over Michaela whose-last-name-she-could-never-remember-and-now-didn't-want-to.

"You didn't kill her," Kit said. "That was a good thing."

Nita stared at him, then flapped her free hand helplessly in the air. "See that?" she said. "You don't even have to know what I'm *thinking* to know what I'm thinking."

Kit started laughing again. "Kind of hard to miss what your face is doing."

"God, am I that *transparent?* How am I any possible use if everybody can tell what I'm thinking all the time?"

"I don't know. Might have saved Michaela deVera's life that you were that transparent. Because word has it that nobody's heard a peep out of her about *you* since she saw the look on your face while you were standing over her on the track."

DeVera. Okay. But it'll probably be ten minutes before I forget her name again, because God *I can't stand her.* "Oh great, thank me for *that* by all means," Nita muttered. "Just don't blame *me* if now she lives long enough to reproduce."

Kit started whooping with laughter, laughing so hard that he had to stop walking and pull Nita over with him to one side, so he could lean on one of the big, sloping, squared pillars of the building they were passing and regain control of himself. "Oh God, oh God," was all he could say for nearly a minute. And then finally, when he had the strength to push himself upright and wipe his eyes, Kit gasped, "Who would — *who* would even be a *part* of that? *Seriously!*"

Nita had to admit that Kit had a point. Michaela had left Nita (and various others) utterly astonished by bragging about Doing It with Mike Kavanagh, when it was well known around school that (a) Mike was totally out of play due to being deep in a Skype-fueled Internet affair with some girl in the south of England, to the point where he wasn't even interested in putting up the usual playing-the-local-field smokescreen, and (b) Michaela's cruel, foul mouth was so well known and disliked that nobody wanted to take the chance of hooking up with her for fear of what would be said about it, *by everyone,* afterward — starting with Michaela.

It took another minute for Kit to fully recover enough breath to say, "Has she ever even done it with *anybody?*"

Nita shook her head. "Maybe not . . ." But Michaela desperately wanted people to *think* she had. Nita had come into the girls' room one afternoon unnoticed and heard one long brag session spinning itself out in excruciating, too-much-information detail, while the group surrounding Michaela down by the sinks at the far end of the room made encouraging (though not necessarily impressed) noises at the graphic stuff. But when they'd noticed Nita coming out of a stall, Michaela had turned their attention to *her,* and the jeering started. And then in gym class when they were outside . . .

She sighed. It hadn't been her proudest moment, but at least Michaela hadn't gotten hurt when she "tripped" in the middle of a hundred-yard dash — just got the wind knocked out of her so hard that she had nothing left to call anybody names with for a while. Nita had been very careful about the placement of the shock-absorbing barrier that cushioned Michaela's spill on the track; it was a variation of what she used to use to protect herself from bullies. "But that's why it's so stupid for her to be in everybody's face about whether they've done it," Nita said. "Or haven't." It was amazing the way the taunts still rang in her ears. *He can't be worth much as a boyfriend if you won't even talk about him. Maybe he can't do it, huh? Or else he won't, he's never going to. Maybe you're making it all up so people will think you're normal. Good luck with* that. Nita concentrated on rhythmic breathing and not getting herself riled up again. *Maybe I need to grow a thicker skin.*

"Your skin is fine," Kit muttered.

She looked at him sidewise.

"Okay, that one I heard," he said. He looked vaguely guilty, which was all wrong.

"It's been coming and going for me too lately," Nita said. *And somehow, never at times when I want it to.* "Sorry."

Kit shook his head. "Don't be. Same here."

They did another half block or so in silence. It was odd, Nita thought, that it seemed easier to talk here, out among all these hundreds of people who were passing them by. *But they don't know us.* Even though the people standing or walking nearest to them might hear what they were saying, it didn't matter; they'd never see any of these people again. And it was also, oddly, more comfortable to talk about this stuff out here than someplace more quiet and private, where things might change suddenly.

"You're irritated again," Kit said.

"I'm not."

There was a short silence, but somehow it wasn't uncomfortable. "You know," he said, "if 'boyfriend' is the wrong word . . ."

"It's *not!* It's just . . ."

She laughed. Kit looked confused. "What?"

"Got a really stupid idea . . ."

"It's probably not."

"Is it possible that, sometimes, with a word . . . you might need a while to break it in? Like new shoes."

Kit gave her a look that suggested he was waiting for more of an explanation.

Nita shrugged. "Just think what we've been through the last few years. The dangerous stuff. We've saved each other's lives how many times now? As friends. And now this . . . it's different. But it's *there.*"

She held her breath again. *Not that there's any real doubt, come on, you know there's not . . .*

"Yeah," Kit said after a moment. "It does take some extra getting used to. Because normally it comes with all these expectations."

Nita nodded, letting that breath out. "How you should look. What you should sound like when you're around each other."

"Or when you're not."

"How you should *be.*"

"God, yeah."

"But we don't have to do it the normal way."

"Normal," Kit said. "Us?" And he laughed.

Nita smiled. *He gets it.* "Exactly."

Kit snickered. "Just do me one favor. Don't let Michaela hear that you're breaking me in."

It was the kind of remark that she normally would have punched him in the arm for. *Well ... breaking this in too, then.* Now Nita quietly laced her fingers through his and squeezed his hand.

Kit grinned at the sidewalk as they came up to the corner of Forty-second and Seventh, then tipped his chin up to regard the traffic. "Where is it again?" Nita said. "Eleventh?"

"And sort of Thirty-sixth: by the Hudson. Not that much farther."

The Sun was bright and the air was warm and there wasn't any need to hurry for a change; they were going to be early for the prejudging anyway. "Not a problem," Nita said, swinging Kit's hand in hers. "Nice day."

"Yeah. We don't get a chance to do this so often when we're not being chased by something."

She chuckled. "Yeah."

"Is it stupid," Kit said, "to think that when everything's going nice like this, something's probably going to happen?"

"With *us*?" Nita laughed. "Smartest thing is just to say 'Let's hurry up and go see what it is.'"

They grinned at each other and started walking faster.

Shortly they were crossing the street in front of Manhattan's great convention center, the huge gleaming frontage of it almost impossible to look at in the sunshine — like three gigantic green-glass boxes set down side by side next to the river, the middle one the tallest. Nita made without hesitation for the center set of doors.

"Upstairs?" Kit said.

"Level three," Nita said, "Hall 3D."

They went up several escalators and came out in a broad, bright metal-and-glass atrium with a food court on one side and some business-oriented stores on the other. On the rear side of the building was the entrance to a huge, high-ceilinged room that stretched in the direction of the river. The view of the room itself was blurred by what seemed to be a translucent curtain hung straight across the entry from the industrial lighting fixtures in the ceiling; and in front of the curtain was a line of five or six tables covered with gold-colored drop cloths, arranged so that they guarded the access to the doors. Out in front of them, and to one side of the gap between a couple of the tables, stood a sign on an easel. It said:

IDAA PRELIMINARY SELECTION SESSION
WELCOME

The amazing thing was that looking at the sign did not make one feel at all welcome. It made you feel as if you first wanted to yawn very hard, then go away and do something else, *anything* else, because standing here was such a waste of time. The font in which the sign was printed was desperately dry, cold, and offputting. Kit found that the mere sight of it made his eyes feel gritty and tired.

Next to him, Nita yawned, and then laughed out loud, impressed. "Wow!" she said. "Can you feel that?"

"Spell," Kit said. He started feeling the need to rub incipient sleep out of his eyes. "Really powerful. Directional, too!" He turned sideways, experimenting, and then turned back again toward it, a little at a time. "When you're not looking at it, it's way less. But when you start turning back toward it —"

"That is *such* great work," Nita said, and rubbed her own eyes. "Somebody knows what they're doing."

Kit grinned: even knowing it was a spell didn't help much — he still felt the urge to go home and take a nap. "Let's get in past it before we fall asleep on our feet."

It took only the few steps in past the sign and toward the tables for the effect to wear off. As they got close, a slim, dark-haired guy in jeans and a white shirt, with a neat little beard, popped out through a slit in the curtain and started rummaging around among some paperwork as if he'd lost something. He glanced up as they came to the table. "*Dai stihó,* cousins! How can I help?"

"We're here for the pre-judging," Nita said.

He smiled at them. "And nice and early, thank you for that, though if you were hoping for peace and quiet to do your picks in, I'm sorry to tell you that the competitors are way ahead of you." He kept turning over papers on the table. "Bear with me a second if you would, seems like nothing's ever where you leave it around here . . ."

Kit looked over his shoulder. "That's an amazing sign."

"It is, isn't it? Sarima Okeke did those for us." The guy paused, apparently surprised at their blank faces. "You don't know Okeke's work? She's a graphics wizard — best there is, if you ask me. Specializes in fonts. Every one of the letters in that sign is a microprinted spell in the Speech. Embedded diagram, condensed phrasing . . . just a work of art. Fuel the spell and print out a few words, and any nonwizard who views it gets the overwhelming urge to take themselves someplace more interesting. The font on that one there — Ennui Sans? Brand new, Okeke designed it for this event. But after this they're putting it in the manual for anyone who needs to use it to keep nonwizards out of things."

"It works really well," Nita said.

"You haven't seen anything," the guy said. "That's the *light* version. If we'd printed that sign in Ennui Overextended, you'd be asleep right now, wizard or no wizard. One of the Planetaries actually dozed off looking at one of those this morning; had to take it down. Okeke has a *gift*."

The guy went back to his rummaging around, this time starting to take apart another pile of paperwork. "Wait, there are Planetaries here?" Kit said. "I mean besides Irina?"

"Yeah, unusual to see them so early, but seems like some people in this round have aroused a bit more curiosity than expected." The table guy, whose nametag said J. W. BYNKIJ, kept on pushing papers around on the table. *Some kind of Slavic name maybe?* Kit thought.

Then Mr. Bynkij straightened, having found what he was after. "Aha! Usual thing, people borrow things and don't put them back where they found them . . ."

It was a WizPad, to judge by the Biteless Apple on the back. Mr. Bynkij tapped at it briefly, and in mid-tap looked up thoughtfully at Kit. "Hey, don't I remember you? . . . Of course I do. You were shooting up aliens on the Moon. Great to see you here." He glanced down at the tablet, apparently scrolling

up and down a list. "Right! So you are Callahan —"
He reached elbow-deep into the empty air beside him
and pulled out a plastic laminated badge on a long blue
woven strap, which he handed to Nita.

"Hey, nice," she said. "And we get lanyards too."

"Lanyards for all," said Mr. Bynkij as he turned
back toward the hole in the air and shoved his arm
into it up to the shoulder, groping around. "Aaaand
Rodriguez." He pulled out another and handed it to
Kit. "Do *not* lose the lanyards. The badges are what
always fall off, even with wizardry, seems to be some
kind of natural law about that, and therefore the access
routines and nothing-to-see-here spells are woven
into the lanyards instead. Please be aware that while
you're wearing these, almost all nonwizards will find
you boring to the point of attempting to avoid you.
Only exceptions to this rule locally are the center's
concession staff, who have the effect dialed back about
eighty percent so they won't care about you particularly but also won't fall asleep in the middle of making
you a latte. If you're expecting a nonwizardly guest,
let me or whoever's working up here know and we'll
get them a waiver pin for their lanyard. Need one of
those now?"

They both shook their heads. "Fine." Mr. Bynkij
looked at his pad again. "The only other thing is
to make sure you've received your mentor's-picks
tokens . . ."

"Got 'em," Kit said. Nita nodded.

"Then go on in and start fulfilling your function." He looked over his shoulder toward the curtain, then turned back to them. "You want to watch out . . . it's a little busted loose in there. Some of the youngest ones are bouncing off the walls." He grinned. "Personally, I think hardhats would do you guys more good than the lanyards, but . . ." He shrugged and waved a hand back toward the curtain.

"Thanks!" they both said, and headed in.

As they passed through the curtain, the sound inside the room burst all around them as if someone had hit the unmute button on a remote. Kit froze for a moment — feeling slightly relieved when Nita did, too — as he found himself looking across the biggest crowd of wizards he'd ever seen when the world wasn't ending.

The space itself was sixty or seventy feet wide and easily more than a couple of hundred feet long, and almost entirely full of people. *Full of* wizards! Kit told himself. It was too easy, in normal times, to think of other wizards either in small groups or scattered all over the planet in the abstract, the way you might think of acquaintances on the Internet: mostly invisible and distant. *But they're not distant now!* Kit thought. The place was alive with them, and all up and down that huge space, from floor to ceiling, the air glowed and flashed with wizardries laid out on show or now in progress, like a small but very enthusiastic fireworks displays.

Next to him, Nita let out a breath. "My God . . ."

"Yeah," Kit murmured. "Come on!"

They started making their way through the crowds. There were as many older wizards as young ones there, gathering in groups down the length of the room to watch contestants who were doing presentations, or to examine setups from which the presenting wizards had stepped away. Kit could see some people standing well up over the heads of the crowd, as if they were on ladders. It took him a moment to realize that levitation was being extensively employed by people looking for someone or something in particular.

"What a zoo!" Nita muttered beside him. "And it's like this *now*? What's it going to turn into later?"

"No kidding. If we're supposed to pick favorite projects, we'd better get going before you can't even move in here anymore."

Nita stared around them. "There has to be some kind of directory . . ."

As it happened, a pair of them hung transparently in the air, one on each side of that end of the room — tall, immaterial signs that could have been mistaken for holograms, except that they were constructs of wizardry. Each was densely lettered in two columns, one in the Speech and one that shifted into

English as they approached. "It must have felt our manuals getting close," Kit said.

"Yeah, nice . . ."

Three hundred and twelve names of competitors were listed on the floating directory, along with the names of their mentors' and their projects. The great majority of these were highlighted with overlaying green bars that (according to the key at the bottom of the display) meant the competitor was onsite. A brighter green meant they were actively presenting. As Kit and Nita watched, a pair of lines flared brighter than all the others, the upper one the brighter of the pair.

"Wait," Kit said, reading it. "Penn's here already?"

Nita's eyes widened. "Mr. Laid-Back, No Hurry? You're kidding." Nita peered at the list. "What number is he?"

The directory promptly faded out all the other listings, enlarged Penn's name and the name of his project, and displayed a map of the floor of the exhibition space with Penn's spot highlighted. He was about a third of the way down on the right-hand side.

Kit peered around the directory. "Yeah, you can just make him out past that—what is that? Looks like somebody's got a bunch of scale-model skyscrapers down there. Wonder what that's about . . ." But sure enough, a couple of spaces past that competitor's display, there was Penn, his spell set out in its showier spherical 3D configuration, rotating gently into and out of the floor. He was talking animatedly to a group of adult and younger wizards gathered around him, and gesturing at his spell in a very smooth and choreographed manner, like a game-show host indicating the virtues of Door Number One.

"I can't believe it," Nita said. "It's got to be eight in the morning for him. Didn't think getting up this early was his style. If he's showing some initiative finally . . ." She shrugged, and turned her attention back to the directory. "As for Dair . . ."

A second later the directory was showing them the space set aside for Dairine and her mentee; but it was dimmed down to show that they weren't there yet, and a countdown clock over their spot showed an ETA of about an hour later. "Well, who knows," Nita said under her breath. "Lunchtime's when they said contestants should plan to be here, and there's a lot of time zones between here and India. They might be stopping at home first."

Kit nodded. "So which side first?"

"This one," Nita said.

Because you want to have a look at Penn right now and get him over with, Kit thought. And if Nita by chance overheard the thought, she gave no sign of it.

They started wandering down the right-hand side of the big room, taking in the competitors' exhibits.

Some of them at first glance looked like the kinds of displays you might see at a high school science fair — a desk- or table-like space with a sign overhead saying what it was supposed to be. But in most of these cases, the signs were floating in the air unsupported, and so were some of the tables. Much more work, however, was being displayed on the beige-and-brown-patterned tile of the floor, or hovering in the air . . . and there, any resemblance to a mundane science fair ended in a hurry. "Is that a *mobile meteor shield?*" Nita said. "That's a pick right there!"

"What, the first thing you see?"

"Why not? It's not like we've got a limit on how many of these things we can give."

"Oh come on, at least wait till you've seen a few!"

But soon enough Kit found that holding back from dropping one Mentors'-Picks token after another was harder than it looked. Some of the spells and wizardly projects were amazingly ambitious, all of them were wildly creative, and the young wizards who were presenting them were across the board so cheerfully excited about their work that it was almost impossible for Kit to walk past without stopping. And every time he stopped, he wanted to drop another token.

The names of the projects alone were enough to do it, sometimes. "Burning the Rain: Why Not? Desalinization with a Side of Subterfuge," for example. That one was about using controlled wizardry-driven ionization and aerosol redirection spells to help make it rain where rain was needed, while also fooling drought-stricken desert countries into thinking that their gradual (and carefully supervised) climatic recovery was an unanticipated, idiosyncratic function of world climate change. The competitor responsible, a dark-skinned blond-dreadlocked twelve-year-old boy in a tank top and surfer jams, stood there laughing and explaining his floor-spread spell diagram to the people gathered around it, while overhead a six-foot-wide cloud like something out of a cartoon continually rained gently down on them all (and an uptake spell underneath the spectators recycled the water and kept it from running all over the floor). Kit saw at least one pair of wizards vanish from in front of the "water feature" and reappear a couple of minutes later in swimsuits.

Then there was "Don't Look *Now!*" which was a new take on stealth shielding for wizards who needed to hide some crucial work in progress. The shield spell, once activated, synced up with a very tightly constrained conditional timeslide wizardry and superimposed a perfect 3D "playback" of what that given area had been like at a previous time of one's choosing—ideally a time when nothing was happening there. But for demonstration purposes the "shielded" area on the exhibition floor was now set to loop back to two minutes before. As a result, spectators were dodging in and out of the project demonstration space like people standing in front of an electronics shop's window to see themselves in the view of a camera — but they were doing it so they could stand next to *themselves* as they'd been two minutes previously. There was a lot of laughter and joking ("Didn't I tell you how those jeans looked from behind? Didn't I *tell* you?"), and almost constant flashing from held-up phones as wizards took selfies with themselves. While this went on, the competitor — a calm, smiling Aboriginal girl — leaned against her "stand" with her arms folded, explaining the intricacies of intratemporal visualization manifestation to anyone who'd hold still long enough.

And as for "Taub-NUT Space Seen as an Answer to Practically Everything" . . . The competitor responsible for it, someone called Marit Horowitz, wasn't minding his or her stand when Kit and Nita passed by. Laid out on a floating table, and flowing over the edges of it to hang down like some kind of glowing lacy tablecloth, was a spell packed so insanely tight with delicate detail that figuring out its major structures at first glance was impossible. The Speech-phrases in it were so fine that they looked like they'd been woven into the structure by a spider with particularly good handwriting and a fondness for heavy theoretical work.

Kit stopped and read the project's prospectus — or

as much of it as he could, since it was mostly mathematical symbols — and then read what he could of it again. Next to him, Nita was doing the same thing. Kit was intensely relieved when she heaved a sigh and shook her head.

"It's something to do with diagnosing the status of local hyperspace, right?" Kit said.

There was a pause. "Yeah, I think so."

Nita's hesitation made Kit feel better. "Most of it, though, I'm not getting. Tell me it's just me."

Nita stood there for the space of a few breaths and then looked at Kit. "Nope," she said, shaking her head. She leaned over the "table" and read the competitor-wizard's personal profile, which was embedded in it. "And he's *eight.*"

Kit opened and closed his mouth. "How do you even have an *Ordeal* at eight?"

Nita shook her head again. "As soon as I can find somebody to explain this to me in baby words," she said, sounding fairly put out, "either him or someone else, I'm giving him a token." And she wandered off down the exhibition space.

Kit waited until Nita was out of sight behind some people in the crowd . . . then dropped his round, Speech-initialed token, glowing, onto the table. The token twinned itself: the twin vanished into the table and the original leaped back into Kit's hand. Kit grinned and went after Nita.

This is all so amazing, he thought as he gradually caught up. There were people redesigning ocean currents and tweaking the Jet Stream, there were young wizards playing around with superconductivity and others building microscopic worldgates into computers to act as concrete data transfer mechanisms; there were kids Kit's age or younger, *seriously* younger — at least by three or four years — playing with dangerous natural forces as if they were Tinkertoys. *Why didn't it feel so dangerous when* I *was doing it?* Kit thought.

Though maybe having company helps . . .

He wandered past a brawny dark-haired guy in a long white robe who was displaying something that had to do with dynamically changing atmospheric density. It apparently had applications for restoring the ozone layer, but most of the kids gathered around the display were using the custom-redensified air so they could quack-talk like people who'd been breathing helium. Avoiding a couple of these who were doubled over with laughter, Kit bumped into Nita from behind. She was standing there with arms folded at the back of a crowd of people, and she wasn't making any move to slip through them.

The reason was Penn, who was walking his tall self up and down the front of the crowd and waving his arms as the spectators examined the spherical-structure version of his spell while it rotated gently up out of the floor and down into it. "Absolutely no way it can miss, my cousins! Drop your tokens here and vote for what three out of four passing wizards have already declared to be the best thing since sliced bread, the best way to redirect the solar wind that anyone's ever come up with, not least because voting for it makes *you . . .* look *. . . great!"*

And with a series of grand curving gestures he traced a flaming Wizard's Knot in the air and started the mockup of his spell running. Its 3D version flared out of view, to be instantly replaced by an underfloor view of the Earth as seen from low Earth orbit. An incoming flood of charged particles from the distant Sun came shooting and sparkling in, blinding-bright as rain caught by lightning — a sudden splendor of inbound solar wind made visible. But at a gesture from Penn the spell went active, and the reality of it as it would appear in operation, rather than the schematic, came burning to life above him. The power conduit between the spell and the Sun started pulling energy into the space around the Earth as the wizardry went fully active. Penn flung his arms up over his head, and an invisible half-dome of repelling power sprang up above him, matching the Earth's curvature, so that the high-energy particles bounced off it like hailstones off a tin roof in dancing curves of light.

Penn stood there with his eyes squeezed shut and a triumphant grin plastered over his face as the crowd gave him a round of applause. Some of them pushed forward to drop pick-tokens in a hot spot at his feet, a glowing circle with pointing neon arrows and a label that said (first in the Speech, but then switching every second to English and other languages) SHOW YOUR SMARTS HERE!

As the crowd started to move on, Penn bowed effusively to them, and bowed again to the new group that was moving up to see what was going on. "Thank you, thankyouverymuch, I'll be here all week . . ."

Kit laughed under his breath. "This is so like him."

"Yeah, it is," Nita said, very low. It was almost a growl. Kit found himself entertaining two very different thoughts as she moved away from him and toward Penn: *If I were him I'd watch what I said to her right now,* and *Why is it that when she sounds like that it's kind of hot?*

A break developed in the crowd in front of them and Nita was already slipping forward to where the basic spell, once again in 3D spherical mode, had reappeared and was once more rotating in and out of the floor. "Ah, Juanita," Penn said, beaming at her, "I see you've been getting the vote out for me. Lots of interest, nice to see you're getting the job done . . ."

"I haven't done a single thing," Nita said. "Ask Kit."

Kit produced the most neutral expression he could

manage and focused on the spell diagram, because he knew that tone of voice; it might sound casual, but he knew better. "Looks like *you* were busy last night, though. Thought you might have decided to sleep in instead . . ."

"Sleep? Sleep is for the weak. Did some light spell work along the lines of some of the stuff you mentioned, watched the Sun come up, decided to come in early and wow the crowds."

Nita smiled. "Think you're gonna have enough energy to carry on like that all day?"

"Oh, don't worry your pretty little head, I'll be pacing myself." He turned his back on her, and so missed the way her eyes went wide. "Kit, my man —"

"Penn," Kit said. If he fist-bumped with Penn, it was reflex. It also distracted Penn from noticing Kit's glance over Penn's shoulder at the disbelieving expression on Nita's face. "That looked pretty good there."

"Yeah, they've been eating it up. Got something like —" Penn picked up his manual, glanced down at one page where a bar graph was showing. "Sixty-eight tokens already. And it's not even lunchtime! If it keeps going like this, there'll be three or four hundred by the time the judging's done. I am gonna *sweep* this thing!"

"Long time between lunchtime and five p.m.," Kit said, "but let's see how it goes." He glanced at his watch as if he had some reason to. "We've got a lot of ground to cover . . . we should go. But we'll look in on you every now and then."

"Aw, come on, stay for one whole run-through and bask in the reflected glory, huh?"

Reflected. Glory. Kit grinned, and hoped it didn't look too fake. "We wouldn't want to distract anyone from the idea that what you're doing's all yours," he said. "Go right on ahead."

"Wouldn't want to deprive you of any reflection, either . . ." Nita said, heading down toward the next exhibitor's space with a slight smile on her face.

Penn turned to watch her go. "Kit," he said after a moment, with the air of someone asking a delicate question among Just Us Guys, "do you find her kind of . . . hard to understand sometimes?"

"Well, every now and then," Kit said, "yeah. But you know what? The Lone Power has *exactly the same problem.*"

And he gave Penn what he hoped would be mistaken for a conspiratorial look and went after Nita.

When Kit caught up with her, Nita was thoughtfully looking over a very compact and elegant spell diagram that was about a tenth the size of Penn's. Kit quietly leaned over her from behind and whispered in her ear, "I'm so sad now."

She didn't turn around. "Sad why?"

"Thought you were gonna pretty-little-head-butt

him into another time zone. I was getting ready to put the manual on record."

Nita gave him a sideways look as they moved on together. "I had something else in mind."

"Oh?"

"Chilling him out a little. Pluto's nice this time of year."

Kit snickered. "That place where you dumped Dairine's bed that time . . ."

"Nice crevasse," Nita said. "Dark. Deep. Cold." Then she sighed. "Kit, he's not worth it. I want to wander around here and look at all these other wizardries."

"Yeah," Kit said. "And drop a bunch more tokens."

Nita nodded, but didn't say anything else for a few moments. Kit stayed quiet.

"I'm done with him," Nita said. "Absolutely done."

"Which could be a problem, since as far as he goes we've barely started." Then it was Kit's turn to sigh. "You know, though, I just had this awful thought."

"Yeah?"

"Think what he's going to be like if he makes it through to the quarter-finals."

Nita covered her eyes briefly. "It is *bad* to secretly wish your mentee will get deselected with extreme prejudice," she said. "So bad."

"When we're supposed to be helping him win? I guess."

"Great. On top of everything else, guilt. I needed guilt so much."

She rubbed her face, then looked up at Kit almost challengingly. "Never mind. He doesn't need us hanging around; we've done everything we can for him. And we've got more things to think about than Penn."

"Yeah. Like where's Dairine?"

Nita laughed. "I really *am* that transparent, aren't I."

"Lucky guess. Come on, let's go admire everyone's stuff and drop tokens all over them to make up for Elvis back there."

10

Javits Center: The Cull

✳

DAIRINE AND MEHRNAZ and Spot popped out in the sheltered green space at the far end of the Callahans' backyard and made their way up through the garden toward the house. *At least it's not raining,* Dairine thought. The weather forecast had mentioned a chance of showers, but there didn't seem to be any in the neighborhood right now. Nothing showed through the leaves of the trees but blue sky and sunshine.

Mehrnaz was staring at everything with absolute delight, and spun around once as they walked toward the back of the house, as if trying to take in everything at once. "Everything's so small and pretty!" she said. "It's like something out of a storybook!"

"Seriously?" Dairine said, and laughed at the thought of anyone considering a suburban New York tract house surrounded by chain-link fencing as being at all charming or cute. "Well, let's get our butts into the storybook house, because I've got to change out of this." She pulled her tunic away from her waist, making a face as she felt it peel away. "I thought I didn't mind humidity. I mean, it gets humid here, but *wow,* in your part of the world it's been raised to an art form. Five minutes outside and look at me!"

"Well, *you* were the one who wanted more *bhajis!*"

"Yeah, thanks for reminding me of that, and *you* are in *so* much trouble for getting me hooked on the ones with the chilies —"

"Oh, this is *my* fault, is it?"

"It is, and I'll tell the world, so don't play innocent." They went out the side gate to the driveway, and Dairine led the way up the steps to the house and unlocked the back door. "Come on, I'll just be a few minutes . . ."

Mehrnaz followed her through the kitchen and dining room, and looked around in wonder. "It's all so *snug!* I could wear it like a coat."

Dairine snickered as she headed up the stairs to her room, because sometimes when the house got full of people, or wizards, or both, it *felt* that tight. "You seriously don't like having all that extra space?"

"Sometimes," Mehrnaz said, following her up. "There are a lot of us, sometimes the place gets awfully full. But it's so empty when everyone's out *doing* things. I start feeling like a bean in a gourd, rattling around . . ."

They chatted while Dairine rifled through her closet for a tank top and a loose shirt to throw over it, now that she was out of an environment where she didn't feel the need to cover up so completely. Mehrnaz bounced on her bed and gazed around at Dairine's desk and books and posters, and Spot clambered up on the bed beside her and watched them both curiously. As she ducked out and down the hall to the bathroom to change, Dairine caught a glance from one of his spare eyes as it stalked around to follow her.

She likes you.

Possibly a good thing, Dairine said silently to Spot as she closed the bathroom door.

And she thinks you might be a friend.

Yeah, I was getting that. The funny thing about it was that Dairine didn't have many of those who were local. *All the people I like are from far away*, she thought. *And sometimes it seems like the farther away they are, the better I like them.*

There's a message there somewhere, Spot said.

Dairine wondered about that while she got out of her sweaty clothes and into the fresh ones. *No question, she's nice. But I don't want to hurt her feelings, don't want her expecting anything from me that's not going to happen. Need to make sure she knows that after this is over, I have to get back to business. Got somebody to find . . .*

She paused long enough to splash some water on

her face and scrub it dry, then headed back to her room. Mehrnaz had gotten up again and was peering out the side window, past the neighbors' driveway and into their messy yard, with the kind of rapt and wistful expression Dairine would normally have expected to see on someone looking through a window into Shangri-La or Middle-earth.

"You ready?" Dairine said. "It's almost twelve-thirty . . . we should get going."

Mehrnaz turned and suddenly Dairine was thrown off balance by the nervousness in those dark eyes. "Is this going to work?" she said. "Truly?"

Is this going to work . . . ? It was a question Dairine remembered from what seemed too long ago. The stakes had been much higher then. *But how do I know what this feels like for her? Except by looking at her.*

"I told you it will," Dairine said. "And I told you I didn't have time to BS you, Mehrnaz. Let's go show 'em how it's done."

She headed for the stairs, and heard Mehrnaz follow her down, and Spot ticking along on all his legs after her. "Spot, set up the transport spot in the back for Javits, we can pop out in their dedicated transport hot spot —"

But from behind her, as she passed through the dining room, came the sound of a soft chime. It was nothing associated with Dairine's phone, or with Spot. She turned around. "Was that yours?"

"Uh, yeah," Mehrnaz said. She'd stopped in the living room, and was staring at her phone and looking a bit shocked. "I lost track of the time, it's Isha already! Is it all right if we go in about fifteen minutes?"

"Sure," Dairine said, "but if you —" And then she paused, because Mehrnaz had promptly shoved one arm deep into the empty air and was now was pulling something long and brightly colored out of an otherspace pocket. "Um. Is that a rug?"

"What? Of course it is."

And suddenly it dawned. "Wait. Do you mean —"

"Well, I'm a Muslimah after all, you knew that. What did you think the hijab's about? It's not because I don't like how my hair looks or something." Mehrnaz giggled. "Look, I need to wash up real quick. Is there a bathroom downstairs? Do you mind if I use it?"

"What? Sure! Down the way you came and straight back, the door right in front of you."

Mehrnaz headed out of the living room. "Thanks. Just a few minutes for ablutions, and then I'll be in here for ten minutes or so, okay?"

"Fine."

Dairine wandered out and went into the kitchen. *I am an* idiot, she thought. *It's not like she was going to stop doing her religious stuff just because we're on the road . . .*

Spot paused in the middle of the kitchen floor

and looked at her curiously. *Should I go wake up the transport spell?*

"Sure," Dairine said. "Put it on standby until we get out there. Fifteen minutes or so . . ."

Right.

Spot headed for the back door, developing a set of manipulating claws as he went, and pushed the screen door open with them. Dairine let out an impatient breath as the door swung closed behind him — she'd been all ready to go. *Well, never mind. Time enough for some tea or something.*

She filled the kettle and put it on the stove, then fished around for a teabag and a mug. In the middle of this process, though, Dairine heard a sound she hadn't been expecting: her dad's car turning into the driveway. *Oh great . . . !* But she got down another mug while she sat waiting.

A minute or so later her dad came in through the back screen door with a pile of mail from the shop. He smooched Dairine on the top of the head as he started to go past her, but she put out an arm to stop him. "Not right now, Daddy."

"I have to change, sweetheart, and then I have to —"

"Okay, fine, but not right this minute. Mehrnaz'll be in there praying."

"Oh." Her dad blinked as the kettle started whistling. "All right. I wanted some coffee anyway, and a sandwich . . ."

They puttered around in the kitchen together for a few minutes. "How's it all going?" her dad said, pulling the sandwich makings out of the fridge: mayonnaise, mustard, ham.

"Not bad, so far." Dairine wrinkled her nose. "How can you *mix* those? So gross."

Her father grinned benevolently. "So finicky. Your friend in there —" He paused while he started to put the sandwich together. "Mehrnaz, is it?"

"That's right."

"Is that an Indian name?"

"Iranian. Her family moved from there to Mumbai after one of the big earthquakes."

"Oh." He went rummaging in a drawer for a knife. "I'm behind on all this stuff you gave me to read. Sorry. You two working together all right?"

"Yeah. She's nice." Dairine sighed. "Her family situation's kind of odd, though."

Her dad put his eyebrows up at that. "Problems?"

"Well, a lot of them are wizards."

"You'd think that would make everything easier."

"I did too, at first."

"But not now?" Dairine's dad looked thoughtful. "Interesting." His eyes flicked in the direction of the living room. "Meantime, just so you know, Nelaid's coming down to the shop tomorrow."

Dairine snickered. "You should hire him."

"I have to say, if he didn't have such a long commute, I'd be tempted. Among other things, he has nothing but praise for a place where people don't try to assassinate him once a week."

Aha, Dairine thought. *He* has *told him. And Daddy hasn't freaked* —

"Which surprises me," her dad went on, intent on eating his sandwich. "I mean, we don't exactly live in paradise here. It amazes me how many aliens who come to visit seem to like our place better than theirs."

"The grass is greener on the other side, maybe?"

"Well, when a *tree* says that to you — or someone who could be mistaken for a tree — you pay attention." He smiled. "Where *is* my favorite decorative planting? Has Filif come along to this thing?"

Dairine shook her head. "He's home on Demisiv, I think. But then this is pretty much an in-system affair. Sker'ret's the only non-Solar I've seen so far, and he was there to ride herd on the worldgating infrastructure."

Her dad laughed in between bites of his sandwich. "Well, if he's still in the neighborhood and he feels like a snack, have him stop by. All those boxes in the shop . . ."

"If I see him, I'll tell him," Dairine said. And she frowned. "Daddy . . ."

"I know that tone," her dad said, putting his sandwich back on its plate. "And that face. What's the problem?"

"Overprotective parents."

"Meaning not *me* for a change?" he said. "Wow."

On sudden impulse Dairine threw her arms around him. "You're absolutely okay!" she said. "Seriously. Way better than most."

"Wow," her dad said again, and hugged her back. "Not every day I get a thumbs-up like that." He gave her a look. "Maybe I'll let you off the hook about this week's shopping. Just this once."

Dairine snorted, let him go, and picked up her tea. "At least, you got that way once you came out of your state of shock about your kids being wizards."

"Well, I like to think Nita took the edge off a little and made things easier for you. You didn't have it all *that* bad, I think."

She wasn't about to admit that he was probably right. "Is that ham okay?"

Her dad threw her a look that said he knew when the subject was being changed on purpose. "Yeah, it's still fine. Not that it wouldn't have been nice to have some of the pastrami that was on the *last* shopping list . . ."

"Oh please, not you too, cut me some slack . . ." Dairine muttered. "And what about this?" She picked up a jar from the counter and shook it at him. "I *wondered* where all my coffee was going so fast!"

"*Your* coffee? And who pays for all the groceries, may I ask? Besides, Tom said I should try it. Blame *him.*"

It was so funny to have her dad using Tom as an excuse that Dairine broke up laughing, and mostly failed at keeping it quiet. And immediately she started to get upset with herself because she wasn't sure Mehrnaz was finished. But right then Mehrnaz peeked in around the kitchen door, smiling, and said, "All done, and it sounds like a good thing too — what did I miss?"

"Absolutely nothing, just my dad stealing my stuff," Dairine said. "Dad, Mehrnaz, Mehrnaz, my dad, now come *on,* we need to get moving or you're going to get missed!"

She allowed Mehrnaz exactly thirty seconds of putting her hands together and bowing and greeting her dad and being greeted back and all the rest of it before hustling her out the door. Once out, they half ran back down the garden together, Dairine leading the way, for she was starting to get excited now and didn't care who knew. "This is going to be the hottest thing. I cannot *wait.* Especially because we're gonna make Nita's guy look utterly *useless* —"

Merhnaz started catching the mood from her and

began giggling. "Is your father going to come along later?"

"He said he wants to if he can spare the time from work."

"Good. He's so nice! *And* so handsome."

"You have *got* to be kidding me," Dairine said. "Don't say that in front of him whatever you do . . . he'll never let me forget it. Anyway, there's our spot. And there's my Spot. You ready, big guy?"

All set.

"Then let's go blow the Invitational open!"

The place was a zoo, as she'd expected. Near the cordoned-off space where Sker'ret or someone else from the Crossings had installed the mini-hexes for the beam-in space was a semicircle of cloth-covered tables: and around these tables easily forty or fifty wizards were crowded in together, checking diagrams and schedules on their manuals or handheld devices and asking the people behind the table for help. On first taking in the hubbub, Mehrnaz froze.

"It's okay," Dairine said, "nothing to worry about, there are still lots of people checking in, we're not late. Go on!" She nudged Mehrnaz from behind.

Mehrnaz moved forward into the group that was gathered around the tables with the hesitant determination of someone walking into a tiger's lair for a chat while uncertain whether the tiger was in a conversational mood. Behind her, Dairine found herself feeling unexpectedly upset on Mehrnaz's behalf. Uncertainty wasn't that much a part of Dairine's makeup most of the time. She tended to plunge into things and deal with the coping part when she was in the midst of the situation; how other people managed their own nerves wasn't normally an issue for her. But suddenly that seemed to have changed. *She wants to be able to deal with this, but because of how her life's been, she has trouble with it.* And what made it worse was that Dairine knew it would be wrong for her to try to shield Mehrnaz from what was going on all around them. *It was the Powers who dumped her into this, or got the Seniors to. And she said yes. So she'll either cope or she'll melt down. All I can do is what the people around her* haven't *been doing: give her space to do one or the other . . .*

The crowd closed in around Mehrnaz and blocked her from sight, and Dairine stayed where she was and gazed around, prepared for any impulsive screaming or fleeing that might ensue. None did, though, and she let herself be distracted by the unfolding craziness. In her arms, Spot wriggled.

"Want to get down?"

Yes, please.

Dairine glanced around again. "Don't get stepped on."

All Spot's currently visible eyes rotated on their

stalks in the gesture he used to simulate an eyeroll. *If it happens, it won't happen twice.*

Dairine chuckled. *Got an eye on something?*

I can feel some computer-associated projects in here. Might as well have a look to see if there's anything that might be of interest to the cousins at the other end of space . . .

"Go on," Dairine said, and watched Spot spider himself away through the crowd, drawing the occasional curious glance from bystanders as he went.

A few moments later Mehrnaz slid out of the crush of people with a couple of badges on lanyards and handed one of them to Dairine. "They've got some fairly heavy-duty wizardries wound up in these lanyards," she said, almost breathless with excitement. "The nonwizards outside will barely notice us if we go out."

"Smart," Dairine said. "Come on, let's check the directory over there and get you set up."

They found the location that had been assigned to Mehrnaz without too much trouble. Mehrnaz stopped before the empty space and looked from one side to the other at the wizards who were already set up; and as she did, Dairine saw her go several shades paler in the space of about a second.

Don't let her freeze, Dairine thought. "Right," Dairine said, "this floating table thing they've got, do you want to keep it? Or push it out of the way, or vanish it? And what about the sign over it? Is it too big?"

"I'm, I'm not sure ..." Mehrnaz said, and she started wringing her hands.

"Well, who do we ask?" Dairine said. "Come on, we need to get this show on the road. Table, yes or no? And let's have the text you want on the sign."

Mehrnaz gulped and recited her project's title, watching as the letters and characters in English and the Speech flowed into being on the surface of the hanging sign, then began to scroll sideways. Moments later the table was covered with the written description of Mehrnaz's spell. And seeing this happening, people who'd been passing by now paused, and some started gathering around.

Dairine looked at Mehrnaz as more and more wizards stopped in front of her stand to see what would happen next. And Mehrnaz looked back at Dairine with an expression that was getting more scared by the second. It was as if she'd imagined everything else about this experience except *this:* real people, standing around and staring at her, waiting for her to do something.

Dairine held her breath, for that second or so as frozen as Mehrnaz's was. *I can't help her past this. I can't. She's got to do it herself.* But the moment kept stretching into a breathless strangled silence, as if everyone around the two of them was waiting for some kind of explosion to occur.

. . . And then Mehrnaz let that breath go. She reached out into the empty air and snatched her wizardry out of it in a tangle of light, whirled herself around once, and spun the complex webwork of the spell around her head as she did, letting it unfurl in air — then cast it outward in front of the first group of onlookers. They all made room and watched the spell-web spin out, settle to the floor, and start annotating itself, and they all went *"Ooooo!"* And there was a patter of applause from some of the older wizards standing in the back of the group.

Mehrnaz's glance met Dairine's, and Mehrnaz grinned. "Fellow wizards and other cousins," she said, "here's what I've got to show you today . . ."

And she was off, and suddenly it was all as easy and calm as it had been in Mehrnaz's home, except that there were a lot more people than Dairine being impressed. *She's got this,* Dairine thought. *She was made for this. The nerves were a blip . . .*

She stood there watching Mehrnaz speak for a minute or so more, in the groove now, concise, confident, smiling, having fun. *She doesn't need me,* Dairine said silently to Spot.

No, Spot said from somewhere down the long hall.

Fine. I'm gonna wander.

She quietly made her way off around and behind

Mehrnaz and around the side of the crowd. Then, some yards down the corridor on that side of the huge hall, Dairine threw a look over her shoulder at Mehrnaz to see if she'd registered Dairine's having left the immediate area. If she had noticed, it didn't show; she was talking animatedly to the people who were watching her, gesturing at the spell that lay before them and already pointing out the most intriguing aspects.

Excellent, Dairine thought. *Let's go see what Neets's guy's doing.*

There was another of the big directories hanging off to one side about halfway down the corridor. Dairine paused in front of it long enough to see that Penn was over on the other side almost directly opposite her. *I could cut across . . . But why not see some more interesting stuff first?*

So Dairine started out the long way, taking her time. But as she passed the tenth or twelfth or twentieth project where she wanted to stop and stare at some fabulous idea she'd never thought of and really should have, she found herself starting to speed up. And it was annoyance that was making her do it. *If only they held this thing more than once every eleven years,* Dairine thought. *I could have been in something like this. I'd have blown them away —*

"Excuse me," someone said from behind her in a rich, deep Caribbean accent.

She turned in surprise to see a very tall, dark,

skinny young guy wearing a polo shirt and, unbelievably, Bermuda shorts. He was clutching what appeared
to be a thick, beat-up paperback book as he looked
down at her. "Ah, excuse me, cousin, but is it possible
that you are, ah, Dairine Callahan?"

"Uh, yeah," she said.

"Could you, I mean, would you, if you have a minute it would be lovely if you would, um, maybe just
sign —"

He cracked open the paperback and held it out to
her, laid open at what was revealed to be a blank manual page. It took Dairine a moment to realize that she
was being asked for her autograph.

She blinked. "Sure," Dairine said, "sure, of
course —" It struck her as she took the manual that
this was exactly what she'd predicted would be happening to Nita sometime during the Invitational. It
hadn't occurred to her that *she* might be a victim too.

Dairine scribbled her signature with one finger;
light trailed after it and burnt her name into the manual interface, glowing there softly when she finished.
"So listen, cousin," she said, tilting her face up to look
at the guy, "how come you're so interested in —"

But the guy snatched the manual out of her hands,
his face set in an expression of terrified admiration.
"Uh, thank you, thank you very much," he said, and
then he turned, fled, and became lost in the crowd a
few seconds later.

Dairine stood with her mouth hanging open. *What was that about?* she thought, completely confused.

. . . And why is it always the tall ones? The ones who're going to give me neck strain?

She stood there for a moment more, waiting to see if maybe Panic-Stricken Bermudian Guy was going to come back. But he didn't, and finally Dairine turned and walked on, trying to work out what had just happened. *Okay, I did some pretty cool and dangerous stuff out on Ordeal, and later, but why would anybody be scared of* me? *I'm nothing to be scared of . . .*

She kept trying to find her balance again, and found it, and then someone else stopped her — a tanned, nearly white-haired, beach-babe-looking girl who might have been Carmela's age or older. She was sporting a bright print sundress and a broad Aussie accent, and this time it was some kind of tablet that was held out for Dairine to sign. And the girl talked at her politely for about five minutes and never met Dairine's eyes once.

Finally Dairine extricated herself and hurried away as a horrible idea hit her. *It's not me these guys are talking to. It's my power rating. Or what it* was. *How is it they can't see past that? Because I'm not that person anymore. I was only that person for about six months.* Not that *that* didn't piss her off to a greater or lesser degree most days. It was simply extra annoying that no one seemed to be looking past the history, past the stuff in the manual, to perceive who Dairine was *now.*

She frowned at herself. *Great. Jumping the gun a little here? From a sample of two? Anyway, look, no one else cares, they're all staring at the projects. This isn't about me.*

And she scowled harder as she made her way along the display spaces full of eager and excited kids . . . *But it* could *have been. It* could *have been about something* I *had some control over, something smart I made or did, instead of something that was an accident, the luck of the draw, just the way things went when I was under pressure and thought we were all going to die.* Dammit —

Dairine's mood, which had been wobbly in response to Mehrnaz's nervousness, now started to veer toward the foul end of the spectrum. *Blood sugar?* she wondered. *Ought to do something about that.*

But she didn't. Instead she headed straight toward Nita's guy. And sure enough, just past a project about covert parasitic wizardly use of the "waste" wind power between city skyscrapers, there he was, with his solar management wizardry rotating flashily in and out of the floor as a big bright glowing globe.

She came quietly up behind the crowd that was watching him. *Which is the problem,* Dairine thought. *It's the spell they should be looking at . . . not that he's making it as easy as it should be.* Penn was extravagantly kitted out in dark skinny jeans and a blindingly bright orange and green urban-camo shirt under a tuxedo jacket that was about a size too small for him, and . . . *Is that a* top hat? *He looks like a clown. Who* dresses *like that when they're doing a serious presentation?* Dairine thought. *Come on. It's gonna take you five minutes to stop analyzing his dress sense and pay any attention to the spell he's laid out.*

And the thing that was the most distracting after his clothes was his presentation — which was as slick as that of a late-night talk show host trying to sell you some kind of slice 'n' dice gadget — and the way he played constantly to the crowd. *They should be looking at the spell,* Dairine thought, *not so much at him. It's like no one paid attention to him when he was little and he's making up for it now . . .*

But for the moment that was fine, as Penn was so preoccupied with the responsiveness of the people in front of him that he never noticed Dairine slipping quietly around the side and behind him to take a closer look at the wizardry proper. It was tidier than it had been, which was certainly Nita's work: she'd told the guy at least part of what needed doing, and he'd done it. *So he's at least that smart. But it's a shame his delivery doesn't at all match the style of the spell. There's this . . . disconnect somehow . . .*

Penn was gesturing and waving at the spell while he went on talking. *Maybe he doesn't so much sound like an infomercial as one of those telemarketers,* Dairine thought, having occasionally picked up the house phone and wound up stuck talking to one. *Like he's reading the same script to everybody and couldn't care less about making it personal.* " . . . With a nod to some traditional legacy structures that date back to the last major shift in the Sun's internal dynamics, around the year 1010 and roughly coinciding with the period called the Oort Minimum, when the Sun's subsurface speeds and flow patterns altered . . ."

Dairine rolled her eyes. *Nice excuse for not finding a more elegant way to get rid of the legacy structures. It's like I told Neets, this guy's lazy . . .*

" . . . possibly secondary to missing structural or energic elements which have 'aged themselves out' of Solar structure as similar surface-weather elements have been aging out on Jupiter and Saturn. My wizardry takes those changes into account and adds a 'total recall' function that alerts a supervising wizard while at the same time autonomously amending the boilerplate on the fly if there's any kind of reassertion shift toward the older subsurface states. Not that anything like that's happened for a while, but good wizardly practice suggests it should be taken into account in spell construction. But it's just a safety feature. Let's look instead at these power structures . . ."

Which are still too fragile, Dairine thought, slipping around to the far side to check out that section of the wizardry. *Dammit, he needs to stop this thing rotating. Is he afraid someone's going to get a close look at it? If the judges get that idea, they're gonna chuck him out on his ear. Hope he has the sense to stop it and lay it out flat when they come along.*

She examined the power structures and saw changes that had been made, but wasn't at all sure they'd been strengthened enough not to snap off when submerged in the Sun's roiling structure. *Well . . . not my problem.* Unquestionably, the guy had some good ideas, but he seriously needed a teacher, someone who'd shake him out of his bad habits. The thought of what Nelaid would do to him made Dairine grin.

She turned away: she'd seen enough. *Put him up one to one against Mehrnaz and she wins,* Dairine thought, walking quietly away around the far side of the crowd, while Penn carried on with his one-man show. *She's got five times the smarts that he has and easily ten times the sincerity. Her spell looks like her personality, like they're connected somehow. His, even after Kit and Nita got him to tidy it . . . it's all over the place, scattered. It's like it has nothing to do with him. Or not enough to do with him.* She made a face as she walked off, wanting to be more engaged with the other projects around her; but her thoughts kept drifting back to work she'd been doing with Nelaid on the management of solar radiation before it got to the surface of the star and started getting out of hand.

Wonder why Thahit's management wizardry doesn't have something like that — these legacy structures that remember previous physical states. Is it too stable to need these? But that seemed unlikely. The main problem with Wellakh's primary lay in how *unstable* it was.

Or maybe there's something like that buried in the stellar simulator back on Wellakh, and now it's taken for granted. Which was likely enough. Even if she'd built it herself, once a spell was in place, Dairine didn't often bother looking twice at its diagramming unless something had stopped working or needed to be changed or debugged. And the interactive simulator on which she worked with Nelaid was a going concern, one that generations of wizards before him had fine-tuned before it had been settled into its present configuration. Tinkering around under its hood would have been the last thing on Dairine's mind, especially when she and Nelaid first got started, for the Sunlord-in-Abeyance had been touchy enough about Dairine and about her connection to his very missing son. They'd got past the worst of it eventually, but at all times the thought of the third party in the relationship, the one who was not there, hovered over all their dealings with each other.

Dairine finally shrugged as she kept walking. *He'd love this,* she thought. *Roshaun would be stalking around through this and approving the good projects in that oh-so-high-and-mighty way of his, and disdaining the bad ones. And what he'd make of Penn . . .*

She had to snicker then, imagining the most likely response: the scornfully raised eyebrow, the long, thoughtful, judging gaze down Roshaun's lengthy, slightly nostril-flared nose . . . and then the crunch of another lollipop destroyed in a moment's princely (no, *kingly* now) irritability at everything that was wrong about Penn. *The guy's a dork,* she thought, unwilling to waste any more time on analysis. *He'll get culled, and everybody'll be relieved, especially Nita, it sounds like. Because he seems like such an overentitled,* under-performing *dork.*

Why do you dislike him so much? something said in the back of Dairine's head.

Not just something: Spot. He was still over on the side of the room, but he would have had to have been light-years and light-years away before he couldn't hear her think.

Dairine laughed. "Don't know," she said. "Don't care. Did you see that skyscraper thing next to him, though? They had a smart computer working as part of that."

I'll have a look.

"Right. Meet you up by the gate hex afterward? I'll go see how Mehrnaz is doing."

Right.

She wandered on down the concourse to pause in front of another display, something to do with making schools safe against attacks by people with firearms. But as she looked the project précis over, it occurred to Dairine that she'd been speaking to Spot in English, and what she'd said to him might not have been strictly true. She *did* care. And the question was a fair one, if a little annoying.

Why do *I dislike Penn so much?*

Over on the opposite side of the concourse, Kit was making his final pass through the exhibits, checking out a last couple of possibilities for token dropping. As time had started to get short before the formal judging began, he and Nita had split up to handle separately the picks that they couldn't agree on. As a result, Kit kept running into other people who were also immersed in last-minute choices, and kept accidentally eavesdropping on conversations that even in this context were unusual. Some of the oddest ones — and the least inhibited — occurred when the competitor wasn't onsite to explain things.

"Why would you want to *do* that to water?"

"To show off?"

"Yeah, well, an eighth matter-state sounds *interesting,* but what's it *for?*"

Or at another stand:

". . . Well, if you ask them the earthworms will tell you they're okay with this, but you have to wonder if they're just sparing his feelings."

"Yeah, this wouldn't constitute quality time for them, would it?" And leaning over the tank, a whisper: *"Come on guys, come clean . . ."*

And at another:

"Just think about it, though. It's an idea whose time has come. Lightning as an antimissile weapon . . ."

"Won't help you with ICBMs."

"Depends on which way you're pointing the lightning, doesn't it?"

That was one of the last places where Kit dropped a token as he came to the far end of the exhibition hall, at the other end from where he and Nita had come in. That whole area down by the restrooms had been set aside as a casual meet-and-greet space, where people could deal with personal or medical needs, get a drink or a bite to eat without having to go out to the food court, and generally take a break from the chaos of the main space.

Kit went and got himself a cola, feeling that he could use a little kick from the caffeine, and moved over to one side to drink it and look at the people around him. There was something so terrific about being in a place full of wizards who weren't in a life-or-death situation: you kept seeing unexpected things, or things that perhaps shouldn't have been unexpected.

He found himself watching a couple of wizards doing what he at first mistook for the beginning of a dance, and then for a session of tai chi. But suddenly he realized they were *signing*. They were leaving long bright trails of power in the air as they traced out words and phrases in a Speech-recension he'd never seen before — something very condensed though no less fluid or graceful than the written forms of the Speech he was used to, and nonetheless looking completely different.

Of course there's a way to use the Speech without speaking, Kit thought. *Why would the Powers leave anybody out of wizardry just because they can't hear? Why has this never occurred to me?*

"I'm an idiot," he said to himself.

"A moment of realization there?" came an amused voice from beside and behind him.

Kit turned to see Tom ambling over with something latte-looking in one hand. "Hey!"

"Been here a while, yeah?"

"How can you tell?"

"You've got that spell-shocked look."

Kit laughed. "Yeah. At first we thought we'd come in early and beat the crowd . . ."

"Good luck with that," Tom said. "I'm not *absolutely* sure, but if you asked the setup staff, I bet they'd tell you that some of these kids were lined up waiting to get in before dawn."

"Wonder what the people who live around here made of that . . ."

Tom chuckled. "Probably not much. Some of the trade shows that come in here, like that big comics convention — they've got so many out-of-the-ordinary people attending them and wandering around outside that our group probably looks dull by comparison."

"I guess so," Kit said. "It's just weird to be doing something wizardly right out in the open."

"Well," Tom said, gazing around, "it's not like New York's not a big tourist destination. Lots of wizards want to come to town for reasons that have nothing to do with the Art. And since all the contestants and mentors involved are on travel subsidy, it kind of makes sense to have this part of the event someplace they might not have the time or energy to spare to get to otherwise. If they're going to take the time and effort to contribute, the supervisory structure may as well give them something back."

Kit nodded. "Anyway," Tom went on, "seen anything particularly worthwhile? The end of pick time is upon us. Not much more than five minutes now . . ."

"A lot of things." And then Kit had to laugh. "You know what kept distracting me, though? Wondering if someone was about to slip somehow and blow everything up."

Tom's grin was edged with good-natured irony.

"As if working with *you* two when you got started wasn't like juggling chainsaws sometimes," he said. "And don't even get me started on Dairine." He took another swig of his coffee. "But don't worry yourself too much. There's a proctoring task force full of very smart Senior Wizards hidden away under the surface of every Invitational. They've signed off on every wizardry individually, and all of the projects taken together, before any of them are allowed into the same room."

Kit put his eyebrows up as the thought occurred to him that Tom's expertise was writing specialized spells and debugging them. "And if I wondered if maybe you were one of the proctors . . ."

Tom smiled slyly. "If I thought you were going to run around announcing the fact, I'd refuse to confirm or deny. But why would you bother? Since the proctors aren't involved in the judging, none of the contestants are going to care."

Kit grinned. "Okay. But seriously . . . how much effect do our picks have on the judging?"

"Exactly what it says in the rules description in the manual," Tom said. "'Picks may come to constitute significant weighting on the judges' choice.'"

"*May.*"

"Look, we may be wizards but we're not omniscient, any more than the Powers are," Tom said. "If something about some spell snags the attention of a whole lot of wizards, even for reasons they can't fully articulate, it merits extra attention from the judges. Any spell may have a secret message buried in it: a hint at something else useful that that wizard's doing. Or something they're not doing that they ought to be — that we *all* ought to be. You can't tell until you look closely, sometimes in a group. Or sometimes only when someone drags you over to a wizardry and makes you look at it extra hard. So we make sure that can happen, if people feel strongly enough about it."

Kit nodded. "Neets did that to me once or twice. Wouldn't take no for an answer."

"Well, you know by now that sometimes she's worth listening to."

"Uh, don't let her hear you say 'sometimes.'"

Tom smiled lightly. "I hear you there."

"So what now?"

"Besides the judging?"

"No — I mean, are they going to throw us out of here for that?"

"No need . . . it'd only increase the stress. Not to mention the ferocity of the last-minute politicking." He gulped down the last of his coffee and chucked the empty cup into a nearby wet-recycle bin. "Because nothing's more dangerous than a wizard who feels passionately about something. And in this crowd . . ."

He looked down the length of the hall. Kit, following his glance, noticed something else: the noise level was rising. It was already considerably louder than when he'd started talking to Tom. Additionally, he could see people on both sides standing around some spell-displays and arguing.

"I'd say there's some passion," Tom said.

The sound of a soft chime echoing through the huge room made everything a touch quieter for a few seconds . . . and immediately, as it faded, the noise of the crowd rose again, louder this time. "Five-minute warning?" Kit said.

Tom nodded.

Over the heads of some people arguing down by one of the nearest exhibits, the one with the lightning, Kit caught sight of Nita and waved at her. She nodded at him, with an amused sideways glance at the people who were more and more loudly arguing the pros and cons of the antimissile defense. Nita rolled her eyes as she passed them. Directly behind her, some other wizard, a swarthy teen in a three-piece suit, walked by and said in a carrying voice, "Increasing *entropyyyyy*, people . . . !"

The argument got only marginally quieter as Nita walked by it, then started to scale up again. She came over to Kit and Tom, shaking her head.

"I'm ready for a break," she said.

"You'll be getting one," Tom said, "and so will they. Half an hour."

"They're going to judge *all this* in half an hour?"

"The judges have been working all day," Tom said. "This is just the crosscheck session, where last-minute developments get dealt with and the picks are factored in. If you're going to get something to drink and find a quiet place, this is the time to do it, because it'll get pretty unquiet back here for that half-hour."

He glanced around him. "Catch you two at the party later?"

"Sure," Nita said.

Tom vanished.

Over at what Kit was now thinking of as the Tame Lightning stand, the argument was getting even louder. Nita was observing this with dubious interest: two wizards, one a big broad-shouldered weightlifting kind of guy and one slimmer and shaggy-haired, were standing almost chest to chest and waving their arms and alternately pointing at the spell and shouting at each other. The argument seemed to have something to do with ionization. The stand's owner, perhaps fortunately, didn't seem to be anywhere close by.

"Have you ever seen anything like that before?" Nita said, sounding scandalized.

"In the middle of a baseball game maybe," Kit said. "Not with wizards."

Nita shook her head. "Don't think anyone's planning to kick dirt over anybody's shoes . . ."

Kit wondered if it would break out into a full-fledged shoving match before or after the prejudging session ended. "Can it be that all these enlightened, magical people we've been working with are actually just human beings after all?"

"'*Just* human beings'?"

"You know what I mean."

Looking bemused, Nita watched the argument roll on. "Maybe it's true that the worst brings out the best in everybody . . ."

"Yeah. And now I'm beginning to think, also vice versa. You wouldn't have seen any of this while the Pullulus situation was going on."

Nita snickered. "Well, the *universe* was about to end! Kind of a different situation . . ."

"Not to judge by some of these guys . . . It's like that saying about football."

"What?"

"Something of Ronan's. 'Football isn't a matter of life and death. It's way more important than that.'"

"The winning thing."

"The being-*seen*-to-be-winning thing . . ."

Nita shook her head again. "I always thought wizards didn't do this kind of stuff."

Kit shrugged. "Maybe it's just the numbers? We haven't worked with all *that* many other wizards really. Maybe we needed a bigger statistical sample."

Nita's expression was amused. "Maybe somebody thinks it's important that we all find out that other wizards are just people."

"Then maybe this should happen more than once every eleven years."

She laughed. Right on the end of the laugh came a second chime, louder. "That's it," Kit said, as the room started to break out in applause. "Should we go find Penn?"

"Probably a good idea, if it's going to get as crowded down here as Tom thinks."

They made their way down the long concourse, mostly against the stream of wizards and other attendees who were gravitating toward the relaxation area (or in some cases, levitating toward it). "Did you see Dairine at all while you were going around?" Kit said.

"Once at a distance, but she was busy," Nita said. "There were about a hundred people around her mentee. It was a real crush, she was answering questions or something . . . I let her be. She didn't look like she needed help."

Kit nodded. Penn's project had attracted a fair amount of attention, too. *But does that even mean anything?* he wondered. "Do we have a plan now?" he said.

"For what to do if he gets culled?" Nita said. She exhaled in a way that suggested she was annoyed at herself. "Resist the urge to celebrate?"

"Yeah," Kit said, "mostly."

"And if he makes it past . . ."

It was Kit's turn to shake his head. *He'll be*

insufferable, he thought, *twice as bad as before.* Three times.

"We're going to have to spend a while thinking about how to handle that," Nita said. "Because I'm wondering if in some ways we've been too hard on him."

Kit blinked. He stopped and stared at her. "*What?*"

"You saw him," Nita said. "Yeah, sure, Mr. I'm a Tough Guy, I Can Handle Anything? When somebody put a *real* sun underneath him, that changed real fast. What was *that* about?"

"Him forgetting to treat you like you were the wizardly version of arm candy, for one thing," Kit said. "I remember *that.*"

Nita gave him a look that was both surprised and perplexed. Kit swallowed. *Uh oh, did I sound too angry just then?*

"Yeah," Nita said, "okay. No argument. But the other thing still worries me. If he goes through to the next round, he's going to be exposed to a lot more examination, a lot more pressure. We need to find out what was going on with that before one of the judges does, and fails him on it. Because if he passes this, he'll be building himself up and up in his head until the next round . . ."

Kit sighed as the still-rotating globe of Penn's spell diagram came into view. He was fairly sure he knew what she was thinking: *And when he gets dropped out, which is likely, he'll fall hard.* This was as much about Nita not wanting the two of them to look bad as anything else.

At least I sure hope it is . . .

He didn't have a chance to take that thought any further. Penn was heading toward them, grinning, pumping one fist in the air. Kit found himself half wishing that in the excitement Penn would knock that ridiculous top hat off himself.

"A hundred and eighty-three tokens!" Penn shouted at them. "Are we brilliant or *what?*"

"It's not what *we* think we are —" Kit said.

"For certain values of 'we,'" said Nita, sounding a bit dry. "The question's going to be how brilliant the *judges* think we are. Or *you*, rather."

"But you saw me out there! No one else came close to that level of class."

"That's so true," Nita said in that innocent tone of voice that Kit had been hearing way too much lately. "Penn, have you had anything to eat all day?"

"Aww, that's so nurturing of you!" Penn said. "Better watch out, can't have you getting Kit nervous!"

Kit closed his eyes for a second. *He doesn't just have a gift for saying the wrong thing,* he thought, *he's got a superpower.* He opened his eyes and was surprised to see Penn still standing there and not scorched to a crisp.

Nita was regarding Penn the way someone might look at an incompletely housebroken puppy who miraculously hadn't yet made a mess on the rug. "You have half an hour to get down to the far end and eat a sandwich and have a smoothie or something," she said. "If you pass out from blood sugar issues in front of all these people when the results come out, you don't want them thinking you fainted from shock."

"Wow, of course, you're absolutely right. As my lady commands," Penn said, and bowed deeply to Nita, sweeping his hat off. He reset it at a jaunty angle and set off down the concourse, nodding regally at everyone he passed.

Kit and Nita watched him go. Then Nita looked up at Kit.

"The Powers That Be," she said, "seriously *owe* me for this one."

"Let me know when you figure out how to collect," Kit said, and they headed after their mentee.

A little while thereafter it seemed to Nita as if all three hundred or so of the competitors were milling around down in the chill-out space, talking and laughing and looking relieved that it was all over — though there were also a lot of people standing around quietly with friends or relatives and looking tense. It was like the aftermath of any big test at school, the SATs or something similar; relief, anxiety, people talking about what they'd done well and more often what they thought they'd screwed up.

Nita spent a few moments glancing around to see where Penn had gone. *Probably looking for someone else to compare token numbers with,* she thought. At least he'd had the sandwich and the smoothie, and was coming down somewhat from the buzz of his final hour of presentation, as she had hoped. But he'd really gotten into the swing of his presentation toward the end. *And if nothing else, he'll never be afraid of hecklers again. If I thought* we'd *given him a hard time . . .* Nita shook her head. There were people who'd picked up on the prescripted quality of Penn's delivery and started asking him questions in exactly the same tone of voice. *Which was when he completely dropped it and started sounding like a normal person. Didn't think he had it in him . . .*

It was then that she noticed that the sound level in the room had changed — all the conversations going increasingly muted. Irina was in the middle of the room.

She was standing in an empty space at the center of things, and quiet was spreading out around her through the crowd like a single ripple in a pond. That quiet spent a few moments becoming deeper, finally turning into a silence broken only by the faint rustle of a few people still moving around. Then they too were still.

"Well," Irina said into the silence, "we're ready. I want to thank everyone for having done a tremendous job. You know you all have — otherwise you wouldn't have made it even this far. To those of you who won't be going along with us any further in this journey, I want to thank you for committing yourselves to make the effort even though you had no certainty of the result, and were very likely to suffer pain if things didn't go your way. You committed yourselves anyway — and that is the heart of errantry." She sounded somber, but not sad. "So: time to reveal the results."

And almost before she'd finished speaking, the room started to fill with every possible kind of audio alert as those who had such things hooked up to their manuals heard them go off.

It was lower-key than Nita had expected. There was no big list posted, no dramatic calling of names. And (as she saw when people near them started comparing results in their manuals) there was no big deal made over the issue of rankings, or where anyone stood in the standings of those who had made it: only the bare fact of whether or not they'd gone through. All through the room, cries of excitement or moans of disappointment began filling the air at the same time as people's manuals, or whatever instrumentalities they used to manage their wizardry, gave them a thumbs-up or thumbs-down. Here and there, groups of friends started to cluster, jumping up and down or commiserating with sad hugs.

Nita looked around to see if she could find Penn. From behind her, Kit leaned in to say very low by her ear, "Just look for the one making a big fuss."

And sure enough, there, past a couple of small groups of hugging teenagers, was one guy, all by himself, leaping and whooping and waving his manual in the air. "We should go congratulate him," Nita said.

"He should be congratulating *you*," Kit said. "Care to bet on that happening?"

Nita laughed. "Wouldn't waste my money," she said. "Come on."

As Penn spotted them coming toward him, he assumed an expression that was impossible to describe in any other way than smug. "Did I tell you?" he shouted. "Did I *tell* you how it was going to go?"

"You did," Kit said, and bumped fists with him. "Now we start the heavy lifting."

"Not right now," Penn said. "Tonight we celebrate!" He held out his hand to Nita. "Well?"

She took it. "You did good," she said.

He started to lift her hand. Nita gave him a look. He stopped, but he didn't let it go. "Don't get cute," Nita said. "You'll spoil it."

Penn dropped her hand and grinned. "But I *am* cute," he said. "By definition."

"We're using *such* different dictionaries," Nita said,

and turned away. "Come on . . . let's go to the losers' party."

On the far side of the room, Dairine and Mehrnaz were standing quietly together, watching the crowd.

Dairine had been carefully controlling her own excitement. When the end-chime had rung and she'd turned to Mehrnaz to congratulate her on the latest of a final series of presentations, each one better than the last, she'd caught a look on Mehrnaz's face that was more than relief. It was fear.

"It's going to be okay," Dairine had said. But Mehrnaz's face hadn't dropped that terrified look. "Whatever happens, you've done great. Seriously!"

"I think I could use some water," Mehrnaz said, sounding a little faint.

They'd made their way down into the crowd and each of them had grabbed and quickly downed a whole bottle of water. "Even though it's not hot in here, the air-conditioning makes it so dry . . ." Dairine said. "You forget how much sometimes."

"I guess so," Mehrnaz said, sounding flat and distracted. She was looking into the middle distance at nothing in particular.

"Mehrnaz," Dairine said, and was moved to put an arm around her and hug her one-armed. "Come on. You got the job done. Now we just have to wait for the result, okay? Don't act like the world's ending. You did a brilliant job."

"I did my best, anyway," Mehrnaz said, sounding dubious.

"Which is all anyone's expecting," Dairine said.

That was when silence fell over the room. From where they were standing, their view of Irina wasn't very good, but her voice carried perfectly. And then the audio alerts started going off.

Mehrnaz nearly jumped out of her skin when her little pink diary-manual began playing a music-box version of "Anitra's Dance." Her eyes went wide and round. She yanked the diary open.

And she stared at it and froze.

"What?" Dairine said, and looked over her shoulder. "What — Wait! You made it! *You made it!*"

Dairine would have started jumping up and down with delight, except that Mehrnaz was still standing there immobile. "Wow, look at the numbers," she said, "way more people got culled than — since when do they cull *more* than half the participants? They hardly ever —"

But Mehrnaz still wasn't moving. The face she finally turned to Dairine was stricken.

"You made it!" Dairine said. "Look, that was the worst Cull in the last ten Invitationals and you survived it!"

She trailed off as Mehrnaz closed her manual. "You're upset?" Dairine said. "Why are you *upset?*"

Mehrnaz finally found her voice. "I didn't — It didn't go the way I wanted it to go." She sounded wretched.

Dairine was flabbergasted. "You made it through the *Cull,* girl, how could this *not* be the way you wanted it to go?"

"It's just that now things are going to get really difficult."

"That's kind of the whole idea," Dairine said, with a sinking feeling in her gut. *What have I missed here? What's the matter?*

"Yes, but not the way it's going to get, Dairine. You don't understand. You don't get it at *all.*"

She turned and walked away with a terrible rigidity to her spine: away from the crowd and down toward the doors that led out of the room.

"Mehrnaz? *Wait!*" Dairine yelled.

She wasn't waiting. She simply disappeared into thin air.

"*Spot!*"

He was there already, having caught her concern.

"Find her," Dairine said, snatching him up. "We've got a problem."

Together, they vanished.

11

New York: The Losers' Party

✴

IT TURNED OUT NOT to be a party *for* the losers, as it happened, but one in their honor: a general celebration of what had happened that day, and a place for those who'd attended the Invitational to relax and let off steam.

Everyone was welcome, which was a good thing, because everyone would certainly have tried to get in on account of where it was being held — the beautiful glass-walled upstairs atrium space that was the jewel of the convention center, with gorgeous views of the Hudson River and the cliffs of the Palisades beyond. Huge amounts of food and all kinds of drinks were laid out, and there were wizards DJ-ing a madly eclectic mix of music from Earth and other worlds entirely. But the main attraction was the atmosphere of sheer unbridled relief — hundreds of wizards and guests recovering from the day's business in a large, very casual gathering in which even the unusually large number of losers couldn't feel *very* lost.

Regardless of the competition's results, none of the competitors would be leaving the Cull without a keepsake of their participation. Along with each detailed project-and-results report in the participants' manuals came a token about the size of a quarter, rather like the markers that Nita and Kit used for the Mentors' Picks event. These glowed green for those who had passed through and blue for those who hadn't, and when held in the hand they silently communicated the name of the competitor's project and any special notes or commendations from the judges, along with the participant's final ranking at the Cull.

As she and Kit headed toward the refreshment tables, Nita saw a lot of these tokens changing hands: groups of people who had been positioned close to each other on the exhibition floor were trading them to remember each other by. Others were simply giving them away to friends or acquaintances. "I bet somebody's going to start collecting these things," she said to Kit.

"Wouldn't surprise me," Kit said. He was looking ahead of them to where Penn was more or less dancing his way through the crowd, singing in time with the music: "We are not the *losers,* we are the *winners,* all the babes love a *winner* — !"

He was still fist-pumping as he boogied, and being

(as far as Nita was concerned) obnoxiously happy. *Babes,* Nita thought, and kept her various other thoughts to herself as Penn found a dance partner to start hip-bumping with. "What are we going to do with him?"

"For the time being," Kit said with a sigh, "let him do his thing. Too many other great people here to focus on him the whole time . . . we've got enough of that ahead of us." He glanced around. "Look, they've got that sour lemon soda of Carmela's."

"You mean the one you're always stealing?"

Kit grinned at her. "Yeah. Make it two?"

"Sounds good."

He headed off toward the nearest drinks table, while Nita breathed out and concentrated on letting herself relax. The feeling of other people doing the same, letting go of the tension, was almost palpable. *Everybody's shoe dropped, but it didn't drop too disastrously: no getting called up in front of the room and embarrassed, like something out of a bad reality show . . .*

She went back to watching the crowd and paused as she thought she saw someone she recognized among the people who'd started dancing, though she couldn't be sure. A girl, tall, dark curly hair . . . *Wait. Lissa??* She waved. *"Lissa!"* she shouted over the escalating roar of laughter and shrieking and music.

No response: too many bodies between them, too

much noise. "This is ridiculous," Nita muttered, and reached for her phone, then had another idea. "Bobo?"

You rang?

"Beep Lissa's manual for me, will you? Tell her I'm over here and I almost didn't recognize her without the orange jumpsuit."

I live to serve.

The sound kept scaling up around her as Nita saw Lissa's head turn from side to side, her face wearing a broad grin. Nita waved again.

A few moments later Lissa came bouncing out of the crowd and jogged over to Nita. She looked fabulous in sparkly leggings, a very short silver skirt, and a very low-cut sparkly top, and they swapped a big hug.

"What a look! Where've you been hiding this stuff?"

"Saving it for a special occasion," Lissa said, and did a twirl.

The skirt had a glittery belt hanging down from it, a chain of dark ovals that turned out to be faceted gems. Nita realized she could feel a slight burn of wizardly power from it. "Have you got *spells* packed in there?" she said, admiringly.

"Saw what you did with your charm bracelet," Lissa said. "That was such a great idea. I got hold of some black quartz crystals and encoded some wizardries into the crystal lattices, you'd be amazed what

you can fit in there, there's so much storage space . . .
Oh, thanks Kit, don't mind if I do!"

Nita burst out laughing as Lissa deftly relieved Kit
of his soda while he was in the act of handing Nita
hers. Kit looked briefly chagrined, but not particularly surprised. "Hey!"

"You've gotta *move faster,* Kit!" Lissa said, and
giggled.

Kit regarded his empty hand with a half smile.
"Looks like it," he said, resigned, and headed back to
the table.

They watched him go. "I hear that last session on
the Moon was really something," Nita said.

"Yeah. Ronan's still crowing about it. And daring
Kit to design something better. But poor Matt! The
bitching's not over yet . . ."

They stood there chatting about the doings of the
rest of the gaming group that Ronan had put together
from the team of wizards that had been investigating
Mars and some of their friends and associates. Lissa
had been one of the wizards who'd spent months
doing image analysis on the planet, combing live
imagery of Mars's surface for any sign of artifacts of
the ancient species who'd died out there millennia
before. There'd been no keeping her out of the gaming
group once Ronan started it — not that anyone would
have wanted to: she had an eagle eye for detail and a

clever aggressive streak that made her the person to have at your back when trouble started.

Lissa was in the middle of giving Nita a deliciously shocking play-by-play about one of the scandals of the day — competitors who'd been revising their project while it was *on display,* and almost got thrown out of the Invitational for it — when Nita suddenly caught sight of somebody waving at her from the river side of the room. It was Dairine. Nita waved back.

She lost sight of her sister in the crowd for a moment, but then Dairine came sliding along between the dancers. "It's Dair," Nita said to Lissa. "Looks like she's got something on her mind . . ." Whatever it was, it didn't look good; Nita could see as Dairine got closer that her frown was set in, hard.

"Sounds like a smart time to hit the dance floor," Lissa said, and started off in that direction. "Later, Neets. Hi, Dairine!"

"Lissa," Dairine said as they passed, and nothing more.

Uh oh, Nita thought, *this is bad: she likes Lissa and she barely gave her the time of day . . . Never mind. Start somewhere neutral.* "So how'd your mentee do?"

"She's in." But Dairine's expression lightened only a little.

Nita hugged Dairine. "That's so great! And even after a Cull like *that.*"

"Yeah, everybody's talking about it. There's hardly any point to the quarter-finals stage now. The numbers are so small, they might as well go straight to the semis."

"Yeah. Tom said there'd be a final call on that in the manuals tomorrow. But where'd you vanish to? Thought I was finally going to get a chance to meet your mentee when she wasn't onstage."

Dairine scowled harder. "'Vanish' is absolutely the word. Mehrnaz transited out right after the announcement. Spot's targeted her and he's going after; when he finds her, he'll hold her still and I'll follow."

Nita was confused. "But what *happened?*"

"Knowing her, something complicated," Dairine said, and turned the word "complicated" into a curse. "I'm not sure yet ... I have to find out more. But I've got my suspicions." She shook her head. "Neets, Mehrnaz's family ... there's some odd stuff going on with them. This isn't the place to get into it. But my God, you should have seen her mother."

"What? Why?"

Dairine was shaking her head, but her expression was grim. Nita's heart clenched. "Wait. You're not saying — she's not being *abused* or anything —" She trailed off, horrified. Not even wizardry necessarily made you proof against that kind of thing.

But Dairine was still shaking her head. "What?

Oh, no. Nothing like that. Or at least not from her mom, I don't think. There're just things going on there that . . ." Dairine rubbed her face. "I've got to find out if she needs help somehow, because her home life, *seriously* . . ."

Dairine spent the next few minutes describing to Nita what essentially sounded like a gilded cage, one alternately overcrowded and bleakly empty. Her first thought was that there might be cultural stuff going on that she didn't understand. But Dairine sounded as if she didn't think that side of things was entirely to blame — that other things were happening. "There hasn't been time to find out *what*, though. At least now that she's gone through, I have an excuse to find out. We'll have a ton of work to do to get ready for the next round . . ."

And so will we, Nita thought. *With a mentee who now has what he's going to take as proof of his belief that he's the best thing since sliced bread.* "So what're you going to do?"

"Tomorrow? I haven't thought that far ahead. Tonight I want to find her and try to settle her down. Afterward, assuming she's not already there, we'll probably go home."

"Home home or Mumbai home?"

"Mumbai," Dairine said. "Her mom's kind of a mother hen . . . don't think she's going to rest easy until she has her baby under lock and key again."

Nita frowned. "You'd better not be speaking literally."

Dairine sighed. "Oh, if Mehrnaz wanted to be out of there, no question, she could be out in a moment. But they've got her not *wanting* to be out of there. Whatever . . . I need more data before I can work out what she needs, and what to do."

Nita sighed. "If you need to stay with her, I can let Daddy know —"

"No, it's okay," Dairine said. "She might just need a dose of normal, or what passes for her as normal, before anything else happens. She's got a few days to relax before we have to start putting together her advanced presentation for the panel assessment stage. Not that she'll have any trouble with that. She knows what she's up to."

"You like her, don't you," Nita said under her breath.

Dairine looked sharply at Nita, as if she expected to be made fun of. "Yeah," she said. "So?"

"Don't look at me like that!" Nita said. "I'm not on your case. For you to like her, she must be nice."

"Yet also somehow completely different from me," Dairine said, sounding both grouchy and amused.

Nita held still and considered that for a moment. "You might have a point," she said. "Suits your personal trend, though. Sentient trees and giant centipedes and alien princes . . ." And Nita laughed. *"Kings,"* she said, absolutely in unison with Dairine's voice as she corrected her. "I keep forgetting . . ."

"*I* don't," Dairine said.

"I know you don't," Nita said, very quietly. "But at the same time . . . It's so unexpected. On the surface, anyway, and from what you've told me, you and he are unalike in every major way."

Dairine just looked at her. "Opposites attract?" she said. "Meanwhile, thank you for not saying 'were.'"

Nita shrugged. "It's not if he's a *was*. He's an *is* . . . we know that for sure now. Just not where, or when."

"Or possibly how . . ." Dairine suddenly gave Nita a curious look. "Neets, have you ever . . ." She trailed off.

"Ever what?"

"Tried to *see* him. Where he is." And Dairine made a finger-wiggling gesture in front of her eyes to indicate that she was talking about Nita's visionary talent.

Nita blinked. It had been difficult enough checking the manual, the first time, to discover for sure whether Roshaun was alive or dead. Her relief at finding that he was something else — though not even the manual seemed sure exactly *what* — had been huge. But she'd left further investigations strictly to Dairine, whose ideas of who had the right to be doing what were sometimes fierce. "I . . . no," Nita said. "But Dair, this isn't something I've had great results with. Or a lot of luck controlling. Mostly at the moment the 'seeing gift' spends its time running me around in circles and showing me things that make no sense. Then Tom tells me to try harder, and Bobo laughs at me."

"Well, fine, I get it, you need more practice. But would you try?"

"Sure!" Nita said. "But I may not get anything for days, or *weeks*. Or till after you solve the problem yourself." She snorted and drank some soda. "It's a good thing I have a reputation for blowing things up . . . I can always fall back on that. Juanita the Destroyer of Stuff."

Dairine stared at her. "Is he *still* calling you Juanita? *Why?*"

"Don't ask me. I'm afraid to ask." Nita rolled her eyes. "He might tell me."

Dairine shook her head in amazement. "Seriously, he hasn't looked at his manual to see what *normal* people call you?"

Nita snickered. "He's kind of a selective reader." Then she grinned. "And I'm pretty sure he's never seen the page that people keep asking me to autograph."

"That's happening to you too, huh?"

"Yeah. Callahan's Untoward Instigation seems to have a lot of fans. Or a lot of people want other people to think they know the spell's inventor."

"Or the person who shot up the Crossings when it was full of hostiles, and got away with it," Dairine said. "You know, you should be proactive about this.

Change specialties! Dump the visionary thing and go into weapons design."

"Bad idea," Nita said, with a grim smile. "Going to be dealing with somebody I'd be tempted to test the designs on . . ."

"If he gives you too much trouble," Dairine said, "let me know."

"No," Nita said, "I think I'm up for this. Did you see his latest outfit, though?"

Dairine covered her eyes briefly with one hand. "Please. *The top hat.* I nearly died."

Then her head came up suddenly. "Wait. He's found her."

"Where is she?"

"As I thought . . . Mumbai."

"I'll tell Dad you might be late."

"Thanks." And Dairine was off in the direction of the room's roped-off gate hex without another word.

Nita stood there considering with some amusement (mostly at herself) that it was possible the Powers That Be actually knew what they were doing. She and Kit might be stuck with a would-be solar specialist when they thought Dairine ought to have had him . . . but Dairine had plainly been put together with someone who needed something *she* had. *And she'll go to the ends of the Earth, or a lot farther, to get it handled.*

. . . Meanwhile. Nita finished her soda and realized she was still thirsty. *But then it's so hot in here*

with the dancing, and with this crowd. Already a lot bigger than it was, people from all over are coming in. She glanced around to search for Kit: she'd bring him one this time. But there was no sign of him. *Maybe he went to get another one, too. Let's see . . .*

She wandered over to the nearest of the drinks tables to find out what was "on ice" there — part of the interest being that absolutely no ice was involved. The top of each table in that row had been equipped with a force field with foot-high walls, and wizardry was maintaining the temperature of everything inside the field at a steady four degrees above zero. The only exception was down at the end of the area shielded by the force field, where a plastic bin full of ice cubes was being maintained at ten below.

Inside the field, bottles of all shapes and sizes and colors were ranked up neatly. One of them didn't seem to be representative of any of the local major brands; the bottle was dark green with a bright green label, and Nita's first thought was that maybe it was beer . . . except that all the other drinks on this table were non-alcoholic.

Curious, she picked up the bottle. Behind the table, the wizard who was managing it — a shaven-skulled guy in his late teens, wearing designer sweats over a Black Widow T-shirt — said to her, "Need help with anything?"

Nita was trying to read the bottle's back label, which was not making a lot of sense. "This is — what's Cel-Ray?"

"Celery soda." The wizard looked indignant at the incredulous expression on Nita's face. "I'm not kidding!" he said. "It's traditional."

"Where's it come from?"

"Brooklyn."

Surprised, Nita shook her head. "I've never lived anywhere but Long Island and I've never heard of this."

"Must've been a pretty sheltered life so far," said the young wizard. He flicked a finger at the bottle and its cap vanished. "Go on, live a little."

Cautiously, Nina drank some. It tasted like . . .

Celery. But fizzy.

Okay. I like celery . . .

"Thanks," Nita said, glancing around once more to try to spot Kit. *Well, no rush, I'll walk around the room once and see.*

So she strolled around the cavernous space in the early evening light, taking a moment by the floor-to-ceiling western windows to watch the Sun going down behind the Palisades, and doing some people watching. It was unusually pleasant to have no need to *do* anything in particular when surrounded by so many wizards. *And others . . .* Because there were all kinds of nonwizardly guests there too, family members and friends of competitors and judges and so forth, snacking and drinking and chatting and laughing.

And it all feels so normal. Yet Nita knew perfectly well that the sense of normalcy was an illusion. Outside — in the streets of the city on the near side of the river, in the suburbs across the river and beyond — *that* was what the world she'd grown up in took for normalcy: a world where magic was a myth, something that might be lovely if it were true, but had nothing to do with hard cold reality.

Nita looked up over the dance floor — where some of the dancers, in reaction to being packed too closely together, had used wizardry to harden the air ten feet up into a broad round platform, and were dancing on *that* — and thought, *I think I like this reality better.*

She started strolling again, making her way between the crowd watching the dancers and the people who were now boogying to something from the nineteen-seventies. For a brief moment, as the last gleam of sunlight shot through the room from across the river, Nita thought that through the crowd and off to the far side of the room she caught a glimpse of a magenta carapace. *Sker'ret? Did he come in to have a look at the gates?* She turned to start making her way in that direction, when from behind her someone grabbed her by the hand and pulled her onto the dance floor.

The next few moments were spent being confused

and concentrating on not losing her balance as she was twirled around several times, but after the twirling stopped, Nita found that the person holding her by the hand was Penn. "You're just in time! Lose the bottle, Juanita, I've got an opening on my dance card and you fit in it *just right*."

Nita sighed at the typical overstated delivery. *Okay, I may prefer this reality but even* this *one has parts I'm not wild about . . .* "Penn, it's been a long day, don't get cute."

"Why not? Your sister says I'm cute! Even *Kit's* sister says I'm cute!"

Nita's first impulse was to quiz him about when and where Dairine had said any such thing, but she discarded it instantly. *Because he's a legend in his own mind, and this is probably another part of it.* Her next thought was *Oh, Carmela's here finally, maybe Kit's with her.* The thought after that was *And as for* you, *our sisters think tree-shaped aliens are cute. In fact, our sisters think six-foot-long metallic centipedes are cute. And in* their *cases, they're right!* You, *however . . .*

She restrained herself. "It's possible they might not mean that the way you think they do," Nita said. "Sorry, Penn, better cross me off."

"Aww, you'll break my heart!"

She shrugged, waggled her Cel-Ray bottle at him in what she hoped was an amiable if otherwise noncommittal manner, and did her best to vanish into the crowd. Fortunately that wasn't too difficult. But when she came out the other side, to the gate hex's roped-off section, she found that Sker'ret had disappeared. *Maybe literally,* she thought. *He's got a lot to keep his eyes on, all of them, no matter where he is. Never mind . . . Any sign of Kit?*

She glanced around but couldn't see him anywhere. On this side there were some chairs and cushioned benches, and kids were relaxing on them, drinking and chatting. Nita wandered along down through the seating area, pausing to take a swig of the celery soda. As she lowered the bottle, her gaze fell on one bench nearby that was empty except for the single guy sitting there, a very average-looking sort — jeans, sneakers, a striped sweater, dark blond hair, a bit stocky and round-faced and carrying some extra weight around the tummy. *Don't know if I'd wear horizontal stripes if I was him,* she thought, *but he seems to pull it off.* He had one of those cheerful faces.

He caught the look and grinned at Nita. "Cousin," he said in the Speech, "I greet thee."

It wasn't the usual salutation, and more to the point, the recension was very formal, very . . . *old.* It wasn't Enactive: Nita had had a good while to get to grips with that version of the Speech while she was doing her first kernel studies. *Wonder where this guy came in from,* she thought: there were people from so many different places onsite that Nita had simply stopped guessing their origins.

"Well, I greet you too, cousin," Nita said. "Taking it easy for a while? Can't blame you." She smiled and wiped her forehead. Even with wizardry helping out the air-conditioning, it was hot in here. "Need a drink of something?"

"Oh, thou needst not serve me, cuz!"

"No problem, I'll be done with this in a moment and I was thinking about another." Which was true enough: the slightly bitter taste of the Cel-Ray had caught her by surprise at first, but it grew on you. "They've got the usual sodas and fruit juice. If you're of drinking age in your jurisdiction and you feel like indulging, there's harder stuff . . ."

"Harder?"

"Well, alcoholic."

"I am not averse to such molecular structures," the guy said, musing. "Yet . . . Would there be water?"

"A bunch of kinds. Get you one?"

"Pray do. With gas, possibly?"

"Fizzy it is."

Nita went off to the nearest drinks table, finished her Cel-Ray, and swapped the empty bottle for a full one. Then she found a sparkling water bottle and wandered back to sit down next to the guy in the striped sweater. She handed him his drink. "Your health," Nita said, holding up her bottle.

He looked at it in slight confusion.

Nita laughed. "Uh, you clunk them together. At least some of us do that around here."

"Oh! I see. *Na'gekh emeirsith*, then."

"Yeah, mud in your eye too, my Advisory always says."

The young guy's mouth quirked up in amusement. They both drank. "So what do you make of the results so far?" Nita said.

"'Tis all a wonder and a confusion, thus far. So many names, so many gifts."

"They've got a postevent analysis app running in the manuals," Nita said. "What's the old saying? 'You can't tell the players without a scorecard'? Something like that. Or you could hunt down one of the wizards who was doing sideline analysis today. They're all in here relaxing now that this round's action is over."

"Nay, I've no wish to trouble them now in their repose. I'm but late-come myself: on me their expertise would be naught but ill spent. Enough it is to look on the gathering as thou dost, at ease."

Nita had to laugh. "You know, cousin, you can loosen up a little, you're among friends . . ."

"Loosen up?"

"The recension," Nita said. "I mean, I get that

you're serious about the older language structure, but . . ." She waved a hand. "Way too formal! Give the tough grammar the evening off."

He giggled. "Oh, okay. I wasn't sure I had permission."

His giggle made her want to laugh too: there was just something generally funny about him. "Honestly," she said, "it's not a problem. No one in *this* crowd's going to stand on ceremony." She looked out over the dance floor as one of the couples up on the hardened-air platform stage-dived out over the surrounding crowd, drifted down onto them as slowly as falling leaves, and were crowd-surfed off to one side.

"Seems you're right," the young guy said, and chuckled. "Those folks over there — what're they doing?"

Nita followed his gaze. "Oh. I think they call that pogoing. It was big a long time ago. Looks like it's coming back . . ."

They sat there chatting for some minutes while Nita split her attention between watching for Kit and trying to figure out where her companion's accent came from. *I don't know why, but he reminds me of somebody,* Nita thought. He hadn't offered a name, and that wasn't a big deal: some wizards were sensitive about personal names, feeling (not without reason) that some aspects of their power might be closely associated with them. *Or do I know him from somewhere else? And if I do, what's the matter with me, because how would I ever meet this guy and not remember him? He's such a trip.*

It was like meeting someone on the street but not knowing who they are because you're seeing them in a different context from usual. *Like that one lady who works over at the big supermarket in Freeport, the time she came into Daddy's shop to buy some flowers, and we just couldn't identify her because she didn't have the store's uniform jacket and the name tag on.* Now, in the same mode, Nita sat there racking her brains. *Did we meet him on the Moon during the Pullulus situation? Or maybe I've seen him somewhere else, dressed differently? Something more formal, not jeans and stripes and . . .*

Wait. Stripes?

It hit her all at once. *Planetaries. Mr. Bynkij said there were* Planetaries *here.*

"Oh my *God,*" Nita said.

Her companion looked at her in slight confusion, but even so, he was smiling. "It's been a while since anyone's made *that* mistake," he said.

Nita felt like an idiot, and didn't care. The humor, the laughter: the *joviality. Oh God. Do I even* listen *to myself?* "I can't believe it. You're *Jupiter.*"

Her companion looked down at his sweater with vague concern. "Was it this?" he said, pulling the sweater out a little from his middle. "Please tell me it wasn't the stripes." He blew out an exasperated breath. "I *told* Saturn this was too much."

I told Saturn. *I can't cope with this . . . !*

Nita tried to get a grip. "What do I call you?" When the wizard mediating for a planet was of another species, that Planetary was often called by his or her or its planet's name: the way European kings or queens used to be called formally by the names of their countries. But this was also a matter of identity, because Jupiter was a being.

"Well," he said after a moment. "Some of your people used to call me Jove . . ."

"Jove," Nita said, trying it on. "Jovie . . ."

He giggled once more, a ridiculously contagious sound. "I don't think anyone's ever put a diminutive on it," said the largest planet in the Solar System. "Jovie, then. And as for you, nondiminutive cuz — for today, wonder of wonders, you're the size of a planet —"

"Nita. Nita Callahan. And please," she said, grinning. "Size jokes? Too many ways to take those wrong. And here I went all the way over to that table to bring you bottled water! You be nice."

Jupiter laughed and drank his water. Nita drank her soda, wondering how much congruency the concept "his" had with what was going on with him. *Or anything else. How do you have a gender when you're made of hydrogen and helium?*

Then again, carbon doesn't come with an automatic

gender either ... In any case, gas giants didn't seem to have all that much trouble becoming sentient. Sometimes they developed extra species to keep them company, but just as often they sailed along their orbits in uncounted millennia of splendid solitude, thinking thoughts no human could easily understand. They had a bent for philosophy, and also for math and physics, given that they were living the physics of their lives on a scale that few other sentient beings did.

"So," Nita said finally, about halfway down her Cel-Ray bottle, "you came all the way up here, and did this —" she waggled her bottle at his shape change, unquestionably a work of art in terms of displacement of mass alone — "just to see what the new intake looks like?"

"Indeed. Sorry, I meant 'yeah.' It's hard, you know, just changing recensions all of a sudden!"

"I know," Nita said. "I've been there." She rolled the bottle back and forth between her hands.

"We work often enough with Earth's wizards, all of us," Jupiter said. "It's wise to know them better as they come fully into their practice." He gave Nita a look. "For you were busy with Mars not too long ago, weren't you?"

Nita blushed. "I was one of the team."

"But it was your work that reforged the planet's kernel," Jupiter said, "and I stood guard over that while the species who'd come to live on Mars slowly found their way back to the One. *That's* why you seemed familiar to me. The name I knew, and the being; but the shape, only at second hand. Because you were in on that group debrief, weren't you, when the intervention was finally finished."

"Yeah," Nita said. She was nervous about admitting that her memories of the debrief were sketchy. Bad enough that Irina had been dissecting their performance, but the presence of an outer Planetary in the conversation, vast, massive, and *old,* had left her feeling very small, nervous, and ephemeral at the time.

"So that explains it," Jupiter said. "The familiarity. At any rate, when all that was handled, I said to myself, 'They did very well on little notice and in a situation they weren't sure how to handle.' So when the Invitational schedule was settled, I thought it might be wise to drop by." He shifted his shoulders a bit. "Though the business of handling the visitation can be a bit complex in terms of the physics . . ."

Nita watched him stretch, with a slight air of discomfort that reminded her of someone wearing jeans that were a size too tight. "Does it hurt for you?"

"What? How do you mean?"

"You're so *big,* usually. And . . . there are so many different kinds of matter involved in you. Does it hurt being crammed down so small?"

"Oh!" He laughed. "No, not at all! So much of my matter's empty space anyway, after all . . . I've just packed things down tighter than usual, locally. And left the rest at home. I mean —" He pulled the striped sweater away from him again, looked at it. "Clothes, that's what you call these?"

"That's right."

"And you have others."

"Sure."

"But you wouldn't normally wear them all at once."

"Uh, no!" Nita laughed. "No, that wouldn't work too well."

"This is like that," Jupiter said. "You wear one thing at a time. If I'd worn all my monatomic hydrogen to this do, there wouldn't be anyplace for anyone *else* to sit down . . ."

Nita had to work at controlling her laughter again. "You said Saturn said something to you about —" She waved her bottle at the shirt. "Are you buddies? Well, wait, of course you would be, you're only an orbit away from each other . . ."

Jupiter smiled. "A bit more than that. We're dating."

"*Really?* Wow." Nita let out a breath of amusement, because since she'd said the B word to Kit, the whole issue of relationships seemed to be stalking her most of the time. "What does that look like for planets?"

He blinked. "Look like?"

"I mean, when you're close. When you . . ." *I'm*

about to discuss sex with a planet. Yes, this is my life. But her curiosity was getting the better of her, as usual. Nita cleared her throat. "I don't even know what I'm . . . When you want to express it. Do you, I don't know, get physical somehow? Get together . . ."

Jupiter's eyes went wide. "You mean . . . *touch* each other?" His mouth opened, and closed, and opened again, until Nita was reminded of one of Carl's koi. "Oh no. No, no, no, we don't do that." And then he looked embarrassed. "I mean, forgive me, I didn't mean to sound judgmental, I know it's normal for a lot of you, of course I know that, but the whole, uh, *reproduction* thing . . ."

"Sorry," Nita said, "sorry, Jovie, didn't mean to put you on the spot!" She was blushing harder than he was.

It was almost as if he hadn't heard. "And as for touching, *physical* touching, oh *no*, no that would be very problematic, if we — you know, if our orbits — started to, you know, *coincide* at all, it would get incredibly messy, the gravity and the tidal effects and the radiation and . . . *No.*"

"Okay," Nita said. And then she had to laugh again, because it was the only way she could think of to break the tension. While she'd understood that putting an alien psychology inside a human form could be exciting, because the form inevitably invokes its own psychology and tries to impose that on the indwelling mind, she'd never seen such an emphatic version of it before. "Are you okay? I didn't want to freak you out!"

"No," Jupiter said, calming down. "No, it's just . . . well."

"You should have seen me the first time I was in another body," Nita said. "I was a wreck half the time, it seems like. Maybe because I wasn't paying enough attention to it."

"What happened?"

She took a moment to think where to start the story, and told him about her first times in whaleshape while being involved with the Song of the Twelve. Nita stuck to the technicalities of running a new body in a crisis situation, but soon enough she had to at least mention the emotional contexts, the blood and the breath of a new body, the feelings that came with it, the different ways in which it reacted to excitement and dread and desire.

Jupiter shuddered a little, the kind of shiver you might get during the middle of a really good horror movie when you saw the Slimy Scary Thing From Wherever sneak up through the darkness on the scientists . . . especially when *you* were safely out of reach of its ickiness. "That's so . . . *biological.*"

The way Jupiter used the word sounded like someone trying out an evil term for a particularly kinky physical act. "Well, okay," Nita said, "guilty as charged. But you must have a way to go about it that's *less* biological."

"Well, yes."

Her curiosity was up and running. "So what do you do, then?"

"We resonate."

It was naturally a word in the Speech: nothing in English could have produced the huge shiver of force and meaning that ran down Nita's spine as Jupiter pronounced it. The single word bore with it a terrible weight of meaning, a long harsh deep whisper of what would have been sound if there had been any medium besides interplanetary space to carry it. Even through that, attenuated, distant, it throbbed, far-separated molecules nudging one another as its message transmitted itself through them. Nita felt like a gong that had been struck: the vibration, the message, the *meaning* shaking her, flesh and bone and brain, the blood in her veins and the air in her lungs, all vibrating together.

But not just with the vibrations of that one note. There was another note, somebody else's, huge and message-freighted like this one. *Bandwidth,* Nita thought, dazed. Huge *bandwidth.* Radiation at a distance, heat, light, gravity, color: it all communicated, it all . . .

Resonated. He's not kidding. She was still trembling with it and couldn't seem to stop, had to put her hands up to her ears, then over her eyes when covering the ears didn't help. Inside the darkness behind closed eyes she could still feel it shaking her, immense, long, *old*. But how could something that had been going on for billions of years feel so young? There was laughter in it, *so* much laughter! The agreement was laid down in curtains of radiation and reaffirmed across hundreds of millions of miles in slight orbital aberrations and gravitational perturbations that not even the most eagle-eyed human astronomer (except for those who were wizards) would ever recognize for what they were — two planets delicately and immaterially poking each other, stroking each other, fields interlacing at the greatest possible distances. Surface patterns changed, features appeared and disappeared as the two worlds wrote each other notes in their upper atmospheres, joked broadly by copying spots and stripes from each other, announcing their relationship across vast distances, uncaring if other planets saw it and rolled their eyes. Some features — the Great Red Spot, the Hexagonal Jet Stream — hadn't gone away since an initial early declaration of relationship, around the time humans first started paying close attention to the sky with instruments better than the naked eye. Now the features were more complex than they had been, true. The dance of hydrogen atmospheres and organic chemistries around the borders of the markings had grown fainter and more nuanced: but each of the two great planets was still more or less wearing a tattoo of the other one's name on its forehead.

Nita regained enough self-awareness to shake her head as the vibration of the two worlds' relationship inside her head began to die back a little and she found more room to breathe. "You guys," was all she could say at first. "*Wow.*"

"We have fun," Jupiter said.

It was a staggering understatement. She could still feel echoing in her body the shadows of the complex dance that Jupiter and Saturn performed with and around each other every second ("How can you be dancing around Saturn when her orbit's outside yours?" "It's a simple topological inversion. Turn your back on the Sun and the inner orbits and include Saturn and everything else, and they're all inside *your* orbit —")

And how did I even hear *that?* Nita thought, dazed.

Resonances, Jupiter thought, and giggled. *There's always room for one more in the dance.*

"Wow," Nita said again, because it was all she could think of to say.

"But you know, they laugh at us, the other planets," Jupiter said. "They say, 'You two have been going around together for *how* long? And you're only *now* noticing it? Are *you* ever obtuse."

At that Nita started laughing again, though this time there was a slight edge to it. "Yeah," she said, recalling various recent conversations with both Dairine and Carmela, "well, don't be embarrassed, you're not the only one who gets that."

"Oh good."

And without any warning the crowd in front of them seemed to part, and Kit came through it in a hurry. He headed over to Nita and stood in front of her with barely a glance at the guy sitting next to her, and bent down toward her with worry written all over his face. "Are you okay? I felt — *something* — right across the room."

"Oh no, no," Nita said. "I'm fine."

"You're sure?" Kit said. And now he turned his head toward Nita's companion. "And who's your friend?"

Nita grinned. "Kit, Jupiter," she said. "Jupiter, Kit." She paused. "Wait a minute, I think I got that backwards. The older one should come first, right?"

Kit's eyes went wide as the full impact of the other's persona hit him. His mouth opened, but no sound came out.

"Better sit down," Nita said. "This is going to take some explaining . . ."

It did. It was dark by the time they left Jovie to his own devices and headed across the room. "That," Kit said, "was . . ." He trailed off. "I don't even know how to begin describing that."

"Me either," Nita said. "I don't know about you, but I could use some *ordinary.* And something to eat."

"Yeah," Kit said.

There were buffet tables in all four corners of the big room. The burritos on offer had a lot of appeal for Nita, and she went through several of them one after another, with another bottle of the Cel-Ray soda. "Your appetite's plainly okay," Kit said, looking suspiciously at the soda, "otherwise I'd start worrying. That stuff smells like metal polish."

"No it doesn't!"

"Yes it does," Kit said. "God only knows what it's doing to your insides."

"Only what it does to the insides of thousands of other New Yorkers," Nita said. "Otherwise they'd have the Board of Health after them. Anyway, if you're worrying about insides, *you* shouldn't keep putting that habanero relish on your burgers. You won't have any stomach lining left."

"Come on, it can't hurt your stomach lining. That's a myth." Nonetheless, Nita observed that he changed over to a ballpark mustard relish for his fourth burger.

"You're going to roll home after that," Nita said.

"Look," Kit said. "I've been on my feet all day! And so have you. And these burgers are small."

Nita smiled. "You're just trying to make up for the lack of blue food," she said. "You don't fool me."

Kit sighed. "I was kind of hoping Sker'ret might've brought something in from the Crossings, but I guess it wouldn't have made sense for him to be doing the catering too . . ."

They wandered back into the main part of the room, where the divide between dancing Invitational guests and nondancing ones was becoming more pronounced as the evening wore on. A lot more people were now sitting or lounging around the walls, the sound of conversation and laughter scaling up into a low roar that competed very successfully with the dance music in the middle of the room. Nita and Kit wandered in a long arc around the room, saying hi to various people they recognized.

"What's going on over there?" Nita said to Kit at one point. "There's a whole bunch of people in a circle on the floor —"

Kit shook his head. The two of them set off in that direction: and then Nita saw Kit register something that made him break out in a grin. "What?"

"It had to happen" was all he said as they made their way over to the group. A shout went up inside the circle, along with cries of "Oh, man, *how* the hell —" and "Deal me out, I'm done!" And among these, one voice with a sharp, abrasive Australian accent rose highest of all. "That's it, ladies and gentlemen, read 'em and weep — !"

Nita threw Kit a look. She knew that voice. "Oh, no —"

"Oh, yes," Kit said. As they approached, Nita saw a thin wiry guy in dark slacks and a shirt plastered with giant Day-Glo flower designs. He was raking toward him a huge pile of the participants' glowing souvenir tokens, blue and green both, while others in the game were throwing down their cards in resignation or disgust. "Who wants to buy in to the next hand, ladies and gentlemen? Who knows, everybody else's luck might change . . ."

"Matt," Nita said, shaking her head. "Only you."

Matt looked up at her, and a grin of delight stretched across his face. *"Nita!"* He jumped up and stepped straight through the circle to her, threw his arms around her, and nearly crushed her in a hug. "Long time no see!"

She hugged him back and ruffled his dark hair, which was all over the place as usual. "Lissa was talking about you before —"

He smiled sourly. "I bet she was!"

"But I didn't realize she meant you were *here!* Are you mentoring?"

"Not me. My mate Dokes." He peered up over the circle of card players and past them into the main part of the room. ". . . Never mind, can't see him. But come on, Nita, you could've found me in a minute. There's an app for that . . ." He reached into his pocket, pulled out a WizPhone, and waved it at her.

"Oh no, don't tell me Darryl's got to you too," Nita muttered.

"Are you kidding? No one can resist him. I'm starting to think he's on commission." Matt laughed. "But never mind that. Care to try your luck?"

"I could get into that," Kit said. And he promptly sat down cross-legged in the circle. "Who'll stake me a few?"

A tux-clad young African-American gent with glasses and a studious look laughed and handed Kit a few. "Glutton for punishment, huh . . ."

"Randy, hush up, you'll scare him off!" said a tall brunette who'd made room for Kit on his other side, handing him some tokens as well. She had a small Siamese cat on her shoulder, and Nita found herself suddenly wondering if Irina was around, and exactly where her parakeet was.

"Looks too late for that, Bex," Matt said. "Kit's just gonna have to take his medicine . . ."

Kit looked up over his shoulder at Nita. "Neets? Want in?"

She shook her head. "Not me," she said. It was a matter of embarrassment to her that though she was good at all kinds of things, no matter how many times she tried to master the rules of poker, she always forgot them five minutes after she'd learned them. "You enjoy yourselves . . ."

"Don't worry," Matt said, stepping back into the circle and sitting down again, "I'll clean him out pretty quick if you're in a rush."

"Wouldn't be too sure of that if I were you," Kit said.

"No, it's okay," Nita said to Matt. "I'm going to lounge around for a while and let my dinner settle . . . I'll come back in a bit." She raised her eyebrows at Kit. "Don't let him have it *all* his way . . ."

Kit grinned. He and Dairine played regularly, and Dairine had pronounced him "pretty competent," which Nita suspected meant "extremely good." *Matt may get a surprise . . . but then Kit's surprised him before.*

And it was surprisingly restful to wander around and take it easy. For the moment, at least, Penn was not in evidence. *Maybe the long day finally caught up with him.*

Or he found somebody to go home with . . . Because there was that sense with Penn that the thought of sex in general, or of hooking up in particular, was always imminent. It was as if he thought that all the innuendo made him interesting. *When what it mostly makes him is a lot tougher to be around,* Nita thought. *You hate to say anything to him for fear it's going to bring something like that up ... Who wants to hear some-body talking about that* all *the time?*

She stopped by the drinks table. The young wizard who'd served her earlier was still standing there, and he smiled at her.

Nita raised her eyebrows at him. "You know what I want."

Without hesitation he handed her a bottle of Cel-Ray, and said, "Just so you can thank me later in life, my name is Frank."

Nita saluted Frank with the bottle and ambled on. It seemed to her that over the last hour or so, the general atmosphere of the party had gone edgier, crazier. She could see that most of the adult wizards seemed to have abandoned the field. That was probably why the tall, dark, shadow-draped shape standing near a padded bench in the room's most dimly-lit corner caught her attention.

So very tall, she thought. *Nobody's that tall, at least nobody from this planet. And so very dark.* Nobody's *that —*

As the thought came to her, Nita stopped where she was and stared. For a second she thought she was looking at the Lone Power. *Except what would* he *be doing here?*

But a moment's more inspection disabused her entirely of the idea. About this figure, there was nothing of that sense of nasty evil amusement that the Lone

Power normally wore. A great still feeling of deep cold seemed wrapped around it, yes. But the cold was . . . uninflected. It didn't mean anything: it just *was.*

Nita swallowed. *One of these days this curiosity's going to get me in trouble,* she thought. But she didn't think this was going to be one of those days. Slowly, casually, she made her way over toward that corner.

She knew from the way it turned slightly that the figure was watching her come. *Humanoid,* she thought. That much its cloak of shadows couldn't conceal. But there was no way to tell much more from that distance.

So Nita walked up to it, parked herself next to it, and nodded hello. *"Dai stihó,"* she said, then leaned against the wall and looked out toward the room while taking a sip of her soda.

"And to you also," said the shadow-wrapped form, *"dai stihó,* young cousin."

Such a very soft voice, such a dark voice; and no way to see the face it belonged to or guess what thoughts were going on behind it. But something in the voice reminded her strongly of Jupiter . . . a quality that said there was much more going on here than just the physical appearance. *I think I'm two for two tonight,* Nita thought. *And is it possible . . . ? Only one way to find out.*

"Why're you over here all by yourself?" She

looked into the shadow. "You should come on out and mingle."

"That's very kind of you," the voice said quietly. "But I'm . . . not that much of a mingler. I'm not from around here."

The words gave her an odd anticipatory feeling in the pit of her stomach . . . though nothing like what Nita felt when Kit was in question, not the always hard-to-analyze stomach flip. It felt a little like fear, yet there was nothing bad about it. *Awe,* Nita thought. *Jovie had this feeling about him too, but you had to sit with him a while to feel it, and his was funnier. This is stronger. More serious.*

". . . You're a capture," Nita said.

It was a guess, but an educated one, and the shadow-veiled head bowed in assent. "Insofar as any capture is ever nonconsensual at such a level," he said. "I knew what I was being captured by." A glint of very dark eyes, more felt than seen. "Or rather, *whom.*"

And when he agreed, that clinched it. "Then I know who you are."

"Do you indeed," the darkness said, sounding not so much surprised as interested.

"Yes," Nita said. "Yes I do. And I just want you to know one thing."

"That being?"

"You'll always be a planet to *me.*"

The dark shape looked at her in astonishment. Then slowly it bowed, and its shadows flared outward around it, almost winglike.

"I'm so sorry about what happened," Nita said. "*I sure wasn't consulted.*"

The darkness shrugged, though it was a most understated, fractional shrug. "It was merely a shift in terminology," Pluto said. "A classification issue. Ontologically it's not particularly significant: I bear no one ill will for it."

"Still," Nita said. "I feel like you were robbed of something. Status, or . . ." She paused. "I don't know. And though I understood the reasons for it when it happened, it made me sad."

Again one of those bows, though not quite as deep this time. "I appreciate your concern." The darkness straightened. "At a time when you surely have much else on your mind . . ."

Nita's glance slid sideways to the spot across the room where she'd left Kit.

"Relationship," that regal darkness murmured. "So often an issue."

Nita burst out laughing, thinking about Dairine's line that what was going on with her could be seen from space. Apparently it could.

"You know," she said, "forgive me, but this is weirder than usual. With Jupiter, with Saturn — that they can think and talk, and be wizardly, and even that they can cram their consciousness down into shapes like these if they want to —" She flapped her arms a little. "It makes sense once you manage to wrap your brain around it. They're life forms. But you, you're — well — you're a rocky body covered with ice."

"Well," Pluto said, "since we're apparently speaking frankly, as is the wont of good cousins who seek truth together, *you're* a sloppy skin-contained sack of carbon compounds and water, slathered all over a silicate frame." She caught a glint of amusement from the eyes hidden inside those enveloping shadows. "But not *just* carbon compounds and water. True, you have highly evolved organs in which various structures and chemical processes mediate emotion and intellection. Yet no one has yet succeeded in determining the location of *mind.* Unless I'm behind in the news . . ."

"Not that far behind, it looks like," Nita said.

"Good to hear. Your practice has been relatively brief, as your species reckons time, but already you have personal experience of some modes of consciousness that do not map at all closely onto the ones your world commonly knows or accepts. One of these — I would not say a natural law, but certainly a tendency — is for accretions of matter over a certain size or mass to acquire or engender a specific type of consciousness. Such an accretion may remain solitary; it may over many ages become gregarious. But whether or not it ever touches another consciousness, it exists."

There was a thoughtful pause. "The One does love to talk to Itself; this would appear to be another mode in which It does so."

Nita nodded, trying to think when she had last been so courteously put in her place. "Okay . . ."

"In any case, it's not unusual for solar systems to have mixed populations — some worlds sentient but without a Planetary, some in which the sentience holds the Planetary position itself, some in which the world's own consciousness fluctuates cyclically. But again, relationship's always an issue. Solar systems aren't simply about orbital mechanics. They're about who's doing what with whom, in what emotional context."

"Like Jupiter and Saturn," Nita said.

Nita could just imagine eyes rolling inside that cool darkness. "Quite. But not always on that scale. You and I, for example; we have history."

Nita's eyes went wide. "Wait, *what?*"

"Oh, come now, my cousin. How should I not recognize you across a room, no matter how crowded it was?" And she didn't have to see, or try to see, the smile growing inside those shadows now: it was quite audible in the dark voice. "Many are the wizards of your kind who've visited me briefly, and once having seen the sights have gone on their way. But only *one* has ever dropped her sister's bed down my very deepest crevasse."

At that Nita burst out laughing so hard that she had to sit down on the nearby bench. The dark shape beside her simply smiled more broadly inside its shadows — laughter possibly being beneath its ancient dignity — and sat down too.

It took a while before Nita could breathe again. When she was able, she said, "Oh, I am so, *so* sorry."

"*I'm* not," said Pluto. "It made my day."

"Meaning about a week around here," Nita said, and snickered. "Well, good. Because she still blames me every time her bed squeaks."

"It could be metal fatigue," Pluto said, as if trying to be helpful.

"Um, you know, probably not. It was there for hours and hours. The cold probably screwed up the crystalline structure of the metal in the springs." Nita wiped her eyes. "Don't tell her I said that."

"It shall remain between us, I assure you."

It took a few moments more for Nita to get herself to stop feeling like she wanted to burst out in giggles. "Okay. Look, I don't want to monopolize you."

"I would say there would have been no fear of that," Pluto said. "Nonetheless I thank you for your consideration: when one is normally used to a more solitary lifestyle, such gatherings can be wearing."

Nita nodded, got up, and stretched. "Are you sticking around for the rest of the Invitational?"

"I will be in and out," Pluto said. "The other

Planetaries and I have matters to discuss, and it's rare enough to have as congenial an opportunity as this — where we can also have a chance to view at close range those with whom our work in this System is so closely associated."

"And who dump bedroom furniture on you without warning," Nita said.

"Yes," Pluto said, "and perhaps we might dispense with that in future? It could adversely affect the neighborhood's property values."

Nita burst out laughing again. *What is it tonight? Tension relief? Or all these amazing things happening?* "No more furniture," she said. "Cross my heart."

The dark Planetary rose up in great majesty and bowed to her again, leaving Nita wondering how mere silent motion could be so thoroughly imbued with gentle sarcasm. "Then may the view of the long Night delight your heart," Pluto said. "And let us meet again before the end."

"Yes," Nita said. "Good night to you too." She bowed in return, then headed back into the room.

She started working her way over in the general direction of the poker corner and took several more slugs of the Cel-Ray, for her mouth had gone dry. Apparently awe could be retroactive. *This,* Nita thought, *has been a most,* most *unusual day.* "Bobo," she said under her breath, "have you been taking notes this evening?"

Meetings with beings of Planetary level or better normally invoke automatic archival activity, Bobo said, *for their reference as well as yours.*

"Oh good," Nita thought. Though she then remembered what Dairine had told her about the Mobiles' archival project, and had to wonder if the best use of it was preserving for all eternity the story of how she'd dumped her sister's bed in Pluto's backyard.

She giggled to herself. *What a day. I can't think when I've laughed so much for so many different reasons* . . . Nita paused briefly by the dance floor, which was packed even tighter now, though the floating hardened-air platforms had been removed, possibly for safety reasons. She shook her head, amused, turned away —

And someone seized her by the elbow. "At last! At *last* our schedules coincide."

Nita's dentist had warned her at her last checkup about gritting her teeth. *I know teenage life is a lot more stressful than it used to be, but seriously, Nita . . .* Now she turned toward Penn and forced her jaw to relax.

"Whatever schedule I have," she said, "I don't believe I even had you *penciled in.*"

But his attention was now on the bottle she was carrying. "Don't tell me you're *still* drinking that stuff!" Penn said. "Seriously, it smells like windshield washer fluid."

"Oh, come on, it does *not,*" Nita said. "I swear,

some people just get so unnerved by anything new and different!"

"Like *me!*" Penn said, throwing his arms wide. "Come on, Juanita! Come dance with me. Everybody else has!"

"Uh, no," Nita said. "Seriously, no thanks ... it's not my thing." Even with people she liked, she wasn't terribly confident about her dancing skills. Except earlier, when a slow dance sequence had started, she'd looked at some of the couples and thought, *Kit...*

"That dreamy look," Penn said, "*I* know what that means ..."

And you honestly think you do, Nita thought. *That's the problem. Or part of it.*

"What you want is to loosen up and let the whole place see how you really feel about me —"

Nita swallowed, as this was beginning to get on her nerves. "That could be interesting," she said, "except we'd probably wind up forfeiting our cleaning deposit."

He wasn't even listening. "— instead of wasting your time talking to spooks in the corner!"

"That was not a *spook*. He was nice," Nita said. *As if that could begin to sum it up.*

Penn clutched his heart histrionically. "Oh, Nita! Are you *two-timing* me?"

Nita's jaw dropped. "What? Penn ... *In your dreams.*"

"I mean it! I'm wounded! That you could even *look* at anybody else right now . . ."

Wounded is exactly what he's going to get if he's not careful — She took a few seconds to finish the Cel-Ray and turned to drop the bottle in a nearby bin, reminding herself about her teeth again as a brief cool breath from the air-conditioning caught her from behind and helped her settle herself. "Penn," Nita said. "I hate having to say this in quite this way —"

"But I cleaned those guys out," said Kit's voice from directly behind her, "and thought I'd come over to see if you wanted to help me celebrate. You busy?"

Nita's eyes went wide as he came up beside her. *Not the air-conditioning, then. Wow.* "Not at all," she said.

"Good," Kit said. "Penn, we're off the clock right now. Was there anything you needed to talk to us about?"

"Nothing," Penn said, "nothing at all."

And he sailed off past the dance floor without another word.

"That," Nita said, "was the *quietest* beam-in I have ever seen you do. You barely made a breeze."

"You do a spell for as long as I've been doing that one," Kit said, "and you're likely to pick up some expertise."

She sighed, smiling at him. "Well, thanks."

"I nearly said 'Is this guy bothering you?' Except that it's such a cliché, and also it's obvious that he *is* bothering you. You okay?"

"Yeah." Nita shook her head. "Kit, seriously, you shouldn't worry about it; I can handle him. Life's given me way too much experience with idiots."

"Maybe so," Kit said. "But you know what? Let's give the idiot some experience for a change."

"What?"

Kit reached out and took her hand. When they started moving, it took Nita a moment to realize that he was leading her toward the dance floor as the music cross-faded from the hip-hop beat into something significantly slower.

Nita's stomach did that flip again. "I might step on you . . ." she said.

"Somehow I think I'll survive," Kit said.

It was amazing the noise that could erupt in your head over so short a walk. *I look stupid I should have worn something nicer everyone's going to get the wrong idea everyone's going to get the right idea but too soon what's the matter with me I wanted this but I didn't know if* he *wanted this or if he wants this for the right reasons and what if I'm bad at it what if he decides this was a bad idea what if what if what if* . . .

The introduction to the slow-dance song was already playing, something Nita didn't recognize: not *too* slow, with a soft-rock eighties kind of backbeat and a female vocal. But that was all she could deal with at the moment, as they were out there now on the wood-tiled dance floor, and she didn't know what to do with her hands, and it felt like the entire planet was staring at her, actually *several* planets, because she was sure both Jupiter and Pluto were still onsite, leaning quietly against one wall or another and watching the humans do peculiar human things. *I wonder what they'll make of this,* she thought as Kit lifted up the one hand he'd taken and put his other hand on her waist. He put his head down by her ear and said conversationally, "You might try grabbing hold of my belt to keep me from running away."

"Yeah, right, makes perfect sense," Nita said, struggling to sound slightly snarky even though she knew she was babbling. Nonetheless it was a good suggestion, and once she'd managed that, they began to move together. Nita was glad to let Kit handle this part of the process, as she wasn't entirely sure where any of her limbs were at the moment; her body seemed almost to belong to someone else, she was in such a state of wonder and shock. *This is happening. I can't believe this is happening. In front of all these people. Oh God.*

The vocalist had started singing, but Nita couldn't make head or tail of it right now, because her hands were sweating and she could feel Kit's muscles moving and it was all a little bit too much and he was looking down at her —

And then she blinked, and laughed.

He was still looking down at her, but the look changed, softened. "Something funny?"

"You're looking down at me. I can't get used to it."

"No?"

"No. Not yet. You were shorter than me for such a long time."

"Stockier than you too," he said. "I wasn't wild about that . . . Didn't think it was a good sign." Kit's smile went very wry. "My dad used to say, 'Either you're going to favor my side of the family, where we all get to be six feet tall, or Mama's side of the family, where they specialize in diminutive-but-fierce.' And every night when I was praying I would say, 'Fierce is good. Diminutive, not so good.'" He made a face. "I mean, I didn't want to order God *around* or anything, I didn't think that would help my case . . ."

"I don't think you have to worry about the diminutive anymore," Nita said. "You've got that handled."

She was relaxing now, the noise in her head pretty much on its way to dying back to nothing: at least enough to start hearing the vocalist as the two of them rocked gently back and forth. *I don't know why I was worrying about stepping on him,* Nita thought; *we're*

not exactly doing the tango. But they didn't need to be.
This was nice enough . . .

> *It's kinda funny,*
> *you were always near,*
> *But who'd have ever thought that we would*
> *end up here?*
> *And every time I've needed you,*
> *You've been there to pull me through;*
> *Now it's clear*
> *I've been waiting for you —*
>
> *Could it be you and I?*
> *I never imagined —*
> *Could it be suddenly*
> *I'm fallin' for you?*
> *Could it be*
> *you were right here beside me*
> *and I never knew?*
> *Could it be, could it be that it's true . . . ?*

Nita gave Kit a look. "You set this up," she said.
Kit blinked, all innocence. "What?"
"The song. You set it up."
"Me?"
"One of the most basic principles of wizardry,"
Nita said. "'There are no accidents.'"

After a moment, the corner of Kit's mouth twisted upward. "It's possible," he said, "there was some kind of agreement with the DJ. Who may or may not be part of a gaming group who's going to be playing Ronan's group in a couple of months, and wanted to see some of our planning notes for the last campaign."

Nita's eyebrows went up.

"They're not classified or anything," Kit said. "Ronan knows. In fact, he may have tweaked them a little."

All Nita could do was shake her head at him. "You have *no shame*."

"That's what the Transcendent Pig said when I ran into it in the practice spaces, back when your mom was sick. Or something like that." Kit looked thoughtful. "It also called me a *twerp*."

Nita laughed. "Did you deserve it?"

"Probably. But I was looking for someone right then, and I needed it to tell me where they were. So maybe I got pushy."

"Okay," Nita said. "But that worked out all right."

"Yep."

"Good." She smiled. "Twerp."

Kit chuckled. Nita put her head down against his shoulder, feeling him hug her a little more tightly, and found that she didn't mind a bit.

The song was gradually reaching its end, and to her surprise Nita found that though when they'd first started dancing she'd wished it was already over, now she was wishing very much that it wouldn't stop. *Make up your mind,* she told herself.

> *— The rest of our lives,*
> *I can see it in your eyes . . .*
> *And it's real, and it's true,*
> *It's just me and you,*
> *Could it be, could it be*
> *that it's you? . . .*

As the song came to its end, Kit bent his head down to Nita's, touched the side of his nose very gently to the side of hers. And then he looked at her, not moving; waiting. His eyes weren't just brown, she saw: there was gold in them. *So close.*

"Here?" he said.

She breathed out. She could feel him do the same. "Not here," she said. It was stupid, and she wasn't going to say it, but somewhere out in that crowd she could feel Penn watching them. "Not the right reason. Not for this."

But still he leaned his forehead against hers, and they smiled at each other.

"Home?" he said.

"Home," Nita said.

12

Mumbai / Shanghai / Elsewhere

THE MORNING SUN was streaming in the windows of Mehrnaz's upstairs flat. Everything looked bright and cheerful; tea was laid out on the table before them, along with a basket of sweet breads and two or three plates of cookies and — set aside, as if someone didn't want the more posh and proper foods to suffer by contagion — a brown paper bag of onion bhajis. It was the best breakfast imaginable, except that Dairine knew that the early morning sunlight meant that for *her* it was really just past midnight. Her stomach was growling, and her head ached, and she didn't understand everything that was going on — which was worst of all.

Next to her on the couch, Spot flipped his lid open to display the restructured Invitational schedule. "By the final count," Dairine said, "they threw out two hundred and eighty of three hundred and thirty projects. That leaves only fifty or so, which is a semi-final kind of total. This was one of those years where the judges seem to have come down hard on every-body. It's happened often enough before, but not in the last few decades."

"What made them *do* that?" Mehrnaz said.

Dairine shrugged. "Bad catering? Insomnia? Sunspots? No idea. Check the manual, you'll see all kinds of theories about why over-deselection might have happened before. But theories are all anyone's got."

She leaned back against the sofa pillows. "So what the Intervention management committee is doing," she said, "is removing the quarter-final stage entirely. We're going straight on to the semis. They'll be happening on the original schedule, which is good, because it gives you more time to prepare. Five extra days, in our case. And since this is the first time you'll be going in front of a live judging panel and having to defend your spell instead of laying it out for examina-tion and talking it up, the extra time is good."

Mehrnaz, sitting cross-legged on the sofa across from Dairine, shook her head. "It still doesn't seem like a lot of time . . ."

"But it's a better schedule," Dairine said.

Mehrnaz didn't say anything, just reached out for her cup of tea and drank some of it in silence.

"So you should take today off," Dairine said,

"because *I'm* sure going to. You did a great job yesterday. You were brilliant, you had everyone eating out of your hand, they couldn't get enough of you. But in the next stage what you're going to need is the ability to describe your spell in very fine detail, to be questioned on it by experts and not panic . . . and to make absolutely sure that it's structurally sound. They are going to test it everywhere that it could be weak, and if they find anything significant you'll be out on your butt."

Dairine stretched her legs out. "I told you about the aschetic space that my sister has access to, didn't I?"

Mehrnaz put the teacup down. "Yes, you did. It sounds intriguing."

"Well, I think the best thing we can do for you is take you and your spell in there and reproduce the very worst earthquake conditions we can find, and test the spell against them. I know yours is kind of regionally specific, because you designed it to intervene in earthquakes around that one slipstrike fault in Iran, and the spell has its historical behavior and tendencies built in. But if we test it against a bunch of other sets of conditions — against San Francisco and Wellington and Tokyo, say — then we can both improve the spell and probably impress the judges, because their intention's always going to be to see how useful this spell is in more than one place."

Mehrnaz nodded and poured more tea.

Dairine took a breath and reached for the bag of bhajis and a couple of the paper napkins sitting by it. "I love these things," she said "but they are so greasy . . ."

She fished a bhaji out of the bag, doing her best to look casual, as she'd spent the last few hours trying to work out the best way to approach the problem. *I'm going to have to come at this sideways, or I'm not going to find out what's happening here.* "There's one thing we have to sort out first," she said. "It would seriously help if you could tell me more about what your problem was last night. Because I get the feeling that we're going to need to handle whatever was going on there before we go much further."

Mehrnaz put her face in her hands. "I panicked," she said into her hands.

Dairine was tempted to believe her. Though at the time, she'd found herself possessed of the feeling that Mehrnaz was *prepared* for this panic.

Mehrnaz dropped her hands now, looking extremely embarrassed. "Maybe it was the time zone lag," she said. "Maybe it was blood sugar, or fatigue, or too much excitement. Or all the people around. Everything just seemed to be too much to bear, all of a sudden. I had to get out . . ."

Dairine sat quiet. She wasn't tempted to try to make Mehrnaz repeat any of this in the Speech. If you volunteered to speak so, that was one thing.

Otherwise, it turned into a rather insulting sort of lie detector test. "Well," she said, "that won't be a problem the next time. You get a panel of seven expert wizards and a quiet room to present your spell and an associated intervention plan. Other than that, if you're having trouble managing stress, there are steps we can take to help you get a handle on that." She sighed. "So is your mom pleased? She should be."

"Oh yes," Mehrnaz said. "Frankly, I think she expected me to be knocked out."

Dairine kept what she was thinking off her face. *My money says she was* hoping *you'd be knocked out,* she thought. *And I don't know where that comes from . . . but I think it has something to do with your meltdown.* "Well, what we expect doesn't always happen," Dairine said. "So she'd better fasten her seatbelt, because I think things are going to get interesting."

"You truly think I have a chance of making it through?" Mehrnaz said.

Dairine laughed. "After a Cull like *that,* are you kidding? I'm beginning to think the people who survived that could walk away from a meteor strike." She folded her legs under her and fished another bhaji out of the bag. "The competition's going to be tough, but all you have to do is beat four out of five of the people you're up against. After that you're in the finals, and whether you win or lose, you're covered with glory."

Mehrnaz shivered. "It sounds so impossible . . ."

"'Impossible' is a dangerous word around our neighborhood," Dairine said. "Look, we'll do whatever it takes to make sure you have a fair shot at getting into the finals. After that . . ." She took a breath. "One thing at a time."

Mehrnaz nodded slowly. "Why is this next stage being held in Canberra?" she asked after a moment. "Was it their turn or something?"

Dairine shook her head. "You know, I looked that up," she said, "and there was nothing but a note that described it as 'mandated.'"

Mehrnaz blinked. "Meaning that the Powers told them to do that."

"I think so." Dairine shrugged. "You could always ask Irina. I assume she knows."

The look Mehrnaz turned on her was shocked.

"What?" Dairine said.

Mehrnaz sat there quietly for a few seconds before lifting her head. "You speak of her so casually," she said. "It's so odd. Like saying you'll have a word with a thunderstorm, or ask the incoming tide to run down to the shops."

"Well, we're wizards, aren't we? We have words with thunderstorms all the time. I don't know that I'd ask the tide to *do* much of anything — mostly it seems to know about going in and out. But seriously, Mehrnaz, this whole thing is about winning a one-year apprenticeship with Irina. She's powerful, yeah, but she's not a force of nature. She's about *managing* them. There's a difference. Irina's a housewife with a baby and a parakeet, and people walk up to her and talk to her every day! And if that's something you don't think you can do, your apprenticeship's going to be kind of uneventful . . ."

Mehrnaz sat blinking at that. Then, slowly, she smiled. "You might have a point there."

"Good," Dairine said. "So what time should I come by tomorrow?"

"Well . . . if you're not too tired right now, I had some thoughts about the intervention plan . . ."

Dairine wasn't quite satisfied that she'd gotten to the bottom of what was bothering Mehrnaz, but at least this was a start. She smiled. "Let's go."

"Shanghai?" Nita stared at Penn. "What do we need to go to *Shanghai* for?"

"To see my Baba," Penn said matter-of-factly. "He wants to see my winner's token."

Nita sighed. *Okay, it* is *just after the Cull . . .* But Penn had been using the word "winner" approximately once every ten minutes since she'd first laid eyes on him this morning.

It had occurred to Nita that things could be a lot worse. She'd been dreading this meeting, but she'd had no choice but to take it alone. It was a school day, and this was one of the two days in the week when her schedule and Kit's got out of sync. But much to her relief, whatever had got into Penn last night — and it occurred to Nita that beer might have had something to do with it — he seemed to have left the oh-my-God-aren't-you-gagging-for-me mood behind. This morning, downstairs in the working basement of his parents' place in San Francisco, he was merely insufferably cheeky. *That I can cope with. God knows, I've been getting it for long enough from Dairine.*

She shook her head and got back on track. "I thought you weren't wild about your grandparents."

Penn waved a hand as he went rummaging around in a chest over to one side of the recreation room. "My folks aren't," he said, "but they'd die rather than admit it. They're still all hung up on the old-fashioned filial piety thing. Baba, though, he doesn't care what they think of him. Come to think of it, he mostly doesn't care what *anybody* thinks of him. Which makes him kind of cool, even though he's not trying."

Penn straightened up from the chest, letting its lid slam down. In his hands he was holding something that looked like a tube made of bamboo slats. He shook it open and dropped it to the floor. As it fell, Nita could see that it was a mat lined with paper and tightly written all over its interior surface both in the Speech and Chinese. It spread itself out on the floor, and from it a worldgating diagram flooded right out to the walls.

"There's a place over there for your name," Penn said, pointing at an empty circular stance locus near the spell's far edge. "Climb on in, add all the detail you feel the need for. It's pretty generic . . ."

"Right," Nita said, and made her way around to where she would stand. *My, aren't we businesslike this morning,* she thought. *Is someone a little nervous about this meeting? I wonder.*

She turned her charm bracelet around on her wrist and felt for the charm that was a capital N. From it she pulled out, in a line of Speech-curlicues burning with pale golden light, the template version of her name that she kept for such off-the-cuff transits. This she dropped into the circle, and then bent over to do a careful double-check. Even though it was her own boilerplate, it was always smart to check it once it was in place in someone else's spell. Sometimes unexpected spell elements could alter your own name's parameters, and if you came out of the other end of a transit with an extra head or something because you *hadn't* checked, you had nobody but yourself to blame.

"Ready?" Penn said, already in his own locus, and impatient.

"Yeah, yeah," Nita said, and was about to add "Keep your pants on" until she stopped herself. There were too many responses Penn might come up with that she didn't want to hear. "Ready."

Penn shoved his hands in his pockets — jeans

pockets, this morning, and just a T-shirt over the jeans with some Chinese characters — and began to read the spell. Swiftly the room around them went quiet as the universe leaned in to hear. A moment later came the slam of air as the transit spell activated —

And then another slam as they came out on the far side. Penn bent down to pick up the little bamboo mat as Nita looked around her. Concrete, a lot of it: concrete ceiling, concrete pillars, concrete floors ... "What is this, a parking structure?"

"Yep," Penn said, rolling up the mat and sticking it in his back pocket. "We're right under the Hyatt on the Bund — that's the big shopping street on this side of the river. Come on —"

He headed for a stairwell and Nita followed. A few moments later they were up at ground level and out on the street, and she gazed around in unease and amazement.

Nita had of course seen images of Shanghai before. They turned up all the time on TV and in movies, the splendid upward-spearing skyline glowing jewel-bright in many colors by night and neon-blue down among the feet of the skyscrapers, where the highways ran like rivers. She knew in a general way that the hypermodern downtown was just one side of a very complicated picture in which old shabby-seeming neighborhoods crouched and sprawled in the shadow of the sheen and gleam of plate glass and the glow of a superilluminated downtown. But here, on the Bund, both sides lay right up against each other, seemingly a little hostile. It unnerved Nita.

And the other thing that amazed her as the two of them started walking away from the Hyatt was the color of the air, and her ability to see the air in the first place. "Penn, my God, the *pollution!* What are people doing about it?"

"Not enough," he said, sounding relatively unconcerned. "Too many people here and not enough wizards, I guess. The amount of energy spent dirtying it up is more than anyone wants to spend cleaning . . ."

Nita shook her head. "Seriously, it reminds me of Titan." Penn threw her a look. "Well, it *does!* The same shade of brown, almost."

"Never wanted to get involved with this myself. Seems hopeless, like shoveling out the ocean . . ."

Nita didn't say anything as they turned the corner between the Hyatt and the next skyscraper over, and almost within a block the neighborhood changed entirely to row after row of three- and four-story apartment buildings with shops on the bottom floor, or locked gates in stucco-faced walls through which tiny courtyards could be glimpsed. She felt the urge to look over her shoulder, back at the skyscrapers towering over them, and then back again at the run-down and tattered buildings in their shadow, to try to make some sense of the disconnect.

Shanghai was a very busy city, the streets full of people, and Nita found herself getting a lot of looks as she followed in Penn's wake. She worked to smile at the people they passed, but it took some doing; those who noticed her almost without fail stared at her with either the kind of curiosity you might bestow on some exotic animal walking down your street, or expressions of mild suspicion or hostility. *This is weird,* Nita thought. *I don't mind this sort of thing in the Crossings. But on Earth . . .* She took a deep breath and instructed herself to ignore it and concentrate on following Penn. Shortly he took a sharp turn onto a side street lined with more of the small apartment buildings, and then another turn onto an even smaller street, which seemed to be lined entirely by blank walls with gates in them. "There's not much of this type of architecture left in the city," Penn said. "Baba's lucky to have a place like this. Though maybe it's not luck. He knows a lot of wizards in town, and it wouldn't surprise me if one of them's on the planning management board."

In front of one gate — a wire-mesh and iron-grilled structure set in an energetically flaking blue-plastered wall — Penn stopped, reached out to touch the padlock hanging from the gate's latch, and murmured a few words in the Speech. The padlock undid itself, and Penn opened the gate and slipped through. Nita followed, and Penn locked the gate behind them.

They were standing in a courtyard about the length and width of Nita's driveway. Narrow cinderblock balconies surrounded it on three sides, and there was a stairway up to one of them. "Over here," Penn said, and led the way.

Nita followed up the stairs, looking around her and trying very hard not to judge, but it was difficult. The place seemed exceedingly run-down, and the balcony, though it was uncluttered, was one long passage of peeling paint and raw, stained concrete, the roof above it discolored again and again with rust marks from dripping water. Finally Penn came up to a door down at the far end of the balcony, with a reinforced iron screen door outside. Penn pulled the screen door and the interior one open, shouting something in Chinese. The Speech rendered it for Nita: "Hey, Baba, the genius is here!"

Nita found herself standing in the middle of a small living room with a sofa and easy chairs that when new would not have looked out of place in any suburban home back in New York, but now were pretty beat up and looked like the kind of thing you put out on the curb and hoped someone would steal. There was a new flat-screen TV opposite the curtained front window, and a scatter of remotes and magazines across a central wooden coffee table along with someone's relatively new laptop.

Penn stood over the coffee table, fumbling around in his pocket, and came out with his token from the Cull. He flipped it onto the table and then pushed past Nita. "I've got to get a few things," he said, "make yourself at home."

He slipped into the next room. Nita looked around a little helplessly. "I thought your grandfather was going to be here."

Penn came back into the room wearing an expression that Nita could not read. *Annoyance? Disdain? Nervousness?* "Oh, he's here," he said, "but he doesn't like me bothering him in the daytime. Claims he's busy. Here —" He opened another door. "You go talk to him if you like."

"But I — if he doesn't want to be —"

"Don't worry, he knows some English. He likes Americans! Thinks they're interesting." Penn's expression let Nita know what he thought of that concept as he more or less shoved Nita into the room and shut the door behind her.

She stood there feeling profoundly embarrassed. And as she glanced around, she realized that he had shoved her into the kitchen.

Nita took a long breath. *I will* kill *him,* she

thought, *without even bothering to use wizardry. Just a nice blunt rock.* She let the breath out, and concentrated on taking in where she was. As kitchens went, it was on the basic and run-down side — cupboards on two sides of the room, a small refrigerator, and a plainly patterned linoleum floor, rather worn and grimy in the middle. Off to one side was a window with a stainless-steel counter running under it, a sink to one side of the window and a double gas burner on the other side, with a wok sitting on one of the burners. In the middle of the floor was a well scrubbed, somewhat scratched and hacked-up wooden dining room table. And sitting in one of the chairs around it was a little old baldheaded man wearing gray tracksuit bottoms and a darker gray hoodie.

Nita stood there for a moment while he looked her over. *And now what do I say?* she thought. *Does he know what Penn's up to? How am I supposed to explain myself?*

"Well, young cousin," he said in English, "don't just stand there. Sit down and tell me what you're doing here."

He had a voice like a rusty hinge, and for some reason it made her want to smile, even though there wasn't anything overtly friendly about it. All she said was, "Thank you, sir," then pulled out the chair opposite him and sat down.

They studied each other for a few moments. Penn's grandfather was on the wiry side but surprisingly unwrinkled, with high cheekbones and a strong jaw. If his age showed anywhere it was in his eyes: the lids drooped. But the gaze with which those eyes favored Nita was sharp, sharp as knives. Beyond that, it was intriguing how someone sitting so straight in his chair could still seem so relaxed. There was a tablet computer off to his side on the table; on top of it, face-down and open, was a paperback book in a dialect of Chinese. Off to the other side was an open bottle of beer, which he had apparently been drinking from the neck. "I'm sorry if I interrupted you," Nita said.

"You didn't interrupt me," the old man said. "*Penn* interrupted me."

"I'm sorry about that," Nita said. "He said he was coming here to show you his passing-through token from the Invitational."

"Knowing Penn," his grandfather said, "it's *you* he came here to show me. We're all supposed to be very impressed by his mentors. Forgive me if I don't give him what he wants. At least, not right away . . ."

Nita had some difficulty keeping herself from laughing. "Impressed with his 'mentors,' plural?" She managed to smile without allowing it to look scornful. "But as for not giving him what he wants, I'm with you on that."

The diminutive figure flashed her a totally unself-conscious smile that was missing some teeth. "You don't like him much."

"He's a challenge," Nita said. "But I have to believe there's a reason."

"Can we use the Speech?" Penn's grandfather said. "It's harder to hide what you're feeling."

Nita nodded. *Bobo,* she said silently, *stay close here. I may need you to fill me in on vocabulary.*

I'll grab your vocal cords if you're about to say something stupid, Bobo said.

Nita smiled. "Interesting," Penn's grandfather said, picking up his beer bottle. "You have an outrider."

He used the specialist phrase in the Speech for a wizard whose thought processes were somehow augmented by those of another sentience. Nita swallowed; though it was a blanket term, Bobo's presence wasn't something she was used to having other people notice. "That's right," she said, also in the Speech. "Not many people pick up on it."

He nodded, as if it was nothing out of the ordinary. "I notice things," Penn's grandfather said. "Though mostly I'm a mathematician." He reached out to pick up the paperback lying on top of the tablet, turned it to face Nita, and she could see it was a Sudoku book. "So tell me. Who else in your family is a wizard?"

"My sister . . ."

"No. Outside of your own generation."

"One of my aunts," Nita said. "That's all, as far as I know."

"You've looked no further back than that?"

"I did once, but we only seem to go back five or six generations, and even then we keep skipping them. We may have been 'outbreak' wizards." She used one of the terms in the Speech for newly established wizardly families, specifically the kind that occur in clusters, geographically or temporally speaking. There was some conjecture that this clustering might be a reflection of the Powers attempting to solve some problem that was about to arise. But there was no way to prove it one way or the other.

"A difference between us, then. Our family has had quite a few generations, going back into the 1500s at least." He smiled slightly, a dry look. "Even family members who don't know we have wizardry in the line always know there's something a little odd about us. Though we do try to keep it quiet." The smile went tighter. "We don't mention it to the government, for one thing."

Nita blinked. "I thought China was supposed to be . . . more culturally accepting of wizardry."

"Sometimes that has been true. But cultures can change very quickly sometimes. And this is one of those times."

"There's supposed to be a saying," Nita said. "They say it's Chinese, anyhow. 'May you live in interesting times . . .'"

Penn's grandfather nodded. "It's Chinese . . . though I'm sure other people have said it, too. Other countries, other empires. The world's changing faster than it ever used to. The change comes from a thousand directions, nowadays, and it leaves you wondering whether you ever actually knew what was going on."

"I know how *that* feels," Nita muttered.

"I looked you up in the Tao." Penn's grandfather said. Nita put her eyebrows up at that. She knew what the Tao was; to consider the wizard's manual as being included in it made perfect sense, since the Tao was everything. "You're older than I thought."

"I'd think it would've told you how old I am," Nita said.

"It told me what age you are. But how *old* you are is another story." He had a swig of his beer. "Some of us seem to get pushed into being older quicker."

It was as if he was almost daring Nita to say something. Finally she took a breath and said, "My mother died not long ago."

She didn't think she had ever put it to anybody quite that bluntly. The look the old man gave her was oddly congratulatory, as if he had been expecting her to soften the declaration somehow. "So did mine," he said. "There seems to be a lot of that going around. The human condition . . ."

Nita was beginning to wonder if there was some kind of secret sport among Chinese wizards that involved being borderline rude all the time, and seeing how much of it you could get away with. If not, and if this was merely a personality thing, then it was definitely something Penn had gotten from his granddad. *Well,* she thought, *two can play at that game.* "People die," Nita said, "people get born. Sometimes even in that order."

He flashed a gap-toothed grin: an expression suggesting that he thought she should win a prize of some kind. "My daughter," he said, "was a wizard of great skill. Weather was her specialty. She died much, much too young. It was an accident; insofar as anything's ever truly an accident. But it was one of those events in which nobody living can see any sense." He stared at a drop of condensation running down the neck of his beer bottle. "Your culture has it too, I think; the saying that the Powers 'called somebody home.' Because it makes no sense, what's happened to them; there's no other reason possible, or palatable, that this person who was walking around warm and vibrant one day is suddenly gone from the world."

He shook his head. "The pain you have to suffer for such a thing — it makes no sense. And when there are young people involved, when you have a boy like Penn who worshiped his mother, and suddenly the world is broken and the Sun is black in his eyes because she's not there anymore —"

Nita swallowed. "Entropy," she said very quietly.

Penn's grandfather nodded.

It occurred to Nita that the Powers That Be had known exactly what they were doing when they sent her as part of a team to mentor Penn. "He became a wizard after that, then?" she said.

"A year and a half later, after his father remarried and they all emigrated. It was a very sudden Ordeal." And then he laughed at himself. "Well, what Ordeal isn't? We'd all thought that perhaps Penn would be a skipped generation. But we were very wrong. Typical of him to show us so noisily *how* wrong we were." He took another drink of his beer, put it down on the table, and turned the bottle around and around on top of one of many water-rings there. "Hell journey," he said.

Nita held very still. *That* was not information the manual would ever have given her — certainly not without Penn's permission, which wasn't likely to have been granted. So-called hell journeys, Ordeal-fueled forays across multiple dimensional barriers, were famously associated with wizards who were very angry, or very stubborn, or very troubled, or all three. "Let me guess," Nita said. "He went to try to get her back."

"Of course he did. And you can guess who met him on the road. He doesn't talk about it much. But what he has said is that the Lone One didn't give him a lot of trouble. And though he's all bluster and brag, our Penn, for some reason I believe him." He picked up the bottle again, stared at the wet label. "Naturally he didn't bring his mother back; when *he* came back he was like someone defeated in battle. Any return from Ordeal is a victory. But he didn't see it that way."

"I guess it might be," Nita said after a moment's thought, "that somebody who had that kind of introduction to wizardry might spend a lot of time later trying to find that first victory that was supposed to happen."

"It very well could be," Penn's grandfather said. "I know little about what he actually *does.* That, too, might go back to his mother; she was usually very private about her practice in casual conversation. It was as if she felt that too much discussion of what she did might possibly attract certain others' attention."

Nita nodded. There were lots of wizards who felt it unwise or even unlucky to discuss with other wizards, let alone family and friends, what they did on errantry. *Personal preference,* she thought; *I don't know that it's made a difference to me one way or the other . . .*

The old man let out a long breath, and glanced around the room with the softened gaze of someone looking into another time. "She did a lot of work in here," he said. "She'd have her version of a page of the Tao rolled out across this table like a drop cloth, a big display of maps and charts and satellite imagery. Half the world's storms would go drifting across here while we tried to have supper around them, and Penn's mama talked some of the worst ones out of what they were doing."

"She was an aeromancer?" Nita said.

"She was." His face twitched up in a gentler smile. "And with her being air, and Penn fire in his way, well, they fed on each other. He was in here a lot, afterward . . ."

After she died. "I have to tell you," Nita said, "except for — some similar recent history — I don't know what the Powers are thinking of by assigning us to him as mentors. He only listens to us about half the time."

"That's half the time better than the rest of us usually get with him. As I said, he doesn't usually want to talk about his own practice much. But who are we to second-guess the Powers?"

Nita snickered. "Lately that's my whole business day."

The door to the kitchen flew open. "Come on, Juanita," Penn said, "I've got the stuff I need. We've gotta get back. Work to do . . ." He went over to his grandfather and grabbed him by the head and kissed him on top of it: then dropped the glowing token on the table in front of him. "There, now you've seen it, satisfied?"

Penn's grandfather peered at it. "If I say that I am, it could shatter your whole image of me."

"Too true, Baba."

"It's smaller than I thought. They should have given you something bigger."

"See that, Juanita! If I'd have gotten culled I'd never have heard the end of it. And when I *don't* get culled, it's *still* not good enough for him!"

Nita thought it smarter not to respond to this. Penn laughed and headed toward the kitchen door. "I'll come back and see you when I'm famous, Baba. Better be nice to me then or it won't happen twice."

"If you don't hurry up it won't even happen once," his grandfather growled. "The Powers might have plans for me, and don't think I'll keep Them waiting just because *you* might drop by." Nita caught a flicker of a wry look from under his bushy dark brows: *You see what I put up with.*

"Respected elder," Nita said, giving him a slight bow, "*dai stihó . . .*"

"Why are you bothering being nice to him?" Penn said, holding the door open and jerking his head impatiently for her to hurry. "He wouldn't have bothered to do it to *you.*"

"'Course he wouldn't," Nita murmured with a last sidewise look at Penn's grandfather, and brushed past Penn without a glance.

Dairine stood in the little spinney of sassafras trees at the far end of the Callahans' backyard. The doorway to the place she wanted to go was hidden, but she knew that Nita had left the aschetic space commissioned and on standby. It was safe enough, after all; the portal proper was keyed to the personalities of Nita and the wizards she was working with, which naturally included Dairine.

It was evening, warm still after the day, with just a slight breeze moving in the trees around her. Nita was off working with Penn, and would be for a while. That suited Dairine perfectly. Right now, right here, she was going to be overstepping her bounds a little, and the last thing she wanted was to have Nita lecturing her.

She spoke the brief coded series of characters in the Speech, like a keypad combination, that popped open the portal to the aschetic space. Access to it was still private; Nita had re-booked it for her own use until the Invitational was over. *Which is interesting,* Dairine thought as she stepped through. *I think she foresees a lot of trouble with Penn . . .*

Foresight, of course: that was more and more the

issue with Nita. Dairine was getting the idea that there were things Nita was afraid to see. She'd come downstairs some mornings lately with a very guarded expression on her face. Only Dairine, who had known her longer than anyone else, would've recognized it for what it was: dread. Nita had seen something that frightened her, and she wasn't discussing it with anybody. *And if I ask her, she's going to deny it,* Dairine thought. *She's afraid that even sharing information about what she's seen might somehow change the future.*

Dairine stood there on the endless, black-and-white checkerboard floor and shook her head. Of all the gifts she would've wanted nothing of, seeing the future badly, or even incompletely, would be chief among them. One of the things she'd always liked best about her big sister was that Nita knew how to make up her mind. She would make a choice, and then she would *go* for it, wholeheartedly. But that wasn't happening so much anymore. Choice was beginning to frighten her. *Or rather, she sees a whole bunch of choices in front of her and she doesn't know which one will make things turn out the way she wants. And so she hesitates . . .*

Like I'm doing now, Dairine thought, laughing softly at herself. She felt around in the malleable space to find the otherspace pocket where its controlling kernel was stored. A few moments later she was holding it. Dairine was nowhere near as expert with this as Nita was; Neets had had so much practice with it before their mom died. But she understood the general principles.

She turned the kernel over and over in her hands, pulled out its recent history strand, which Nita had thoughtfully tagged with the image of a clock, and ran her fingers down its nodes until she found the settings for her last session in there with Penn. Dairine squeezed the node, and Penn's spell spread itself out across the floor.

She looked it over with satisfaction as she noted that Nita had instructed this display of the spell to sync itself with Penn's most recent version, the edited and cleaned-up wizardry that he'd presented at the Cull. It was much neater now, much more concise than the original work, but there were still things about it that bothered her.

Dairine stood there in silence, then started walking around the spell, letting it sink in. This kind of analysis was something she'd been working on with Nelaid. What frustrated her at such times, though, was how *easy* he made it look.

And Roshaun had been even better at it. The easy fluency of the way he handled fire, that sense that he and his element were one and understood each other intimately — Dairine wondered rather desperately if she was ever going to have that. *In fact,* she thought, *let's be honest with ourselves here, shall we? I will never be as good as he is.*

Anyway, there was so much more to the way Roshaun had been than mere expertise. *Courage,* she thought. In her mind, Dairine saw again that terrible abyss of fire over which she and Filif and Sker'ret and Roshaun had hung, all the while knowing that they might die doing what they were trying to do — tinkering with the insides of a living star to keep it from flaring and destroying half the life on Earth. But it was a death that would've been over in the blink of an eye. One moment they'd have been breathing, and in the next, they'd all have been sitting in Timeheart, wondering what they'd got wrong.

Roshaun, though, hadn't been content to sit tight and let death come to him. He'd walked down willingly into that danger, barely shielded, as calmly as someone going downstairs in the middle of the night for a drink of water. And Dairine had seen the look in his eyes before he went — and had known why he did it. It was almost too much of a burden to bear: the passage of time made it harder, not easier.

She shook her head. *Not the time to be thinking about that . . .* Right now the issue was Penn's spell. Something about it had been bothering her since she had first laid eyes on it. *Something that I'm missing.* It wasn't strictly structural, or at least she didn't think so. But she was having trouble identifying what was wrong, and part of the difficulty was in the way Penn diagrammed his spells. *He just keeps leaving these big messy blanks all over them . . .*

Dairine stood still again, staring down. *Big messy blanks, she thought. Life seems full of those lately.* The big messy blank left where her mother had been. The big messy blank left where Roshaun had been. One of them, at least, she might be able to do something about. If only she could handle these damn blank spots . . .

It's not a blank space, Mehrnaz's voice suddenly said in memory. *It's a lacuna.*

Dairine laughed under her breath. *See, there's another one.*

Except . . .

No. Just a coincidence.

But still . . . There are no coincidences.

Dairine held still. *It's a legacy structure,* Penn had said in his presentation. And Dairine remembered thinking, *I wonder, does Thahit have one of those?*

Spot, she said.

He was in the house, but that wasn't a problem where communication between them was concerned. *Need something?*

Can you do me a favor? I need the diagrams for the underlying spell suite for Thahit's solar simulator.

Kind of complicated, that, Spot said. *Might take an hour or so to process it down. The simulator itself incorporates something like six or seven hundred smaller spells, after all —*

Okay, Dairine said, *maybe that's not what I need. I want you to look for any sign of structures that might've been left over or held over from previous versions of the simulator, or previous versions of the individual spells. Stuff that's been tagged to be saved on purpose. Can you do that?*

No problem, Spot said. *Leave it with me for a while.*

Hours?

More like minutes. Scanning for something specific will take a lot less time than porting in the entire suite.

Fine.

Dairine resumed walking around the spell, continuing to take it in. She got sufficiently lost in it that it startled her somewhat when Spot spoke to her far sooner than she'd expected. *I have three such incidences,* he said.

Really! Dairine said. *Lay them out for me.*

Overlaid, or separately?

Separately.

Off to one side, beyond Penn's spell circle, three smaller circles appeared. Dairine went to look at them and found that each one was densely interwritten with the Speech, as she'd expected. But each had a space in it that had once been left open. In all three circles, however, the space was now filled.

So Thahit doesn't have this feature now, she thought. *But it did once. The only problem is . . . what are these for?* The Speech-writing itself gave no clue. It merely seemed to indicate that these would be useful as the container for some unspecified energy.

Dairine stood there and scowled in frustration at one of the circles. *Great,* she thought. *Another dead end.* She examined the other two circles, but the result was the same. *This is some kind of safety valve, probably, in case of abnormal energy fluctuations: a place to store an overload until it can be safely released.* The encapsulations would serve the same purpose as when someone dredged a stream or watercourse to make sure that, even in flood conditions, it would never burst its banks. Dairine sighed heavily. Whatever the answer she was looking for might be, this wasn't it. She walked away.

On a sudden urge she again turned the kernel over in her hands and felt around for another node in its recent history. Finding it, she gave it a squeeze, and that ravening, deadly sea of fire that Nita had made for Penn spread itself away to the edges of visible existence, swimming with sunspots, prominence-lashed: the naked Sun, deadly, beautiful, the anchor and source of all life in the System. *I used to think it was going to be easy to master you,* she thought. *Now I know it's going to take a long time . . . if I ever manage it at all.*

She sighed, squeezed the node again. The Sun went out, leaving her looking dully at the spell diagrams. *Oh, Ro,* she thought, and simply stood there and *ached.* Her eyes burned with missing him.

Not that it helped in the slightest.

. . . Shall I get rid of these? Spot said after a few moments.

Dairine shrugged. *No, store them,* she said. *I might need them for something later, and I'm still curious about who left them in place. I can always ask Nelaid about it when I see him next.*

She put the space's kernel back in its storage pocket and then stood for a few more seconds staring down at Penn's spell. *I hate this guy,* Dairine thought. *Because even when he's screwing up, he's better than I am. Even though I'm trying and he's not.*

And there's not a damn thing I can do about it. It's like it was with Roshaun. It was an astonishingly bitter realization for someone whose motto had always been *I can do that.*

Slowly Dairine walked away toward the portal, stepped through, and waved it closed behind her.

Nita dreamed.

She was upstairs in the shopping center a couple of towns over, on the food-court level, strolling slowly around the big circle of it and smelling the sweet-and-sour of Chinese food and the beany scent of burritos and the aroma of frying fat. Bright-colored plastic chairs and tables were scattered around, littered with empty trays and crumpled fast food containers and tipped-over paper cups; the garbage bins placed here and there among them were mostly overflowing. "What a mess," Nita murmured, looking idly around to see if there were any cleanup staff working on the situation. But the place was empty except for her and the one walking next to her, in step, easy and casual.

It was Roshaun. And in the dream, this was nothing unusual. She saw him as Dairine had described him when he last visited here with her and Sker'ret and Filif: ridiculously tall, the long, long blond hair that made him look like an animated character or movie elf hanging down before and behind, the golden eyes narrowed in amusement at the plebeian surroundings, hands shoved deep in the pockets of the Earth clothing he was wearing as a disguise — jeans and an oversize floppy T-shirt that said FERMILAB MUON COLLIDER SLO-PITCH SOFTBALL.

"Yes," he said, "dreadfully untidy. The servants should be disciplined without delay." And his gaze slid sideways to meet hers. There was only one problem with that. The mind looking out of those eyes at her was not Roshaun's.

"Oh, no," Nita said. "Not *you* again."

"But we're such old associates!" the Lone Power

said. It looked at her sideways again through Roshaun's eyes. "And you've done so much for me!"

"If by that you mean I helped give you a chance to be something different," Nita said, "and that since then I've stood in your way a bunch of times when you wanted to keep screwing things up the old-fashioned way, then yeah, I *have* done a lot for you. You'd think you might show some gratitude."

"But I am!" said the Lone One. "I'm helping you right now."

"The only thing you're doing now, as far as I can tell, is slowing me down. Or making fun of something I've got on my mind." She gave him a pointed look, glancing up and down the long, lean shape of the (more or less) late King of Wellakh, and turned away with an annoyed breath.

"Well, you must know that *that's* a fool's errand," said the Lone Power. "Surely you know you have other things to be looking for right now. Much more *important* things. I can't imagine why you're wasting your time searching for the hopelessly lost when you want to be concentrating on keeping someone much closer to home from getting lost in the first place."

The images flashed before Nita's mind again: Carmela shaking with terror, stammering with fear of something that was about to happen. Kit, looking for her, finding her, and then suddenly and terribly falling down into darkness. And Nita shivered all over, because this was so peculiar. *A dream within a dream . . . When the levels nest this deep, how will you know when you wake up? How will you know the difference between the vision and reality? And what happens when you can't* tell *anymore? What are you then? There's a word for that, and it's not "visionary" . . .*

"Yes," said the Lone One. "Such a common problem for people with a specialty like yours. They lose their way. They get overconfident, and go wandering off among the paths of vision one time too many, and after that they never come out." It wore an amused smile that was a parody of expressions Nita had seen Roshaun wear.

"I wouldn't say that overconfidence is the problem here," Nita muttered.

"Well, no," the Lone One said, "because you do keep changing specialties, don't you? Can't seem to make up your mind. Try one thing . . . can't make it work . . . try something else. You seem unable to *settle*."

"Can this not be about *me* for the time being?" Nita said. "I'm trying hard to be useful to somebody else here."

"Yet the visionary who fails to include herself as a point of reference in her vision can't possibly see clearly or effectively," the Lone Power said. "There is no seeing without the one who sees. And if the medium through which one sees is clouded, all the visions will be clouded, too. If the medium's left clouded on purpose, the question then becomes what good you're going to be to anybody."

That had the sound of something that Tom or Carl might have said, and for some reason that annoyed Nita even more. "You know," she said, "nobody with a brain would trust anything you say. You're all about the lies. The smartest thing might be to do the *opposite* of everything you're saying. And to assume that this is all some attempt to lead me off into the wrong direction."

The Lone Power in Roshaun's shape actually rolled Its eyes at Nita. This, too, was an expression she'd seen on the original, frequently when the royalty in question had a lollipop stick hanging out of his face. "The reverse psychology argument?" It said. "Truly, I thought better of you. *You're* the one eager to throw it into my face that I've been given a chance to change. If you're not willing to at least entertain the possibility that I might honestly be trying to be of assistance to you, then what's been the point of this whole exercise? *You're* the one keeping *me* stuck in the old role. And if you won't avail yourself of available help, then *I* can't be blamed. I did my best . . ."

It didn't sound wistful; It didn't sound smug. It sounded blasé. And something about that tone caught Nita's attention. She wasn't about to give up being alert for her old enemy's trickery, but she did have to give It a chance.

"Okay," she said, doing her best to sound as blasé as It had. "What have you got for me?"

They walked along again quietly for a few steps. Then, in an altered tone, as if suddenly dealing with an entirely different subject, the Lone One said, "What's the old saying — that every wizard is the answer to a problem? And that every intervention, every wizardry, solves not only its own problem but others that you may never even know about?"

"'All is done for each,'" Nita said. She hadn't quite known what to make of that concept the first time that Tom mentioned it to her. Later, the more she'd thought about it, the more it had unsettled her, even as she came to understand that it was a simple expression of a quantum reality: that all events in the universe, at least theoretically, were interconnected on levels that beings functioning only in three or four or five dimensions were ill-equipped to grasp.

"Sheer laziness, that's all it is," said the being walking beside her. It was a growl of pure irritation. "The One may try to *pretend* that It simply hates wasted motion, but It's not fooling anyone. All this finagling around with the structure of reality to have everybody possible be happy when they don't even particularly *deserve* to be —"

Nita cleared her throat. "Less bitching, please?" she said.

The Power that invented death stopped in mid-stride and looked at Nita out of Roshaun's eyes with the strangest expression of appreciation. "You have no idea," it said, "how *disappointing* it is that you chose the side you did to work on. We could've been so good together."

This struck Nita as some of the most backhanded flattery she'd ever received. *At least until Penn came along* . . . "I know this is a dream, but try to focus, okay?"

It heaved a sigh and started walking again. "Right. Problem solving. There probably ought to be some irony in the concept that while you're being the solution to someone else's problem, they're being the solution to *yours.*"

"As long as the problems get solved," Nita said, "I can cope with that."

"Actually, no, you can't. And that's where I get my fun. So very often, humans who're wizards and humans who aren't get so intent on having the solution come out their way that they mess up what the other side is doing, and *nobody* gets what they want." It smiled a lazy smile at her.

"So you're telling me that's something that might start happening . . ."

"Oh no. I'm telling you that it's something that's happening right now."

Nita frowned. "And of course you're not going to tell me exactly *how* this is happening."

"Where would be the fun in that? For either of us." It smiled more broadly. "Besides, you like to think of yourself as a smart person. I'm sure you'll figure it out eventually."

"But ideally," Nita said, "not before I screw it up."

The Lone One bowed Its head to her to indicate she'd got that right.

Nita took a deep breath and let it out again. "Okay," she said. "Thanks for that."

The being walking beside her in Roshaun's body threw Nita a rather testy look. "You know," it said, "you're a lot more fun when you're less controlled."

"It's funny you should say that," Nita said. "Because normally when we're playing the game, you and I, and I lose my temper, things don't always go real well for you."

"Yes, well," the Lone One said, "at least there's someone to play the game *with*. Nonwizards don't even know they're playing, half the time. And wizards . . ." It shrugged. "Even they forget. They get into their day-to-day practice and the minutiae of problem solving — do a spell to move this piece here or that piece there — and they stop bothering to look up, across the board, and remember who they're playing with."

And that time it was Nita who stopped walking. She stood still, and looked down at the dusty, rocky ground; and for that moment didn't need to glance up to see the butterscotch sky. *Mars*, she thought, on one level; *how did we wind up here?* But there was something else going on, something she hadn't been meant to hear, or to understand, about the one who walked in the shape beside her. *A long time ago . . .* Nita thought. *Who did you think wasn't noticing you enough when you made things,* did *things? When did you start getting the idea that Somebody thought others were more important than you? And so you did something that would get everyone's attention once and for all . . .*

It was the most bizarre concept. Far away in the depths of time, a great Power, one of the very greatest, moving through the darkness and thinking thoughts that were eccentric and terrible and profound — yet also feeling so *alone,* sure that others thought It was lesser than they and wouldn't include It in their games. And so It went away and invented a new game, one with unending pain and danger at its heart, a level of threat that no other Power had ever contemplated, and a terrible prize for the losers.

A chill ran down Nita's spine. *You can never let on that you suspect this,* something whispered in her ear. *Your anger, that It can cope with. That It courts. But if It catches you* pitying *It . . . then for you and everybody around you, it might be better if you'd all never been born. The only way to win this game is to pretend you don't know what the other player's thinking.*

She looked up into Its eyes, then, and searched them. The expression was unconcerned. Nonchalant again. "Well," Nita said, "how about this. *I* won't forget you. Who looks across the board and tells you that to your face? Sure, it's sensible to be scared of what you can do. Think what you've already done to me. But you know what? That's no reason to stop playing. Maybe *I'll* win the next round. Unless you keep playing, there's no way to find out."

For a long moment, the other's face was unrevealing. "If you're conceiving of this as some clever plan to get me to treat you more kindly —"

"Oh, come on, reverse psychology again?" Nita gave It a look of kindly scorn. "I thought that was off the table. I'm serious. Let's play."

The laughter It forced through Roshaun's throat at that was appalling, meant to unnerve her. But it had an unexpected effect. Something struck Nita very abruptly, a jolt down her spine like half-expected lightning. In the laughter's wake, reflections of a thousand possibilities teemed around her, rustling against one another like leaves in a high wind — as if she stood in a forest of mirroring probabilities. *A dream within a dream . . .* But in this second she surprisingly felt no fear of getting lost among the levels, within the reflections: she was right where she needed to be, utterly centered. "And listen," Nita said. "That working together thing?"

It turned the most confused expression possible on her.

"Don't give up on that," Nita said. "It might happen yet."

The Lone One gaped at her, and Its jaw dropped. "*What?*"

And just like that Nita was awake, gasping for breath and her heart pounding, her eyes wide open, staring at the window in the wall beyond the end of her bed, and the dawn light seeping through the Venetian blinds.

What did I just tell it? Nita thought in shock. *What was that?* Yet her feeling in the dream hadn't been at all one of concern. What she'd said had struck her at the time as *funny*. It had almost been a joke.

But not entirely. It had also absolutely been the truth.

Nita sat up in bed, still staring at the far wall as if it held some clue to what was going on. *Mars. Why does this keep coming back to Mars?*

But that's a minor issue. There's something more

important going on here. She rubbed the sleep out of her eyes and flopped back down against the pillows. "Bobo?"

On deck, boss.

"Good. That last one — *boy,* have I got some context for you. Let's make these notes and get moving."

13

Canberra

★

THEY WERE NERVOUS. They were *both* nervous. Maybe *that* was the source of the problem.

"Why's it doing that, Mehrnaz? I thought we fixed this!"

"Yes, well, I'm not sure it was actually broken," Mehrnaz said.

It was raining and humid outside the flat, and inside the air-conditioning wasn't functioning as it should, and they were on edge. This was now the fourth of the five extra days the restructuring of the Invitational schedule had provided to the new semifinalists. Two of those days had been schooldays for Dairine, and she'd spent all her evening and homework time here. The other two had been weekend days, and she'd spent both of them here, too. She was tired, she was frayed, she was seriously time-zone-lagged, and (to her horror) she was getting bored with onion bhajis.

She was also getting sick of looking at Mehrnaz's spell. The complexities of it were significant to begin with, as might be expected when you were trying to keep two very large pieces of the Earth — each one fragmented into hundreds or sometimes thousands of smaller pieces, subtly or chaotically balanced against each other — from grinding one another into powder and killing thousands if not hundreds of thousands of the unfortunate humans who lived on top of them. And as she tried to keep all the particulars straight, every now and then Dairine found herself falling into that sort of hazy state where one group of symbols or set of diagrams looked exactly like the one right next to it — interchangeable if not meaningless.

And no sooner had Dairine snapped herself out of one of these states than she would find that Mehrnaz had moved something away from a place in the spell where it was working perfectly well, and had been doing so since they started. *And here we go again . . .* "But *you* were the one who suggested that the main slipstrike routine needed to be subdivided. And so we subdivided it. You had a lovely reason for that, it stood up under scrutiny, we did the role-playing thing and tried to pick it apart the way the panel will, and we couldn't do it. And now you want to go back to the way it was to begin with, which was frankly kind of vulnerable to failure if any of the other major working parts of the spell got deranged?"

"Yes," Mehrnaz said, standing on the far side of the diagram with her hands on her hips. She was actually managing to look belligerent. *I wonder if all the tea she's been drinking is getting to her,* Dairine thought. "It was starting to look ... I don't know ... unnecessarily complicated. I think a more straightforward approach might be smarter."

Dairine was tempted to throw her hands in the air and tell Mehrnaz what she really thought of her indecisiveness. This had been getting especially bad over the last day or so. At one point she had been trying to get Dairine make the changes herself, until Dairine suddenly noticed a very odd little smile that popped out briefly on Mehrnaz's face when she was about to shift a spell's subroutine into a less effective position. It was like something naughty at the back of Mehrnaz's mind had peeked out at Dairine and smirked at her, amused that it was getting its way. At that point Dairine had started to dig her heels in and resist all these changes, some of them genuinely sweeping.

It makes no sense, she thought as she started to marshal her arguments against this newest change, or rather, rollback. *The whole purpose of the initial round is to get the big changes dealt with in front of an audience that wants to help and isn't interested in marking you down. And we've done all that. Who wants to make more work for themselves? Why would anyone want to tire themselves out and screw up all the good work they've done so far?*

Dairine's frustration level was increasing so much that she started thinking out loud. "It's almost like what already works isn't good enough, like you have to find the perfect solution and so merely good won't do, almost like . . ." She fumbled for words, turned away.

Like you're sabotaging yourself, said something in the back of her brain. *Like you truly don't want to go any further. Like you're planning to have things come undone now.*

And in a horrified split second it all laid itself out in front of Dairine, clear as crystal, like a chess problem written down, like a maze solved. "Something didn't go right" was what Mehrnaz had said at the end of the first round. But that, as Nelaid had warned her, was code. What Mehrnaz really meant was, *I won when I was supposed to have lost.* And more to the point: *I want to lose.*

She has some reason to want to fail this, Dairine thought, not for the first time. *It's something to do with the family, I* know *it is.* And thinking this, Dairine started to get angry. *We like each other, yeah, but she doesn't trust me enough to tell me.* That started to make her angry too.

Well, there are a couple ways to handle this . . . But Dairine knew instinctively that one of them was *not* going to be confronting Mehrnaz directly. *Not yet, anyway. I've got to let her play it out, and just refuse to let her screw it all up. Who knows, she might give in to the idea of winning if I wear her down. But after all this work I've done, I will not lie back and let her screw it up on purpose!*

"Like what?" Mehrnaz said.

"Sorry," Dairine said, "lost my train of thought. Let me see the fault analysis routine again. There was something on the power-feed segment of that routine that got me confused."

But wow, this is going to be a long, long day or two. Remind me again why I signed up for this?

On the morning of the semifinals, Nita sat up in her bed, gasping again. It was dawn.

It took her several minutes to get control of her breathing. "I'm starting to hate this," she said silently to Bobo. "I can't remember when I had a stupid *meaningless* dream anymore. Like being in school and suddenly realizing I haven't studied for a test."

Or that strange one where your teeth fall out.

Nita shuddered. "Why'd you have to remind me? I was just forgetting about that one."

Sorry . . .

"Never mind," Nita said.

Have you got context for me?

"Yeah," Nita said. She had to take an instant to swallow — her mouth was dry at the memory of her dream from last night.

The imagery had been arresting, because when the dream started, it had seemed like one of those ordinary inconsequential dreams. She'd been heading over to Kit's house because his mom was going to be making that chicken dish she did so well. And she got to the house, and she went in the back door, and Kit was there in the kitchen, getting something out of his refrigerator. He turned to her . . .

And his eyes were empty. There was no one there, no one inside. It wasn't as if the stare was blank or zombielike. It was just that Kit was *missing* somehow. None of the expressions that normally lived in his eyes were there.

She shivered. That was not something she ever wanted to see again. And what was worse, in the dream she could hear echoes of that earlier dream with Carmela, where Kit's sister had begged her "not to let them get Kit." In this morning's dream, she remembered being overtaken by a wave of utmost dread, because she realized that it was too late, they *had* gotten Kit, and there was nothing she could do about it. The sheer horror of it had snapped her awake and upright in a flash of hot and cold adrenaline.

Anything else? Bobo asked.

Nita shook her head. "Not sure I want anything else, frankly. It's made me feel a little sick to my stomach."

Probably you should have some of that peppermint tea.

"Better let my insides settle first," she said.

Nita got up and got dressed. *What's this all about?* she thought as she put the kettle on. *Is this something to do with The B Word? Is my subconscious terrified that Kit won't be Kit anymore if he's my boyfriend instead of just my friend?* Because there was no avoiding the whispers and rumors and suggestions, at school, in books, on TV shows, that if you took that extra step too far you could "ruin it" and never ever get back again what you had before. Usually, before this, she'd have scoffed at the idea. She and Kit had been through way too much trouble together, and though there'd been misunderstandings and disagreements along the way, they'd always come out okay on the other side.

But those eyes, those empty eyes . . . The memory of them creeped Nita out. They made her feel like the solutions that had worked in the past might not be good enough for the present, let alone the future . . .

She eventually managed to push the image away. But she wasn't going to be terribly happy with life until Kit came over later in the morning and she saw his eyes, and that he was inside them.

She'd just finished making herself some of the peppermint tea and was halfway down the mug when her dad came in, found himself a mug, and started going through the cupboards. Nita was paging through her manual and not paying much attention to him until it occurred to her that the rummaging was taking a lot longer than it usually did for him. *It's not like he doesn't know where the coffee is. Or else —* "Coffee or tea?" Nita said.

"Coffee."

"Did she drink it all already? Wow, she must really be having trouble with the zone lag."

"What? Oh."

Her dad was staring straight at the glass jar of Dairine's coffee, but it was as if he couldn't see it. Nita reached into the cupboard past him, grabbed it, and handed it to him. "Here," she said. "I won't let her know you had any. Just grab another jar of it from the store when you go by there."

Her dad made himself some coffee, and then once it was made, leaned against the counter and stood staring into his mug for a while as he stirred. *He looks so concerned,* Nita thought. *What's going on with him?*

"Nita," he said. "You have a moment?"

"What? Sure."

"Okay. Good." And he took a breath. "You and Kit —"

With a shock Nita realized what was coming. *Oh no*, she thought. *Not right now. Not on top of everything else!*

Nita held her breath.

"How's it been going?" her dad said.

She had no idea where he'd been planning to start, but this was so low-key, even for her dad, that Nita was tempted to laugh out loud. Except that would probably throw him right off his stride when he needed to talk to her about this, and she didn't want to do that. This was going to be weird and difficult enough for them both as it was.

In any case there was no point in trying to pretend she didn't know what subject he was trying to broach. "We're fine," she said. "A little freaked, maybe."

"Both of you?" he said, giving her a curious look. "Kit's been playing it pretty calm."

"Playing it, yeah," said Nita.

Her dad smiled half a smile. It was an expression that Nita remembered her mom wearing a lot, and now she found herself wondering which of her parents had come up with it first and how long it had taken to rub off on the other one. After a moment he said, "Has anything. . ."

". . . *Happened?*" Nita gave him a look that she hoped would be dry without being too snotty.

Her dad had the grace to look embarrassed at asking so baldly. "Uh. Maybe I, uh . . ."

Nita simply leaned on the counter and regarded him, wondering how deep a hole he was about to dig for himself and how long he'd take to stop digging.

"Um." He looked up. "In baseball terms?"

Nita paused to give this some consideration. "First base?" she said.

Her dad made a face that suggested this was probably okay.

"Might have stolen first a few times," Nita said. "And thought about stealing second . . ."

At that, unexpectedly, he laughed. "Um. All right. But you *do* know . . ."

"Almost *certainly*, Daddy." She was wishing that he'd get the hint and let the subject drop, but there didn't seem to be much chance of that.

"That there are parts of what you're getting into that are, uh . . . they have life consequences . . ."

"Dad," Nita said. "We had all this in school. *It's okay.*"

"Yes," her dad said, "about the mechanics, I *know* you know about that —"

Nita had to smile. "You remember that time when Kit was getting the TV set up for PeculiarSat . . .?" This was the household code for GalacNet and the other major extraterrestrial image and data feeds to which wizards had access. ". . . And Mom was playing around with the remote and she stumbled across the TentaclErotica channel?"

Her father put down the coffee mug and covered his face. *"Oh God,"* he said.

"You knew *then* that I already knew everything I needed to know about this," Nita said.

"Excuse me," her father said, and picked up the mug again, and he was actually *blushing*, "I knew that you already knew everything anybody possibly needed to know about *tentacly things from alpha Centauri* doing it! Because the explanations —"

"Aldebaran VIIa, actually," Nita said.

"— Nearly gave me a coronary!"

"They've got a lot of sexes," Nita said. "They have a lot of sex. If you go there on business, you have to be prepared. But everybody in that was *consenting,* Daddy! That's the important thing. *Hvurkh* means *hvurkh!"*

Her dad started laughing. "Okay," he said, "fine. That's about a third of the talk I wanted to have . . ."

"Oh good," Nita said, unable to stop dreading whatever the other two-thirds were going to be.

"So, beyond the, you know, the just *doing* it . . ." Her dad stopped, cleared his throat. "Look, wizardry aside — you're just getting started in life. College is coming." Nita winced and groaned softly: too well she knew it. "And even though you're as strong and smart as anyone could hope for their daughter to be . . . it's going to be a good while yet before you've got the emotional maturity to deal with parenthood."

"Please," Nita said. "I have exactly *zero* plans for that for the next ten years. Or twenty."

"Well," her dad said, "planning is kind of the issue, isn't it? And not forgetting to have the planning in place when, um, when things *do* happen. *If* they do."

His embarrassment was so profound that Nita would have done almost anything to spare him this. It didn't seem the time, though, to get into the various management strategies available to a wizard who wasn't ready to reproduce. "We know what we need to do," Nita said. "Or not do. Honest, Daddy. You don't need to worry." She stopped herself before she could have a chance to say *We'll be careful* or any other of about twenty other reassuring phrases that could be terribly misunderstood.

"Okay," her dad said. "Most of the rest of it . . ." He actually shrugged. "It was going to be about keeping your options open. A lot can happen in ten years. Or twenty." He looked up, favouring her with an expression that was a bit challenging.

This was harder to cope with, harder to be reassuring about. At the moment Nita was equally torn between not being able to define what was going on with her and Kit, and not being able to believe that the way they were with each other could ever possibly happen with anyone else. Knowing this in the abstract was completely different from the inextricably intertwined senses of fluttery nervousness and total certainty that she got when she looked at Kit. She couldn't explain it to herself, and she despaired of explaining it to anyone else, especially her father.

"Because you can't always be sure," her dad said after a moment. He drank some coffee and looked at something over the top of the cup: not Nita. "I wasn't sure with your mom for a long time."

Nita blinked at that. "Really?" It seemed impossible, somehow. And certainly impossible that the two of them had ever been with anyone else.

Her dad shook his head. "We met a fair number of times before we started getting serious," he said. "At first she thought I was a jock. Well, I *was,* then." He grinned a little: his college-football time, to hear him tell it, had been one of the best parts of his life. "And at first I thought she was a snotty stuck-up elitist. *Ballet* . . ." Her dad snorted. ". . . But then after a while things shifted, and it all made sense. *We* made sense — when I'd have sworn just a few months before that it never could. *We* never could. Just . . ." He shrugged. "Give things room to move if they need to."

"Okay," Nita said. "I'll try."

He nodded, then, and drank some more coffee.

"So," Nita said. "And . . . you're okay with everything?" Because she suddenly realized that it was important that he was: surprisingly important.

"Do I have a choice?" her dad said.

Nita didn't have an answer for that.

He was looking down into the coffee mug again, swirling the coffee. "There was a time," her dad said, "when I realized . . ." He sighed. "It was that night at the beach, when you told us the truth about what you and Kit were up to. And at first we were just too shocked to believe it. Because honestly, how could we? *Magic?* Come on." He shook his head. "But after it started sinking in, I had just the worst possible moment. It was something Kit said that triggered it. And I realized — and so did your mom — that no matter what we said or did, if you were intent on doing this dangerous thing, there was nothing we could do to stop you. *Nothing.*"

"It was hard," Nita said after a moment, and wasn't certain whether she was thinking more about the effect of that night on her mom and dad, or on her. "But I knew you'd be okay with it sooner or later."

"It was hard," her dad said, sounding very somber. "But we did get our brains wrapped around it, finally." He looked up from his coffee. "This is like that, in a way. Even if you *weren't* a wizard and you wanted to get it on with somebody, realistically there's no way we could — I could stop you. What, am I supposed to keep you in a cage? And probably there's no way I could even know about it if you absolutely set your mind on keeping it secret."

This struck Nita as the wrong moment to agree with him. She kept quiet.

"But there comes a point where you have to just decide to trust people," her dad said. "No matter what age they are. And in your case, yeah, you have a set of priorities that your mom and I never could have predicted. But you're still our daughter, and I know how we brought you up, and I think you'll do the right thing without me having to watch you day and night." He laughed a little helplessly. "Even if I could."

In the face of a vote of confidence like that, there wasn't much Nita could do but put her cold tea down and go hug him.

Her dad smooched her on the top of her head and hugged her back. "There," he said. "Wasn't as bad as I thought it would be."

"Good." Nita grinned at his relief, let him go, and shoved her tea in the microwave, pushing the button that would give it a minute to heat up. "So are we okay?"

"For the moment," her dad said.

Nita threw him an *oh no, what now?* look.

"Well, I'm not sure it's responsible to have this talk just *once*," her dad said. "The whole idea that you can just get it over with . . . As if conditions might not change in the future, for you, for me . . ." He shrugged. "Remember when you were six or so and we had that talk about you not crossing the street without looking both ways?"

Nita had no memory of that at all. "It was kind of a long time ago . . ."

Her dad gave Nita a look that suggested her attempt to deflect his question without hurting him had been noticed, appreciated, and was being allowed to pass without comment. "But it's not like, having given you that long talk, I was just going to *stop worrying forever* about whether you were crossing the street safely, right? What kind of sense with that make? Of course I'm going to keep worrying about it. And we might need to talk again some time when you have more data. Or things change some other way. But I'll leave that with you."

"Okay," Nita said.

Her dad finished the last of his coffee, ran some water into the mug and left it in the sink. "Gotta go," he said. He felt around in his pockets for his car keys. "Seeing Dairine? I keep missing her, her hours are so strange right now."

"Yeah, probably I will."

"Thank her for getting the garbage out, okay?"

"Sure."

Her dad kissed her again and headed out the back door: it slammed behind him.

Ten minutes of the birds and the bees, Nita thought as the microwave pinged at her. *Just before I get ready to gate halfway around the planet. What is my life*

. . .? She'd calmed down a bit by the time Kit turned up: though her dream of this morning was still very much on her mind as he came in and she spent a few moments looking carefully into his eyes.

The look he gave her in return was bemused. "Is there something on my face?"

"One of your normal expressions," Nita said. "Which I'm glad to see."

"Another of those dreams . . . ?"

"Yeah," Nita said. She turned away.

"Pancakes?" Kit said.

"Not today," Nita said. "Sticking to toast. Want some tea?"

"What's that, the peppermint stuff? Yeah."

She made him a cup and they sat. "So," Kit said. "Tonight's the night."

"Yeah. We're due at Penn's when?"

"Four o'clock, our time. Then over to Canberra."

Nita nodded. "You know," she said, "I'm thinking those unworthy thoughts again."

"What? Wishing that he'll get knocked out?"

"Well, the odds are a lot better this time . . ."

"For us, you mean."

"Yeah."

Kit sighed. "True. You want to know what's kind of embarrassing?"

"Tell me."

"That I'm wishing that too."

"So it's not just *my* nerves he's getting on more and more . . ."

"Not so much him," Kit said. "But you know, I'm not so excited about going to the far side of the Moon."

Nita reached out and stroked Kit's arm. "I know. And you know what? Neither is Dairine."

"Similar reasons, I guess," Kit said.

"Yeah." Roshaun's terrifying disappearance had come mere minutes before Ponch's climactic battle with the Wolf That Ate the Stars.

"But if she's going," Kit said, "I need to go too. If only to remind her that happy endings are possible . . ."

All Nita could do was sit there for a moment regarding him in shameless admiration. "You know," she said, "you're not only a terrific wizard, but you're a nice person."

Kit threw her a look that was skeptical on the surface of it, but he was still smiling. "So," he said. "Onward to the semis."

"Yeah. But I'm betting that before that, we'll have at least a few other things to distract us."

"Such as?"

"Penn being a jerk," Nita said. "Again, and again, and again . . ."

• • •

"And if I can get you lovely ladies to turn your ever-so-fickle attention to the unique power control segment —"

"*Penn!*" Nita said.

He looked at her brightly. "And there's a question from one of them now!"

Dear Powers That Be, give me strength. "Penn, I truly almost hate to break this to you," Nita said, "but even though more than half of the people judging you today are going to be female, an even more significant portion of them, say a *hundred percent* or so, are going to be more *experienced* than you. And another significant percentage, kind of hard to evaluate but let's be kind and just say *most,* are going to be smarter than you as well. So you need to amend your attitude right now or you are *not going to do well.*"

"You're taking this way too seriously, way too personally! But it's not your fault you can't see how easy this is going to be for me." Penn's tone was almost pitying. "I know you've always had to try hard, it's written all over your service history, but some of us just don't have to go down that road. It's going to be okay, Juanita, seriously, you're worrying way too much about this —"

"Penn," Kit said sharply, "it's not funny, and it's not cute. They'll laugh you out of there. If you call Irina Mladen a 'lovely lady' to her face, after she's done with you you're going to wind up wishing that the Earth would open up and swallow you. In fact, considering her specialty, the odds are better than even that it *will*."

In turn, Penn threw Kit a sly look. "I see what the problem is," he said. "She's been getting to you." He glanced at Nita. "It's okay . . . I know what you're really thinking."

Kit covered his face.

Nita waved her arms and pushed herself away from the wall at the side of Penn's downstairs rec room where she'd been leaning. "Nope," she said. "Nope, nope, nope. Kit? You mind if I go ahead?"

The slightly wistful look he gave her suggested that he wished he'd thought of it first. "No, go on," Kit said.

"Mmm," Penn said to her, "can't stand the heat?"

"Don't go there, Penn," Nita said. She pulled her transit circle out of her charm bracelet — preloaded with the coordinates for the venue in Canberra — and dropped it, glowing, to the floor around her. To Kit she said, "A couple hours?"

"Yeah."

Nita breathed in, breathed out very hard, and said the activation word for the transit circle before she could be tempted to stick around and reduce the number of semifinalists by one.

• • •

The arrangement for the wizardly space at the convention center in Canberra was much the same as it had been in New York: a spell-shielded area to keep the nonwizards at bay, various meeting rooms, and a big, beautiful, airy public space conducive to a large number of people getting together after the business of the meeting was done. It was a smaller space, though, than the New York venue had been. With only fifty or so participants presenting projects privately to a panel of judges instead of out in the open, there wasn't any need for a huge space that would resemble a carnival fairway.

With all the appealing outdoor terraces around the convention center where people who felt inclined could bask in the sunshine, and with the lovely warm weather then prevailing, the whole feeling of the event seemed to Nita to have taken a more leisurely turn. This struck her as a good thing, as the tension level had ratcheted up a great deal. Quite a lot of people, especially Australian wizards, had come in to take part in the proceedings and see who went through to the finals. These attendees had started arriving early to learn how the initial rankings stacked up. But there was no mistaking the casual guests for the competitors, who all had a twitchy look to them that instantly set them apart.

There was a good reason for this: the drastic results of the previous round had led a lot of people to suspect that the trend toward unusually hard judging was likely to continue. And when the four core judges were announced, this theory was instantly confirmed. One of the core group was naturally Irina Mladen. Another was Jarrah Corowa, possibly one of the most famous wizards of Aboriginal origin on the planet, and an expert in spells that had to do with materials technologies. A third was the venerable Yi Ling Harrie from Singapore, at ninety-three one of the oldest and best-known aeromancers still in active practice; and the fourth was Malak Marouane, Moroccan-born but practicing mostly in animal communications in Central Africa. Nita, looking over their images in her manual, thought with anticipation of the response should Penn call any one of them a "lovely lady." *It'd be memorable . . .*

The problem was that she wouldn't get to see it, as mentors were not permitted in their mentees' judging sessions. Penn and his spell would stand in front of the four core judges and three others selected for their expertise in the field of wizardry in which his spell was positioned. He and that spell would stand or fall together on their own merits — which suited Nita entirely.

Nita was wandering down the long concourse that faced onto the nearby lakes when about halfway toward the end she spotted a familiar orange jumpsuit. "You're kind of early," Nita said as she came up behind Lissa and patted her on the back. "What time is it in Toronto?"

"Don't ask me," Lissa said. "I've been here for three days."

Nita looked at her in bemusement. "No tan?"

"I don't do tan," Lissa said. "I hate the beach, it gets you full of sand. But there are lakes here, and I like to row and talk to the fish." She glanced around. "Where's Kit?"

"Not here yet," Nita said. "In a couple of hours."

"Zone lag?"

Nita shook her head. "Annoying mentee syndrome."

"Yeah, you've got a hard case with that one," Lissa said. "Well, never mind him. Come on out to the terrace! It's full of wizards."

"Nobody else?"

"Nope, they put up signs with that boring font out there and then they had to fine-tune where the signs were pointing, because we started having sleeping kookaburras fall out of the trees on people." They went out through automatic doors into blinding sunshine. "A lot of the local crowd's here. Some of the game group, too. Matt's here, but he lives down the road, why wouldn't he be, and his boyfriend, that little guy in the duster. And there's Adele, and those German twins —"

Nita paused to try to figure out who in the crowd had a dust cloth, and the only little guy in sight was wearing a long coat — Then she blinked. "His boyfriend?"

"Yeah, name's Daki or Doki or something, I always get it wrong when I try to remember. Did I mention Adele? She . . ."

"Yeah, Adele," Nita said, losing the thread for a moment while the back of her brain shouted at her, *Yes, here I am again, your old friend the universe, and I'm stalking you and making everybody talk about sex things all of a sudden! And how did you not know Matt had a boyfriend? Were you purposely not noticing because thinking the word made you nervous? Were you —*

"Shut *up*," she said under her breath to the universe.

"What?"

"Oh! Sorry! Not you."

"Oh, your invisible friend?"

Nita started to say yes, more or less out of habit, and then stopped herself. "Might as well be."

"Well, let's get you and him a smoothie or something, you look parched!"

And within a few minutes Nita was sitting on one of a circle of loungers under the shade afforded by the projecting eaves of the building, stirring a mango smoothie with a straw and looking at a wizardly projection of the morning session's results so far. The quiet interlude was welcome, as she was still reacting to what Lissa had told her about Matt. *How did I never realize he was gay?* She took a long drink. *I feel like an idiot.* And then she laughed at herself. *Well, it wouldn't be the first time I've missed something like that. Guess it's too much to hope it'll be the last . . .*

"Well, this looks sybaritic," said a familiar voice from overhead.

Nita looked up in surprise. "Carl!" she said. And sure enough, there was her other Supervisory wizard in a white linen shirt and khaki shorts and Ray-Bans and sneakers, and carrying some kind of orange-creamsicle-colored drink with a little umbrella in it. "Are you proctoring?" Then Nita thought again. "No, wait, they don't need to do that for this round, do they?"

Carl sat down on the lounger next to hers. "No, the judging panels handle any security that the spells need when they're examining them. Today I'm here for the networking." He smiled slyly at her. "And because of neighborhood interest."

"Oh, okay."

"But also, I meant to look you up," Carl said.

Nita found herself wondering guiltily if a Supervisory could hear you thinking about killing your mentee. "Uh —"

"You're not in any trouble," Carl said.

She gave him a suspicious sideways glance. "How do you do that?"

"By having been your age once," Carl said, "and being able to see your face."

Nita snorted. "Okay."

He took a long pull on the straw in his drink. "I was curious, after the first round, to ask you whether you were contemplating a change of focus."

She was mystified. "Focus? . . . And I didn't see you at the first round."

Carl chuckled. "I have my sources. Have you given any thought to whom you've spent a significant portion of your time hanging out with so far? I mean, planets. To the exclusion of both Kit and your own mentee, sometimes."

She shrugged. "Kit's been wandering around meeting people. We both have; that's how I ran into Jovie and Pluto."

"'Jovie,'" Carl said, and grinned into his drink.

"He didn't mind."

"No," Carl said, "he wouldn't have."

"And as for my own mentee, he's a pain in the ass and doesn't want to listen to me any more than he has to. I'm the wrong sex or something."

Carl gave her a resigned look. "Cultural?"

"Personal."

"Oh well."

"But Carl, seriously . . . What do you do when your mentee doesn't want to be mentored? I mean, without breaking the commitment?"

He looked out toward the lake and thought about it. "Why are you so intent on staying in it?"

The question caught her briefly by surprise. "Well, the Powers That Be put me in this position. Normally they've got reasons for that kind of thing."

"That's true," Carl said. "But it's not as if they're requiring blind obedience of you. There are cases in which a mentor can do the person they're mentoring more good by walking than they can by staying stubbornly in place. You're the only one who can make that judgment call, and the Powers trust you to do that."

Nita sniffed and drank some more of her smoothie. "Don't make it sound too good," she said.

Carl laughed. "In our time working together," he said, "have I ever been shy about giving you bad news when it was necessary?"

An image rose in Nita's mind: a South Shore beach, with the Sun shining down on the sand and the water and a young girl who was in the process of realizing that she had made a promise that was almost certainly going to be deadly for her to keep. "No," Nita said. "That hasn't been a problem."

"So you can make some assumptions about the

good news, then. Assuming it actually *is* good. Problem is, you're the only one who can decide that."

Nita smiled and sucked down the last of her smoothie so that the straw gurgled. "I was about to start complaining about you and the Powers treating me like a grownup who knows the right thing to do," she said. "Maybe I changed my mind."

Carl leaned back and stretched out his legs. "The truth is that not all the situations the Powers put us into are optimal," he said. "They may have great insight and be able to see deeper into causality than we routinely can at our level, but they're not omniscient and they've never pretended to be. They'll make a judgment call sometimes, as in this case, that a good result is likely if you put a given combination of people together. And since they hate to waste energy, they'll routinely make sure that it's the best possible result that can be achieved, and that it will do as many people good as possible. You may be having an effect on your mentee that isn't obvious to you. The difficulty, of course, is that since *we're* not omniscient either, we may sometimes do our jobs and think we've failed . . . and still have done massive good to someone that we may never be aware of."

"I prefer to be aware of it," Nita said.

"So do we all," Carl said. "I'd also prefer it to rain chocolate-frosted donuts in my kitchen on Sunday mornings, but I don't seem to be getting a lot of that. Plainly the universe is mismanaged."

Nita snickered. "So you're saying I should keep doing what I'm doing and hope for the best."

"There's always the chance that the one who's being done good by this is you," said Carl.

She gave him a sideways look. "By being told over and over that no matter how smart I act, I'm really some airhead whose highest purpose is to hang off some guy's arm?"

"If your mentee's telling you that over and over," Carl said, with a very grim small smile, "I think it's very likely that you may sooner or later respond in a way that changes his mind. If only by repetition."

Nita's gaze went to the lake. "Pity that's not the ocean. I could drop him in it. I've got friends out there. With teeth."

Carl shook his head. "Do what you normally do," he said. "Leave the rest to the Powers. And if you feel you absolutely must go, trust that that's what's needed. You can't get this wrong."

And then he sat up straight. "Whoops," he said, "incoming!"

And just like that he vanished.

Nita shook her head, both because he'd just done that in full view of the road between the convention center and the lake — *but then they'll have this whole side of the place spell-shielded* — and because he had done it soundlessly. She sat up a little straighter, looking around. *Kit?*

No answer. Not that she always got one by silent communications these days, especially since things had begun to shift between them.

The automatic doors to the building opened, and Penn came bursting out in flowered beach jams, some kind of brocaded vest, and flip-flops. As he stood there looking almost frantically from side to side, it was only with the greatest difficulty that Nita kept herself from laughing out loud. *The way he dresses,* she thought, *there has to be a word . . .*

Penn spotted her and immediately headed her way. *Flamboyant,* Nita thought. *That's a good word. But no Kit? Interesting . . .*

"Juanita!"

She rolled her eyes. It wasn't the normal stagy delivery of her name, though. Penn sounded upset.

As he came over to stand by her chair, Nita tilted her head up and did her best to betray nothing more than mild curiosity. "What?"

"I'm, uh," Penn said. "I'm due in there pretty soon —"

She glanced at her watch. "About ten minutes," Nita said. "And?" She glanced toward the doors, but there was no action there. "Where's Kit?"

"Uh," Penn said, not looking Nita in the eye, and

plainly not wanting to. "He, uh, he said he had other things to do."

Better *things to do,* Nita's mind instantly supplied. *He got angry at something Penn said, and he dumped him. Did Carl know this was happening? There are no accidents . . .*

"You pissed him off, didn't you," Nita said. "Penn, one of these days you're going to stop being so certain you know what people are thinking before they open their mouths, and your life's going to get a whole lot simpler."

Slowly and reluctantly Penn sat down sideways on the lounger that Carl had vacated.

"I, uh," he said, and then seemed to run out of words.

"Yes?" Nita said.

". . . I'm not sure I can go through with this."

All right, Nita thought, *here we go.* There had been something about Penn's mood the last couple of days that had been ringing alarm bells for her. But whether he was likely to want to talk to *her* about it now was another question. "What's going on?" she said.

"I don't know," Penn said, bending half over and rubbing his hands through his hair. "I don't *know!* This morning, and then later, just now, after Kit left . . . I keep having these times when, I don't know, I look at the spell and it doesn't seem to make any sense. And that's ridiculous! *How can it not make sense?*"

Nita sighed. "Haven't you ever had the thing," she said, "where you look at a sentence after you've read it too many times, and it doesn't mean anything? Or you say your own name too many times, and it turns into this gibberish word. There's a wizardly version of that too."

"No," Penn said miserably. "If only Kit was here!"

If only, Nita thought. *He'd love to see this: he'd laugh so hard.* "Penn," she said. "Am I or am I not one of your mentors?"

"Uh, yeah."

"Then be quiet, because I'm about to explain it all to you. You're getting cold feet."

Penn stared at his flip-flops in confusion.

"Cold feet!" Nita said. "It's finally sunk in for you that you're coming up against something that a flashy presentation and some fast talking won't be enough to get you through. This isn't just about knowing how to handle hecklers or deflect difficult questions, or be flashy or showy or cute. You're going to be standing in front of seven wizards who're going to scare you spitless. And you know what? They'll be doing that to *everybody* they judge today. Just this once, you're going to get to act like *everybody else.* You're going to be *scared.*"

He stared at Nita with an expression of utter dismay that suggested he was getting a head start.

"And then you're going to push through it," Nita

said. "You're going to walk into that judging room and take a deep breath and say to yourself, *I am scared but I'm going to do this anyway.* Wizards do this every day. *People* do this every day. I've done it, Kit's done it, and now it's your turn."

She got up off her lounger. "Come on," she said.

Penn didn't move.

She glared at him. "Have some dignity, Penn," she said. "Get up and walk. Don't make me levitate you. Because under your own power or with assistance, *you are going into that room.* And what state you're in when you come out of it is going to be entirely up to you."

Very slowly he got up and started to make for the doors. Nita waited until he caught up with her. "Stop hanging your head like that!" she said as they walked. "Hold your head up. It makes you braver."

"What?"

"There are physiological changes," Nita said. "Not gonna start explaining them now. Take a deep breath. Yeah. Let it out now. Have you got your manual?"

"Uh. In a pocket."

"Good. Got the basic version of the spell cued up in it?"

"Yeah."

"Breathe again. Just get in the habit of it, I can't be in the room with you to remind you."

He sucked air in, let it out again as they went

through the doors into the main concourse. "You're doing fine," Nita said. "Once you're rolling, this will pass. You know your subject, I *know* you do. The only reason you're experiencing a panic is that you've realized you can't sweet-talk or swindle these judges into giving you the benefit of the doubt. And you don't have to. They'll listen to you if you just *talk to them about the spell.* Right? Tell them what you built. And tell them why you built it. Remember how you explained the difference it was going to make for people? Tell them about that."

Nita had passed the judging rooms on the way out to the terrace and knew where they were. Two of them had message boards that said, in the Speech, UNSCHEDULED. The third was blank. Nita stopped by its closed doors, and exactly as she and Penn paused there, the signboard outside the door lit up with Penn's name in English and Chinese and the Speech.

He stared at his name as if he'd never seen it before. "I, I can't . . ."

"You *can*," Nita said. "You can do this, Penn. And you're *going* to. Now remember: always take a breath when somebody asks you a question — it gives you extra time to think. See your spell in your head, now? Good."

The door opened before him.

"In," Nita said. "And good luck, cousin."

Penn hesitated. Then, like someone sleepwalking, in he went.

The door closed.

Nita sagged, passed a hand over her face, and laughed at herself. *Poor guy,* she thought. *Who knew he was going to freeze up like that?*

From inside her otherspace pocket, Nita's manual pinged softly.

She moved off to one side of the doors, unzipped the air, pulled the manual out and checked its messaging section. As she opened up to the section with its edges flashing blue, words were already spelling themselves out across its first page.

Is he there?

Nita laughed. "Yeah."

Did he go in?

"Finally."

Under his own power?

"Believe it or not, yeah. Look, get over here when you can ... we're going to need to present a united front when he comes out of there."

Be there in twenty.

"See you," Nita said. She closed the manual and put it away, then headed for the doors to the outside terrace.

Dairine made her way down to the prejudging area in the convention center where she'd agreed to meet

Mehrnaz that afternoon. There were a lot of wizards and other guests hanging around, looking at the results of those coming out of judging and the rankings as they stood. Maybe half of the semifinalists had been through the judging by now, and Mehrnaz was scheduled in about half an hour. *It's a good time to be scheduled: less reason to panic . . .*

Dairine put Spot down while she looked through the crowd, and after a moment caught sight of Mehrnaz. But she wasn't alone. Next to her stood an imposingly tall and darkly handsome woman in a rusty-colored silk hijab and a long below-the-knee tunic, subtly patterned in dun and gold, over dark designer jeans and sandals. She had huge dark eyes and a long pretty face, but her mouth had a set of lines around it on each side that suggested her lips were more normally drawn down in an expression of disappointment.

All right, now *what?* Dairine thought, and hung back to get a sense of what was going on.

"Why are they making you wait like this?" the woman said. "It's disgraceful."

"There are people scheduled ahead of me, *ameh,*" Merhnaz said. "Everybody has to wait their turn."

"I don't see why," said the woman, sounding most annoyed. "Surely they must know who they're keeping waiting, who you're affiliated with; why would you be here otherwise?"

There was a pause at that, and Dairine saw Mehrnaz's glance go sideways, as if there was something she didn't want the woman to see there. "Well, the spell, *ameh . . .*"

"Oh, but you know that's not the issue at all, because the family doesn't waste time on these things anymore, do we?" It was a soft, warm voice, but so dismissive, and the woman's expression suggested that she was amused at how *simple-minded* Mehrnaz was. "Not that it's not a nice gesture, I suppose, but there are so many uncertainties in that whole scholium of wizardries. No way to guarantee the results . . . so many ways to *fail.* And who bothers with anything that they can't be sure will work? It's wasted effort, though I'm sure it's nice of you to make the attempt to keep up the old family tradition, your Uncle Khorazir does love that kind of thing and it's no wonder you'd want to please him, he knows so many useful people . . ."

That is the stupidest reason to specialize in one kind of wizardry that I've ever heard, Dairine thought, folding her arms.

"But *ameh,* that's not what it's about. If someone just —"

The woman looked down at Mehrnaz with affectionate disbelief. "You're truly going to tell me that you thought you might be able to work out how to do something about the old homeplace's slipstrike faults when generations of your family weren't able to do a *thing?* Even great wizards like your grandfather Bardia? He gave up on it after a year, said the very idea was hopeless. Surely you don't think you can do what *he* couldn't do! Though it's brave of you to try, but there's no point in you trying to prove anything to us *that* way. We know it's taken you longer than everyone else in the family to find a specialty, there's no reason for you to wear yourself out over impossibilities. Everybody moves at their own speed, we know you're a bit slow, but it's absolutely all right, you have to manage what you can. And even if —"

The woman looked amused at the idea that seemed just to have come to her. "Even *if* you got somewhere along those lines . . . well, you wouldn't like to embarrass your grandfather, would you? He'd be so hurt. None of us would want that."

Mehrnaz turned away again, looked at the ground. "I just . . ." she said, and trailed off.

This is it, Dairine realized. *This is why she melted down after the Cull.* This *is the source of the trouble.*

"You wanted to do your best," the woman said, in that particular sympathetic tone that says someone's trying to be kind to you while also implying that you're a fool, and not listening to anything you say or caring about what you want. "I know, I know! And it's understandable, the way things go so wrong for you most of the time! Well, the whole point now is to make these people hurry *up* so that you can get this demonstration over with and come home. There are much more important things for you to be doing —"

This attitude, Spot said silently, *is not very supportive of function for any wizard, successful or not.*

"No kidding," Dairine said softly, unfolding her arms. "Come on."

She headed over toward the two of them, not rushing, with Spot ambling along behind her. Dairine could feel Spot's stalky eyes fixed on the tall dark woman, and it was his regard, interestingly, that first got the woman's attention as they approached. She gave him a look like someone who's seen an unusually large bug on the kitchen floor and is considering the best way to step on it.

Dairine noted this. Her eyes narrowed. "Mehrnaz," she said, ignoring the tall woman and focusing all her attention on her mentee. "Problem here?"

Mehrnaz looked suddenly panicked. "What? Oh, no, it's all right, Dairine, everything's fine, we're just —"

"Waiting for the organizers to get their act together and stop wasting our time," the woman said in a tone abruptly gone very sharp.

"Well, it's all kind of hurry-up-and-wait at this point for everyone," Dairine said.

"Not for *everyone,*" the woman said, disdainfully.

"Don't you know who I am?" And the implication was as much "Because I'm important and famous!" as "Because I can't believe she hasn't told you."

Dairine simply put her eyebrows up. *I could make a pretty good guess,* she thought, *but let's see how far into your mouth you're willing to stick your foot before I have to commit myself.*

Mehrnaz's face was a study in immobility. "This is my aunt," she said. *"Ameh,* this is my Invitational mentor, Dairine Callahan."

The woman looked down at Dairine from her considerable height. Dairine, who before now had been looked down on by experts — up to and including the Lone Power — stood there with her head tilted up, matching her gaze for gaze.

The woman emitted an indignant sniff. "Afsoun Farrahi," she said, as if that should have been sufficient.

"'No education is ever complete,'" Dairine said, "'and enhancement of one's own is always to Life's advantage.'" The phrase in the Speech was very neutral, and implied a willingness to receive more data without you having to regret that you didn't know what was going on, or having to say "sorry" about anything. *Because I get a feeling that the only thing I'm going to be sorry about is that we've met. Seriously, you look like you just drank a pint of vinegar.*

"I am the daughter of Bardia Mazandarani and

the wife of Dalir Farrahi," Mehrnaz's aunt said, "the granddaughter of Asek Jahanshah and Baharak Gol, the *great*-granddaughter of Mehredem Khadem; and thereby a member of three of the foremost families of wizardry in all the East." Dairine noted in passing that she didn't appear to be in a big hurry to be the *aunt* of anybody. "So, little one, you ought now to recognize your place, and pay proper respect to your elder wizard." And she looked haughtily down at Dairine, waiting.

Dairine knew there were traditions of wizardry in which younger ones performed physical gestures of respect to older ones. But right now she had no particular taste for cross-cultural courtesies, as she was concentrating on holding perfectly still while the back of her mind shouted things like *You're not* my *elder wizard* and *My* place?? and *Little one? LITTLE ONE?*

Very slowly she let out the breath she'd been holding.

While there were many equivalents in the Speech for "pleased to meet you," Dairine had no intention of using any of them, especially since right now they wouldn't be true. So, "Madam," she said. The word in the Speech was *talif'*, a polite-enough generic feminine-gender title, and was normally used for non-wizards or Speech-users whose enacture status you weren't sure of. As such, used on someone you *knew* was a wizard — and one who was making a big deal of it — the title was as exquisite an insult as the hearer cared to make it.

Afsoun's eyes had already started to go wide. *Good. Hang on, lady, because we're just getting started.* "I hear your asserted ranking," Dairine said. "Now hear mine. I am the daughter of Harold Edward Callahan, friend and confidant of kings and Planetaries, and of Elizabeth Kathryn Callahan, who walks with the Powers and whose name is known to the Transcendent Pig." *Which is true enough, Neets saw them together . . . someplace . . . and such visions don't arrive unauthorized.* "And in my own right and of my own wizardry I am the Mother of Mobiles, and of the world they have made for themselves." She used the Speech-name that the Mobile species had after some thousands of seconds' deliberation chosen for itself, *Eles'ha;* and *am'Merensheh-ta-Eles'havesh* rolled very nicely off the tongue, especially when the listener's annoyed eyes went a little wider against her will.

Then Dairine smiled gently. "But out of regard for my friend and colleague, to whom you have the privilege of being related," and she tilted her head in a friendly nod in Mehrnaz's direction, "I permit you to omit the traditional obeisance to one of significantly senior rank or experience. You may continue to stand in my presence." And her gaze flickered up and down Afsoun in amusement. "Because it's such a pain when the kneeling gets the knees of such nice jeans all *baggy.*"

Dairine spent the next few seconds concentrating hard on keeping her face straight as Afsoun's jaw dropped. *"Just who do you think you are?"*

"Thought we'd already established that," Dairine said. *"You,* we're still working on." Then she applied a carefully puzzled look. "Or was the vocabulary in a recension you haven't mastered yet? You should work on that, someone your age." Afsoun's eyes got even bigger, and Dairine smiled in satisfaction, realizing that she'd hit at least one tender spot, probably more. "Either way, I said it in the Speech; you know it's true. So you can stop trotting out how many generations of wizards you're descended from, blah de blah de blah. I know people from much older, longer lines who make *way* less fuss about it." She could still hear Roshaun saying *ke Nelaid am Seriv am Teliuyve am Meseph am Veliz am Teriaust am det Wellakhit:* but for him it had been like reciting his credit card number.

Afsoun was working her mouth like a fish out of water. Dairine grinned. "In the meantime, while I'm sure there must be somebody here who'd just *looooove* to have you hang around and try to pick up a few pointers while pretending to critique wizardries you don't understand, our prep time for this event is at a premium and so we're going to have to say goodbye." She grabbed Mehrnaz's arm. "So, goodbye!"

And she glanced down at Spot. A short-hop transit circle flared into life around the three of them, and everything winked out, including Aunt Afsoun's face, gone all blotchy with rage.

They popped out right across the concourse, with Dairine working hard to stifle her laughter, as she didn't want their position given away. "Spot," she said, "stealth-field us. I don't want her able to see us or hear us or figure out where we are until Mehrnaz is in the judging room and you have to kill the spell to keep it from interfering."

No problem.

Under her hand, Dairine could feel that Mehrnaz was shaking. When she let her arm go, Mehrnaz rubbed at it in a frightened way, as if she thought it might fall off. Her expression, meanwhile, was torn between terror and delight. "Oh sweet Powers — oh Dairine — *what did you just do?*"

"Not half of what she's got coming," Dairine said. "And come on, tell me that you haven't wanted to do that since you were old enough to talk! Because it's been going on that long, hasn't it? Come on, Mehrnaz, say it in the Speech."

Mehrnaz opened her mouth, closed it again.

"But I get it now," Dairine said.

"Get what?"

Dairine frowned. Whatever problems she'd had in her home life, one of them had *not* been having the people around her assuming that she couldn't do things. Her mom and dad had always been in the "Yes you can, get on with it" department. Sometimes she had shocked them, sure, by how far she'd go to get on with things. But no one would tell her "No you can't" unless it was things like "No you can't take the barbecue apart while there are briquettes in it that are on fire!"

Dairine smiled dryly to herself. *Not that* that *stopped me either . . .* But what Mehrnaz had here, she now realized, was another problem entirely.

If this woman starts interfering, Dairine thought, *I'm gonna get her butt kicked out of here so hard she'll feel the universe slam on it on the way out, and I'll laugh for hours while she complains.*

For the moment, Dairine simply shook her head. "Leave it for now," she said. "We've got twenty minutes or so, and I want to see what you did with that force-diffusion routine. Let's have a look . . ."

Mehrnaz was in the judging room for nearly forty minutes. Dairine spent a good while pacing up and down outside it, waiting for any sign of Aunt Afsoun: but there wasn't any. *And maybe she's gone home. Good riddance, then.*

She was just turning around to pace one more leg in front of the doors when the message board changed. JUDGING, it had said over Mehrnaz's picture and her name in English and the Speech and Farsi. But now it went *flick* and said PASSED.

"*Yes!!*" Dairine exclaimed, and waited for the doors to open. A moment later they did, and Mehrnaz walked out . . .

And it was clear that something was terribly wrong, for Mehrnaz was coming out into the concourse with that terrible rigid-spine posture that Dairine had seen before. *God, she looks like someone who's about to get beaten up —*

In that instant Dairine remembered Nita's horrible conjecture. *Not even wizards are proof against that . . .*

Mehrnaz walked right past Dairine, didn't even stop. Dairine froze, for a moment, then went after Mehrnaz in a hurry.

"Mehrnaz," she said, because the girl wasn't stopping. "*Mehr!* Wait up!"

It's not possible, not possible that her own family would do that to her. They're wizards. *And even if they were doing that — she could stop them, she'd —*

She caught up with Mehrnaz, caught her by the arm. "Mehrnaz!"

She didn't shake off Dairine's hand, but the way she stopped suggested that she wanted to. "What," she said in a dead-flat voice.

"Mehrnaz," Dairine said. "I don't — *listen* to me! They're not — What's the matter? You *passed*. You're in the finals!"

"Yes," Mehrnaz said, very softly. "That's the problem."

Dairine found herself trembling. "Nobody at home's getting physically violent with you, are they? You don't have to put up with that. If that's going on, I don't care who's doing it to you, I swear I'll take them apart like Lego!"

Mehrnaz held very still. "Touch me? Of course they won't touch me. That would speed up entropy." Dairine didn't think she had ever heard the phrase used with such bitterness. "But you still don't get it, do you? None of my family expected me to make it past the first Cull. I was supposed to fail."

Dairine stood there dumbfounded.

"They don't have to touch me," Mehrnaz said. "There's more than one kind of abuse. If I'd have lost today, that wouldn't have been so bad. Oh, they'd make fun of me for a few weeks, a month, until they got bored with it. It would be the big joke in the family. How Mehrnaz almost got it right, but then screwed up in front of the whole world. Because she would, wouldn't she? That's her style."

She stood there hunched, her fists clenched. It was a creepy stance for someone who was usually so fluid and graceful, so quick and easy in her movements. "But now, *now* I've done something *really* bad. Now I've made them all look like idiots. Because all my relatives have been telling their friends, and other people in the family, that this was going to be it for me. Everyone's committed themselves to being sure that this would be as far as I could go. And you know why they say that? My grandfather, the famous one, you remember him? He made it past the Cull when he was in the Invitational, but he never got any further. And this isn't even the quarter-finals, now. It's *so* much worse. It's the *semis.* Now I've made *him* look bad. That whole side of the family is cursing me now. They have to. It's a loyalty thing." She sounded resigned.

"Oh, God," Dairine muttered.

"Yes," Mehrnaz said. She smiled, but there was nothing remotely happy or funny about the expression. "Now on we go to the finals. And the whole family will be saying to everybody *outside* the family, oh, we're so pleased, yes, we didn't think she had it in her, isn't it wonderful, talent will out, after all! It must be the stress, put one of our people in a crisis situation and they rise to meet it —"

She laughed bitterly. "But inside the house, they're going to be ripping each other up. My grandfather's side of the family is going to be all over my mama, saying, 'You meant for this to happen, didn't you? You set this up on purpose to make us look bad. Here you were claiming that you never thought she'd make it that far, but now see what's happened!' And my mother's going to deny it, but they won't believe her.

They'll be furious with her. And *she'll* be furious with *me* ... Though she'll never show it in front of them! While I'm around, she'll support me, to annoy them. But the moment the doors close, when I'm home trying to have some peace, she'll find a hundred ways to make my life a little hell. And I get to put up with that, without complaining, and to be a good girl, with the pressure getting worse all the time until the finals come. Five days of every look, every word, everything that everybody does around me, being code for 'You screwed it up. And now we're going to punish you.'"

Dairine was still shaking all over with her own tension. "You could come live in my basement," she said. "The last guests we had down there gave it rave reviews."

"No," Mehrnaz said. Some of the stiffness and anger went out of her posture when she raised her head and met Dairine's eyes. It was, however, a more challenging look. "I have to tough it out on my own ground," she said. "Because this isn't just about competing in the Invitational proper, is it? This is about handling what goes on outside the competition, *around* the competition. The strains, and the pressures. It's a test, all of it ... *another* test, another game, that takes place outside the competition space. Isn't it? The Powers are playing this game with the Lone Power. And we're the pieces on the board."

"Not the usual board game, is it?" Dairine said after a moment. "When the pieces have a voice . . ."

"Not at all," Mehrnaz said. She was standing straighter. "It's okay. I can play that game. No matter what happens in the competition space, this time I can refuse to let my family browbeat me into doing what I usually do."

But then she sagged a little. "At least I think I can," she said. "Because sometimes I get so tired . . ."

"Come on," Dairine said. "For a while, anyway, let's go relax someplace where nobody's going to beat you up."

14

Canberra: The Post-Semis Mixer

✶

THERE WAS A MIXER that night in one of the bigger function rooms of the convention center, and it spilled out onto yet another of the terraces facing the lake. At least a few hundred people were there: wizards and their guests, people who'd fallen out of the first round but were continuing to follow the event, or others who were attending for the first time because things were getting more exciting.

Possibly the most relaxed people were the forty or so contestants who headed the deselected in this stage. Bigger and slightly more ornate deselection tokens had been handed out — they glowed silver — and some discreet trading was going on. Some of it was less discreet: Nita could see that the poker group had once again convened over in one of the corners, and a pile of blue- and green-glowing tokens from the previous round now had some sparks of silver in it.

Not quite so relaxed, of course, were the five finalists. Nita stood there shaking her head once more in amazement that Penn had managed to make it through. It was hard to reconcile the trembling, freaked-out guy she had nearly had to shove into the judging room with the judges' brief assessment, published at the end of the round, of "a promising and generally well-constructed wizardry presented with some style and élan by a forthright and well-spoken contestant." *They must have really seen something there, though,* Nita thought. *I guess all that work that Kit and Dair and I did has paid off. But after this, it's all up to him. And the spell...*

Penn had recovered enough to be laughing and joking and showboating around the room the way he had on the night of the first round, swanning out onto the dance floor to bump and grind and boogie with anyone who would hold still long enough to let him get close. Nita noticed with some amusement that he was doing a lot better at finding dance partners as a finalist than he had as a survivor of the first round. *Well, maybe that'll keep him out of trouble for a while.*

As for Mehrnaz, maybe she preferred not to dance, and as Nita looked around, she didn't see her at all. Two of the three other finalists were standing by one of the food and drink tables, deep in conversation. *Wonder if we've got a little something else besides competition going on there,* Nita thought. One of the pair, a handsome, dark, broad-featured Finnish guy whose first name was Joona and whose second name had so many vowels that Nita had stopped trying to say it after the fourth or fifth attempt, was laughing as he drank some kind of near-beer, and was gazing out at the room as if he still couldn't quite believe what had happened to him. The other one, a tall, willowy Indonesian girl named Susila Pertiwi, was drinking coconut water on the rocks and talking quietly to Joona between fits of laughter. This intrigued Nita, as both their projects had been highly involved and detailed — Susila's having to do with microgravity management framed as a technology that conventional scientists would be able to "stumble across" in decades to come, and Joona's involving the rerouting of cold water currents in the Atlantic to rejuvenate the Gulf Stream and heal the somewhat damaged southern Atlantic "heat-pump engine" that maintained healthy ocean temperatures but had recently been suffering on account of climate change.

Right now, though, the two of them seemed mostly occupied with making eyes at each other. Nita thought it was very cute. She hoped the fifth finalist, an Iowan guy whose name she thought was Maxwell and whose project she couldn't remember for the life of her, was having as good a time.

"Yeah," said a familiar voice in her ear, "they're a real pair of lovebirds, aren't they?"

Nita snickered at Carmela's whisper. "Wondered when you'd get here," she said. "I thought you'd decided to take another shopping day."

"Woman does not live by shopping alone," Carmela said. "Sometimes the excitement is elsewhere."

The first sentiment struck Nita as ridiculous coming from Carmela, and she was opening her mouth to say so when she saw a slim, tall, dark-haired figure in black jeans and black T-shirt weaving through the crowd toward them with a dark drink in one hand. "Aha," Nita said. "Might've known."

"And what are *you* two plotting and planning?" Ronan said as he eased up to them, walking carefully to spare his pint of Guinness.

"The fall of empires, the destruction of civilization as we know it, the usual," Nita said. "When did you get in?"

"Oh, just now. I was about to go to bed when suddenly the idea came to me, 'Why don't I transit halfway around the planet and completely screw up my internal scheduling for no particular reason?'" He took a solicitous slurp through the head of his pint and paused to wipe away the mustache.

"Well, I don't care about the reasons. It's nice you could make it."

"And why wouldn't I come? Seeing as somehow both you *and* Kit have managed to come out winners in this thing."

Nita shook her head. "We're not winners yet . . ." She swallowed. It was silly to think about things like jinxes; they didn't exist. Still, she didn't want to talk about the possibilities too much just yet.

"All the same," Ronan said. "Thought I'd see you guys before the real stress begins."

"And speaking of stress, what have you done to your *head*?" For Ronan had developed a bold silver-white streak springing from his part in the front.

"Took all the white hairs this one's giving me and put them in one place," Ronan said, flicking his gaze toward Carmela.

"I'm missing something," Nita said.

"He's going in with me on a trading venture," said Carmela.

Ronan waggled his eyebrows at Nita. "Chocolate."

"Oh *God*," Nita said. Chocolate was unique to Earth, and fulfilled numerous roles among a multitude of alien species: currency, drug, priceless collectible, aphrodisiac . . . The sudden image of Ronan and Carmela as some kind of Han Solo and Princess Leia, transiting stealthily from one star system to another with cargoes of contraband cocoa, suddenly sank itself into her brain. "Maybe," Nita said, "the less I know about this the better. Listen, have you seen Dairine?"

Carmela pointed over her shoulder to another table at the far end of the room. "She was after an iced coffee or something."

"Okay. You going to be here for a while?"

"Till closing time. I'm looking to add some part-ners."

"I'll catch you later, then."

She headed over to where Dairine was pouring cream into a tall glass of coffee and ice. "Feeling the strain, Dair?"

Her sister sighed. "It's either this or those energy drinks, and they all taste awful. You okay?"

Nita nodded. "Not too bad."

Off to the side, someone in the circle of guys and girls in the nearest corner said in a broad Aussie accent, "Dealer's choice. Five card stud . . ."

It was Matt. "I'm in."

"James, you're always in. A veritable rock of inno-cence in a suspicious world."

"Stop buttering him up, Matt. I'm in too."

"Sarah! Good woman, you. Lesser beings have refused to come back for another round after such punishment."

A tall blond lady slipped into the circle and got herself comfortable. "Hey, wait for me, Matt!"

"Couldn't possibly start without you, Emily, wouldn't be the same without your lovely carping when I clean you out."

A hand reached down into the circle from behind Emily and handed her a diet Coke. "You're going to want this."

"Thanks, Rivka . . ."

Nita smiled, turned away from what was sure to be another bloodbath. "Where's Mehrnaz?"

"Taking some personal time. She's had . . . an interesting day so far." Dairine glanced around and noticed the group sitting in the corner for the first time. "Wait, what are they up to over there?"

Oh no. Nita was all too aware of where Dairine had been getting a significant portion of her pocket money since she was in about fourth grade. *"Dair . . ."*

"What? Why shouldn't I sit in?"

Nita could think of any number of reasons. "Dairine. They're our *cousins.* Be merciful to them."

Dairine cracked her knuckles. "No prisoners," she said.

Oh God, Nita thought, glancing out the windows toward the lake as the dusk settled in, *she's going to own them* all *by the time the night is out.* "I'd still like to talk to Mehrnaz . . . there's hardly been any time."

"She'll be around later. I'll tell her you were asking." And Dairine was off, heading toward the poker game.

Nita sighed and sauntered off with what was left of her smoothie, and made her way around the dance floor. Benches and conversation pits were built into the walls on the side, and on one of the benches she spotted Penn taking a breather.

She wandered over to him. "How're you holding up?" Nita said. "Feeling better?"

"Yeah." He rubbed the back of his neck, a nervous gesture. "Thanks. It's just that . . ." He shook his head. "There are times when, I don't know, crowds get to me."

She raised her eyebrows. "I'd have thought that would've been more of a problem for you in the first round. That place was really crammed."

"I think at first I was too buzzed. Later in the day, it did start to get to me, and I kind of pushed through it . . ."

"Maybe it's cumulative."

"Yeah, maybe." He looked up at Nita. "Because somehow, this morning when I went in there, I started seeing all those *eyes* looking at me. It felt like they were going to see something. Maybe something I didn't want them to know."

"I've had that," Nita admitted. "Especially with the really powerful wizards, the Senior ones . . . Sometimes you get this feeling that they can climb inside your head. Or that they've done it already." She laughed. "Doesn't help that in some cases, they *can* . . ."

"Well, anyway," Penn said, "thanks. You were terrific this morning."

She was touched. "Thank you" was not something anyone heard often from Penn. "You're welcome."

And he grinned at her. "Maybe even as terrific as *me!*"

Nita narrowed her eyes at him, but still managed to find this funny. "Knew it couldn't last. *There's* the Penn we know . . ."

Too late she realized the opening she'd left him. "— and *loooove?*"

"All done now, Penn," she said, waved airily, and walked away.

She went off to get herself yet another smoothie — *I'm going to be so* healthy *this week, once this is over and I dump all the stress* — and ran into Matt on the way back through the crowd. It was so surprising to see him not in the poker game that she laughed. "Bathroom break?"

"I wish! Your *sister,* not to name any names, cleaned me out."

Nita shook her head. "She's not safe to be around, Matt," she said. "Ask the Lone One."

"Don't need to! Doki warned me when he saw her getting dealt in."

Nita laughed. *As good a time as any to deal with this.* "Matt, I feel like a real idiot."

"Why? Unless it's too much hanging around with Bonzo Boy there. That'd do it for sure."

He was looking back across the room at Penn, who was out on the dance floor again. "Not that," said

Nita. "It's . . . well . . . I didn't even realize you *had* a boyfriend!"

Matt laughed at her. "Don't see why it should've jumped out at you! Last time you saw me, I was kinda busy saving *that* long gonzer's life." He jerked his chin at Ronan, who was just sitting down in the poker game, while Dairine favored him with a pleased and predatory look. "And then I buggered straight off. Didn't have time to say 'Hi I'm here to fix the hole in your chest caused by a magic spear and by the way I'm gay!'" And he started laughing harder. "I should get a T-shirt. Save a ton of time."

"This would be the part of the evening where I die of embarrassment," Nita said.

"Absolutely no reason," Matt said. "He'd like you. You should come chat when you have time. But right now I think you're probably busy keeping an eye on Bonzo."

"He's on my mind," Nita said.

"How much?" Matt said, giving her a thoughtful look.

"What?"

"Wouldn't want to worry some people," Matt said.

Nita blinked. "What?" she said again. "Wait. You mean — you mean Kit? Worry about *Penn?*" She laughed at Matt. "*Not the slightest chance.*"

"Okay," Matt said. "Just checking." And he patted her on the arm and headed off.

Nita stood there for a moment, confused, and then went off to look for Kit.

Dairine had no intention of staying in the poker game very long . . . only long enough to distract herself from the stress of the previous hours. Mehrnaz's distress had hit her hard.

It's funny, she thought as she went over to the nearest food and drink table, where she acquired another iced coffee and a chicken salad sandwich. *There she is, with her family so wealthy that she has to* think *about whether she's rich or not. And all the times at home when Dad's been short of money, and I'd think, If we just had a lot of money, everything would be okay. Except that all of a sudden it's obvious that you can have lots and lots of money, but if your family's not on your side . . .*

Dairine sat down and disposed of the sandwich in about two minutes. She hadn't realized how hungry she was. *My meals have been all over the place the last couple weeks,* she thought. *And when this is over I may need to take a vacation from onion bhajis for a while.*

"I think this is maybe the first time I've seen you sitting down since this started," said a voice above her.

Dairine looked up to see Irina standing there looking down at her, wearing a long, casual sundress in a bright floral print, and the usual baby-sling. The yellow parakeet was sitting on her shoulder, gazing around with vague interest. "Oh," she said. "Yeah, everything has been kind of busy . . ."

"I just wanted to have a quick word with you about the Farrahi business earlier," Irina said.

"She and her people are really not good to Mehrnaz, Irina," Dairine said. "They're putting her through all kinds of crap, and it's not *right*."

"They're also, unfortunately, fairly influential in that part of the world," Irina said. She let out a long, annoyed-sounding breath. "You need to understand that what happens at an Invitational can be seen as sanctioned by the supervisory structure . . . And if what happens is embarrassing to a wizard or group of wizards who have significant influence over others, that can in turn affect who works with whom on what interventions, or who's willing to cooperate or volunteer when there's a problem. It can make a difference, regrettably, to the way the world works."

Dairine put her plate aside and stood up. "Irina, if you had to apologize to her about me," she said, "then I'm sorry. But the way they're treating Mehrnaz is *terrible*. Her family is screwed up and her home life is one giant head game. They're kicking her around like, I don't know, a football or something, and if it doesn't stop they're going to screw up somebody who could be a really powerful wizard, really *useful*. More useful than the whole bunch of *them*." She scowled. "And that aunt . . . She is a *complete* waste of time."

Irina stood quiet for a moment. "I remember seeing something in one of your personality précis about your tendency to speak truth to power," she said. "It wasn't exaggerated." And Irina smiled. "Or the bit about your loyalty, once you've decided someone's worthy of it. Those qualities are all very well. But if it turns out the situation warrants it, and I can't calm things down, I may require you to apologize formally to Mehrnaz's aunt."

Dairine scowled at her. "If I have to," she said, "I'll do it. But at a price."

Irina's eyebrows went up. The parakeet stared at Dairine and made a scratchy little scolding noise.

"I want somebody to look into her situation," Dairine said. "Somebody who's got the power to do something about it. It's not fair for her to have to suffer like this."

That smile came back again. "Not the kind of price one might have expected," Irina said. " . . . But I think we can agree on that. Meantime, you can help me out by writing up a description of what instigated the exchange. Be thorough. Give me at least three sets of reasons for what you did, each one better than the last."

"Shouldn't be hard," Dairine said.

"Have it to me tomorrow morning, then," Irina

said. And she nodded to Dairine, resettled the baby sling, and walked off.

Dairine swallowed as it hit her what she'd said and done just a few minutes earlier. *And Nita thinks* her *temper's something,* Dairine thought. *Maybe the stress is getting to me . . .*

She went off with her iced coffee to tour slowly around the room, looking for Mehrnaz. She was getting a sense, now, that Mehrnaz liked to be on the edge of things where she could see what was going on and make the decision whether or not she wanted to be drawn in. Sure enough, after five minutes or so Dairine spotted her over by the room's back wall, leaning against it with her hands cupped in front of her and looking vague.

Dairine headed over to her. "You okay?"

"Sure. Just making dua."

"Making do with what?"

"No! Making *dua,*" Mehrnaz said, amused. "Talking to God." She shrugged.

"Oh."

Mehrnaz laughed at Dairine. "What? It's not like *you're* not always saying 'oh God' this and 'oh God' that!" She smiled. "It's not a big deal, I know it's just how you talk. But God likes it when you make time for conversation. Likes to be asked for things, told what you need, told what you're thinking. I mean, isn't that some of why we're here? It's not like Allah *needs* anything. He likes to hear from us, that's all. Is that iced tea?"

"Oh, no, coffee. The ice kind of watered it down."

"Tea, I really need some tea . . ."

"Then let's go get you some. I just had a talk with Irina . . . best you know what happened."

The evening went on. Kit had spent a while letting himself be drawn into new groups, chatting with people he hadn't seen since the Pullulus War. *It's very relaxing. Which is a bit of a surprise: sometimes I get so stressed meeting people. But these are* my *people. Wizards . . .*

He'd purposely been trying to give Nita some space today. Some remark she'd made to him earlier about the two of them "living sheltered lives" had stuck with him. *She doesn't need me looking over her shoulder all the time. There have to be people here she'd rather be talking to without me standing there hanging on every word!* Still, his eyes kept roving, seeking her out . . .

Like now. Across the room Kit caught sight of Nita talking briefly to Penn as he was coming off the dance floor. Something inside him squeezed uncomfortably at that. First of all, she looked so good. She'd dressed for summery weather in a little flowery skirt and a kind of low-cut pink top and pink flats, and she looked altogether . . .

Hot. The word you're looking for is hot. *Admit it.*

The problem was, he had trouble admitting it. There were lots of girls he thought of That Way, but it wasn't until recently that he'd ever found himself looking at *Nita* That Way.

And it was so *strange.* Sometimes it was all perfectly natural, and he saw her looking back at him and got the sense that she really *liked* him looking at her That Way. On Mars, for example: the old Martians' casual daywear, what there was of it, had suited Nita brilliantly — the glint of precious metals in the bodice and hip harness, the flow of translucent veils in that thin Martian wind. *Mmf!* he thought, flushing a little at the thought.

Then Kit laughed at himself. *I'm like some cartoon character with my eyes bugging out.* But at the same time, there was no point in pretending otherwise: he liked the feeling. And he'd started wondering, in a casual way, what kinds of feelings *she* might like. It wasn't something he spent more than a few hours a week on the Internet researching, and he always made sure to scrub his search history very thoroughly afterward. Where Carmela was concerned, Internet privacy was a concept that afflicted only lesser minds.

He saw Nita make a laughing, dismissive gesture at Penn, a sort of go-away wave, turn her back on him, and walk off. *Better,* Kit thought. *Because as for* him

. . . even if she were interested in him, which she's not, he's nowhere near good enough for her. He doesn't even know how to see her as a human being. The things he says, honestly . . . somebody should kick him.

Kit sighed and kept on wandering. *Why do I see her more clearly when we're around other people? It's weird.*

Meantime, there were additional distractions. The music of all the voices around him, all the different accents, sometimes using the Speech, sometimes in English, fascinated him. One group of voices, briefly laughing raucously, got his attention, and one voice, recently gone deeper than he remembered it, dominated.

"She is getting hotter by the minute," it said, "but a wise wizard wouldn't get *too* closely involved. She's armed and dangerous. In fact she's dangerous whether she's armed or not."

"Terrific, though."

"A real looker."

"You'd have to wonder what she'd be like."

"Just look at her, are you *kidding?*"

"Now, now, kind of objectifying there . . ."

"I would say the divine Ms. Rodriguez is absolutely *worth* objectifying."

"With that hair . . ."

"And that butt . . ."

"I can think of somewhere she could sit that down!"

Kit's eyes widened. He slipped quietly close to the group from behind.

"Excuse me," he said softly, "but are some of you guys discussing *hitting on my sister?*"

A shocked silence fell as all eyes present turned toward him. Some of them went confused. Some went embarrassed. "*More* than hitting on her!" Kit said. "That was *sex* being discussed!"

The silence got deeper.

"I mean, seriously, have a little *respect,*" Kit muttered into it.

Most of the group looked abashed. Ronan looked innocent.

"No, he's absolutely right!" Matt said, looking around. "*Completely* inappropriate! So cut it out and let's talk about something besides Carmela's sex life."

Kit breathed out a sigh of relief.

"Let's talk about *Kit's* sex life."

Kit stopped breathing.

Penn, Nita thought, shaking her head.

She visited one of the drinks tables again — *I am so smoothied out, no more of* those — and found some kind of unfamiliar Australian lemonade, extremely sharp and very refreshing. With this she strolled to the outside terrace and leaned on the railing there, watching the lights of the city twinkle on the water of the lake across the road.

Down the railing, something moved. Nita glanced that way and got a glimpse in the dimness of an orange jumpsuit. "Liss!"

"It's getting warm in there again," she said. "Even here they don't seem to have the hang of the air-conditioning . . ."

Nita laughed and made her way down the terrace. "More kinds of heat going 'round in there than one," Nita said.

"Uh oh," Lissa said. "Don't tell me. Penn?"

"He keeps getting weird with me and I'm not sure how to handle it."

Lissa sighed. "Well, I don't know that I'm the right one to be asking for advice," she said, "as I've got absolutely no interest in any boys that way, so I'm short on data."

That made Nita blink. *Oh my God, is she like Matt and* again *I haven't noticed?* "Yeah, I know, he —"

"Or any girls, either. Or anybody."

"Oh," Nita said. *I am such an idiot. She's a virgin and she's perfectly okay with me knowing that, she is so brave* — And then she lost her train of thought, because Lissa had kind of an unexpected smile on her face.

"Because the sex thing," Lissa said, "I don't do that."

"Yeah, I thought I was getting that," Nita said.

"I didn't say I *hadn't* done it," Lissa said. "I didn't say I *couldn't* do it. I said, I *don't* do it."

"Uh. You're . . . you're, uh, celibate?" Nita had meant it to come out as a statement. But instead it came out as a question as Lissa's smile changed again and she seemed positively amused.

"Nope, I'm ace," she said. Nita blinked.

"Asexual," Lissa said.

Nita took a breath. *"Wow"* was all she could think of to say. *I keep saying that lately. To everything. I am the least interesting person in the world.*

But Lissa was grinning, and now she burst out laughing. "That is the best reaction," she said, "the very *best* — !" And peal after peal of her laughter rang out and she wrapped her arms around herself. "Perfect, just perfect, what a breath of fresh air!"

Nita felt both relieved and somehow obscurely annoyed. "Have I been some kind of idiot again?" she said. "Please say no."

"No," Lissa said.

"Relationship and physicality," said a dark voice from off to one side, sounding a touch amused. "Always so fraught . . ."

They both looked farther down the railing. Darkness loomed in darkness there, wrapped in shadows.

"Uh, hi," Lissa said, sounding uncertain.

"Pluto, Lissa," Nita said. "Lissa, Pluto."

Lissa's eyes went wide in the darkness and the near-full moonlight on the water. "As in the Planetary?"

"That's him," Nita said. "Come on over, elder cousin, don't be shy. . . ."

The shadows moved closer, coming to rest at Nita's left elbow. "I wouldn't like to intrude."

"You're not." She looked up into that darkness, trying again to catch a glimpse of the difficult-to-see eyes. "Relationships, though . . . Don't tell me *you've* got trouble that way. Sounded like you didn't mind what Jupiter and Saturn had going . . ."

"Of course not. They're of consenting age," Pluto said. "When one's over two billion or so, what one does with another body is one's own business."

Lissa spluttered with delight.

"But out in the further reaches it can be different, the distances are so great. One can feel a bit left out. Even in my original system, I was the furthest distant. The last formed . . . all the best elements pretty much gone at that point." He paused. "You gather yourself together as best you can from what's available. And then start circling, doing the eternal Round: trying to find out what's going to happen in your life . . ."

Nita looked over at Lissa. "Left out . . . You ever feel that way?"

Lissa shook her head. "About sex? No. Do you feel dragged in?"

Nita laughed helplessly. "God *yes!* And not by Kit. By other people."

Lissa nodded. "So did I until I realized it just wasn't for me. But once I found a special friend, someone who mattered without the sex being what it was about . . ." She smiled. "Things got sorted."

Nita looked over to the darkness at her elbow. "You're so far out there," she said, "and you can't do the resonance thing quite the way Jupiter and Saturn do . . ."

"There are differences," Pluto said. "Neptune and I have an old periorbital relationship; the occasional amiable gravitational interaction . . . two neighbors waving as they pass on opposite sies of the street." There was a slight smile to be sensed inside that darkness. "But there are many other consolations, other ways to fulfill your passions and be intimate with the universe in singularity: for even great distance need not imply isolation. In my place, you learn darkness, and the uses of it. Cold, and the mastery of it. Emptiness, and the secrets it holds. You learn strength: the certainty of iron, the stability of stone. You hold those places, those states, as a reference for others. Let stone melt to magma elsewhere, let iron melt to slag: *you* know solidity, and hold the reference true. And because that's what Life's given you to do, you do it well and steadfastly. There's joy in that." He was silent for a bit: but then, all his words seemed to

Nita to rise out of a great silence. "And if sometimes you yearn for closeness to the inner circle, you learn to know that you already *have* that closeness in the work Life's given you. You guard the outer boundary of the circles of Life, sweeping up matter that could come to threaten lives closer to the warm heart of things. In their name you hold the space of Strength in Emptiness, and gladly make your rounds ... and *maintain.*"

Lissa nodded. "I did that for a long time," she said. "Just kind of waited, you know? I always knew something else was going on with me but I didn't know the words for it. It wasn't anything to do with not being able to be in love! God, I crushed as hard as anyone else. But the whole physical end of things? Pff." She waved a hand in the air. "No interest."

"But then things changed," Nita said.

"Yeah, I found the Special One," Lissa said. "The one who got that there were other ways to be close." Her voice went quiet and musing. "Kind of sudden and unexpected. But I *should* have expected it, really. Change is what life's about . . ."

"It was so for me as well," Pluto said. "When I was a far smaller planitesimal, my star died. Oh, nothing spectacular! It swelled, it ate its inner worlds; then everything collapsed and went cold. So I waited: maintained, as I'd always done. And things shifted, as they always do. Turbulence in the starstream, gravitational fields shifting; benevolent chaos brushes up against you. A black hole wandered by from the madder spaces near the Galaxy's heart. It knocked me loose and sent me tumbling out into the dark. And then I traveled hopefully, as they say, for a long time. And finally, there came that first brush of gravity and warmth, out at the edge of the Sun's radiopause. Such a kind eager little star, so small and solid and golden. It reached for me and drew me in, and so I found a home again in the outer reaches, among many others; some of whom have become one with me since."

"All that time by yourself, though . . ." Nita said.

"It was worth that wait," Pluto said. "I am home now."

"Definitely worth it," Lissa said, "even if finding the way takes a while. There's always somebody that you're the Special One for."

"Patience," Pluto said, "is key . . ."

They were all quiet for a few moments. "Your Penn guy — he's looking for the Special One, too, maybe? But not waiting. Just grabbing at whatever gets close enough . . ."

"Could be," Nita said. "Or trying to find something to replace something he's lost. Not that *I* want to get close enough to find out. Because —" She paused. "There's something else. Gut feeling — a visionary's supposed to trust that, I think." She shivered. "But right now I feel like a TV with a busted remote. Half the time, I get every channel but the one I want. And some of the ones I see, right now, I *really* don't like."

"But without getting into that," Lissa said, "you were going to say you think Penn's got something different going on with him."

"Maybe." And it flared again in Nita's mind, that image of the stranger-Kit, staring at her with empty eyes. And Carmela, near tears, grabbing her, shaking her, begging her not to let them get Kit, whatever she did. Nita shivered. "And I don't know where to go with that."

Lissa shook her head.

"Stay in the Now," said the dark regard fixed on Nita from the other side. "The Now is where all useful work is done. To plan for the future, to anticipate it: these are prudent. But to *live* in it? For those of us grounded in the world of time and matter, that's mere folly. The Now is where we and the One brush shoulders. The only place." And then Nita got a sudden sense of uncertainty from that otherwise very solid and grounded presence. "Was that the right idiom? 'Shoulders'?"

"It's usually 'rub,'" she said, and smiled. "Close, though."

And from inside, then, came a sudden roar of applause.

"Huh," Lissa said. "What's going on in there?" She peered toward the doors. "Some kind of big circle —"

A bare second later, something went through the back of Nita's mind like a hot needle: the feel of a spell getting ready to fire.

"Oh my God," Nita said softly. "Kit. *What is he doing?*"

The evening was wandering gently along to what Kit thought was probably going to be its conclusion. The dance floor was emptier than it had been; people had started saying their good nights an hour or so before. Matt and the other guys whom Kit had been speaking to earlier, except for Ronan, had already left. Carmela had left as well, apparently for the Crossings, to talk to Sker'ret about furthering one or another of her nefarious schemes.

Kit yawned — it had been a long day — and headed over to the drinks table to see if he could find one of those canned iced coffees before going to find Nita. He was rummaging around in the very depleted magical cold drinks bin, unable to locate anything there but beer, which he didn't want — when the voice said from behind him, "Looking for a nightcap?"

Penn. Kit sighed. From what Nita had told him about his state this morning, he was pretty much fully recovered now, getting bolder and braggier by the hour as he forgot how embarrassed he'd been. Kit moved the last few cans around, found one of the little skinny beige-and-brown coffee cans, grabbed it, and popped its top. "Nope," he said, having a drink, "I think I'm about done. Gonna find Nita and call it a night."

"I can see why you might want to," Penn said. "Finally, I can see it. She was so strong with me this morning, and I never saw that in her before." He had a sip out of the bottle he was carrying. "I guess I'm big enough to admit I was a bit wrong about some stuff. Her power levels, anyway. And what she knows how to do with them. The manual doesn't lie, after all."

"So you can read," Kit said, amused. "Nice to hear."

"Yeah, I can," Penn said. "But can you read what's going on right in front of you? You don't deserve her, Kit. You've been taking her for granted for a long time."

He was getting loud, and some heads were beginning to turn. Kit's mouth quirked a little in distaste. "Penn," he said, "this isn't a conversation I want to have with you. We've got a lot of work to do in the next few days before the finals . . . so let's finish this up for tonight and head home, okay?"

Penn gave Kit a narrow-eyed look. "Yeah, I bet you don't want to have this conversation," he said, more loudly. "Because what I'm saying's true, isn't it? Anybody who *appreciated* what he had would've made a move by now."

More heads were turning nearby. Even some people on the dance floor now, sensing the sudden tension in the room, had stopped to stare. In the increasing quiet, Kit's voice became a lot more audible. "Another wizard," Kit said, "another person, isn't someone you can *have.* They might share themselves with you. But if you're going to get all grabby-hands about them, then you deserve to be dumped on your butt."

Kit couldn't help glancing at the bottle Penn was holding. Penn's expression went belligerent. "Oh, come on," he said. "I don't need to be drinking to be brave enough to take you on!"

"Not what I was thinking," Kit said. He shook his head. "I don't want to do this, Penn . . ."

"Of course you don't. Nobody likes to lose."

The silence around them was increasing. "If you don't want me as your mentor," Kit said, "say the word and I'll step away."

"Go right ahead," Penn said. "Nita's committed. I'll keep her."

Kit just looked at him.

"And why shouldn't I? Because admit it, you're on the downhill slide. Your high-powered days are behind you now. That's why you're mentoring, after all." Penn smiled. "Those who can't do . . . teach."

Around them, the quiet went dead silent.

Kit felt the flush rising to his face. *And to think we had the idea that maybe he was done being a jerk,* he thought. *Okay, then. He's spoiling for it. Time to teach him some manners.*

"Fine," Kit said, raising his voice into the stillness. "I really don't need to be listening to this. We've got hard work ahead of us at the finals, and there's no point in letting stuff fester. So let's find someplace where the ground suits."

All around them, there was the sound of breath being pulled in. "Does the ground suit?" was the question asked by a wizard offering another one the opportunity to duel.

"Right here'll do," Penn said, glancing around them. "Even *you've* got enough expertise not to damage anything."

"Let's make double sure," Kit said. "Keep it inside a force field. Who'll hold it for us?"

Ronan came striding with some urgency from the far side of the room and stopped in front of Kit, bending his head down. "Are you seriously going to waste your time on this little twat?"

"No more than about five minutes of it," Kit said.

"You are bloody buggering insane, have you ever even *done* this before?"

He hadn't, but the phrase *I'll keep her* was ringing over and over again in Kit's head like a gong and making it impossible for him to feel anything but a deep, cold anger. "First time for everything," Kit said. "So are you going to hold the force field or not?"

Ronan stepped back a couple of paces, shaking his head. "Clear back, people," was all he said.

Murmuring, the people who'd been in the center of the room started backing away. Penn walked out into the space they'd left and Kit followed, wishing Penn would change his mind. But it plainly wasn't going to happen.

In the center of the empty space, they turned to face each other, and Kit swallowed. He'd been the one to offer the challenge phrase, so it was Penn's right to pick the manner in which the duel would be conducted. "What's the paradigm?" Kit said

Penn was grinning. "Elemental," he said. "Pick two elements, stay inside them. No sliding out; changing into a nonelected element disqualifies you immediately. Best four falls out of seven. Leaving the agreed space is an instant forfeit. Winner's the one who forces the other out of an element or makes it impossible for them to change between the two. Agreed?"

"Agreed," Kit said.

"Pick your two," said Penn.

"Earth and water," Kit said.

"So passive-aggressive," Penn said. "Perfect. Air and fire for me."

Kit rolled his eyes. "If the ground suits," he said, "shut up and get on with it." He shifted his gaze to Ronan. "Got the field sorted?" he said.

Ronan had his eyes closed as he consulted his Knowledge-based version of the manual. Now he flipped his hands open in a "Not *my* problem now, you idiots ..." gesture, and the faint shimmer of a hemispherical force field domed up around them.

Penn vanished, or seemed to.

Kit closed his eyes and whispered the words he needed, dissolving.

The principle behind the kind of shape change you used for this sort of duel was uncomfortably simple. You dissociated your consciousness from your body's matter, and used that as raw material to mimic other kinds, states and masses of matter. Key to coming back to your own form after such a bout was making sure that you had your own bodily structure and elemental construction locked down correctly before you shifted out.

That was a simple business for someone who was used to working with the Mason's Word, and there were few spells Kit knew better. *Or maybe one,* he thought. *Save that for later ...* Before the force field was even up, he'd had the coded matrix for his own body's structure laid out in his mind, and he'd saved all the pertinent data to it. It was fail-safed as well: should he be incapacitated, his mind would find its way back to his reconstituted body automatically.

Okay, Kit thought. *Let's start out basic.* He'd been immaterial for a few moments, and already the space inside the force field was being buffeted by a ferocious wind meant to keep him from coalescing. *Don't think so*, Kit thought, and pulled up into the forefront of his mind the structure of a large granite boulder —

All around him he could feel the wind changing tack, blowing at him with force and pressure impossible except in places like Venus. And here came the heat, too. Between the wind and the fire, flakes and granules of sand were being eroded swiftly off the structure of his granite. The air inside the force field went thick and gritty with his own substance that was being stolen from him. If this went on for more than a minute or so there wouldn't be much of him left —

He shifted elements, letting go of the hard lattices of stone and letting all his atoms slide into liquid state, into water, completely filling the body of the force field. *Wind can't blow if there's nowhere to blow to —*

He heard a screech of frustration, much dulled by the weight of the water. *Okay, let's see what you've got next —*

Terrible actinic light erupted inside Kit, blinding him and stabbing him with pain. It was plasma, burning the water in the middle of the dome, combusting it away to hydrogen and oxygen. Gas started to fill the upper part of the dome, and Kit could feel Penn starting to pressurize it, meaning to break the force field and push Kit's water form out past its boundaries to make it forfeit.

Nope, Kit thought, *no way,* and shifted elements again, back to earth this time in the form of the extraordinarily energy-resistant green metal that the Martians had used. It flowed gleaming green in the space and solidified into the shape of one of the Martians' giant scorpion-pets, a heavily-clawed and armed *sathak.*

Instantly fire flowed around him, but the sathak-constructs that Kit was mimicking were impervious to that. *It's so perfect,* Kit thought. *He wants to go big and flashy. He thinks water and earth are weak because they're not violent and showy —*

Kit, Nita yelled at him, *what the hell are you* doing?!

Who was it who said he needed some slapping down? Kit said. The temperature of the fire was increasing, but he could resist it for the moment.

Not like this!!

Are you kidding? Just like this! This is the first time he's fully engaged with anything since we've met. He's always held something back so he can concentrate on playing Most Alpha Guy On The Block. Not now, though!

Then Kit realized he'd better start paying attention again, as Penn had switched tactics and was now blasting his metal scorpion with pure oxygen and sulfide gases. Between them Kit was being simultaneously bathed in acid and rusted away in huge unnerving flakes. *Okay, not good,* Kit thought, *what's a good response* — ?

You shouldn't be doing this! Nita was shouting at him. *You're enjoying it* way *too much!*

I absolutely am *enjoying it.* Incredibly. *And you would be too if you'd heard the kind of things he was saying about you. In fact you'd be helping!*

She didn't answer, just stood there fuming. *Fuming,* Kit thought, *there's a good idea. Let's get volatile. Sodium? Naah, too quiet.*

Magnesium —

Kit's scorpion slumped into a dusty pile of silvery metal grains. The acids and the pure oxygen hit it and its surface began instantly to bubble. Kit felt the instant shock of alarm go through Penn as he tried to change into something less reactive, but too late, the magnesium ignited —

The explosion that followed was tremendous and deafening, even inside the force field. For a moment things were quiet: then came a scream of rage, followed by the force field being filled entirely by a ravening ball of compressed plasma, pure star-core.

Kit screamed with the burn of it. But he still had an answer as his magnesium atoms started to burn away. *Just enough left, and don't forget the gravity damper* —

A second later the inside of the force field was completely coated with the thinnest imaginable skin of collapsed matter, so dense and dead black it could hardly be seen. *Because there's more than one kind of star-core, little boy!*

Inside the shell Kit could hear Penn raging and screaming in plasma form, but there was nothing he could do: he was trapped. Very slowly Kit began to collapse the skin of hyperdense matter around him, and inside it the plasma started to burn lower under the increased pressure. Penn was choking as Kit slowly put his fire out.

Give up, Penn, Kit said silently.

No!

Kit squeezed tighter. The shell collapsed smaller and thicker every moment: the size of a beach ball, the size of a basketball. *Say it!*

No —

Penn's voice was weaker, the fire was almost entirely out now, he was gasping —

— the size of a softball, and there was hardly a spark of plasma left burning in it now. *Say it!*

A final desperate gasp, and then — *The ground's yours!* Penn whispered. *The ground's yours, let me —*

Kit let the spell go and called his matter back to make up his body again.

The force field vanished. Kit was lying there on

top of Penn in clothes that were acid-burned and sandblasted and very much the worse for wear. Penn's clothes were scorched and stained and his flipflops were melted. Kit started getting up —

To find himself staring up into the furious face of Irina Mladen, and the outraged parakeet on her shoulder, which was flapping its wings and shrieking at him. The baby, surprisingly, was asleep.

"Up," Irina said, "both of you."

Kit and Penn struggled to their feet.

"Your team is suspended until I decide whether you should be allowed to compete further," Irina said. "Go home. I want to see you both tomorrow. I'll send for you."

And she disappeared.

Penn threw Kit a withering glance, turned his back on him, and took a few steps toward Nita. "Did you see what I —"

"*Don't*," Nita said in a voice like someone contemplating murder. "This is *your* fault."

"What do you mean? *I* didn't do anything, *he* started it, everyone here saw it —"

"Penn, shut up! This wasn't about you, don't pretend this was about him, this was about *me* somehow. *Why are you so damn* fixated *on me?*"

"*Because you have something I need!*"

It was a cry of pure rage and anguish that froze Kit where he was, it was so unexpected.

Nita didn't sound impressed. "Well, *what?*"

"I don't *know!*"

And a dead silence fell.

Nita seemed powerless to do anything but stand there and shake her head. "Look," she said, "I'm done with you for today. Actually I'm done with *both* of you at the moment, but *him* I'll forgive. I guess," she said, pointing at Kit. Then she glared at him. "When I get over being fought over like some prize out of a bubblegum machine!"

She swung on Penn. "And as for you! I made a promise, and if Irina lets me keep it I'll keep mentoring you with Kit if it kills me. If it kills *both* of us, because all this crap has to be about *something.* Now go the hell home and don't let me see either of you until you're done with Irina!"

And she vanished, too.

Kit and Penn stood there staring at each other, then sullenly turned their backs on each other and walked away.

I don't get it, Kit thought. *That was for her. Why doesn't she get it?*

. . . Girls!!

15

Antarctica and Daedalus

✴

"To describe this whole event as unbelievably witless and profoundly distasteful would probably be an understatement of considerable magnitude."

The Planetary Wizard for Earth lived in a third floor apartment in a very average suburb of Prague. The flat had beautiful high ceilings and a hardwood floor and five or six rooms that opened in and out of one another through tall double doors. The living room had six tall windows, a fireplace in the far wall, and shag rugs and brightly colored baby toys scattered across the floor. Over on one side was a crib, in which a baby in a diaper and a T-shirt with a picture of Donald Duck was lying on his back, sound asleep. The rest of the room was filled with comfortable furniture, none of which Kit or Penn was sitting on. They were standing in the middle of that hard wooden floor, shifting uncomfortably from foot to foot, while the woman who was arguably the most powerful wizard on Earth glowered at them from across the dining room table where she was working.

She sighed the exasperated sigh of someone with too many chores to do in too short a time. All around her on the table were piles of paperwork, books that might or might not have been wizards' manuals, and empty coffee cups. With one hand Irina was rubbing her forehead. With the other she held a pen she was using to tap more or less constantly on a legal pad, where many notes were written in a tiny, neat hand.

"You," Irina said, pointing at Kit. "I'm sure I don't know why I need to keep having these talks with *you*. You came to me very highly recommended. Tom Swale, whose opinion I trust implicitly, spoke very highly of you. But now I have to go back to Tom and say, 'How can you be sending me this person to work with when he behaves the way he behaved last night?' You've embarrassed Tom, you've embarrassed me, and as for what the Powers That Be make of it —" She stared at the ceiling as if begging for help.

"And about *you*," she said, pointing at Penn, "I've no particular reports at all. You do your work, you go on errantry when it's required of you, and generally speaking you do an okay job! But the problem seems to be that when you're not on errantry, you feel yourself at liberty to share your opinions about things. And some of these opinions . . ." She shook her head rather helplessly. "I'm not sure what century they come from. They remind me more of ancient Babylon than anything else. And the Babylonians may have had some terrific wizards, but as a civilization they had a long way to go before they started treating people like human beings."

Irina glared at them both again. "Wizards are in general expected by the Powers That Be to exhibit good sense. Courteous behavior. Intelligence! But I'm looking in vain for any sign of any of those from you two after —" and she glanced at the legal pad she'd been writing on —"9:48 Canberra time last night. You could've done serious damage to the convention center. You could've done serious damage to *each other.* The spell you were using, yes, it's very well known, and if you're familiar with it and careful with it one can usually recover from it even under fairly dire circumstances, but I question whether either of you was being careful last night. At least you had the smidgen of good sense to ask for a force field. I wish that Ronan had exerted more pressure on you to to stop what you were doing, but it's possible he correctly perceived that at that point there was no stopping either of you, short of dropping the roof on your heads."

She dropped the pen on her legal pad so that she could rub her forehead with both hands. "There's no point in asking either of you what you were thinking, as you plainly weren't thinking," Irina said, as with a whirr of wings the parakeet flew onto the table, wobbled over to the pad, and picked up the pen in its beak. It started to walk off with it, and Irina reached out and took the pen back, then dropped it on the legal pad again. "Thought was in fact the furthest thing from either of your minds. Other organs appear to have been in play that are not very useful for thought. Yes, I know that at your age everyone gets very hormonal, there's no way to avoid it. But combining that particular set of hormones with wizardry can be as irresponsible and counterproductive as combining wizardry with alcohol or drugs." And she glared at Penn. "Understand me: We have room for passionate wizards, we have room for sexual wizards, we have room for wizards who act on impulse — because sometimes impulse is the right thing to act on. But we have no room, *none*, for idiotic wizards. And you two have somehow managed to combine cleverness about the way you use spells and manage your wizardly practice with occasional flashes of the most extraordinary idiocy. I really begin to wonder if it might not be smartest to take you out of circulation for a while."

Kit and Penn stared at each other in confusion and dread.

Irina let them stand there like that for a few moments. "You have to understand," she said, "that because of my position as Planetary, I have wide latitude over the practice of wizardry on this planet. I am sometimes in a position to recommend to the Powers That Be that they *offer* wizardry to a specific person. And I'm also in a position, sometimes with the greatest regret, to request the Powers to *withdraw* wizardry from a person. The withdrawal can be very short-term, or very, *very* long, if necessary."

The parakeet was attempting to make off with Irina's ballpoint pen again. She took it back and once more began tapping on the legal pad with it while the parakeet made grabs for it.

"I hate doing that to younger wizards," she said, "because all their good habits and expertise they've acquired during the early practice tend to get mislaid during a prolonged ban. Often they're never again quite the wizards they were. And you can guess what such a ban does to relationships that these individuals might have with *other* wizards."

Kit had never had a referent before for the phrase "his blood ran cold," but he had one now.

"I wouldn't like Nita to suffer as a result of such a ban," Irina said. "She's done nothing but try hard to keep you two on an even keel. But the way you work with each other, or I should say fail to do so, is making that effort increasingly difficult. I need to find a solution to this problem fairly quickly, because the finals of the Invitational are fast approaching. And we have never, *never* yet had a finalist chucked out for behavioral issues. Other reasons, sometimes, yes. But not that."

She paused. "If either of you has anything useful to say to me here that does not involve some imbecilic attempt to blame the other guy, I'd be happy to hear it now. Anything."

Kit fought with his own urges briefly before finally saying, "Nita's been seeing some kinds of disturbing things in her dreams. And I think maybe I've been getting kind of disturbed by them too."

Irina sat looking thoughtfully at him. "You two are fairly close," she said.

Kit blushed, twitched a bit where he stood, and looked away. "Not like *that*," Irina said. "I have no interest in where you are in that regard. It's not my business. But your mental connection has sometimes been quite strong. I understand that that's in flux right now — which is normal for this age, and for this type of relationship. But how have *your* dreams been?"

Kit shook his head slowly. "I'm not sure," he said. "Usually I don't remember most of my dreams. But right at the moment — I'm not remembering any of them."

"Is that so," Irina said. "Then may I make a suggestion? If at some point in the near future you have a dream that you *do* remember more vividly than usual — please share it with one or the other of your Supervisories. I'd like to have it screened. She made a note. "But this isn't germane to the immediate problem. There is no question that the piece of work that *you* have brought to us —" and she pointed at Penn —"is superior. We weren't kidding when we wrote our evaluation. This is one of a possible suite of solutions to a problem that's going to become more and more of an issue as Earth becomes ever more surrounded by fancy electronics on which the daily lives of billions and billions of people rely."

Irina leaned back in her chair. "You have a right to be credited for that work and to continue to do it — so I'm reluctant to ban you. But I'm not yet entirely decided whether I want to let you present in the Invitational. Your behavior has not been best representative of the kind of talent and mastery both of oneself and one's art that we expect of people who function at this level. And as for you, Kit, I mean —"

She shook her head again. "You've come through in the past under extremely peculiar circumstances. Yet I have to ask myself whether it is wise for me to keep sending you into situations in which one day your impulsiveness may mean you don't come back. If that were to happen to you because I cleared you for errantry in the face of evidence that you can't be relied on to act wisely, your blood would be on my hands."

She looked at one of those hands. "There's enough of that as there is," she said very softly. "On my instructions wizards go to their deaths — not exactly *every* day, but it would be rare for a couple of weeks to pass during which someone out on errantry does not wind up in Timeheart because I sent them into harm's way. Bad enough when it happens to adults. When it happens to our younger wizards . . ."

She looked away and let them stand there for a few minutes more while she folded her hands, rested her head on them, and stared at the legal pad.

After another moment she stood up, walked past Kit and Penn to the crib, and leaned over it. The baby had awakened and was looking at her with clear gray eyes. Irina picked him up and put him over her shoulder, then walked back to the table. She leaned against it while the baby made little gurgling noises. "Sasha here," she said, "might not be alive right now except that a wizard working closely on human blood chemistries was able to cure him of neonatal leukemia. That wizard was a presenter at the last Invitational. He found a way to leak some of the nonwizardly modalities of his treatment into the public domain, and as a result, neonatal leukemia death rates are starting to drop." She rubbed Sasha's back. "So I very much dislike keeping any particular piece of work out of the Invitational once it's past the semifinal stage. There tend to be reasons why such works wind up there . . .

reasons we don't always understand. Sometimes the Powers don't understand them either."

She looked at the baby. Sasha turned in her arms, put his hand on her mouth, and stuck a finger up her nose. ". . . So I think I'm going to let you present," she said, looking at Penn. "But if I hear so much as a *whisper* about you being any less than unfailingly polite —"

"But I *am* polite!"

"Only in the most offensive way possible," Irina said. "Truly, it's a gift! But so is what you've been building. So present it. And while you're doing that, you will do *whatever* Nita and Kit tell you to do. If they say 'Jump,' the only answer I expect from you is 'Into which dimension?' I expect your presentation to go off without a hitch. Otherwise, all kinds of hell will break loose. Am I understood?"

"Yes, Planetary," Penn said.

"And as for you," she said to Kit, "stay grounded, all right? Nita is at a pivotal place in terms of her wizardly career. She needs someone solid behind her. The element of earth you chose last night — ?" Irina laughed ironically. "Well, you got that right. Stick with it."

She sat down at the table again, still holding Sasha. "So I'll see you in four days, on the Moon. Now go away, and let me get on with —" she waved one hand in the air —"the rest of the planet. Go well, you two."

And they vanished.

. . .

The crater Daedalus on the Moon's far, "dark" side is one of the largest craters on the body, if not *the* largest, and is positioned almost exactly in the middle of the side that's permanently turned away from Earth. Its floor is surprisingly smooth, broken only by a scatter of small flattish, central peaks; and the neatness of the crater's positioning has caused some earthbound astronomers to suggest that this would be a perfect location for an installation of radio telescopes, protected by the Moon from the never-ending racket of radio emissions from Earth, or even a vast liquid-mirror optical telescope that could see farther away in space, and farther back in time, than any other.

Wizards, of course, have had other uses for it. Not too long ago it had been used to stage the last defense of Earth against the inbound darkness of the Pullulus: the inhabitants of the defended planet could see nothing of the heroism or tragedy that ensued. Now, though, the space had been prepped and reclaimed for the Invitational, as it had been a number of times before.

Up on the mountainous rim of the crater, a teenager in a personal force field shield looked down into the heart of the crater and saw something shining and iridescent as a soap bubble resting over the peaks at the crater's center. An area about the size of Manhattan Island, in terms of square mileage, had been domed over with wizardry, filled with air, and warmed:

and in that space she could see the movement of the Invitational's spectators, getting themselves settled.

There were other things going on. Much closer to the rim, near where Nita was standing, someone had laid out a baseball field in the gray regolith, and batting practice was in progress.

"Come on, put it over the plate —"

"No hitter, no hitter!"

Nita watched one solidly hit fastball arch up and out into the darkness, wondering idly how hard you had to hit a ball up here to make sure it reached escape velocity.

Two point three eight kilometers per second, Bobo said.

"Thanks for that," Nita said. "I have no idea what that's going to feel like when you're batting . . ."

Probably about like a triple against the centerfield wall.

"I'll take your word for it," Nita said.

She became aware that someone was standing beside her. An older teenager, wearing a portable mechanical force field generator belted into the small of her back, was holding up a sleek black tablet-camera and photographing the batting practice.

"If I didn't know better," Nita said to Carmela, "I'd think you were stalking me."

"Kind of too busy for that," Carmela said, turning

the tablet in her hands from portrait to landscape orientation and grabbing another shot of the baseball field.

Nita gazed at the device admiringly. "Where did you get that?"

"At the Crossings," Carmela said. "Sker'ret got it for me. Take a look at this —" She flashed its shiny black front face at Nita. "That whole *thing* is a camera. Perfect definition, like looking through a window. Standalone 3D, you name it . . . it's fabulous. Sker'ret wants lots of video."

"Want me to give you a lift down to the center?" Nita said. "My dad's down there . . . I want to check on him before I go back down to Antartica."

"I'll give you one if you like," Carmela said. "Sker's given me a point-and-shoot gating locus, it hooks into the hex he's installed down there."

"Sure."

A few minutes later they were stepping out of the bold blue tracery of the Daedalus gate hex and looking around at the crowds. The center section, closest to one of the in-crater peaks, was empty at the moment, reserved for the competitors, their support teams, and the wizardries that would be worked there. But around the reserved center, a huge crowd of people were standing, sitting, lounging, or just hanging around, waiting for the event to begin.

Nita parted company with Carmela and went wandering along toward where she'd left her dad and Nelaid. As she was getting close to their location, some activity off to one side caught her eye, and when the figures causing it got close enough she could see Matt at the head of them, bounding along through the gray dust of the crater toward her. *Like a kangaroo,* she thought, amused. A crowd of others came along with him, among them the twychild Tuyet and Nguyet and Matt's small dark Egyptian boyfriend Doki, whom Nita was glad to meet at last.

"Looking for the best spot?" Matt said. "You might try up the crater's slope a ways, the view's a bit more panoramic . . ."

"Nope," Nita said, "I've got my people settled. If I can just keep my dad from filling every available container with Moon rocks to take home, everything'll be fine."

Matt laughed, then looked at Nita keenly. "And how are *you* holding up? You were having some weird dreams, I hear."

"You on the clock for medical support already?"

"Not yet. Soon, though. And anyway, thought I'd check."

She shrugged. "Just par for the course, lately."

"Okay," Matt said. "You know, though, anything starts bothering you, you shouldn't hesitate to call."

"Yeah," Nita said. "Irina sent along a message about that after she got done reaming Kit and Penn out."

"Would've liked to have been a fly on the wall for that one," Matt said.

Nita smiled sourly. "You're not alone."

"Where's Kit?"

"Down in the Blue Room right now. Mostly he's keeping Penn calm."

Matt raised his eyebrows. "Wow, kind of a role switch. That was your job, I thought."

"Well, Kit's gotten better at doing it. Fortunately they won't have to keep it up much longer . . . they're both going crazy being kind to each other to stay on Irina's good side. I'm scared one of them's going to sprain something." Matt snorted. "Meanwhile, Irina sent me up to have a look at the crowd and see if they were settled in." Nita looked out across the expanse of the crater. "I have to confess, all these lawn chairs make me laugh."

And there were a lot of them. Nita's manual told her that three thousand, eight hundred and sixty-three humans were up here to see the Invitational's final phase, along with various cats, dogs, dolphins, and a few stray whales. Since the whole center of the crater had been domed over and climate-controlled with wizardry, the human visitors had been extremely proactive about bringing the comforts of home with them: the whole place had the look of a rather monochrome tailgate picnic. Even Nita's dad had made arrangements to bring supplies when he came up with Nelaid, and had arrived with his own lawn chairs and a beer cooler.

"It is kind of crazy," Matt said. "Worth enjoying while it lasts. But listen, before you go, I've got something to show you —"

Doki and the twychild were suddenly all attention. Matt pulled his jacket open. Inside it was a dark blue T-shirt that said in white letters:

HI THERE
I'M HERE TO
SAVE YOUR LIFE
AND BY THE WAY
I'M GAY

Nita covered her face and laughed helplessly. "Oh, God, Matt. You're wearing this to torment me. *Take it off!*"

The Twychild laughed uproariously. "Ooooo, Nita!"

"I might have to explain!"

"When two guys —"

"Or girls —"

"Or whatever —"

"Love each other a whole lot —"

"Then they get *snuggly* —"

"And sometimes if one of them asks the other to, you know, take their clothes off —"

"It could be misunderstood!"

"Which is why you should always use the Speech in such discussions —"

"Because then you can use the phrase *me'hei tha sam'te* instead of 'take it off'—"

"Which there are just too many ways to misunderstand in what's laughably called Our Common Tongue."

"Yeah, ask about the time I knocked Kit up —"

"Matt," Nita said.

"Mmm?"

"Kindly shut them up."

The twychild dissolved in laughter and took themselves away.

Nita had to wipe her eyes, she'd been laughing so hard. "Okay," she said. "I should get down there again. I think we're probably about ready to start. You going to stick around afterward?"

"Wouldn't miss it for the world," Matt said. "Cleanup's half the fun. I'll see you up here after your guy kicks ass."

Nita high-fived him. "We'll see how it goes," she said. Matt and Doki waved and headed off.

Nita went bouncing along a ways farther until

she found her dad's spot. He and Nelaid were already stretched out on the loungers — Nelaid hanging out somewhat over the end of his: no one on Earth had yet made a lounger long enough to take a Wellakhit — and both looked extremely relaxed.

"They about ready to start?" her dad asked.

"Very soon now," Nita said. "You guys all set?"

"We have all the comforts of home," Nelaid said. "It's hard to think how our enjoyment could be enhanced."

"Well, stay comfy," Nita said, and bent down to smooch her dad on the head. "I'm going to go downside and make sure our bundle of nerves is ready to go."

"You think he has a chance of winning?" her father said.

Nita shook her head. "One in five," she said. "Keep your fingers crossed."

And she vanished.

In Antarctica, on the Knox Coast, it was around sundown, under a rising full Moon.

"It's not so much a green room as a blue room," someone had said when the space was getting set up, and that observation had provoked an immediate change of name for the venue and a fair amount of laughter. But there wasn't any laughter right now. The space that had been so full of cheerfulness and nerves when they'd all first met inside it weeks ago was now simply full of nerves: bundles of them. There were five of these, along with eight others, their mentors, and one woman with a baby and a parakeet.

Everyone was sitting over in one of the conversation pits that was big enough to take fifteen or twenty people. Centrally positioned in the group, standing, was Irina. "The first thing you all need to know," she said, "is how extraordinarily proud I am of you. All five of you have risen superbly to the challenge. Wizards who've done the Invitational for a century and more are all agreed that this is the single best group of finalists' spells they've ever seen. All of you are going in the manual; and all of your spells are going to be named after you, which as you know, in this business, is about as famous as anybody gets." She smiled. "The work you've done is going to make a difference to people all over this planet, and in some cases to people on other planets as well, where the technologies can logically be extended so far. You have increased knowledge, and there is nothing in the world more valuable than that."

Off to one side, Dairine was sitting beside Mehrnaz and rubbing her back to try to work a few of the knots out of it. Mehrnaz was thrumming with tension; her hands were clasped together until the knuckles went white, and there were circles under her eyes. She hadn't slept well for the last few nights.

"I told you you should've come and stayed in

my basement," Dairine said. "Plenty of room, good food —"

"No bhajis," Mehrnaz said.

"Which is fine."

"I was *afraid* you'd get ruined for them . . ."

"My fault, not yours," Dairine said. "Meanwhile, my sister makes pretty good pancakes when the stove's not acting up. Promise me you'll come."

"I promise I will," Mehrnaz said, "assuming I survive . . ."

Nita appeared quietly at the far end of the room and walked down toward the conversation pit. Irina turned toward her. "How is it up there?"

"I think they're about as ready as they're going to be," Nita said. She looked over at Kit and Penn. Penn was hunched over, rubbing his hands together. Kit was watching him, not touching him or getting too close; but he had a concerned look in his eye as he glanced up at Nita.

"All right," Irina said. "Roll call. Joona?"

Joona Tiilikainen, with his tilted dark eyes and his close-cropped dark hair, exchanged a glance with Susila Pertiwi next to him. "All set."

"Rick?"

Rick Maxwell, a tall, raw-boned blond guy with a broad Midwest accent, nodded. "Ready when you are."

"Susila?"

Susila threw her long dark hair back over her shoulder. "Let's go."

"Mehrnaz?"

Next to Dairine, Mehrnaz nodded hard twice. "Yes."

"Penn?"

He raised his head, tilted his chin up. Dairine saw Nita smile at that for some reason. "Let's do it."

"Then let's go topside," Irina said. "Everybody into the transit hex: and the Powers be with you!"

A moment later, darkness full of stars was arching over them.

Kit took a deep breath. Beside him, Penn took one too, almost certainly for very different reasons.

A roar of welcome went up from the spectators at the sight of the group appearing in the hex. Kit looked all around, wondering where Nita's dad and Nelaid might be. Three thousand people didn't seem like a lot when you thought of a modern sports stadium; but packed into this bubbled-over intimate space, the crowd seemed huge.

"Cousins and friends and welcome guests." Irina's voice rang out, artificially amplified by wizardry. "Please acknowledge and greet the participants in the final round of the 1241st Interventional Development, Assessment and Adjudication Sessions: the Wizards' Invitational!"

A thunder of applause, a huge cheer.

"Our competitors are the best of the best, chosen by a rigorous testing and evaluation scheme from among a field of more than three hundred of the best and brightest young wizards from around the world. Over the past fourteen days they and their custom-designed interventions have passed through day-long all-comers evaluations and *viva voce* panel judgings designed to reveal weaknesses and hidden strengths, and determine how effective these spells will be when used in daily practice. The contestants will now demonstrate their spells live, activating for the first time what have until now been strictly theoretical interventions untested at full scale in physical reality."

Irina looked around at the contestants. "We'll start with the usual random number selection to determine the order of presentation. Each competitor's manual or similar instrumentation has been requested to generate a random number. Low number goes first, next to lowest number goes next, and so forth. Will you please display your manuals."

They did. Irina walked down the line of five finalists, regarding the book or roll or device that each one held out to her.

"All right," she said. "First will be Rick Maxwell, who will be demonstrating a magma management and redirection technique for volcanoes located near urban centers, intended to prevent pyroclastic flow and similar dangerous phenomena." Rick waved at the crowd and the cheering began.

After a moment the crowd settled down. "Presenting second will be Joona Tiilikainen, who will demonstrate a new Atlantic conveyor protocol for deep ocean convection management." Joona waved and jogged around a little like a Rocky clone, which produced some laughter and more cheering.

"Presenting third will be Penn Shao-Feng —"

"Third," Penn was muttering, "third is good, third is a great spot —"

"Yes it is," Kit murmured. "Now just hang onto yourself, don't lose it. You're gonna be fine, right? Stay focused."

"Presenting fourth," Irina said, "will be Mehrnaz Farrahi, who will demonstrate an energy cancellation and displacement protocol for management of slipstrike and similar earthquake faults —" Kit saw Dairine put both hands on Mehrnaz's shoulders from behind, holding her down as if she was likely to ascend into the air; and she leaned over and whispered something in her ear.

"Third," Penn was saying. "Gives me a little extra time to get ready."

"Yeah it does," Kit said. "So get into your head, not too deeply now, start going through the outer inclusion circles of the spell —"

"And presenting fifth will be Susila Pertiwi with a

planned-subterfuge microgravity acquisition program for release into the wild." Applause for that.

"Can I now ask all but the first contestant to take their seats. Will the implementation support team please set up for the first presentation?"

A group of wizards in casual dress came in from one side and arranged themselves around the cleared central space. "I need to remind the spectators," Irina said, "that the effects you're about to see are physical-force virtual duplicates of real effects on Earth, manufactured here by wizardry with one-to-one correspondence in terms of mass, weight, and other physical qualities. They are reproduced here so that there's no chance of endangering or alarming communities on Earth, and they will look and feel real. Even though these effects can be classified as an amazing reproduction, they are not immaterial . . . And since the human mind is a funny thing, in this next demonstration in particular, we urge you not to play with the lava."

That produced some slightly unnerved laughter from the audience.

The unnerved noises got considerably louder when a smallish but terribly real, full-size volcano appeared in the middle of the cleared space and began to erupt. And then Rick Maxwell, in his polo shirt and jeans and loafers, walked over in front of the foot of the volcano, threw his arms wide, and began to chant in the Speech.

The lava slid directly down at him, and gasps went up all around; but Rick paid the lava no particular attention, just kept speaking the trigger phrases for his predesigned wizardry. The spell that began to spread out around him was a masterwork of structure, elegantly constructed to trap and hold stone in solid form by way of clever temperature changes and gas nullification routines. Kit watched it with admiration. Penn watched it too . . .

And then Kit was horrified to hear Penn mutter under his breath, "This was a horrible idea. I can't compete with that."

"Yes, you can," Kit said. "It's nice, Penn, but you're in another league. You're dealing with much bigger natural forces . . ."

"A very bad idea . . ." Penn was whispering. "I can't do it."

Kit looked at Nita with dismay.

She crossed over to them from where she'd been standing off to one side. "Penn . . ." she said.

"I can't!"

Kit and Nita stared at each other.

Oh God, Kit said silently to Nita. *He's freezing up again.* Now *what??*

"Look at that," Mehrnaz was murmuring. "It's fabulous."

"It is," Dairine said, watching with pleasure as the

lava ran down, slowed, and was halted by wizardry and will. She laughed at the sight of it, reminded of the toy volcano she'd built for one of her school science fairs a long time ago. "But you know what? What you've got is hotter."

"It is, isn't it?" Mehrnaz said.

"Absolutely."

"And when I make it work," Mehrnaz continued, "my aunt is simply going to bust a blood vessel somewhere."

"Ideally at the end of her nose," Dairine said.

Mehrnaz snickered softly. "I'm done with her," she said. "After this . . . we're all finished."

"Finished how?"

"I was thinking about moving out."

"Kind of a big concept right away," Dairine said. "Don't worry about her right this minute. Or the family. Pay attention to what you came to deal with. The spell."

"But that's part of it," Mehrnaz said. "My auntie always wanted to do this, Dairine. The other relatives all convinced her she never could, and she fell in line."

"But not you," Dairine said. "Trendsetter." She grinned.

"This is *my* dream now," Mehrnaz said, low and fierce. "She gave hers up. I found this one and I'm not going to let it go."

"Right," Dairine said. "Look now. He's almost fin-

ished. He did a great job with that. But not like you're
gonna do. Two more people and it's your turn . . ."

A roar of applause was going up all around them for
the perfectly stalled volcano. Rick Maxwell was taking
a bow. The threat management wizards came forward
and spoke a pre-prepared spell: the volcano promptly
and obediently vanished.

"Next," Irina said, "Joona Tiilikainen . . ."

Joona stepped forward into the newly cleared
space, bowed his head, and waited.

Another group of threat management wizards
came out, encircled the space: stood quietly for a
moment, then started speaking.

And within seconds the whole space was a column
of cold green seawater hundreds of feet across and at
least a hundred feet high, with Joona buried under that
terrible depth and weight of water, right at the bottom
and standing there like a statue with only a thin force
field protecting him.

Nita noted how the tagged hot and cold currents,
lighter blue, darker green, were moving in the column.
Joona, fighting the tremendous pressure slowly and
with difficulty, held out his arms on both sides and
began slowly forcing out the words of the spell he'd
designed. Gradually, it flowed out from him, carpet-
ing the bottom of that huge cylinder of water, then
spreading upward into the water like a webwork or

tangle of light, impelling the water into configurations that, once started, would self-manage and self-perpetuate. Cold water flowed under warmer current, warmer polluted water was sucked out where natural processes could decontaminate it . . .

This is fabulous, Nita thought. Her own work with water was mostly beginners' stuff compared to this. *He's good, this guy. But Penn* —

Penn was staring at what Joona was doing, and the look of upset on his face was getting worse by the second.

Nita leaned down to him. "Penn," she said, urgently, "remember what happened to you in the semis. This is just that all over again."

"But this is different," he whispered. "Something's coming. Something's going to happen. *I can't do the spell* —"

Nita's mouth suddenly went dry, for she realizd that she could feel it, feel what he felt: that sense of impending danger. "I get it," she said. "You saw it coming. You had a weird dream, didn't you?"

Kit was looking at Nita with with growing concern. "You get *what?*"

She blinked, trying to stay anchored in the reality of the moment. "I can see why he freaked. I can *feel* why he freaked. He's right, something's coming —"

"But what?"

Out of nowhere there were too many answers. "Something awful," Nita said. "But it's not what he thinks."

Then he's just panicking again!

"Yeah, that's part of it," Nita said out loud.

And he's expecting you to save him again, to give him the answer? He's supposed to be doing this himself, but he knows you'll drag him where he needs to be again —

And it was like a bolt of lightning jolting through her. The image from the dream of the Other who'd been wearing Roshaun's body, saying *No one looks at me across the board.* And then the image of fire. Something burning, striving, trying to escape —

"Yes. *Yes* I have the answer, you're absolutely right! Oh God, you are so perfect!" And she grabbed Kit and pulled him close to hug him. *"How are you always right?!"*

He was staring at her in total perplexity. "That's not what you were saying before."

"But you know. And *it* knows. The *seeing* knows, the vision . . ."

There was fear attached to this for her, too. If Kit was right about this, then he was also right about the danger that Nita had seen coming toward him and Carmela. Her mouth went even dryer as she realized there was no cherry-picking this scenario for an answer she liked better. You had to take the vision whole or not at all. *Oh God — !*

But one thing at a time. Just one!

The applause for Joona was starting up now as he finished his work and walked out the side of the column of water, waving at the crowd. The threat management wizards were already moving forward to decommission the water: a moment later the whole massive column of it was gone.

Penn was staring at where it had been. He whispered, "I can't."

"Yes, you can!" Kit repeated.

And Nita grabbed Penn by his shoulders and stared into his eyes.

"You have to," she said.

"But in the dream I had —"

Nita swallowed. "I know what's in that dream, a little. We're all stuck in it now. If you don't do this spell, something *really bad* is going to happen. Lives are going to be saved or lost because of you finishing this thing or not finishing it. Winning, losing, it doesn't matter. The *demonstration* is what matters. You have got to produce the result."

He sat there shaking his head. "But what if I can't —"

"I've been down this road, believe me," Nita said. "Once upon a time I had to produce a result after I swore to do it. It felt like it took me forever to do what I had to, to make up my mind to it. Good thing I had a lot of help, because I was seriously ready to fold. But the help was there." She took a long breath. "And I just about got myself where I needed to be when someone stepped in . . ." *Or swam*, said her memory, in a darker voice. She could still see herself hanging in water that burned bright, somewhere else entirely, while overhead cruised a shape brighter than the water, glancing down at her with one dark dispassionate eye — Death passing her over, passing her by, in pleased and deadly dignity.

"And presenting next," said Irina's voice, "Penn Shao-Feng —"

"Get up," Nita said, "and do it."

Penn got up, shaking but suddenly determined, and walked out into the cleared circle. He looked like someone walking to his doom.

Kit watched him go, and abruptly realized that he was shaking too. Beside him, Nita was trembling as well with the force of something that hadn't happened yet but was about to.

"What happens now?" he whispered.

Nita shook her head. "It all depends on him . . ."

The threat management wizards were standing around the borders of the circle now, reciting together. Above the space where they were working, the solar wind slowly became visible, spilling past the Moon in great waves and folds like the curtains of aurorae in Earth's upper atmosphere: but these were white, not green or blue, because there were no atmospheric gases for them to react with. They lashed and rippled close to the Moon's surface as dangerous solar storm weather would lash and lick at the Earth when the solar wind was too strong.

Penn took a huge breath, closed his eyes, and held out his arms to either side. All around him, blue-glowing on the dusty ground, it began to appear — the spell Kit and Nita had seen and debugged a hundred times now, the one Kit thought he could probably draw in his sleep.

Very quietly, almost in a whisper, Penn began to recite the spell.

From the diagram, long, graceful, frondlike golden structures began to rear up, the local wavefront guides that would push the solar radiation away from the Moon for demonstration purposes. And from the core of the spell came winding upward another, bigger structure, wavering gracefully: the spell's power conduit, the part that was meant to be sunk into the Sun to power the redirection. The fins at the top of it, the power collectors, looked like the broad petals of a flower, and the main power conduit that would enable the redirection of the solar wind was its stem.

Slowly and lazily the gigantic, glowing, immaterial flower of energy began to twine upward . . .

And then it started to move faster. And faster. It burst upward through the sheltering dome and out past it, curving around the lunar horizon, heading with terrible speed into space . . . and toward the glow of the Sun, away past the dark circle of the new Earth.

There were shouts of alarm from some of the wizards in the audience and on the staff, because this wasn't supposed to be happening. The integrity of the wizardly dome was holding — it had been designed to allow energy constructs to pass. But the amount of energy now passing upward through it was already frightening, far more than expected, even though — the wizardry not being impeded by minor matters such as light speed — the conduit was still barely halfway to the Sun. And shortly the incoming energy would be more appalling still, for the power collectors on their ever-stretching conduit were arrowing toward the solar surface with ever-increasing speed. They would sink into the Sun, they would pull power from it, and that awful power would be conducted back here to the surface of the Moon —

"*Shut it down!*" Irina shouted.

But Penn had finished the recitation and was now frozen where he stood. Irina moved forward, sudden power trembling about her hands as she flung them up and with one huge gesture brought another force shield into being between Penn's spell circle and the surrounding audience.

Barely a second later, a horrifying spill of raw plasma came blasting down the conduit from its far end, already inside Mercury's orbit, and slagged down the lunar surface for hundreds of yards around. Penn fell, vanished away in a blaze of eye-hurting white fire.

And Nita realized that while she stood here watching this terror in the waking world, she was also standing inside one of her dreams.

16

Sol IIIa, Sol, Sol III

✳

OH NO. IT'S STARTING. *It's starting now.*

I'm not ready *for this!*

And then Nita got a grip. *Of course I'm ready for this. I'm a visionary. I will handle this thing, because I can see at least some of what's going to happen. Which is more than most of the people here can do . . .*

And then, instantaneously, she had that terrible sensation she'd experienced occasionally before — that she was standing on a knife-edge, and huge forces were waiting to see which way she moved. *This is how it was the first time,* she thought, remembering what happened to Kit's first Edsel-antenna in Grand Central Terminal all that while ago, at the end of the Ordeal that first made them wizards: the smoking abyss full of terrible, hungry eyes anticipating their fall, the sword-bridge that the noon-forged steel became and that they both had to cross. They had been over that bridge in other forms many times since.

Now everything was different, everything was changing. *But some things are still the same,* Nita thought. *Have to be. Have to be!*

She lifted her gaze to Kit. Their eyes locked.

"Whatever you have to do," Kit said, "do it. I'm with you."

She turned away from Kit and went over to Penn and took his hands. He gasped in air and stared at her in shock.

"I am looking at you," she said. "*I am looking at you across the board.* Do you see me here? Do you understand me? *I'm looking at you.* If you're going to do something, if what you said to me was for real, *this would be the moment.*"

Penn stared at Nita in astonishment and terror, uncomprehending. Close behind her, she could feel Kit staring at her, not understanding either, and very afraid.

But still not moving. Not saying a word, holding still, letting her keep her balance. Trusting her —

"Just hold still," she said to Penn, and closed her eyes.

Because you have to see this. I can see it now. Everything's come together and I can see it at last. The choice to see *became* the vision, and it blinded her and spilled over out of her. Fire, fire everywhere, flurrying like wings, like something trapped in a cage and beating its wings against the bars of the cage to get out. And crying out in a voice like fire, the voice from her dreams, *Let me out, let me go —*

Fire, fire that flies. All the stories about the phoenix, the fire that burned out and then rekindled itself in a blaze of magic: this force was the source of them. *Not stories after all, and not just magic. The nearest star, the Sun —*

Something living in the Sun. Something that was part of the Sun; a living thing, its soul, the way the soul lives in a body. But also, something that left, that went voyaging. And then got caught away from home . . . got lost. That got trapped somewhere it shouldn't have.

And in a flash, literally a flash of light, Nita understood it.

I have a problem with crowds, Penn had said to her once.

Nita swallowed. *And why wouldn't you,* she thought, *if something inside you was used to this kind of life? Solitary, so alone, built to be that way, happy to be that way. But stuffed into a place where you couldn't get out, where you were trapped and crammed in tight and tied down by thought and emotion, by fear and pain . . .* She thought about how Ronan had been, sometimes, his edginess and troublesome ways when the Michael Power had been inhabiting him, an immortal crammed into so small a space, physically and temporally. *Of course Ronan's still a pain in the butt sometimes but it wasn't all* him *being the pain all the time —*

Nita thought about Penn's grandfather, too. *You have an outrider,* he'd said, practically the moment he laid eyes on her. *And his grandson . . . how long did he suspect?* Nita thought. *Is this why Penn never wanted to spend time with him? Because his grandfather knew, but didn't know what to do? Just hoped, maybe, that in another culture what was inside him would either find a way to sleep peacefully and leave his grandson alone — or else escape at last?*

And now, here, finally, concentrated, was all that power — everything it needed to break its prison, to get free. *And the spell was in sync with it. The spell's been trying to break the connection, to let it go!* "Do you *get* it now, Penn?" Nita said. "You've had it exactly *backwards.* You don't want to be controlling anything to do with the Sun. You want to be taking the control structures *away!* You've got something in you that's been in your family for a long, long time, stuck in your souls one after another, generation after generation, and it's never been strong enough to get away before. *But now it is!* You've got the connection, you've got the spell! Turn it loose, let it go, *set it free!*"

He stared at Nita, shaking his head. "I don't —"

"You *do!* You said I had something that you needed. *This is it!* What you needed is what I see!"

She could hardly see him through the blaze of fire, the great wings beating. All she could do was grip his hands until he squeezed his eyes shut with the pain, and had no choice but to see what she was seeing. The spell was active, the linkage was there, the vision ran down the linkage and Nita felt it shock through Penn as if her hands were a live wire he'd grabbed.

The shock hit her too; Nita fell to her knees, shaken, as the vision departed from her. She felt Kit come up behind her to help her as Penn went staggering away from them toward the core of the spell, the Speech-notation all around him flaring with furious golden fire as he stumbled through it, disturbing its power flow.

There at the core of the spell, Penn reeled a moment in panic or indecision. Then he fell, collapsing onto the innermost power control statements, obscuring them, taking them out of the circuit. And as he fell, fire flowered upward.

Nita had to laugh out loud from delight now, looking up at the huge and blinding shape towering over them, throwing its wings wide, first one pair, and then another even larger. *This* was the fulfillment of the visions of burning that had been haunting her dreams. *Flamboyant,* Nita thought, *isn't that what I said about him all that time ago? Now I know why!* The immense shape kept growing, rearing up and up from the lunar surface like a great fierce bird. It beat those massive burning wings so that shadows fled and flickered among the craters in the mountain peaks, as if the whole surface of the dark side of the Moon was alive with fire. *It's a good thing we're turned the other way right now, because if they could see this from Earth . . . !*

The fire burst higher upward, and as it did, it found a voice and roared with joy. *Free,* it cried. *At last, at last!*

Like everyone else on that crater-plain, Nita stood transfixed. She thought she had never heard a more beautiful voice. It was warm; it was glad; it was fierce with incalculable power. And it was *female.*

If Nita could've spared breath for anything but wonder, she would've burst out laughing. *Oh,* Penn. *Is* this *why you've always been trying so hard to impress the ladies? Or were you just overcompensating . . . ?*

But the urge to laugh left Nita as that impassioned and startling regard turned from the great company gathered around them to fix on her. Nita held very still. She didn't *quite* feel like a mouse under the eye of a hawk, but that fiery gaze was profoundly unnerving nonetheless.

One who sees, said the fiery shape — immensely grave, immeasurably joyous — *take my thanks. Not until I was seen again could I be found. Not until I was found again could I be freed.*

All Nita could think to do was bow: Who knew

what the protocol was for this kind of meeting? If there even was any. "Elder sister," she said, "go to your place, and go well."

I go! the great voice cried. And the form of fire launched itself up into cislunar space, and then arced around inward and made for the Sun.

And not far away, on the other side of Penn's spell, Dairine stood staring down at it. The wizardry lay there still burning, afire with power, discharging like crazy: it was hard to make out anything definite from it. The whole thing was alight like a —

Wait, Dairine thought. Because one place where the semiconscious Penn wasn't lying was *not* alight. Or rather, its boundaries were: but not the empty inside of it. Nothing was written there: no power moved.

It's a lacuna.

You always have to leave a little wiggle room for the elemental presences, Mehrnaz had said, as if it was something very basic and elementary and it was surprising that Dairine didn't know it.

And even Penn had mentioned it. *A way we remember when the Sun was different, when it breathed differently.* And all the characters of the Speech in that spot had been faded down into conditional status, into *and/or.* Something had been there once, something that wasn't there now.

A lacuna, a loophole, a place where something isn't.

Except that something is. Because otherwise, why would his spell be misbehaving like this?

Because there had been something else in the lacuna. Something that wasn't *supposed* to be in the lacuna. Something that wasn't designed for it. And whatever happened here, whatever that creature was — *an elemental presence,* Mehrnaz's voice whispered again — it was now heading for the Sun to fill the real physical space or place that the spell-lacuna represented.

And when it gets there, whatever's in there right now will be destroyed!

For a second Dairine was struck speechless and numb by sheer dread. Then she bent down and scooped up Spot, able to think of nothing but how the Sun had tried speaking to her once and she hadn't understood it but *Roshaun* had, even though something had been wrong, something had been *missing* that she couldn't understand. *There's something wrong here,* Sker'ret had said; he'd been monitoring the wizardry they were working. *Something's interfering with the magnetic flow at this level. A darkness...*

An empty place that should not have been empty. The memory in Penn's spell of a space waiting to be refilled. *For the elemental presence to reassert itself...* And then Roshaun's spell on the Moon that had failed when he was pulling energy out of the Sun while fighting the Pullulus, even though the spell *should* have worked, it really should have. *Except his data was skewed because there should have been something in the Sun and it* wasn't —

"We need the coordinates for where we did the spell," Dairine said as soon as she could find some breath again: she felt like she'd been punched, and even now she was fighting for air. "The one where we fixed the Sun when he was visiting and it was acting up! Project the solar rotation forward to now. Then pull the structural and locational data from the lacuna subset into the calculation, come on, hurry up, *Spot — !*"

Done, he said. *Execute it?*

"*Yes!!*"

They vanished.

Seconds later Dairine stood above the boiling, roiling surface and stared down into it, shaking all over. All alone now, no one but Spot to help her, no other backstop. Below her, nothing but the fire that would destroy her if the fragile force-field bubble protecting her should fail. Strong as the wizardry was that was keeping it in place, it wouldn't last forever. Even with four other wizards holding it with her, the last time Dairine had been party to this wizardry, it had always been in danger of collapsing within a matter of minutes.

And out there, somewhere between here and the Moon, another danger was approaching. She had very little time. If that shape of fire got here before she'd done what she had to do —

She refused to think about that. "Okay," she said to Spot. "One of the things I need, I've got. The other's at home. I need you to open a very narrow transit window to my bedroom and get me the Sunstone."

That . . . It was very rarely that she heard Spot hesitate. *That is going to be dangerous. If it breaches the force field —*

I knew I should have brought it with me. Dammit, I knew. "Never mind, *do it now*," Dairine said, and held out her hand, waiting.

Spot was silent.

The next thing she felt was a flash of nearly unbearable heat. Stunned, Dairine opened her mouth to cry out, probably the last sound she would ever make —

And something heavy fell into her hand: a heavy gold collar, with a big cabochon stone set in the front of it, its pale yellow color almost completely washed out in the light blasting up from the star around her.

"Right," she muttered, and managed with a struggle to get the collar around her neck. The wizardries embedded in the stone weren't so much the issue here: its real value at the moment was as a targeting device.

The perception of heat around her was increasing nonetheless. There was only so much power built into the force field: if the local temperature flared, if she had to spend too long here, the force field would fail and she would cease to exist a millisecond later. To try to conserve some power Dairine whispered a few words in the Speech to tighten the field, snugging it in around her and Spot until it was barely more than a sheath around her clothes and skin. There wasn't a lot of air stored in it, the wizardry that ran the shield would only run it as long as she was conscious, and when she used up the last of her oxygen —

Never mind. There in that torrential brilliance Dairine closed her eyes — not that this helped that much, such was the awful potency of the light around her — and did her best to get into sync with the Sunstone. She'd spent months teaching it to be sensitive to the Sun's moods. Now, though, it was another set of moods she was searching for. A former user's —

Dairine held still, *listened.* It was hard. As the Stone's sympathy with the star around her settled in deeper, the noise of its burning, of its life, became more and more inescapable, more deafening every second. Dairine squeezed her eyes shut, concentrated, did her best to block out that noise. It was other life she was more interested in.

Local temperature is increasing past shield tolerance, Spot said softly.

"Ask me if I care," Dairine muttered, concentrating on the stone. The noise around her, the roar of the star, kept getting louder and louder. *The Sunstone's not enough. It's been too long since he's been in contact with it* — She'd been afraid of that, but she had to try the stone first, because if she tried the stone and her other solution and neither of them worked, then she would have to give up. And if she had to give up . . .

From out of her pocket, Dairine pulled the thing she was hoping she wouldn't have to use: the chain of emeralds held together with a single strand of the Speech — the gems Roshaun had given her, saying, *They're like your world's color, everything's so green, I always think of you when I see these.* And the chain —

She tucked Spot under her arm, stripped the round emeralds off it and stretched the long chainlike sentence in the Speech between her hands. It was two names, actually; a long version of hers restated in the Wellakhit style, *Dairine daughter of Elizabeth daughter of Pearl* and so on back ten generations and more to match his: *Roshaun ke Nelaid ke Teriaufv ke Umren . . .* But in his strand of the chain were words and concepts and feelings that did not appear in the public version of his name, just as there were in hers — things no one else knew but they two alone. At first Dairine thought about pulling the two strands apart. Then she thought, *And what if this* doesn't *work? If I've got to go, I'm going with them still wrapped around each other.*

She wrapped the twinned strand of Speech-made-concrete around the fist of the hand that was holding Spot to her, and gripped the Sunstone with the other, closed her eyes again, and concentrated. That ridiculous lazy drawl of his, the long, graceful gait, the truly silly height of him, the bizarre dress sense, that supercilious smile: all these things she summoned up. And the way his eyes softened and went strangely quiet that time he said *"Just" friendship? A poor modifier for so high and honorable a state.*

Under her the fire roiled, the subsurface turbulence growing. *Local temperature increasing sharply,* Spot said. *Survivability index is decreasing. Force field duration estimated fifteen seconds . . .*

"Going to use another ten of those looking," Dairine muttered. *And maybe another five . . .*

— and just kept listening, *listening.* That voice, laughing, scorning, speaking in anger or pain; *you are the only one who hears me. The only one.* Around her the fire licked and blasted at her shield, and Dairine hung on, stopped breathing, turned off the life support because it was eating energy, the roar scaled up —

And she heard it. *The whisper.* So weak, so faint.

Down! she said to the force field. Obediently, it sank further into the Sun's roiling plasma. The whisper was weaker. But it was also closer.

Down!

She sank faster. The heat began to pierce the shield now. *Nonsurvivable in five seconds,* Spot said.

Dairine let go of the Sunstone, thrust her arm out into the fire, reached, felt around —

Her hand touched something that wasn't plasma.

Dairine clutched it, desperate. *Get us out!* she screamed to Spot as all around a new wave of turbulence rose up around her as if from a sea suddenly agitated to storm.

The roaring scaled up once more until it obliterated everything. White fire utterly blinded her as the shield began to collapse.

She felt the familiar fizz of a last-ditch transit spell folding in around her. From light, everything abruptly flashed into darkness as a great burning winged shape came diving in past her through the corona and arrowed into the surface of the Sun as if into a pool.

Under Dairine the chromosphere heaved and rippled like the liquid it was. The enraged corona lashed at her as everything went black. And the last thing Dairine knew was the sense of something heavy, inescapable as gravity, dragging her down . . .

A bare moment later she came down on something hard and cold with a heavy weight clutched in her arms, crushing her. *I can't breathe. Am I in vacuum?* But she didn't care; the coldest vacuum to be found from one end of the universe to the other couldn't have kept her from opening her eyes right then. Wheezing, her chest tight with fear or anoxia, she didn't care which, Dairine opened her eyes to see what she held.

It was something in humanoid shape, long,

lean, still afire with terrible light, too bright to look at — limbs splayed every which way, a heavy dead weight. Dairine gasped again, struggled up from beneath, desperately blinked her tearing eyes to try to see something besides a blur. As she tried to sit up, long hair fell into her face — sun-golden, silken fine. In anguished haste she pushed it away, squinting and wincing into the raging glow around what she held, trying to see something that mattered more than hair — a face, eyes with life in them, a chest with breath in it —

What Dairine held stirred weakly against her. She felt a heart beating, she heard a wheeze of breath. And now the tears in her eyes weren't entirely to do with the light, though that blazed still. "Oh God!" she moaned, trying again to sit upright, but he was too heavy, and she was too tired all of a sudden, it was all hitting her at once . . .

An instant later there was a shape bending over her, even taller, nearly as lean after months of pain suffered for the one who'd been lost. He helped her with the weight, shifted it so that Dairine could at least sit up. Nelaid was holding her in one arm and his son in another, gasping with shock as awful as Dairine's. He looked up into the dark of the space above the Moon and cried, *"Miril!"*

And barely a gasp later Roshaun's mother was

there in a spill of silver-fair hair, taking everything in, pulling off her long outer robe and wrapping her son in it. Roshaun shone through it like a candle. Nelaid and Miril bowed themselves over him, holding him tightly, shaking with their own anguish and relief. "He's breathing," the Lady Miril was whispering, "O Aethyrs be thanked, he's *breathing . . . !*" And then she threw her arms around Dairine. "Daughter, he's breathing, what did you *do . . . ?*"

"What I taught him," Nelaid said, his voice muffled as he once more held his son close.

"What he taught me," Dairine muttered, and rubbed at her eyes, still tearing uncontrollably. But it wasn't so much because of the light now. That was slowly fading, and even through the blurring of her eyes Dairine could make out the long nose, the clean-cut features. There was a slight frown stamped on them.

Someone came astronaut-bouncing along toward them, a little clumsily. "Sorry," Dairine's dad said, thumping to his knees beside them, "I keep thinking I'm getting the hang of this and then I fall over again. Dair, what the hell *was* that, what did you just *do* there?"

"Got in trouble," Dairine said between heaves of breath.

"You have no idea," her dad said, "*no* idea how grounded you are!"

"Okay," Dairine said, and fell over on him.

He caught her and held her in a way not too much different from the way Nelaid was holding Roshaun. Nelaid's voice was choked. "Oh, my son, how are you even here, how does this come to be, what have you been *doing?*"

A long, long silence. And then, though his eyes stayed squeezed shut, then came words at last, raw and difficult, in a voice unused for so long:

"Holding . . . someone's . . . place."

"Take him home," Dairine gasped. "I'll be right behind you."

"You will *not*," her father said. "You will stay *right here* until Nel comes back for you."

"Okay," Dairine said, and slumped back onto her dad again.

"*Nita? Kit!*" she heard him shout.

"*Roshaun,*" Dairine said, and fainted with a smile on her face.

A crowd of medical wizards was already gathering around Roshaun and Dairine and Penn, Matt being one of the first to arrive. Nita knew she had nothing to add to their expertise: she stood back and let them get on with it. Besides, she was in a state of shock of her own, though she didn't require medical assistance.

"I can't believe it," she said. "Oh, I can't *believe* it —"

"I think you'd better," Kit said behind her, hushed.

"But *finally . . .*" Nita said. So many of the things she'd seen in her head, the terrors, the things she didn't understand: in terms of *this,* they made sense. This was what had been coming. *This* was what she had been afraid of — *Wow, was I dim!*

"So all that worrying you were doing," Kit said, "turns out to have been for nothing."

"Not for nothing," she said, so torn between annoyance and relief that she was having trouble pushing the words out. "For *this.* It was all part of the process. *Everything counts.*" Just for that moment, the vision was staggering, and Nita saw it *whole;* event and causality with joined hands, dancing, dipping each other, taking turns leading, deadly serious but laughing, too. It was too big for her to take in, but Nita knew suddenly that it wouldn't always be. *I'll get the hang of this. It may take forever but it's going to be* so much fun *when it isn't scaring me to death . . .*

"Oh," Kit said, "you mean all the times you nearly killed Penn?" Already the teasing was climbing into his voice.

"Yeah, those, apparently," Nita said, somewhat annoyed with herself. *Me and my temper . . .*

"The time when you charred all those pancakes?"

"Look, you know that was the burner, it's got a short in it somewhere, we need to —"

"Or the time after the Cull when you were freaking out on the dance floor?"

So close. And the gold in his eyes . . .

He was laughing now. "Or no, wait, I know, the time when —"

She turned around and grabbed him by the shoulders and kissed him.

Kit shut up. His eyes went wide. Then they closed.

Some seconds later Nita pulled back and regarded him with shivery satisfaction. "*That* worked," she said.

"Uhh," Kit said. It was the sound of someone who'd briefly forgotten how to talk. He opened his eyes, and then they widened again at the sight of something behind Nita.

"What?" she said.

From behind her there came a soft throat-clearing noise. Kit made a face that suggested that Nita needed to sort herself out and turn around.

She put a little air between herself and Kit, and turned. Irina was standing there looking at them, jiggling her baby in his sling. Her parakeet was sitting on her head, looking behind her and far above at where that shape of fire had been. "You know," Irina said, "I don't know if we should let you participate in any more group projects. Things keep *happening*."

Nita blushed. "Look," she said, "I'm sorry, everything sort of all came together and —"

"If you're sorry," Irina said, "I'm not sure I under-stand why. The Simurgh has been missing for a long, *long* time; it's kind of nice to discover where it's been."

Nita and Kit stared at each other. "It's not like stars can't do *without* a soul fragment," Irina said. "Lots of them do. There's even a technical term for it, because some stars just have it in them to wander, and the attempt to repress that tendency is usually counterproductive. Sooner or later the star Exhales a soul-fragment and lets it go wandering around for a while, and eventually, after getting the urge out of its system, it makes its way back home. Sometimes these stars go a long way away first, and sometimes they get lost. But this is the first case I've ever heard of where an Exhalation got lost inside a *human*."

"Really?" Nita said.

"Yes," Irina said. "And by the way, do you know the Chinese name for that star-bird in the old stories?"

They shook their heads.

"Peng," Irina said. "Usually these days Anglicized to 'Penn.'" She paused a moment to let that sink in. "Anyway, the Simurgh used to have a fairly regu-lar schedule — it would journey for twelve thousand years or so, a 'Simurgh year,' and then come home to roost. But then it went missing. At least now we know *where*. And there are those who'll use today's events to suggest that one of the reasons the Sun has been behaving so unpredictably of late is that it was starting to suffer ill effects from its Exhalation being gone so long. Or from being in the very near neighborhood but never coming home." In his sling, Sasha moved a little and made a plaintive noise; Irina jiggled him a bit harder.

"Oh," Kit said.

"Yes," Irina said with an air of great patience. "So we're going to have to wait a while to see if that's the case. In the meantime, we've got to recess for a couple of hours and clean this place up enough to do the remaining two demonstrations. And since the live demo of your mentee's spell has revealed a serious functional flaw, he's going to have to revise it and submit it for testing before the manual steering committee allows it to be listed for public use. When he's up to it, anyway." She glanced over toward where Penn was sitting, being checked over by the medical staff and looking thoroughly shattered. "In the meantime, I'd appreciate it very much if in the next few days you two would make time for me to debrief you, *again* —" She gave them both a stern look. "And after that, please go home and *try* not to do anything destabilizing for the next month or so, all right? I have a family holiday planned."

"My dad's going to want to barbecue for you again," Nita said.

At that, Irina smiled. "That I won't mind," she said. "Meanwhile, I'd appreciate it if you did a pre-debrief

report for me in your manuals. Nothing too detailed
. . . five or ten pages each will do."

Nita and Kit both groaned.

"Sorry," Irina said. "If you're going to routinely be
a force for good, you'd better get used to the paperwork."

And she disappeared without even a puff of dust to
mark where she had stood.

Kit heaved a long breath of relief.

"Yeah," Nita said. She rubbed her face. "Come on,
let's go see if Dair's recovered a little."

But one more thing apparently wanted to be handled before she left. Matt extricated himself from
among the crowd of medical people, and with him,
Penn stood up. The two of them, bouncing very shal-
lowly so as to stay stable, made their way over to Nita
and Kit.

"Gonna take this one back to San Francisco," Matt
said, "and let him get some rest."

"But I . . ." Penn was rubbing the back of his neck
in a way that seemed to have nothing to do with trying to put his hair to rights. He looked mortified. "I
feel so different."

"I bet you do," Nita said. "After having what you
had stuck inside you for all your life get out all of a
sudden . . ." She shivered. "It has to leave behind, I
don't know . . ."

"A lacuna?" Penn said.

Nita had to laugh at that. But the laughter trailed off as she realized Penn was looking at her as if he'd never really seen her before.

"Yeah," Penn said. "My head feels, I don't know, a lot less — *crowded.*"

"I think you need to talk to our buddy Ronan," Kit said. "He's been through something, well, it's not *just* like this, but he might be able to shed some light on what it's going to be like for you now."

Penn nodded, looking around him in an unfocused way. Then he looked back at Kit and Nita with an extremely unnerved expression. It was like the face of a person of exquisite taste and coolness who had suddenly realized he'd left the house wearing nothing below the waist.

"Have I, uh," Penn said, "have I been a complete jerk?"

Nita and Kit traded glances and then turned back to him. "*Every waking minute,*" Nita said.

"To both of us," said Kit. "But mostly to *her.*"

"No way, more to *him!*" Nita said. "You provoked him into a duel!" Then she sighed. "I guess *some* of your trouble's been secondary to having a frustrated Exhalation stuck inside you. But I wouldn't blame her for *everything.* She had to have some raw material to work with . . ."

A little dejected, Penn looked back and forth between the two of them. "Does this mean you're not going to mentor me anymore?"

Nita gazed at him in shock and wasn't surprised to see Kit doing the same. For his part, Kit burst out laughing. "Penn," he said, "you don't *need* us now! You've got the full attention of the Invitational's finals panel, and they'll put you in touch with wizards who'll be way better than us at helping you debug your spell for the manual." He raised his eyebrows at Nita. "Maybe they can set you up with Dairine."

"Nooooo," Nita said, glancing sideways at the small crowd around her. "I think Dairine is going to be busy. Better talk to Irina and see who she recommends."

"Okay," Penn said. "Well, listen ... I'm really sorry. I wish this had gone better."

Nita shook her head and smiled, glancing over again at Dairine. "Penn," she said, "don't sell yourself *too* short. You've been a pain in the butt, but this has gone *way* better than you think. So you get going, okay? And go incredibly well."

He smiled sheepishly, and looked surprised and pleased when Kit put a fist up to bump. But when Nita moved forward and put her arms around him and gave him a big squeeze, his mouth fell open.

"Go on," she said as she let him go, noting with

amusement Kit's slightly widened eyes. "Get out of here and go get some rest."

"Yeah," Penn said. "Yeah. *Dai stihó . . .*"

He and Matt moved off together and dropped out of sight. When they were gone, Kit regarded her with astonishment. "You willingly touched him," he said.

"Yes, I did," Nita said. "Doesn't mean I'm ever going to do it again . . ."

"*Good,*" Kit said, with such emphasis that Nita gave him a cockeyed look.

"Not the jealousy thing!" Nita said. "You have *zero* need for that. Meanwhile, we have other things to think about." And she looked around them. "One of them being that I think I've got my sister back . . ."

Dairine was sitting up among her own medical people, who were leaving her one by one. She looked white and drawn and incredibly tired, but her eyes were bright, and the grin of absolute joy spread across her face gave Nita a pang of happiness. She dropped to her knees in the moondust and threw her arms around her sister and whispered in her ear, "I am *so happy.*"

Dairine hugged her back. "So am I," she said. "You have no idea."

"And still in big trouble," their dad remarked.

Dairine threw her hands in the air. "Okay!" she

said. "Okay! I did a dangerous thing! But look how well it turned out!"

Her father covered his eyes and shook his head. "You are plainly too drunk on adrenaline and happiness for us to have this conversation right now," he said. "And I am too relieved to see Roshaun back, and happy for Nelaid and Miril, and amazed that I have lived to see a Phoenix rise from the ashes, more or less, and blown away that I'm standing on the surface of the *Moon* while this whole thing is going on, even though I keep falling down every time I try to get anywhere —"

"That would be because your pockets are full of Moon rocks," Nita said. "They still have *mass*, Daddy, and when you —"

"Don't interrupt. — And I'm completely covered with dust and need a *shower* —"

"Yes, you do. So why don't you take Dairine home? Nelaid'll come and get her as soon as they've got Roshaun sorted out."

Nita's sister was staring at her with a thoughtful kind of astonishment. "And this has been really good for *you*," Dairine said, "because I have *never* heard you speak so much good sense at any one time in my life." She leaned up against Nita. "And *you* were the one who told me to stick with this, even though I was jet-lagged out of my mind. Now I'm wondering if I'd even have made all these connections without being so wired from exhaustion and pissed off at Mehrnaz's people!" And she laughed wearily. "Maybe not. Maybe the Powers know what they're doing . . ."

Nita smiled at her. "From you," she said, "that's some concession."

A movement off to one side caught Nita's eye. She turned and saw Mehrnaz Moon-bouncing in their direction, and within a few moments she had joined Nita on her knees next to Dairine and thrown her arms around her. "I told you," she said, "I *told* you how awesome you were. Do you believe me now?" She turned to Nita. "She went in the *Sun!* That is so amazing!"

Dairine laughed. "You think *that* was amazing," she said to Nita, "you should have heard me tell off her aunt. *That* was something."

Mehrnaz clapped her hands in delight. "It truly was! You should have seen her face afterward. It would have curdled milk for *hours.*"

"The only problem I have with that now," Dairine said, "is that it's probably going to make more trouble for you with your family."

"It's *not*," Mehrnaz said. "There are people in my family who have been wanting to do that for *decades*. And Irina called my mother herself and told her —" Mehrnaz blushed. "Well, a lot of good things about me. So it's all going to be okay. The World Earthquake Management Group has already messaged me about my spell, they want to use it as a jumping-off point for some other implementations . . ." Then her expression changed and she said nervously, "But I have to present next and you won't *be* here!"

"Listen," Dairine said, "you know I'm always right. Didn't I tell you that you were going to make a difference in people's lives? And see, you're doing it already. So now I'm telling you you're going to be fine, and I'm right about that too. So go get an energy drink or something and get ready to present. I have to go, I *have* to . . . but I'll watch on the live manual hookup." She patted Mehrnaz's back. "And don't forget your spell-casting thing! You're such a *star.*"

"You made me shine," Mehrnaz said, and leaned over and kissed Dairine's forehead.

Dairine smiled. "Go on, get out of here before I faint some more."

Mehrnaz bounced up, made a little baby-wave at Dairine, bowed to everyone else, and vanished.

"I think that's all the cute I can stand for one day," Dairine said. "Can I please go home and have some *coffee* before I leave for Wellakh?"

Nita rolled her eyes at her dad. "She's all yours . . ."

Nita wandered back to where Kit had been watching this farewell and others. "I've just about had it," she said. "Too much excitement. Shall we stick around for Mehrnaz and the other guy, or should we wander?"

"You could convince me," Kit said — and then paused, suddenly going stiff and tense. "Except . . ."

Nita stared at him. "What's the matter?"

Kit pointed. About fifty yards away, a tall dark shape draped all in shadows was standing quite still and watching them.

Nita laughed. "Feel around you," she said. "It's not our old friend. This is . . . someone different. Come on . . ."

She bounced over to him, Kit following her. When they came to a stop and the dust was settling, Nita said, "Pluto, Kit. Kit, Pluto." She smiled. "See, I got it in the right order that time."

Kit's eyes widened. "Excellent Planetary," he said, with a bow, "greetings, and may our orbits cross without too great a perturbation."

He bowed to Kit in turn. "Always a pleasure to meet a cousin who is learned in the protocols," he said. "I hope you'll forgive me." He turned to Nita. "Third time's the charm, they say. May I have a word?"

"Sure," she said, mystified, and moved a short distance away.

He followed her in his drift of shadows. "My own sphere calls me," he said, "and I won't be here much longer: just until the last two have presented. But before I leave I feel I should warn you that some of us who've been here have not merely been scouting new talent. Some of us are investigating possible future colleagues."

Nita stared.

The shadowy shape looked down at her with an amused glint in its darker-than-dark eyes. "There is a sort of . . . I think in your idiom the phrase would be 'steering committee.' Those of us who have experience of more than one solar system lead it, as we're thought to be less invested in the inevitable in-system politicking: more objective. In years when the Invitational's held, normally one or another of us will be in attendance, looking for wizards who might be suited to such a role. Ideally, these are individuals who are not overawed by size or power, who've survived fairly broad or deep experience acquired rather early. Frequent change of specialties can be an indicator in some cases, or dissatisfaction with one area of study that leads to research into another. Sometimes personal crises are involved, but that's not necessarily a diagnostic."

"Uh. Pluto . . ."

"Call me Aidoneus if you like," said the Planetary, enthroning itself on a nearby rock. (There was no way, Nita thought, in which the way it settled itself in majesty amidst its enfurling shadows could merely be thought of as "sitting down.") "Still one of your words, but perhaps a bit more targeted. The other word has more to do with concept surrounding wealth. Not really my department . . ."

"Wow. Aidoneus. Okay." Nita was fighting to keep about four different things from coming out of her mouth, any one of which would have made her sound like a needy six-year-old if it turned out that she was wrong. "Uh, when you say 'such a role'—"

He said nothing, merely looked at her gravely.

You're not gonna help me out at all here, are you, Nita thought. *No, of course not. I'm gonna make myself look like an idiot in front of one of the oldest bodies in the Solar System. Probably older than the Sun. Oh, who the hell cares? Compared to this guy, Jupiter really is a spotty teenager.* "I just want to make sure I've got the right end of this," Nita said. "'Colleagues?' As in Planetaries."

"Candidates for the position," Aidoneus said. "Yes. There are routinely a number of beings in differing degrees of candidacy, or training for it, as no inhabited planet can be left without a Planetary for very long. Yet in the normal course of events, as I think you might guess, the position is hardly something that happens to someone overnight. Not even as *I* reckon overnight." There was a dry smile somewhere inside that darkness: Nita could sense it. "Aptitude is the main issue. Though to be sure it needs a certain type of personality; or a range of personality traits that work together. A certain flexibility."

"You're thinking I might have that," Nita said.

"You'd know best," the dark Planetary murmured. "In any case, it's something to think about in the long term, as you pursue other avenues of practice."

"You wouldn't even be mentioning this if you didn't think I had a chance, would you?"

"It's never wise to raise hopes without some possibility of them being fulfilled," said Pluto. "Entropy is thereby increased. You might never come to that position, despite a lifetime of candidacy. You also know, I suspect, that the work is dangerous and wearing, and that Planetaries on your world can be relatively short-lived if circumstance and their own natures join to conspire against them."

Nita did know that. She thought of Angelina Pellegrino, Planetary at twenty-two and dead at thirty-seven. She thought of Atiehwa:ta and Delacroix and Henoseki, who'd been mighty in the position and had fallen before their time. But also there were people like Asegaff and Davidson who'd worked as Planetaries and lived to a great old age, dying old and full of honor, among wizards at least. *And is there any other kind of honor I'd care about?*

Nita sat quiet for a moment. "I'm nowhere near ready for this."

"That's a matter for debate," Aidoneus said. "But the assessment rests with you for the time being; others' opinions, except for mine right now, and Irina's of course, have no particular bearing on the process as it unfolds. Let's just say that there's interest, and if you choose to pursue the various courses of study needed for prequalification, you would find no opposition. That," and Nita could actually feel Pluto's Planetary grimacing, "normally comes later. When things start getting political."

Nita let out an exasperated breath. "Do not even *try* telling me that there's politics involved in this."

"Sentient beings are involved in this," Aidoneus said. "Of *course* there's politics. Motivation and countermotivation, ebbing and flowing and chafing against one another: how else can things be? But we do what we can to make it work regardless."

And it smiled at her inside those shadows. "In the meantime," Aidoneus said, "consider your options. There's no rush. And come see me."

Nita smiled back. "I will." She nodded back at Kit. "Can he come too?"

"Of course," said the darkness of the outermost Solar System as it faded away. " . . . But *no furniture*."

Shortly thereafter Nelaid and Miril departed for Wellakh with the still only partially conscious Roshaun, taking Dairine and Nita's dad with them for the first short hop to Earth; and the cleanup crews got busy putting the crater Daedalus in order for the Invitational's last two presentations.

Out of a sense of sisterly loyalty (and because in a wholly nonvisionary manner she foresaw Dairine giving her endless grief if she didn't), Nita decided to hang around long enough to see Mehrnaz's presentation. There in company with the astonished thousands in the crater, an hour or so later, she and Kit watched the senior geomancers present trigger a violent earthquake that (while sparing the crater) shook the Moon for hundreds of miles around. But hardly had it begun before Dairine's protegée flung the huge and dazzling network of her spell out across the lunar surface to its full extent, powered it up, and stopped the quake cold in a splendid anticlimax closely resembling a gigantic and devastating sneeze that had failed to go off.

The roar of applause that went up as the ground outside the crater quieted made Nita grin in triumph. But at the same time she felt the weariness coming down on her more and more heavily. And there was a peculiar flickering of images going on at the edge of her vision, a remnant of the kind of thing she'd briefly seen when Penn's internal guest broke loose. She turned to Kit.

"So now what?" he said, knowing — she suspected — perfectly well.

"I'm wrecked," she said. "I want to go home and

do something really ordinary. Sit down, have something to drink . . ."

"Pitanga juice? Celery soda? Aussie lemonade?"

Nita punched him in the shoulder in the good old-fashioned way. *"Tea."*

The two of them were just sitting down at the dining room table when the doorbell rang.

Kit pushed his mug off to one side and bent over to thump his forehead on the table. "Nooooo . . . ."

"Oh, *now* what," Nita muttered, and got up to answer the bell. But as she opened the front door and realized who was standing there, her mood of slight annoyance fell right off. "Carl!" she said. "I thought Tom said you were off doing supervisory stuff again."

"Nope," he said. "Can I come in?"

"Sure," Nita said, leading him into the dining room. "Want some of your coffee?"

"Thanks, but no need. I'll only be here a few minutes. Hi, Kit."

"Hey, Carl!"

He sat down at the table with them. "I wanted you to know that I'm available for counseling services over the next week or so should you require them," he said, "because from the sound of it, and from even the *short* version of the report on the Invitational before they had to recess for the site cleanup, I can't think offhand of anyone more likely to need them."

"Well, Penn, possibly," Kit said. "He's going to have a ton of issues."

"One of his local Supervisories will be handling that with him," Carl said.

"Or maybe Dairine," Nita said.

"Though she's got an above-Supervisory wizard on hand already," Carl said, "I suspect Nelaid would recuse himself. So extend the offer to her on my behalf, if you would."

"No problem," Nita said. "I'll take care of it."

"And I'll drop a note in her manual as well. Meanwhile, how're you holding up?"

Nita shivered. "I'm starting to see all kinds of things. Way better than usual, when I concentrate on them."

"I think that's partly due to exercising the talent in a crisis situation so close to a major shift in wizardly power balances," Carl said. "Everybody who was in the neighborhood for the Simurgh's release will be having similar surges . . . But you did something else, too. If I read your own précis correctly, when you were in a liminal state in the run-up to the finals, you extended an unusual kindness to an old enemy. And apparently had it returned in an unusual mode."

Nita nodded slowly. "Yeah," she said.

"Dangerous game," Carl said, looking at her

thoughtfully. "But sometimes it pays off. So some of that energy will be coming back to you too. Has started to already, from the sound of it. What you want to see, for the next little while, you'll probably find a lot easier to visualize. That'll fade in the near future, so don't let it spook you either way."

"Okay."

"And about Dairine," Carl said. "What's your take on how she's holding up?"

Nita closed her eyes. "Well . . ."

On a splendidly upholstered couch, somewhere very far away, a long, lean form lay all wrapped up in the silken bedclothes of another world, as someone sat by the bed and looked down at him, practically vibrating with concern. And under the weight of that regard, eyes slowly opened — eyes colored a very pale gold — and gazed into the gray ones that watched.

The face was very still, almost bemused. Then its lips parted.

"Whatever *took* you so long?" Roshaun said.

A second later a pillow hit him in the face.

Nita opened her eyes again, acutely aware from unspoken context that a fierce bout of hugging was about to start, and she didn't need to be there. "I think she'll be fine," she said. "Anyway, this isn't so bad, for as long as it lasts."

"Let's just hope what you're able to see stays at

about this level before it starts falling off," Carl said. "I know a visionary who had a surge and started receiving other planets' sports channels on his interior antennae. Not exactly a picnic."

"No, I didn't mean that. It's just, if now I'm supposed to be doing this *other* thing, then I guess this won't stay . . ."

Carl looked at her quizzically. "What other thing?"

"Well, I mean, the Planetary thing. When all this time Tom's been pushing me toward the visionary stuff . . ."

Carl looked at her with incredulity. "*Pushing* you? You're kidding, right? You were *always* a visionary, Nita. You presented that tendency as part of your Ordeal! Almost — if I've got the timing right from what you've told me — almost before your Ordeal even got properly started. You fell asleep on top of your wizard's manual and threw a prophetic dream right off the bat."

"Well, yeah . . ."

"So this is one of your ground-of-being states. Of course it'll always need sharpening: no gift's ever perfect right out of the box. But you're in no danger of losing it if you start concentrating on something else. In fact the two disciplines will probably help each other. If you did decide to go into Planetary work — and you're talking about a course that would last decades, like a doctorate you get to keep doing over and over — then having the visionary talent overlaid on it can only be useful."

Nita sighed. "Okay," she said. "But I'm going to need a while to think this over."

"So think," Carl said. "Take your time. The Planetaries aren't going anywhere." Then he grinned. "Except around in big circles."

"You mean ellipses."

He gave her an amused look that said both *You're correcting a Supervisory?* and *Good, about time.*

Then something went *ping!* and Nita and Kit looked at each other in confusion, as it wasn't an alert that belonged to either of their phones.

"Sorry, just me," Carl said, and went fishing in his pockets. A moment later he came up with his phone and peered at it.

"Huh," he said, resigned. "So much for rooting for the home team."

"What?" Nita said.

"Tiilikainen got it."

"What?" said Kit.

"The second fella who presented," Carl said, turning the phone around to show Nita and Kit the list of scores and rankings from the Moon. "The one with the solution for the Gulf Stream convection problem. He took it on points."

Nita peered at the phone's screen. "I could never say his name . . ."

"All those vowels," Carl said.

"But Penn came in third," Kit said.

"And Mehrnaz came in second!" Nita said. "Dairine'll be glad."

Carl nodded. "So that's that for another eleven years," he said. He turned off the phone and stuffed it back in his pocket. "By the way," he said to Kit as he did so, "this reminds me. I meant to have a word with you about your sister."

"Oh God," Kit said in dread. "What's she done *now?*"

"I wanted to let you know that while everybody was up on the Moon, Carmela was videoing the final rounds. She got some wonderful footage of the Simurgh going home, and that's already hitting the intergalactic Nets. She's probably going to clean up on it. I know she's a very sensible person, as a rule, and God knows I don't care to squash anyone's entrepreneurial spirit. But do me a favor and make sure she doesn't post it on the Web, all right?"

Kit covered his face and moaned.

Carl stood up, grinning. "A word to the wise, that's all," he said. "So you two have a good evening. Sit tight . . . I'll let myself out."

And he made for the front door and a moment later shut it behind him.

"Oh sweet Powers That Be in a bucket," Kit said,

staring into what was left of his tea and rubbing his hands through his hair. "When I catch up with her, we are going to have *such words*."

"Might help you with that," Nita said, as she got up and walked over to the sink with the cups. "Let's go take care of it. Your mama cooking tonight?"

"I think we can talk her into it." He held a hand out to her.

She took it.

Shortly thereafter a casual observer of suburban life would have seen a couple of teenagers walking down the street together, hand in hand in the deepening dusk, with the full Moon rising behind them. As they reached the nearby corner, one of them stood still, glancing back at that Moon, and then looked up at the other. Their faces were coming closer together in the dimness when the quiet around them was broken by one of their phones beeping for attention.

"Oh, come *on* now . . ."

"Go on, you might as well get it."

A pause.

"What is it?"

"Oh no."

"*What?* Let me see."

A moment's silence. And then the words:

"She didn't."

"She *did*."

"And it's going to be all over school in about a minute!"

There was a pause. "If I were her," the deeper of the two voices said, "I would head for the most distant possible planet *right now!*"

And hand in hand they jogged around the corner and out of sight.